West with Giraffes

West with Giraffes

A Novel

LYNDA RUTLEDGE

LAKE UNION
PUBLISHING

Published by Lake Union Publishing, Seattle
www.apub.com

Amazon, the Amazon logo, and Lake Union Publishing are trademarks of Amazon.com, Inc., or its affiliates.

ISBN-13: 9781542021746 (hardcover)
ISBN-10: 154202174X (hardcover)
ISBN-13: 9781542023344 (paperback)
ISBN-10: 1542023343 (paperback)

Cover design by Kimberly Glyder

Printed in the United States of America

First edition

To the real hurricane giraffes

Until one has loved an animal, a part of one's soul remains unawakened.

—Anatole France, Nobel Laureate, 1921

The admirablest and fairest beast ever I sawe was a jarraff . . . prince of all the beasts.

—John Sanderson, traveler, 1595

New York World-Telegram

SEPTEMBER 22, 1938

MIRACLE GIRAFFES RIDE HURRICANE AT SEA

NEW YORK—Sept. 22 (Special edition). After riding through The Great Hurricane that decimated the Eastern Seaboard yesterday, the SS *Robin Goodfellow* limped into New York Harbor this morning along with two giraffes left for dead . . .

Compiled from Sep. 23, 1938, news reports

. . . In one of the few accounts ever recorded of hurricane survival at sea, the merchant marine freighter SS *Robin Goodfellow* rode straight into this week's cataclysmic storm off the coast of Haiti. Witnesses describe swells blocking out the sky, fish swimming in the air, and winds whipping waves into water spouts as seamen caught on deck helplessly watched one snatch a crewman into the void. Crawling to the hold where their mates pulled them in, they had no choice but to abandon two crated Baringo giraffes to face the hurricane's full force . . . Within minutes the ship went into a half-roll starboard and stayed that way for 6 hours of pelting waves and winds, abruptly righting itself as the hurricane passed. On deck, all seemed lost save for one battered giraffe still standing in its lashed crate, its companion's crushed crate found in debris jammed sideways against the ship rail with only the gigantic beast's lifeless head in view. But as the crew gathered to push the carcass overboard, the downed giraffe stirred and opened its eyes . . .

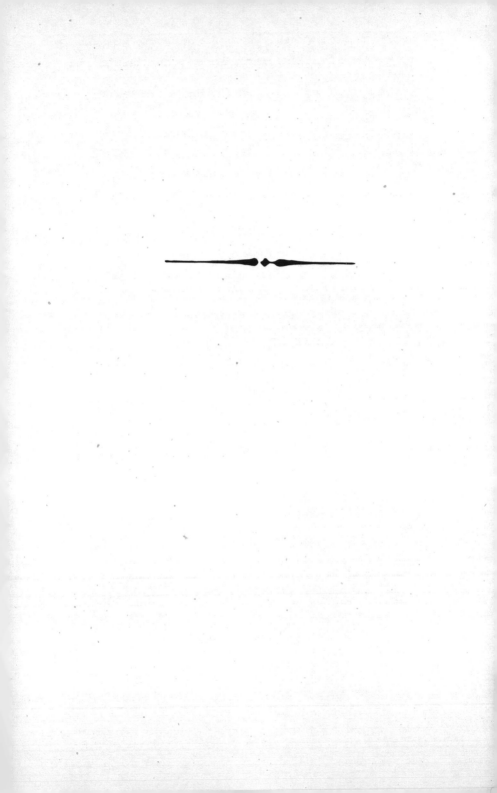

Few true friends have I known and two were giraffes . . .

—Woodrow Wilson Nickel

PROLOGUE

Woodrow Wilson Nickel died in the year 2025, on a usual day, in the usual way, at the rather unusual age of 105.

A century and a nickel.

The young VA hospital long-term care liaison assigned to dispatch his worldly possessions to survivors—which in Woodrow Wilson Nickel's case was an ancient military footlocker and no survivors at all—stood in his vacant room. Determined to keep on schedule, she checked the time. Her job made her feel like some Gatekeeper of Things Left Behind, especially with centenarians gone long before their hearts stopped beating. They were the only ones with footlockers anymore. And old footlockers with nowhere to go were the worst, their contents full of mortal meaning departed with the departed as if she could actually see the past vanish into thin air. So she took a deep breath and opened the old trunk, expecting to find the usual musty uniforms and faded photographs.

Instead she found a giraffe.

The footlocker was full of ruled writing pads, dozens of them, stacked in bundles bound with twine. Perched on top with a yellowed newspaper article was the giraffe, a tiny antique porcelain souvenir from the San Diego Zoo. Despite herself, she smiled wistfully and picked it up. As a child, she'd seen a whole group of the tall, gentle giants at the zoo before they'd become so horribly rare.

Gently setting down the giraffe, she picked up the first batch of pads to move them aside when the top pad's large old-man scrawl caught her eye. She eased onto the edge of the bed and read it closer:

Few true friends have I known and two were giraffes, one that didn't kick me dead and one that saved my worthless orphan life and your worthy, precious one.

They're both long gone. And soon I'll be gone, which will be no great loss to be sure. But the man on the TV just said that soon there'll be no more giraffes in the world at all, gone with the tigers and the elephants and the Old Man's sky-blanketing pigeons. Even as I punched the screen to shut him up, I knew it could be true.

Somehow, though, I know there is still you. And there is still this story that's yours as good as mine. If it goes extinct, too, with my old bag of bones, that'd be a crying shame—*my* shame. Because if ever I could claim to have seen the face of God, it was in the colossal faces of those giraffes. And if ever I should be leaving something behind, it's this story for them and for you.

So, here and now, before it's too late, I am writing it all down on the chance a good soul reads these words and helps them find their way to you.

With that, the VA liaison untied the first batch and, forgetting all about her schedule, began to read . . .

. . . I'm older than dirt.

And when you're older than dirt, you can get lost in time, in memory, even in space.

I'm inside my tiny four-wall room with the feeling that I've been . . . gone. I'm not even sure how long I've been sitting here. All night I think, since stirring from my foggy mind to find myself surrounded by other old farts staring at a fancy TV. I remember the man on the screen talking about the last giraffes on earth and rushing over in my wheelchair to punch him. I remember being pushed back here quick and a nurse bandaging my bleeding knuckles.

Then I remember an orderly making me swallow a calm-down pill I didn't want to take.

But that's the last time I'll be doing that. Because right now, pencil in this shaky hand, I aim to write down one singular memory.

Fast as I can.

I could spend what I feel in my bones is my life's last clear hours to tell you of the Dust Bowl. Or the War. Or the French peonies. Or my wives, so many wives. Or the graves, so many graves. Or the goodbyes, so many goodbyes. Those memories come and go here at the end, if they come at all anymore. But not this memory. *This* memory is always with me, always alive, always within reach, and always in living technicolor from deadly start to bittersweet finish, no matter how old I keep getting. And—Red, Old Man, sweet Wild Boy and Girl—oh, how I miss you.

All I have to do is close my worn-out eyes for the smallest of moments.

And it begins.

1

New York Harbor

Boats were flying through the air, streets were flowing like rivers, electric lines were exploding like fireworks, and houses of shrieking people were being blown out to sea—the date was September 21, the day of the Great Hurricane of 1938. The entire coast from New York Harbor to Maine got smacked so hard it was the stuff of legend, seven hundred souls gone to their final reward as wet as mackerels.

Back then, you got no warning. You'd notice a storm over the water and you'd be worrying how bad that cloud looks when the banshee wind and rain hits and you're scrambling for your life. The dock piling I'd wrapped my scrawny young self around got whipped airborne. Next thing I know I'm waking up in a ditch with a tramp yanking on my cowboy boots. Seeing me rise from the dead, he yelped and ran. I was still in one piece somehow, if black, blue, and bloody, with only my suspenders popped off and gone. So as the rest of the living world began hollering for help or hearses, I wiped the dried blood off my face, grabbed hold of my trousers, and struggled to my feet. The boathouse where I'd been standing had blown away along with Cuz, my third-cousin boss. Found him in a shallow pool of boat shards, a sloop's mast stuck straight through him. I wasn't much to look at even before my hurricane-wallop—an overgrown farmboy with a face newly scarred and a neck sporting a birthmark the size of a state fair prize yam—but I sure looked better than Cuz. I'd say I was lucky, but I hadn't had enough of a relationship with the word to use it. I'd say it was the worst day of my life, yet it was already far from it. I can say this. I never thought I'd see a bigger eyeful than that hurricane as long as I lived.

But I was wrong.

Because the last thing you think you're going to see in the middle of flipped boats and buildings afire and bodies dangling and sirens wailing is a couple of giraffes.

I'd been there not six weeks, Dust Bowl dirt still coating my young rowdy's lungs—and despite my God-fearing ma, that's what I was, a dirt-farm rowdy, pure as a cow pie, cunning as a wild hog, and already well acquainted with the county sheriff, the dust layering my every breath leaving little room for the Holy Spirit to breathe on me. Cuz's bilge-rat boathouse was where I landed after the Dirty Thirties blew so fierce in my corner of the Texas Panhandle that every nester and sharecropper for miles was flung clean off the map. Some like my ma, pa, and baby sister left the hard way, six feet under. Some hit the road with the Okies to California. The rest, like me, headed toward any kin who'd take them in. The only family I had left in the world was an East Coast stranger to me named Cuz, who might as well have been the man in the moon to a seventeen-year-old Panhandle boy. But there's being alone and there's being an orphan alone in an empty wasteland digging graves for all you ever loved with no one to ask for help except the sheriff—which I dared not do for reasons I cannot yet bear to confess.

Sitting there by my ma's, pa's, and baby sister's graves, I let evening turn to morning. Still covered with the dead dirt that had killed us all, I dug up my ma's Mason jar of coins from her withered garden and stumbled dry-eyed toward the highway. Not until a long hauler stopped his truck to ask me where I was headed did I find out I was mute.

"You an Okie?"

I tried to answer. Nothing came out.

"Cat got your tongue, kid?" the driver said.

Still I couldn't spit out a word. Eyeing me good, he jerked a thumb toward his empty truck bed and dumped me at the Muleshoe train station . . . right across from the sheriff's office. I waited for the next train east with one eye back at his door, knowing I was unfit to answer questions he'd surely have if he saw me, and just as the train pulled away, the sheriff strode out to look straight at me looking straight back at him.

Jumpy at every stop after that, I got as far as Chattanooga with my ma's coins. From there, I hopped a boxcar until I saw some tramps fling a bum off the train after stealing his shoes. Then I swiped a motorcycle and rode it until it ran out of gas, snitching food along the way like a stray dog, until I had some snitched from me by a bum with a straight razor. That got me hitching straight to Cuz, where I found myself eye to eye with more water than my thirsty eyes could take in. When Cuz asked me who the hell I was, I had to scrawl my answer with a coal lump on the dock, to which he harrumphed, "Figures I'd get a dumb one, being from that side of the family," and put me straight to work for my supper. For forty silent days and nights, I called a moldy cot in the back of the boathouse home. Now I didn't even have that. Nobody was left to come look for me and nobody was newly dead I'd mourn, Cuz proving himself to be such stone-hearted scum I was already plotting to snatch his cash and run.

Holding up my pants in the hurricane rubble, I stood wobbly over what was left of the man I'd traveled half the USA to find, then reached around the bloody mast pole and picked his dead pockets. When I found nothing but his lucky rabbit's foot, I started kicking him so full of my own hurricane fury that I kicked myself back to speech—I was kicking and cussing Cuz, the gray sky, the black ocean, the putrid air, my ma's precious Jesus and his cruel God Almighty Father—until I slipped and landed on my backside, eyes to the drizzling sky. With that, the logjam inside me busted wide, and I lay there sobbing like the lost boy I was.

Finally, I struggled up on my boots again, tied up my trousers with a piece of soggy boat tether, and wandered back to the dock.

There I sat, pure miserable, watching ship after ship limp into harbor.

Until I saw the giraffes.

Up the dock, a storm-clobbered freighter was unloading. I don't remember getting to my feet or moving. I only remember standing in the middle of the freighter's crew in their blue dungaree uniforms, staring. There, before me, were two giraffes under a dangling crane that had just unloaded them like a pack of tires. One was alive and swaying inside a cracked but upright crate, the colossal beast's head thrusting up treetop tall, the other, lifeless, sprawled across the entire width of the dock, its crate crushed around it like an accordion. Back then, nobody knew much about giraffes, but in the little schooling I had before the dust came, I'd seen a picture of one, so I was able to put a name to the wonder. Staring at the downed one, I was sure I was gazing at a real-life carcass of a real-dead giraffe . . . until the carcass opened a brown-apple eye to gaze up at me. And the deathly look in that eye sent a familiar shiver down my young spine.

I knew all about animals. Some you worked, some you milked, some you ate, some you shot, and that was that. You learned early not to make a pig a pal or your pa would soon be forcing you to thank Jesus for the blessing of eating everything but its squeal. Even feeding a stray dog would get you a whipping for taking food out of the family's mouth. "What's wrong with you? It's just an animal!" my pa kept saying. There was no room for such weakness past being a boy in knickers, especially when, at the risk of hellfire, the worst two-legged human was better than any soulless four-legged animal—or so I was taught. Problem was, whenever I locked eyes with an animal I felt something more soulful than I ever felt from the humans I knew, and what I saw in that sprawled giraffe's eye made me ache to the bone. The giraffe's eye had stopped moving, taking on a pallor I'd seen too many times in an animal's eyes right before my pa would be deciding whether to eat, bury, or burn them. I pushed in closer, waiting for the seamen, all looking like damp hell themselves, to shove me back where I belonged.

Instead they were suddenly parting like a dirty-blue Red Sea.

Coming right at us was a shiny new truck with a wood contraption strapped to its long flatbed that would've made Rube Goldberg proud. Shaped like a squatty *T*, it looked like a two-story homemade boxcar plopped down on the entire length of the truck bed, wooden window openings along the top, trapdoors along the bottom, and a short step-up ladder nailed on each side. I jumped out of the way as the driver— a goober-looking guy with cauliflower ears and enough Dapper Dan pomade on his hair to grease an engine—jerked the rig to a halt.

The passenger door swung wide, and out crawled a leathery old man with a face like a mule. That's what I've called him all these years— the "Old Man"—but here and now as I write, older than old myself, I'd bet the farm he wasn't much past fifty. He had on a rumpled jacket, a yellowed white shirt, and hangdog tie. One of his hands looked gnarled, and propped on the back of his head was an old fedora that looked like it'd been stomped on so much it had forgotten whether it was pork-pied or pinched.

Slamming the door, he seemed headed toward the mutton-chopped harbormaster, who was waving what seemed to be a couple of telegrams his way. Instead the Old Man tromped right past, striding to the giraffes as if unaware of any other living thing on the dock but the giants before him.

First, he went to the upright crate with the standing, swaying giraffe—the male—and started talking to it low like secrets. The giraffe slowed. The Old Man reached in to gently stroke it, and the giraffe's swaying stopped. Getting down on his haunches by the sprawled female, he started up the same soft giraffe-speak. She began to quiver. He put his hand through the crushed crate slats to touch her, and as the giraffe lay still as doom, he began stroking her big head with that gnarly hand until she closed her eyes. For a moment, the only sound in the world was the giraffe's labored breathing and the Old Man's cooing against the waves lapping against the dock. Then the harbormaster stomped over to shove the telegrams under the Old Man's nose. The Old Man took one look at them and tossed them to the ground, a fury flit crossing his face I knew far too well—he had him a temper, too.

Right then, the ship captain appeared from the harbormaster's hut, his uniform ripped and face bruised, and the dungarees turned toward him as one.

The Old Man glared his way. "You kill my giraffe?"

"Mister," the harbormaster cut in, "they lost one of their mates out there and it's a miracle they made it in with or without your fancy animals if that means a thing to you."

The Old Man's face made it clear it did not.

With that, the dungarees were all in a lather. I thought they just might pounce on him. From the look on his face, I thought he just might want it.

"We got her here . . . ," a voice rang out, and you could almost hear the words left hanging in the air: *Now save her, ya bastard.*

The Old Man, his hand still on the downed one's great head, didn't move.

As the grumbling grew louder, though, a dented gray panel truck came rattling toward the rig from the street with a sign on its door so faded I could only make out the word "Zoo." Out from it hopped a stubby, well-scrubbed college-boy type in a white coat clutching a black doctor bag. He strode past us like he was on a holiday, headed to the Old Man.

"We've got to get her on her feet or she's done," the zoo doc said by way of hello. The Old Man motioned to the harbormaster, who whistled over a couple of longshoremen with crowbars, who started yanking at the crushed crate around the tangled giraffe. But it wasn't fast enough for the Old Man. He started pulling at the smashed planks himself, gnarled hand and all. When there was nothing more to yank, the crane's harness—still around planks under her body and feet—went taut, groaning like it was alive as it pulled the giraffe upright. When she faltered, the dungarees rushed by me, plunging their hands in to help the Old Man steady her. With one more tug, everything went full upright and the harnessed female was up on three of her four feet in a flash, violently so, everyone but the Old Man jumping back. And there it was. Her back right leg, from knee to fetlock, looked as if someone had taken a ball-peen hammer to it. She wobbled, fighting to stay up on her three good spindly legs.

"Steady . . . girl . . . steady . . . ," the Old Man purred as the zoo doc felt along her body.

"Her internal organs seem intact," he said. "This leg's the telltale."

I thought it was good news until I remembered they shoot horses for less.

Opening his black bag, he cleaned, splinted, and wrapped the leg, then stepped back as the longshoremen lashed freight panels snug around her. When they were done, the Old Man, still cooing his giraffe-speak, reached in and uncinched the crane's harness.

The girl teetered. Then she was standing on her own.

Seeing that, the Old Man and the zoo doc started talking fast and low. I inched closer.

"But if I reject her as unfit, it's a death sentence and you know it!" the Old Man was saying.

The zoo doc frowned back at the T-shaped boxcar rig. "How long you hoping to take to get there?"

"Two weeks if we make good time."

The zoo doc shook his head. "Better cut that in half."

The Old Man threw up his hands. "How can I do that? We got to go slow—even slower now because of that leg!"

"I'm saying a week tops *because* of that leg. You better start think-ing how."

"*Fine.* So?"

Glancing back at sirens in the distance, the zoo doc fumed. "Go ahead and sign off for both. Don't want to disappoint Mrs. Benchley yet. They've got the time in quarantine to see if the young female stays tall—if we even get *there*. But, Jones, if I were you, I'd tell Mrs. Benchley the whole truth, that even if the female's still upright before you hit the road, odds are your road trip will still do her in. Better if Mrs. Benchley hears it now instead of when you're figuring out what to do with a dead giraffe on the road."

As the zoo doc left, the Old Man marched over to the harbormaster and signed some papers. Then the crane grabbed the patched crates and swung the giraffes over to a harbor flatbed, where longshoremen tied them down. With that, the backslapping dungarees scattered, the Old Man popped the rig's hood signaling a let's-go to the goober driver as he climbed in, and I watched it all pass—two colossal storybook animals from the other side of the world on the back of a harbor flatbed with a contraption rig trailing behind.

I stared after the giraffes, knowing the moment I wasn't thinking about them I'd be forced to face my sudden return to life as a stray-dog boy. Other creatures' miracles don't mean a thing when you're still working on your own. As the trucks got smaller and smaller, my wan-dering, wretched future got bigger and bigger. I took a breath. My ribs throbbed, and as the trucks kept on shrinking from view, I thought I might retch.

Feeling something squish under my bootheel, I looked down. I was standing on the telegrams the Old Man had tossed on the wet dock. Scooping them up, I read them quick and remember them whole.

Said the first:

WESTERN UNION

22 SEP 38 = 0600A

To: MRS. BELLE BENCHLEY
SAN DIEGO ZOO
SAN DIEGO, CALIFORNIA

HURRICANE DAMAGED SHIPMENT. GIRAFFES
ALIVE. ADVISE ON DELIVERY.

                        EAST AFR SHIPPING CO.

Said the second:

WESTERN UNION

22 SEP 38 = 0715A

To: MR. RILEY JONES
HARBORMASTER
NEW YORK HARBOR, NEW YORK

[HOLD]

MEET BRONX ZOO DVM AT DOCK TO ADVISE
ON FITNESS FOR ROAD TO CALIFORNIA.

                                    BB

The wet telegrams turned to mush and slipped through my fingers. But my eyes were still seeing that final bright and shiny word—a word with more storybook meaning than *giraffe* for a Dust Bowl boy.

California.

The giraffes were bound for the land of milk and honey. Moses and the Chosen People couldn't have longed for the Promised Land any more than hardscrabble farm folks longed for "Californy." Everybody knew all you had to do was find your way there without dying on the road or rail, and you'd live like a king plucking fruit from the trees and grapes from the vine.

And how could anybody lose the way following a couple of giraffes?

I felt my eyes grow as big as the thoughts I was thinking. I was miserable-damp, I had an eye that was half-swollen, a couple of teeth loose, a rib throbbing like a tom-tom, and an arm that wasn't working quite right. But it didn't matter a bit. Because with that one bright, shiny word dancing before my eyes, I had something no Dust Bowl orphan had any business having. Although I was living in a time when such a thing was as likely to kill you as save you—I had a flickering hope.

The giraffes turned the corner and vanished from sight.

So I started to run, splashing through the water and the muck after them as fast as my bunged-up bones would go.

For a mile, I ran along the cobblestones following the giraffes. Workers clearing the streets dropped their shovels to gawk. Firemen pulling a body by its arms from a storm drain stopped to gape. Linemen working on dangling electric lines paused in the sizzle to stare. Block after block, as storm-woozy people hung from windows calling to their pals to come look, I kept running behind the slow rigs, not knowing where we were going or what to do next. At the blocked Holland Tunnel exit, the rigs stopped just as a motorcycle cop came roaring up, shouting at the rig drivers to follow him uptown, even though there were elevateds that way the high-riding crates would have to squeeze under—lots of them.

At the Ninth Avenue elevated, a man riding with the flatbed jumped from the truck, pole in hand, brushed back a sizzling live wire, and measured the clearance.

"Eighth of an inch," he yelled back. The flatbed slipped slowly under.

The rig moved on to the next one a few blocks down. Again the pole man jumped out. "Fourth of an inch," he called back.

Another couple of blocks—

"Half!"

On we went, this way and that, edging up through the city, minutes turning into hours. The East River was still flooding the nearby streets, and a factory was ablaze in between, so the cop kept us west. We skimmed Central Park, dozens of woebegone folks and wide-eyed ragamuffins gaping at the passing giraffes from under soaked boards and walkways as if watching a dream. On we still went, until the George Washington Bridge was straight ahead. The cop was leading us to New Jersey. I panicked. I couldn't run over a bridge.

Across the street, I saw a joe hop off a motorcycle outside a storefront and rush inside, pointing back at the giraffes, the machine sliding to the puddled pavement like it was a two-bit bicycle. It had barely hit the ground before I found my legs wrapped around it. With one eye on that motorcycle cop, I pumped that electric horse twice, skidded left then right like some bucking bronco—and held on.

By the time I caught up with the giraffes on the bridge, half a dozen reporter cars appeared out of nowhere, sandwiching in around me, their camera guys hanging out the windows, flashbulbs flashing against the gloomy skies.

On the other side, two New Jersey cycle cops took up the escort, dodging the storm's flotsam and jetsam, until the two big rigs bumped over a track by a deserted depot and stopped in front of a gated sign: **US QUARANTINE**. Behind the gate were gabled tin-roofed brick barns spread out as far as the eye could see. We were at the federal quarantine station, where animals shipped into the country were inspected, from cows and horses to camels and oxen, and now, giraffes.

As the guard waved the two big trucks through, the reporters swarmed the gate. I stopped by a massive uprooted oak near the road and had barely turned off the cycle before they'd all rushed back to their cars, except for a fancy green Packard bumping to a stop behind me. A reporter in suit and tie with a fedora cocked just right got out of the driver's side and headed for the guard hut.

"Wait here," he called up to his camera guy, who was crawling up on the Packard's hood. And the sight seared itself whole and perfect in my eyes, it's sparkling so fresh even now in my old man's memory—because the camera guy was a camera gal.

Much younger than the duded-up reporter, she had red curls all over her head, a fiery halo of raging waves she surely battled into submission every morning, and she was wearing trousers—the first woman I'd ever seen doing so in real life. There she stood, snapping pictures on the Packard's hood in her white girly shirt, two-tone shoes, and two-legged trousers. And there I stood, feeling like I'd been hurricane-walloped again. If it wasn't love at first sight, it was sure something painfully akin to it.

"Oh, hello, Stretch. Are you here for the giraffes, too?" Red said, looking down at me with eyes that about knocked me out on their own. They were hazel and I must have moved closer in their sway. Because as she snapped a picture, she popped a flashbulb bright enough to blind a blind man—and me.

"Lionel! Come quick!" I heard her yell.

"*Hey!* Get away from her!" the reporter yelled, shoving me as I blinked back to sight. Stumbling, I scrambled away.

"What'd you do that for!" I heard her say as I ducked behind the downed oak. "I only thought you'd want to talk to him for the story, Mr. Big Reporter!"

"*For God's sake*, Augie, that kid's nothing but a tramping punk who'd slit your throat for chump change. Don't be naive—he was looking at *you*," the reporter said back. "Let's go. The guard said the giraffes are quarantined for twelve days. I've got all I need, and you've got time to get all you need without entertaining vagrants."

A minute later, they were gone. The cops were gone. The giraffes were gone. And I was miles from anywhere I knew, with night coming on, clueless for what to do next.

I stowed the cycle behind the toppled oak, and I crouched down to watch and wait near a cow carcass. Just as I'd had all I could take of the skeeters feasting on my hide, the gray panel zoo truck jolted to a stop at the gate. As the guard waved the stubby zoo doc through, I started worrying whether the lame giraffe had stayed tall. I decided to see for myself.

Spying where a raccoon had burrowed under the fence, I squeezed under. Mud caked down my backside, I hustled toward the biggest, tallest barn as the zoo truck, the empty harbor flatbed, and some joes in khaki work-duds were leaving. I peeked inside. The barn was full of shadows, its walls lined with haystacks. On the left was a cot, in the middle was the rig, and on the right was a sky-high wire pen holding both giraffes. The splinted girl giraffe had stayed tall. Finally out of their crates, they were facing each other, necks touching, scooched so close you couldn't tell where one ended and the other began. Like they couldn't much believe they were alive and were circling the wagons to keep it that way.

The Old Man—Mr. Riley Jones, according to the telegram—was nowhere to be seen, but the driver had grabbed a big juicy apple from the truck's cab and was leaning against the rig eating it. I watched him chomp it down to nothing, then pitch the core into the hay, and I marked the spot. I hadn't eaten since before the hurricane, so even an apple core covered with goober spit could soon start looking good. During the Hard Times, being hungry was a basic state of being, least for most folks I knew. After the dust killed off the livestock, Dust Bowlers were eating prairie dogs and rattlesnakes and making soup from tumbleweeds. When you don't know where your next meal is coming from, that's all life is—you're nothing but a feral thing chasing your hunger every minute of the day.

Wiping his mouth with the back of his sleeve, the goober driver strutted over and rattled the pen's fence, spooking the giraffes, then *laughed* and did it again. Rocking on my bootheels, fists clenched, I wanted so bad to relieve him of his front teeth that I didn't hear the Old Man returning until it was too late. I had to duck inside, diving behind a hay pile.

Already barking orders at the driver, the Old Man marched right past. "Earl!" he yelled. "Come here!"

Next thing I know he's telling the driver to leave for the night and pushing the squeak-squawking barn doors shut behind him . . . trapping me inside. Cussing my fool self, I settled in to wait until I could figure out how to sneak out unseen.

As night fell, the only sounds in the barn were the giraffes snorting and stomping. The Old Man flipped a metal lever on a wall panel near his cot, the dangling electric light lamps came on, and the place turned bright as day. And there I cowered, nothing between me and him but hay. If he'd looked my way, he would've seen me for sure. But he only had eyes for the giraffes. Watching the giraffes in a tenderhearted way I couldn't quite figure for such a man, he started cooing his giraffe-speak so soothingly it was calming *me* down. When he stopped, only the giraffes' quiet snuffling filled the air. He pulled the switch, the lights went off, and the barn went full dark except for an outside light streaming through the high wire windows, casting shadows across the barn. Then the Old Man flopped on the cot and was soon snoring like a buzz saw.

Of course, that was my chance to sneak out. But there was still the matter of the produce waiting for the taking, and I *had* to take. So I headed quiet but quick to the rig's blindside, stepped on the running board, and spied two gunnysacks on the cab's seat, one with apples, the other sweet onions. Grabbing one from both, I stuffed the onion in my pocket and shoved the apple in my chompers, all but swallowing the thing whole.

As I grabbed another onion, though, I felt eyes on me.

Readying for a scrap, I spun around to see I had an audience. Not a dozen steps away, the giraffes had moved near the pen's fence, and they had both turned their long necks to stare at me. There are lots of things that can make a body freeze in its tracks. Having a couple of two-ton beasts eyeing you from behind a flimsy piece of fencing is surely one of them. I should have been backing away. Instead I inched nearer until I was by the pen studying the living magnitude of them—from their huge hooves to their wide bodies and up, up, up their spotty necks to their knobby horns. I got a crick in my own long neck staring up at the giraffes' colossalness. *They could knock this pen down,* I recall thinking. Yet they weren't doing any such thing. In fact, the boy giraffe had now shut his eyes. *He's sleep-standing like my old mare,* I realized, wincing at the memory. The girl, though, was still staring at me with those round brown-apple eyes exactly like she'd done at the dock, except now she was staring down. Way down.

Have you ever looked straight into the eyes of an animal? A tame one's figuring you out, what you're going to do and what that means to it. A wild one can chill you to the bone, surveying you for either supper or survival. But the gaze of that giraffe was different. It seemed to hold neither fear nor design. Her cantaloupe-sized nostrils snuffled the top of my head through the wire fence and I let them, if only because I couldn't make my legs work. Blowing warm stink breath, she left my hair damp with giraffe spit. Then she bumped the fence with her snout, trying to get to the onion I was still clutching. I held it up. Her long tongue snaked through the wire and snatched it back through the fence, her neck rising to send it sliding down her long throat with a mighty gulp, then she inched near again until the smell of her surrounded me. She smelled of fur . . . and ocean . . . and sweet foreign farm dung. Before I knew what I was doing, I'd reached my hand through the wire to touch a spot on her flank as big as a granny's butt in the shape of a sideways heart.

For the longest moment, we stood there like that, the rough feel of her warm pelt full on my outstretched hand—until I felt another tongue licking my fingers. It was the wild boy, his long neck stretching over the back of the wild girl to me. I jerked my hand out of the fence wire and his tongue followed, poking it through the fence to lick at my britches' pocket. He wanted my stashed onion. So I dug in my pocket to get it for him—and out came Cuz's lucky rabbit's foot with it, falling right through the fence wire to land by the girl's huge hoof. Not until I felt the boy's tongue flicking at my fist could I tear my eyes away from my lost lucky charm and serve up the onion.

As both giraffes stomped and swished their tails at the onion delights, my eyes wandered back to Cuz's rabbit's foot still lying by the wild girl's hoof. Needing all the luck I could get, never mind how dead "lucky" Cuz was, I decided I had to get that rabbit's foot back.

Ducking through the fence's opening, I was cocksure I could grab it quick and slick. As I closed my fingers around the rabbit fur, though, Wild Girl shuffled her hooves—and her wounded leg thumped *me*. Swiveling her big haunch, she bumped me so mightily that when I landed I bounced. Scrambling backward, I flung myself out of the pen. When I glanced back, she was giving me a look so offended that it had me all but begging her pardon.

Just then, the Old Man snort-snored loud enough to wake the next county and broke me out of my giraffe spell. Cramming the rabbit's foot in my pocket, I lurched toward the barn doors. I was halfway to them when I remembered the driver's produce free for the taking and, damn me, I had to take. Sneaking over to the truck's cab, I had loaded up my arms when I realized I wasn't hearing the Old Man's snores anymore—I was hearing the clomp of his boots. He was going to catch me where I stood unless I dropped the produce and ran.

And I wasn't about to drop that produce.

To my left, waist high, was one of the contraption rig's trapdoors. Juggling the goober's food, I gave it a yank and, to my young shock, it opened. So I dove inside, landing in a mound of peat moss, produce falling everywhere. With no time to shut the trapdoor behind me, I waited to be yanked out by my ears, my heart pumping wild.

But nothing happened. Hearing the Old Man's sweet giraffe-cooing, I eased the trapdoor shut. In a moment, his boots shuffled past again, his snores started back up, and my heart slowed. Wolfing down all the produce I could find, I leaned my bunged-up bones back into the padding to rest a minute before trying to sneak out again. Instead my eyes closed on their own—there was no fighting it—that day of days had its way.

And as I fell into the sleep of the dead, I was sure I was already dreaming because I thought I heard the giraffes *humming* to each other. It was a low, purring, rumbling *thhhhhhrummmm* . . . and it was as soothing as the Old Man's giraffe-speak.

New York Sun

SEPTEMBER 22, 1938

HURRICANE GIRAFFES TO QUARANTINE

ATHENIA, NJ—Sept. 22 (Evening special edition). The miracle giraffes who survived the killer hurricane on the high seas had to make their way through the flooded and blocked streets of Manhattan today in order to get to the United States Bureau of Animal Industry Quarantine Station in Athenia, New Jersey. After passing quarantine, they will attempt a daring road trip cross-country to the San Diego Zoo, on the orders of its famous lady director, Mrs. Belle Benchley.

. . . "Morning, sunshine! Time for breakfast."

Someone's busting through the door behind me and it jolts me from these scribbles so hard my heart jumps.

Rubbing my chest, I start to yell GO AWAY at the orderly when out of the corner of my eye I see Wild Girl—her long neck has reached in my fifth-floor window and she's blowing a snuffling spitball my way. Gaping at the impossible wonder of her, I feel the same clutch around my heart on first spying her and Boy down the dock, and I'm glad to still be alive to feel it again.

"I heard you were a bad boy last night. Punching the TV? My good-ness!" the orderly is saying, standing there in his starchy whites. "And now you're late for breakfast." It's an orderly I do not like. He's greasy-haired like Earl the driver and talks to me like I'm simple, his voice as irritating as crotch itch. He's only inches from Wild Girl and I worry he'll spook her.

"Not going," I say quick.

He grabs my wheelchair handles. "Sure you are. C'mon."

I grab the desk. "I can't go, I'm too—" busy, I try to say, but my heart stutters mmmphgh and I almost drop my pencil.

Greasy steps back. "OK, OK."

Clutching the blessed wooden thing, I glance at Wild Girl, who is shooting me the stink eye. "Don't give me that look," I wheeze. "I'm not stopping, I swear. I'm going to tell her the whole thing," I say, writing this down. "See, Girl?"

"What girl?" Greasy says as I scribble. "Who you talking to, sunshine?"

Another orderly pokes his nose in from the hall. "*That* shriveled-up beanpole busted the TV?" he whispers to Greasy, thinking I can't hear.

"Yeah, and now he's talking to a dead girl," whispers Greasy.

"You gonna report it?" whispers Hall Voice.

"Nah. We'd be reporting them all," whispers Greasy.

"Just shoot me if I get *that* old," Hall Voice goes on. "I tell you one thing, you don't want him so worked up he checks out on your shift. It's gross. One did it to me yesterday. Hey, what's he doing now? He's writing like a fool on fire over there . . . wait, he's not writing down what I just said, is he?"

"You *bet* I *am*!" I say, scribbling faster.

"Now, now, sunshine," croons Greasy, "we're leaving, OK?"

"And shut the door!" I yell. "I'm stuck in the rig and we've got to hit the road!"

2

In Athenia

Hush-a-bye / Don't you cry / Go to sleep, little baby.
Brown-apple eyes stare . . . the rifle fires . . .
"Woody Nickel, tell me what happened out there
and tell me now!"

The next morning, angry voices jerked me out of the nightmare dogging me every time I fell asleep since leaving home.

"Slow down on the apples and sweet onions, Earl!"

"But I swear I ain't et more'n my share, Mr. Jones!"

"Who else's been eating them? The giraffes?"

I sat up dazed and bug-eyed, until I remembered where I was and why. Light was streaming in the trap window above me. I'd slept the whole night. Groaning, I fell back into the peat moss padding. Unless I made a run for it, my sorry hide was stuck inside the rig's traveling giraffe crate for the whole day.

There were worse places, though, for a Dust Bowl boy to be stuck. It was dry and so was I for the first time in two days. So, shaking the peat moss out of my pants, I took my first good look around. The contraption was less a big crate than a boxcar suite, a fancy Pullman car for giraffes, with a wide slit between the sides for the giraffes to see each other. Railriders would never leave a boxcar so nice. The crate's walls were so padded with plump burlap and the floors piled so high with moss that I knew I'd be doing worse in any hurricane shelter, or in the back of Cuz's boathouse—hell, even in my shack of a farmhouse back home, what with the constant wind blowing through the slats to drive even a saint insane.

Climbing up on the two-by-four bracing the crate's wall, I cracked open one of the trap windows enough to see the giraffe pen. The giraffes were standing with their necks touching again. Earl had schlupped over with full water buckets, and while Wild Boy was as mellow as milk, Wild Girl seemed to have a burr up her butt enough for both of them. Because, to my delight, when he stepped in the pen to set down the buckets, she charged him. He scrambled out so fast he landed flat on his back. Then, grumbling at Earl, the Old Man entered the pen and inched around Girl's back leg to check the bandaged splint. The zoo doc had wrapped it good, maybe too good, because Girl's long neck started swaying, left, right, left, right, and when the Old Man touched the splint, she raised that hurt back leg and kicked *sideways*—

WHOP

—whacking the Old Man's thigh so hard, it sent him and his fedora flying.

I cringed. Giraffes *kick*. That could've been *me* the night before. A kicking mule can kill or cripple a man for life, much less a kicking two-ton giraffe, so I expected the Old Man to either be dead or wishing he was. While a mule has one kicking gear, though, the giraffe seemed to have plenty of gears to express its displeasure that weren't so deadly. Because instead of being dead or worse, the Old Man was grabbing his hat and scrambling out of the pen. If a mule kicked Pa, Pa'd let him have it with an ax handle. Not the Old Man. He didn't even utter a harsh word toward the giraffe.

The driver skittered over to help, but the Old Man waved him away, like he got kicked by a giraffe every day. "I need to send a telegram," he grunted, popping the fedora back on his head. Then, trying not to limp, he headed for the barn doors.

Hearing the barn doors' squawk, I knew it was my chance to go. But then I felt the rig jostle and I peeked out. Earl was standing on the running board again, reaching into the truck cab. He came out with a flask. He took a mighty swig, then stashed it back in his hiding place. When I heard him flop down on the cot out of sight, I eased open the trapdoor and crawled out backward, searching for the ground . . .

. . . just as the squawk of those blasted barn doors filled the air.

And I met the Old Man.

"WHAT the—!"

As my boots hit the dirt, I felt him grab my arm, and I did what I always did when I got grabbed. I threw a punch. The Old Man saw it coming and slapped it away. So I did the only thing left to do—I rushed right at him, knocking us both on the ground.

Scrambling up, I ran out the barn doors to the sound of him bawling out "Earl!" at the top of his lungs.

At my raccoon hole, I slid under and ran until I couldn't see the quarantine station anymore. Then I leaned on a broken tree trunk to catch my breath and think. Following the giraffes to California wasn't going to be a cinch any longer. The Old Man had seen me. I was at a loss for what to do, so I started walking, the sort of aimless kind of walking that drifting, vacant-eyed joes did back in the Hard Times, putting one foot in front of the other, over and over, until I wandered into a country store and tried snitching a loaf of bread.

"I saw that, you piece of road trash!" the grocer hollered, grabbing my shirt and ripping it clean off my back at the door, sending the bread flying into a puddle. I kept moving. But not before scooping up that muddy loaf.

"That's it!" yelled the grocer. "I'm calling the sheriff to clear your kind out again!"

With the word *sheriff* thundering in my ears, I stuffed both cheeks with soggy bread and ran until I felt safe. Feeling as low as a snake, my bony chest now bare to the wind except for my holey undershirt, I wandered into a tramp camp near a side track as a freight train was passing by—and I knew this was what the grocer meant when he said "your kind." Gulping down the last of the filthy bread, I watched a tramp running for a boxcar already full of railriders, high-stepping to keep from being dragged under, and my stray-dog future hit me in the face. Who was I fooling thinking I could buck it?

Yet I couldn't shake the longing for milk and honey the Californy-bound giraffes had given me, and I felt my flickering hope turn flaming do-or-die. That's what the tiniest speck of hope did to you back then. Got you making plans and dreaming dreams in the face of a fool's folly that hung on a couple of giraffes. You clutched it, nursed it, kept it safe and warm, because that was the only difference between you and the vacant-eyed joes aimlessly walking, dead before their time.

So, soon I found my way back to the deserted depot in front of the quarantine station's gate, where nothing had changed at all, including the hurricane-whopped cow. Even my thieved cycle was where I'd hid it behind the big toppled oak.

What I didn't expect was the green Packard.

Red and the duded-up reporter were stopped exactly where I'd last seen them. I snuck within a few feet of them again, crouching behind the oak. They were standing by the Packard, and I didn't much like the way he was talking to her.

"Lionel Abraham Lowe—*Life* magazine!" she was saying as she reloaded her camera.

"For the love of God, will you shut up about it? Now let's go. I did you a favor driving you out here again. But no more."

"You know I can't drive," she answered, lifting her camera, "and I have to have more. It's *Life* magazine!"

"Augie, I've got to go!"

When she didn't stop, the reporter did something I couldn't abide—he grabbed her arm. Before I knew I was even doing it, I'd run over and punched him.

Howling, he fell back against the Packard, grabbing his nose. "*You!* You're going to *jail*, you little *shit!*" he sputtered. "Augusta, take his picture and then get the guard to call the *cops!*"

Red, though, was staring at me still standing there staring back, fists up. I was so besotted with her, I'd punched but forgotten to run.

"*Dammit*, my shirt's ruined!" the reporter moaned, whipping out a handkerchief to staunch the blood. "Augie, I said snap this sonuvabitch!"

But instead of taking my picture, she mouthed *Go!*

And I finally remembered to run.

As I waited for the giraffes to hit the road, I spent the afternoons snitching food from anybody but the country grocer, and I spent the nights huddled on the deserted depot's platform fighting off sleep for fear of my nightmare. Since leaving home, the hours awake in the dark alone with my thoughts hadn't been much better than my haunted sleep. My mind would wander back to the sights of my family's graves and the sounds of my ma's and baby sister's gasps as the dust pneumonia slowly strangled them dead. There was no waking up from that.

Lying under the stars that first night at the depot, though, I wasn't seeing graves and hearing death rattles. I was seeing the wondrous sights and sounds of Red and the giraffes. Even then, I knew I was probably better off never seeing Red again since I'd punched the reporter. Telling myself it was to protect my Californy plan, though, I wished I could visit the giraffes. As I lay there thinking about it, sleepless but less lonely, I kept feeling them snuffling my hair and nibbling at my pocket, unaware the giraffes were already working their giraffe magic on me far beyond my orphaned-boy scheme for them.

By the next afternoon, I'd swiped a shirt from a clothesline to fend off nightly skeeters before I returned to the depot. Once there, the time passed slow. I swatted flies and shifted with the wind as the bloated cow ripened. I watched the guard chew and spit. I watched trucks come and go. That was it.

Until Red appeared. Alone—and driving. Badly.

Bouncing that fancy Packard over the tracks, she jerked to a grinding halt, all but stripping the gears. For the longest time, she stared toward the gate with a far-off look, not even taking a picture, and I drank in the fiery sight of her doing it, my insides turning to mush with each red curl she pushed off her face.

When she finally got out to take photos by the gate, I found myself peeking in the Packard's open window. I'd have said I was scrounging for food if caught, but that wasn't why. I wanted more. More of *her*. I'd have been happy with only a whiff of her eau de toilette in the air, but there on the seat was a brand-new notepad.

When she drove away without noticing it was gone, I hunkered down, notepad in hand, beside the tree trunk and opened it. Stuck inside the front page was a fresh news clipping, written by Lionel Abraham Lowe, "Mr. Big Reporter":

New York World-Telegram

SEPTEMBER 22, 1938

MIRACLE GIRAFFES RIDE HURRICANE AT SEA

NEW YORK—Sept. 22 (Special edition). After riding through The Great Hurricane that decimated the Eastern Seaboard yesterday, the SS *Robin Goodfellow* limped into New York Harbor this morning along with two giraffes left for dead . . .

The next page was filled with her scribbled notes:

Hurricane sea survival miracle . . . Manhattan floods afire . : . Cycle cops . . . NY and NJ.
Normal truck . . . custom-built bed.
Putrid bloated cow . . . guernsey.
Bronx Zoo vet . . . why?
Tall, gaunt, battered, handsome boy with a nice uppercut . . . who?
First CA giraffes. First female zoo director.
First USA cross-country. Lincoln or Lee Highway . . . how?
12 days to figure.

Red had mentioned *me*. Even better, she'd called me *handsome*—nobody'd ever done that before. Hoping for more, I turned the page, but there was nothing else until the very last page, where she'd started a list:

THINGS I'M DOING BEFORE I DIE
- Meet:
    - Margaret Bourke-White
    - Amelia Earhart
    - Eleanor Roosevelt
    - Belle Benchley
- Touch a giraffe
- See the world, starting with Africa
- Speak French
- Learn to drive
- Have a daughter
- See my photos in Life magazine

It looked like what people nowadays call a bucket list, as in things to do before kicking the bucket. I'd soon find out, though, that was not the half of it.

The next day she came back, and when she wasn't looking, I dropped the notepad back into the Packard window. Her smile when she found it was pure glory.

After that, waiting for her to appear kept me at the depot as much as waiting on the giraffes. The daily sight of her turned my depot nights fighting off nightmares and dark Panhandle memories into hours of recalling her instead. I'd start with her hair, memorizing every fiery curl. I'd study the memory of her smile, the widow's peak on her forehead, each freckle on her nose, the curve of her face and figure, savoring every little detail from silky white shirt to tailored trousers and two-tone shoes, even the camera she clutched like a lover, until I'd stop and drown for a while in the memory of her hazel-eyed gaze. Then, as the nights wore on, I began imagining how I might kiss her. Besotted as I was, I wasn't fool enough to think I'd ever kiss Red for real. For all I knew I'd never get that close to her again. Yet I whiled away untroubled hours working on it all—how I'd place my hand on the back of those flaming curls. How I'd lace my fingers through their thick strands. How I'd either come in slow and sweet and tender or sweep her up planting a big one on her, fearless and lusty, like a full-grown man. I'm not ashamed to admit that it's warming up a scribbling old man right now as I remember the remembering. And when I'd feel myself getting sleepy huddled there on the depot's platform, I'd start over.

But nobody can run from sleep forever. After a few nights, despite all my efforts, I nodded off—and the familiar old nightmare came.

> *Hush-a-bye / Don't you cry / Go to sleep, little baby.*
> *"It's time I made a man outa you!"*
> *"Woody Nickel, tell me what happened out there*
>   *and tell me now!"*
> *Brown-apple eyes stare . . . the* rifle *fires . . .*
> *and rushing waters roar . . .*
> *. . . "Li'l one, who* you *talking to?"*

Bolting to my feet, I started pacing. I could still hear the parts of the nightmare I'd come to know too well—my ma singing, my pa yelling, and my rifle firing, surprised like always not to feel the county sheriff yanking me off the Muleshoe train. This time, though, in the same old nightmare there was something new.

And it shook me up good.

There's a family story my ma loved to tell, how as a toddler I kept slipping from my slatboard crib only to be found in the barn with the mare, jabbering away. "Li'l one, who you talking to?" my ma'd say. When I'd point to the mare, she'd sweep me up singing the hush-a-bye lullaby. Other times she'd find me jabbering out near the prairie high grass, and when she'd say, "Li'l one, who you talking to?" I'd point to the edge of the high grass where there'd be a rabbit or a lizard or a field rat scuttling away. But when my naptime jabbering started being about things beyond my ken, like the preacher coming or a storm brewing or the rooster croaking, Pa's jaw muscles would quiver as Ma praised Jesus, calling it the gift of second sight just like her aunt Beulah, who talked to the birds. So Pa set about breaking me of it.

That's all it ever was, only a story Ma'd tell . . . until I was blown speechless by the dust only to be whopped senseless by a hurricane and found myself pacing the deserted depot. Because not only had I just heard Ma's *Li'l one* question, but I'd also heard rushing water—and if there's one thing we didn't have in the Panhandle it was *water*, rushing or otherwise. So, as I paced, bug-eyed over sudden thoughts of Aunt Beulah and her second sight, I swore to never sleep again. Not even thoughts of the giraffes or kissing Red could calm me.

After that, sleepless and twitchy, I counted down the rest of the days and nights waiting for the giraffes to hit the road. I barely left the depot for fear I'd miss them.

Finally, the zoo doc's truck appeared and disappeared through the gate.

It was time.

Sprinting to my raccoon hole, I squeezed under and rushed to the tall barn. The big doors were yawning wide, and there was the zoo doc's truck. Lurking near the doc's truck, I should have been worrying about being seen, but I'd have had to drive a cattle truck into the barn for any of them to look around, especially the Old Man. He had bigger problems. He was trying to board the giraffes and the giraffes weren't having it.

The rig was pulled up close to the pen and the entire side of the rig's boxcar-T contraption was open, including the top. I hadn't seen it could do that. With swinging hinges on the bottom and latches along the top, the entire side lay down to the ground. It made the padded crates look big, wide, even inviting. Two short sloping chutes had been placed between the pen and the rig to guide the giraffes into their new traveling compartments. But those giraffes knew what a crate was, nice or not, and they sure knew what a truck was. They'd both taken two steps into the chutes, saw where they were headed, and stopped cold.

How long they'd been in the chutes I couldn't say, but from how worn-out the Old Man looked, it had been awhile. Fidgeting with his fedora, he was sitting on his haunches in his undershirt, staring at the giraffes. The zoo doc was standing by the chutes, staring at Girl's splint. Earl was standing by some joes in khaki work-duds, all breathing hard. The Old Man got to his feet. Looking pure frustrated, he stalked over and grabbed some rope, and he, the zoo doc, and the khaki joes tried roping the giraffes like calves to pull them in. Still, the big beasts didn't budge, and the Old Man slid back to the ground, looking clean out of ideas.

Then Wild Girl's nostrils started quivering, her neck stretching toward the rig compartment where I'd slept. She took a step. Then another. Sticking her big snout into the open compartment's corner, she came up chomping. She'd found one of the onions I'd lost in the padding.

The Old Man, no fool, was back up on his boots. Grabbing the gunnysack from the cab, he began pitching onions into the boxcar suite, and lickety-split, Girl strode right into the peat moss searching for the produce. The Old Man pitched the rest into the other compartment, and there went Boy.

At that, everybody rushed in to raise both sides and latch them tight. When the two giraffes stuck their big heads out their windows, licking their lips for the last taste of their onions, the Old Man took off his hat and heaved a great sigh. Then he and the zoo doc marched toward the doc's truck, right where I hid. I scrambled behind a barrel.

"You're going to have to reapply the sulfa to the wound on the road," the zoo doc was saying. "How many times depends on the roughness of the ride and how long you're forced to ride. If you can stave off infection, she's got a fighting chance." He grabbed an extra black bag from the truck and popped it on the hood to show off the contents—bandages, splints, and medicine bottles—then handed it to the Old Man. "Packed this for them. With extra for the two of *you*." The zoo doc shook the Old Man's hand, got in the truck, and with a last "Good luck," drove away.

The Old Man let the giraffes get used to their traveling boxcar suites for the rest of the day, so I settled in behind the barrel and waited through the night.

Before dawn, the Old Man threw the barn doors open. Earl was already behind the rig's wheel, engine idling, and the giraffes' heads were out. With a last look back, the Old Man climbed in the truck cab and the rig rolled out the doors.

Rushing to my fence squeeze-hole, I all but beat them to the front gate. Their lights flashing in the predawn dark, two New Jersey state cycle cops were waiting and escorted the giraffe rig onto the road.

I dragged the thieved cycle from under the downed oak, cranked it sputtering, spewing, backfiring to life, and, after a mighty rub of Cuz's rabbit's foot, I followed. *Californy, here we come,* I thought. With nothing between but the entire USA, sea to shining sea.

Little did I know I wasn't the only one with plans for the giraffes, and worse, that those plans included never getting to California at all.

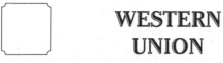

WESTERN UNION

5 OCT 38 = 0334P

TO: MRS. BELLE BENCHLEY
SAN DIEGO ZOO
SAN DIEGO, CALIFORNIA

GIRAFFES IN TRUCK. LEAVE DAWN.

RJ

WESTERN UNION

5 OCT 38 = 0402P

TO: MR. RILEY JONES
US QUARANTINE STATION
ATHENIA, NEW JERSEY

[HOLD]

GODSPEED. CONTACT AS CAN.

BB

WESTERN
UNION

5 OCT 38 = 0501P

TO: MRS. BELLE BENCHLEY
SAN DIEGO ZOO
SAN DIEGO, CALIFORNIA

TRAVEL COVERAGE APPROVED FREIGHTING
TWO GIRAFFES VIA
OUTFITTED TRUCK. ADDENDED: BLOWOUTS.
ACTS OF GOD. TORNADOES
DUST STORMS. FLOODS. WIRED $150
PREMIUM WILL PUT INTO
EFFECT.

A. PETTIGREW
LLOYD'S OF LONDON
12 LEADENHALL STREET
LONDON EC3

Newark Evening News

OCTOBER 6, 1938

HURRICANE GIRAFFES HIT ROAD
Pair to Cross New Jersey Today Toward California

ATHENIA, NJ—Oct. 6 (Special edition). The two miracle giraffes who survived the recent hurricane at sea will now be the first giraffes ever to cross the continent by truck. They leave the federal animal quarantine at Athenia today for the San Diego Zoo, California, 3,200 miles away.

The giraffes will crisscross New Jersey this morning, so state police are offering escort and warning citizens to keep their eyes peeled for the "giraffe road Pullman."

Chicago Tribune

OCTOBER 7, 1938

SAN DIEGO GIRAFFES IN CROSS-COUNTRY DASH

NEW YORK—Oct. 7. Transcontinental giraffe hauling was inaugurated today, opening a new era in the history of shipping, animal husbandry, and trouble. San Diego Zoo's Mrs. Belle Benchley, the world's first female zoo director, has tasked her most experienced man, Riley Jones, with the feat, made hazardous by the height of the cargo and the delicacy of a giraffe's bones. If Jones can get the lanky treasures through subways, viaducts, covered bridges, and low-hanging branches, it will be the first time in the history of giraffes that anyone ever hauled two of them, or even one of them, from one coast to the other.

"They're young. They don't have all their height yet, so we've got 12 feet 8 inches' clearance," Jones said, having scouted the routes himself, "and if need be I can let some air out of the tires."

Asked to comment on the odyssey, Edward Bean, Chicago's Brookfield Zoo director said, "Jones is a good man. If he's got himself a good driver, he'll get them through . . ."

. . . "Hon?"

Someone's at my door *again*, jangling me out of my scribbling. Before I can do a thing about it, in strides another orderly. I start to growl at him, but it's a her. She's flame-haired. Familiar.

Then I remember. She's the big-boned redheaded gal I like—Rose? Rosie? Yeah, *Rosie.*

"You didn't come to breakfast, hon. The chaplain will be here soon for chapel. Why don't you let me to take you down?"

It's Sunday morning. I never go. Which doesn't keep them from asking. It's a kindness in their minds to offer, seeing as each Sunday could be the last chance for us old reprobates to rectify. Today may *be* my last chance. But these scribbles are my rectifying. I study her face a second and then turn back to my writing pad. "I'm busy."

"Hon, do you *recognize* me?" she says next.

"'Course I do," I mutter over my shoulder.

"Oh, hon, it's been such a long time! You used to make me play a game of dominoes and hear a story before you'd take your pills, remember?" she is saying. "I heard about the giraffes. I'm so sorry." But then I hear her reach over and close the window.

Whirling around too fast, my wheelchair bumps the bedstead and I almost fall out. "OPEN IT—OPEN IT!"

She pushes the window back up. Wild Girl is still there. My heart starts stuttering *mmmphgh* again and I rub it.

Rosie notices. "I better call the nurse right now to give you a pill."

"No! No *nurses*. No *pills*. I got to think straight to write it all down for her!"

Rosie settles her hands on her sturdy hips to look me up and down, exactly like the Old Man used to do. Pushing a graying strand of hair behind her ear, she says, "OK, but I'm staying until you calm down."

"Suit yourself," I say, calm as a clam, then return to my writing pad, hoping that will hush her. It does not.

"Hon, who is 'her'? Who are you 'writing it all down' for?"

I don't answer.

"Is it Augusta Red?"

I almost jerk my neck off looking around. "How do you know about Red?"

"She's in all the stories you told me while we played dominoes. Augusta Red, the Old Man, and the giraffes. Is that what you're writing down—your trip? But you always said it didn't matter."

"I was wrong," I mumble. Calmly. And start back writing.

For a few minutes, she perches her big self on the edge of the bed. Then, hearing her get up, I watch her close the door behind her, remembering it all.

A game of dominoes and a story . . .

3

Across New Jersey and Delaware

So we hit the road.

Being on the road's no song, though. Not if you're a stray. There's nothing more pitiful than a wandering creature who was never meant to be wild. By the time a stray dog showed up at our Panhandle farm, it had that scary all-is-lost look that made even my saintly Christian ma run it off. She'd never have believed she'd turn away a stray boy, though, and I know you'd want to believe you'd do the same. But there were thousands of us back then, wandering, hapless, and reckless. What if you lived by the tracks? Or the highway? What if your place got marked as the home of a kindhearted Christian or a Roosevelt bleeding heart so that you had dirty bums and feral boys knocking on your screen door night and day? Would you lock your doors and close your curtains? Would you hide your little ones in your own house? What if a tramp starts waving a straight razor or glass shard at the competition hiding in your shrubbery? Would you call the police or reach for your shotgun?

You won't remember all that back then—and I'm glad of it. I've tried to forget what it was like as a stray boy heading toward Cuz. I was barely human after the first wretched few days, and as time went on I cared less about being so. When your shriveled stomach's aching with hunger, you forget all about your hungry heart. And you keep on forgetting it a little each day until a stray dog has more heart or soul than you.

Then, there were the roads themselves. What we called highways were barely tolerable for transporting people much less chauffeuring giraffes. The country's only two "transcontinental auto trails" were so singular they had names—the Lincoln and the Lee—and we weren't near either of them. Most town-to-town roads still had little more than a gas station guy pointing you the right way or the dead-and-gone wrong. During the Hard Times, taking them any stretch at all could mean taking your life into your own hands—which I was aiming to avoid by following the giraffes.

So, while I should have been quaking at the thought of hitting the road again, I was OK as long as I could see the rig. As the sun came up, though, it began to wobble. It was as if, spooked by daylight, the giraffes didn't know where to stand in this new fresh hell they were in, their heads popping in and out, the back of the rig swaying and rocking, one time even lifting the tires right off the road so bad I thought they might flip over and finish themselves off before we'd even got started. The Old Man, though, started screaming at Earl until the rig slowed to a crawl, the giraffes got their balance, and everything simmered down.

With that, the cycle cops started poking us down the entire length of New Jersey.

In the first burg, people were so surprised, a few sleepy neck-twisting guffaws were all anybody could muster before we were gone.

By the second, though, the people seemed to know the giraffes were coming. The rig was met by the local patrol car at the city limits. As the cops and the rig inched turtle-slow through town, I found myself in a sudden parade. Cars and bicycles fell in behind. Old men waved from stools and steps and bungalow porches. Women in housedresses stood on verandas holding up babies. Townspeople lining the sidewalks were holding up newspapers, and a boy running alongside me kept waving one in my face, so I snatched it, giving the front page a quick glance as we kept rolling. While I didn't pay it much mind at the time, the top headline was one for the ages:

HITLER STOPPED—"PEACE IN OUR TIMES"

Thinking of that headline now, I get a shiver. It was talking about the Munich Agreement, a thing that sounds like something nobody would remember this side of schoolbooks, but the whole world would soon be remembering it far too well. Hitler had seized Austria and was now wanting a chunk of Czechoslovakia, promising peace if he could have it. The spooked Allies handed it right over, believing in fairy tales told by a madman. Back then, though, what was that to me on the other side of the world? Giving Adolph Hitler no thought at all, I flipped the paper over and there was the story everybody but me had already seen:

HURRICANE GIRAFFES HIT ROAD

I pulled over to the curb to read it, but I didn't get past the head-line. Because, out of the corner of my eye, I caught a sight that made me drop the paper and jerk my head clean around—a green Packard. There it went, right by me, with Red hanging out the window snapping pictures and the reporter behind the wheel. As we left the town behind, I kept expecting it to peel off and disappear home again, like before, but it kept following.

So now I was following it, too.

We moved on like that all morning in a sort of rhythm: farmland quiet, dumbstruck hitchhikers, small towns, local cops, sudden parades, and jubilating townies yelling the same geehaws:

"How's the weather up *there*?"

"I'm seeing *spots* before my eyes!"

"Low *bridge*!"

Then, with no warning, the New Jersey cycle cops gave one last salute to the Old Man and vanished back the way they came. We were at the state line. Which was all good and fine, except the state line was a river and there wasn't any bridge to the other side. There was a ferry. A boat. Taking us over water. And *that* was no small thing, considering water had tried to kill both the giraffes and me.

The Old Man didn't look too happy about it, either. As the rig came to a stop at the landing, he hopped out and held up the line until getting some sort of satisfaction from the ferryman. He took off that grungy fedora, wiped at his brow with the back of his sleeve, and watched as the ferryman guided Earl to roll the rig on. When it came to a stop, the Old Man put his hat back on, heaved a great fume, and stepped on board himself. As other cars filled in behind, I bided my time. Then, with a rub of my rabbit's foot, I took a deep breath and walked the cycle on.

As we pushed off, every last person on that ferry silently got out of their cars to gaze at the giraffes. The sight of those big giraffe heads stuck out their windows against the reflection of the smooth river made me go silent, too, inside and out. It was a magical thing. My rowdy young self fought the warm feeling, but I remember the moment as wondrous. We were moving across the Delaware River with giraffes and I think we could have done it without a motor. The calmest of us all seemed the giraffes themselves. Whether the river's flow was so still they didn't notice it was water or whether they'd made peace with their road Pullman, they were riding free and easy.

I looked around for Red, hoping she was snapping pictures of it, but the green Packard wasn't on the ferry. Spinning around, I scanned the shoreline. There it was, still on the landing. Red and the reporter were in front of it, and my warm feeling turned into flitting fury at what I saw next.

He motioned toward the car.

She threw up her hands.

He grabbed her arm again.

She jerked it back.

He got back in the car, slammed the door, and gunned the motor, waiting for her to follow.

But she didn't. Not at first.

Instead she turned and stared back at the giraffes.

I studied Red's gaze as we moved farther and farther away, her face full of things I did not understand yet was desperate to remember before she vanished from sight. I was certain I'd never see her again . . . and I watched long after I could no longer make out the green of the car or the fire of her hair.

When the ferry landed on the other side, everybody made way for the giraffes and their rig, like the Old Man was the king of Siam with passing wonders to behold. As the giraffes' heads disappeared over the riverbank, nobody moved. Under the spell of giraffes and ferries and rolling river, they stayed that way for so long I thought I'd never get off. Snaking around them all, I revved the cycle, fearing I'd lose sight of the giraffes, but there they were, those giraffe heads high, proud, and impossible to miss, and I slowed back to a calm putter.

Soon, we crossed another state line, which seemed to be coming as quick as county lines in Texas. **WELCOME TO MARYLAND**, the sign said. The rig slowed down even more, the road curving this way and that, with tractors, pickups, and even a horse-drawn wagon pulling in and out between us. Then the road took a sharp bend and the rig disappeared.

Next thing I heard was the sound of screeching tires . . . followed by a sickening thud and a deathly howl. My flesh crawling, I inched around that curve and what I saw made me veer for the cover of the ditch's overgrowth. The rig was stopped dead in the middle of the road, and something big was lying by its right fender, spun halfway into the ditch. I was sure Earl had hit a hitchhiker. But it was a mangy stray dog, as big as a pony, and its bowels were hanging out of its bloody, shredded fur.

Ordering Earl to stay put, the Old Man took the rifle from the cab's gunrack and moved toward it. He eased down by the dying dog, gun in his lap, as the dog went full into its death jerks. When the panting and jerking kept on going and going, the Old Man rose and cocked the rifle. Between one panting jerk and the next, though, the dog went still. Lowering the gun, the Old Man paused. Then, hunkering down again, he laid a hand on the dead dog's fur and left it there, like he was offering up some sort of Old Man benediction.

As I watched, in my mind's eye I was in the Panhandle driving Pa's pickup as we hit something yellow and saw it tumble into the brush. Pa got out to cuss the dented fender, and I'd just taken the rifle from the gunrack when Pa turned his cusses on me: *God-DAMN it, son! Where you going? If it's a coyote, we shoot coyotes for being coyotes. If it's a stray dog, we ain't wasting a bullet on it. Stop acting like you're still in knickers. They're just animals!*

Up ahead, the Old Man got to his feet, grabbed the cur's leg, and dragged the carcass full off the road. The giraffes were watching, their heads out their windows. So he climbed up to give them both a pat on their necks, his giraffe-speak wafting back to me on the wind, then he crawled back in the cab and the rig moved on, vanishing around the next curve. I eased the cycle past the carcass, storing the scene away to ponder.

With the next turn of the road, though, I had bigger worries. The cycle's gas gauge was hazarding empty and there I was without a dime or a dollar.

I kept on following. What else could I do?

With me riding on fumes and sundown on its way, we were closing in on a town called Conowingo, which sticks in my memory for more reasons than the peculiar sound of it. Trees lining the right, the road veered near a quick-moving river on the left and stayed.

Then came the signs:

ONE WAY BRIDGE, said the first one.

LOW WATER CROSSING, warned the next.

I could barely believe it. Were they really going to drive those giraffes right into the river?

From one second to the next, though, none of that mattered a whit, since that was the moment the cycle gulped, chugged, and clunked to a stop.

Pounding the clutch, I jumped up and down on the throttle like I could pump ethyl into the cycle with just my hopping, and I kept it up beyond all good sense, wearing myself clean out.

Sucking wind, I stared after the shrinking rig, realizing, like a stab to the heart, I was about to say goodbye to my California plan. *It's over,* I told myself, thinking how I'd sell my soul for it not to be—and considering I hadn't yet quite become acquainted with my soul, that was a surprising thought. So, fueled by the same do-or-die fury I'd felt on the dock, I started running, thinking I might as well die from the running than the standing and watching my flickering hope fade.

But then, this side of the bridge, the rig slowed to a crawl and I began to wonder if I *had* bargained away my worthless thieving soul. Because the rig disappeared into the trees past a sign that said,

AUTO CAMP & CABINS
TURN HERE

Sprinting back to the cycle, I started pushing the dead machine toward the sign, my heart pumping so hard I was gulping air.

By the time I made it to the entrance, the rig was idling by the office that also doubled as an eight-stool lunch counter serving up supper from the looks of the backsides parked on the stools.

Hustling out of sight, I saw the Old Man and the manager appear from inside. As the manager pointed the way, they rolled the giraffes toward the last of a handful of tiny cabins, each barely big enough for a bed, parking the road Pullman under a spreading sycamore tree. I pushed the motorcycle through the underbrush and crept behind a boulder to watch the Old Man open the rig's top and the giraffes' big snouts stretch to nibble at the sycamore.

In mid-nibble, though, both giraffes turned their quivering snouts my way—like they'd gotten a whiff of my ripe young self on the wind. I ducked out of sight, but when I looked back, they were still doing it. Wild Girl's snout was even swaying, like she was jockeying for a better smell. I was so sure they were going to give me away, I ducked full behind the boulder and stayed there until I heard the trapdoors flop open and the Old Man order Earl to water the giraffes. I could see the giraffes' hooves through the trapdoors. The driver shoved in Wild Boy's water bucket with no problem. But when he shoved in Girl's, her hoof popped his arm hard enough to make him cuss and stumble back, which pleased me greatly.

Then, determined to check that bandaged splint, the Old Man went into his own dance with Wild Girl. He waited until her splinted fetlock was near the opening, then reached in. She kicked. He dodged, she kicked again, and he plunked down on the running board to glare at Earl, who was standing so far away he was halfway to me.

That's when the manager marched up with a pile of hamburgers from the lunch counter and brought everybody with him. Trailing behind came all the diners, including the driver of a shiny dairy truck parked near the road who offered up jugs of fresh milk to go with the burgers. The hamburger smell was making me crazy, so I pulled out a pilfered potato and ate it raw to keep from doing anything stupid. When the manager shooed everybody away, I knew the whole county was about to hear what was parked at the camp. As the sun went on down, the giraffes kept nibbling from the sycamore, but with each change of the breeze, they were still turning their sniffing snouts toward me. So I stayed put until the only light was from the office lamp pole streaming through the trees.

Peeking out, I saw the Old Man wave Earl to the cabin, ease down on the truck's running board, and pat himself a cigarette from a Lucky Strike pack. That he could afford store-bought smokes, instead of rolling his own, was an impressive sight for my farmboy eyes. As he flicked open his Zippo and lit up, I decided everybody in California must be as rich as a Rockefeller, which made me ache all the more to keep on following. I eyed that dairy truck, dreaming of milk if not honey, and I took another bite of my potato, picking sweet grapes from a Californy vine in my mind. Finding a mossy soft spot against the boulder, I settled in to watch as the Old Man smoked one Lucky after the other, lighting the new one from the butt of the old. As always, I wasn't about to let myself fall asleep if I could help it, so I stayed up hour after hour with the Old Man, spending the time plotting how I could keep following them.

Since I wasn't much good at planning ahead, my ideas stunk . . . I could use the gas pump out front, but I'd have to first find a dime or a dollar in somebody else's pocket. I could snitch another vehicle, but the snitch-worthy ones were already gone. The only other vehicle at the camp was the dairy truck, which would fill my stomach but wasn't exactly prime thieving material. The later it got, the more desperate and stupid my ideas got. When I was seriously considering jumping on the back of the rig like I'd jump a freight train, I gave up.

By and by, the Old Man woke Earl for his watch, ordered him to close the rig's top, and then disappeared inside the cabin. Putting a chaw of tobacco in his jaw, Earl slicked back his hair with both hands. Then, forgetting all about closing the top, he did what I feared he'd do. With a last look back at the Old Man's cabin, he pulled out the hidden flask and started tippling, swigging right past that tobacco juice, a combination only a souser could love. When he parked himself on the running board, both giraffes poked their heads out their windows, took one look down at Earl, and pulled their heads right back in. But not before Girl quivered her big nostrils one last time my way.

For the next hour, I watched Earl tipple and spit until he was leaning his lolling head against the rig's door. The only thing keeping him upright was his tobacco juice making him hack and cough—which might have been his goober plan.

Finally, when he slumped over sideways, I thought I heard sniggering somewhere beyond the rig. That got me up on my boots. From the shadows, three yahoos appeared, one of them with enough meat on his bones to make two of me, another one in nothing but overalls, and the third one a pipsqueak with a pudding-bowl haircut. After nudging Earl's slumped lump, which upped the yahoos' sniggering, the jumbo one rapped a knuckle on the road Pullman. Both trap windows flew open and out came the giraffes' heads. Taking one look at the yahoos, the giraffes had the good sense to pull their heads back in, like they'd done with Earl. So the pipsqueak decided to climb up the rig to look in the windows at *them*. With a leg up from the jumbo yahoo, there he went. The pipsqueak kept climbing while the other yahoos kept sniggering.

Then everything went bad.

Real bad.

The giraffes began stomping and snorting and shaking the rig so much the pipsqueak fell off and then got right back on.

That's when I saw what the pipsqueak saw and what the giraffes already knew . . . the top was still open. The pipsqueak was headed straight for it.

Still hearing Pa's voice in my head on top of survival lessons from the road, I stood there in the dark, clenching and unclenching my fists. I was a rowdy of the sneaky coyote variety. Even when my temper got the best of me, I never did more than punch and run, and *never* more than one guy at a time.

As the pipsqueak climbed, he whopped the rig again. With that, the giraffes shoved their heads out their windows to stare my way with eyes terrified and pleading.

Then the pipsqueak hit the top.

What happened next all but defeats my poor powers to relate. Having nowhere to go, nothing to kick, and no one to defend them, the giraffes must have thought all was lost. Because from them came a caterwaul so bone-chilling I still despair at its memory. People say giraffes don't make sounds. But I'm here to tell you they do—and this one was a moaning, bellowing, wailing piece of giraffe-terror that surely had met the hurricane itself. It was a sound only the lion at their throats must hear. I put my hands over my ears, but it didn't help—the sound was vibrating in my chest, making me feel the giraffes' terror as if it were my own. I couldn't take it a second more. Before I even knew I was doing it, I'd sprinted to the rig, dodged jumbo, punched overalls, and, with a flying leap, grabbed at the pipsqueak's leg. The two on the ground then grabbed *my* legs and spread them like a wishbone. But as they were about to make a wish, the giraffes rocked the rig and the pipsqueak fell in.

Next thing I heard over the giraffe's caterwaul was a lot of giraffe-kicking and pipsqueak-howling—followed by a sound I'd heard a thousand times before. The click-clack of a cranking shotgun.

There stood the Old Man in his skivvies, shotgun up.

The pipsqueak popped from the top like a bottle rocket, the yahoos scrambled for the cover of the trees, and I dove back behind my boulder just as the shotgun blast echoed through the woods, stunning everything silent, including, to my deep relief, the giraffe-terror caterwaul.

Hearing the Old Man reloading, I forced myself to look. The rig was still rocking, the giraffes snuffling and stomping, and the Old Man had the shotgun stuck halfway up Earl's nose.

"Where the hell *were* you!" the Old Man yelled.

"Right here . . . ," Earl sputtered. "You see me."

"I *smell* you, too, you sumbitch. You been tippling!" Swinging the shotgun under an arm, the Old Man found Earl's flask. I thought he might smack Earl with it. Instead he pitched it into the dark. "The only thing I abide less than a liar and a thief is a *boozer*."

Earl got wobbly to his feet. "I ain't drunk! I can hold my liquor. Stack of Bibles!"

"Sit back *down*," the Old Man ordered.

Earl sat back down.

"If anything happens to the giraffes because of your tippling, I swear to God I'll shoot you full of holes. Then I'll let Mrs. Benchley have a crack at ya," the Old Man said. "You hear *me*!"

Earl nodded, not moving a muscle except to look longingly after his lost flask.

Shotgun under an arm, the Old Man climbed up the rig's side to coo his giraffe-speak until the giraffes calmed all the way down. Closing the top himself, he eased to the ground. "We might as well get going before any more native sons show up," he said to Earl, who still hadn't moved. "Water 'em while I get my pants on and use the phone to call the town cop. That is, if you think you can drive. If not, you better get that way fast or I'll turn you over to the copper quicker'n you can say Jack Robinson, buddy boy." With that, shotgun still in hand, he tromped back to the cabin.

At the mention of cops, Earl began muttering. He looked scared sober enough now. A shotgun in your face can do that. But he proved he was no such thing. Still grumbling, he got up and looked around for the water bucket. When he couldn't find it, he opened Girl's trapdoor, stuck his nose in, and . . .

WHOP

. . . there went Earl, landing spread-eagle on the ground, blood trickling out his snoot and into his ears.

The Old Man came running back, shotgun once again up, and then he saw Earl. Fuming, he stared down at his driver lying there looking mighty dead. He nudged him with his boot. Earl didn't move. So the Old Man parked his gun against the rig, picked up Girl's water bucket perched in its rightful place by the water jugs, filled it from a nearby water pump, and threw the contents on Earl.

And the goober came back to life.

Both hands over his mangled nose, Earl staggered to his feet to howl and stomp and cuss all at the same time. "That giraffe tried to kill me!" he bawled, blood seeping through his fingers. "It b-broke my *nose!*"

The Old Man glanced at the open trapdoor. "Well, what the hell was your nose doing in there? *Jesus-Joseph-Mary*, what kind of rummy idiot did I hire on?" he said, picking up the shotgun. "Get yourself cleaned up. We got to go."

"But I'm seeing *double*—"

"No, you're *not*." The Old Man leveled his gaze. "You've got to drive this rig. You know full *well* I can't, and we don't have a minute to lose if we want a chance to get the female there alive. You heard the doc."

"But that giraffe wants to *kill* me!" Earl howled.

"She's not gonna kill you," the Old Man groused. "She'd have cracked your skull like a nut if she really wanted to. You've seen what she does to me and I'm still standing."

"*No*, I quit!" moaned Earl.

The Old Man whirled that shotgun up like a six-shooter. "We're on the road, you sodden sumbitch. You're not leaving us in the lurch. Now shut your trap."

Earl shut his trap.

"Sit your worthless ass back down."

Earl sat his worthless ass back down.

The Old Man lowered his gun. "I'll get you coffee and some bandages. You'll be fine or wish you were. You're driving. We've got no
choice."

Then he stalked off toward the office.

Down by the road, a truck's headlights came on. It was the dairy
truck, readying to head out. As it roared to life, Earl's head whipped
around, and with one hand still over his bloody nose, he headed straight
for it. Faster than you'd ever think a kicked, bloodied, half-drunk goober could move, he threw the passenger door wide and hopped in just
as it was rolling onto the road headed back the way we came. It happened so fast, I don't think I could have caught him even if I'd wanted
to, which I surely did not.

From the office came the Old Man, hands full of coffee and bandages, shotgun parked under an arm. As he got closer, he stared at where
Earl was supposed to be, not quite believing he wasn't there. Hearing
the dairy truck's passenger door slam as it pulled onto the road, he must
have put two and two together. Dropping the coffee and bandages, he
ran toward the road, half aiming the shotgun at the disappearing truck.

I was sure the next thing I'd hear was another shotgun blast. The
Old Man, though, stopped. And stared. Shotgun dangling. It was like
the sight of his driver vanishing was registering in inches. When it hit
home full, he spit and sputtered at the road as if anger alone could
conjure Earl back in front of him again. He began to pace, dirt clods
flying, shouting words to turn the black air blue—"sorry shit-faced sodden sumbitch" being the repeatable of the lot—until he marched back
to the rig, sank down on the running board, dropped the shotgun in
the dirt, and put his head in his hands.

He sat that way for a long time. Then, picking up the gun, he got
to his feet, straightened his spine, and headed toward the cabin.

Busting with a new idea, I made a beeline for the rig. With Wild
Boy and Girl watching, I hopped on the running board and stuck my

head in the cab's window to study the rig's gearbox, hard and long. Too long. When I jumped back to the ground, the Old Man and his raised shotgun were waiting.

I threw up my hands. "DON'T SHOOT!" I yelped, which even scared me since it was the first thing I'd said out loud since cussing and kicking Cuz. "I'm not with those yahoos! *It's me.* Remember—from *quarantine*?"

Lowering the shotgun, he squinted at the sight I surely was, standing there in my raggedy clothes caked with dried quarantine mud.

"What the . . . ," the Old Man managed. "Are you *following* us?" He moved that shotgun to his other hand, and I saw why he couldn't drive. The gnarly hand I'd noticed back at the dock was his right hand. His gear hand. So I blurted out my new and mighty idea that was still forming even as it was coming out of my mouth. "I can do it," I blurted. "You can't go all the way by yourself with Wild Boy and Girl."

"Who?"

"The giraffes—I can drive you to Callforny."

At that, he raised one of his bushy eyebrows so high I thought it'd take flight. "Who the hell asked you? And what the hell makes you think I'd want you?"

I nodded toward the road. "Because your driver just left you in a lurch, that's why. Mister, I can flat drive circles around any man alive, hand to God. I don't much sleep, I'm not a yahoo, and I sure don't booze. You can trust me."

"Trust you? I don't even know you!" The Old Man looked my raggedy self up and down, pausing at my rope-tied hand-me-down britches barely covering the tops of my boots. "How old are you?"

"Eighteen," I lied. "I can drive anything that moves, and I'm a genius with engines, I am."

"I suppose you're going to tell me you're a genius with giraffes, too?" the Old Man said.

I stuck out my chin. "Better than your driver."

"What makes you think that?"

I eased my hand into my pocket. "For starters, I know not to poke my nose near an animal's hooves," I lied again, having done exactly that fetching Cuz's rabbit's foot, which at that moment I was rubbing bald.

The Old Man looked past me. "How did you get here?"

"Motorcycle." I nodded to the cycle in the shadows.

He squinted. "Is that yours? I cannot abide a thief or a liar."

"I got it, don't I?" I answered, proving myself both.

A patrol car pulled up under the office's light pole, and I stepped back into the shadows.

The Old Man noticed.

"Enough," he growled. Stuffing the gun under his arm again, he marched to my thieved cycle, reached in, and ripped out a handful of wires, then marched back to the rig. "If I see you again I got a lawman in every town I can hand you over to. I'm guessing you don't want that. And, *Jesus-Joseph-Mary*, were you raised in a barn? Take a bath! There's a river right there. The smell coming off you is stinging my eyes." Climbing behind the wheel, he stashed the gun back on the rack. Then, pulling that beat-up fedora low over his brow, he ground every last gear until he found one that worked, bouncing and jerking the rig and the giraffes onto the road.

Slipping to the ground, I stared at the dangling wires on my out-of-gas cycle, clean out of gas myself. Because there wasn't going to be any fixing that motorcycle. Least not by me. I didn't know a thing about engines beyond kick-starting the occasional thieveable cycle. I would have told the Old Man I could raise the dead if I thought it would've kept me on the road with them. And my big idea about driving the rig? I believed, in the way only a young fool can, that the part about driving anything with wheels was bona fide. Never mind the fact that I hadn't driven anything bigger than my pa's worn-out Model T truck. And never mind that the farthest I'd ever driven it was the twenty miles into town on a Panhandle highway so straight a nearsighted granny could do it. I wasn't through with my California dreaming, though, and while I didn't know it at the time, neither were the giraffes through with me.

Salvation of any stripe is a matter of degrees.

So there I sat on my backside by that useless cycle, listening to the Old Man grinding those gears in the distance. When one of those grinds lasted a full minute, I got light-headed from wincing—and I found myself off my ass and back to doing or-dying. Where the liar in me had failed, the thief in me hadn't, but it didn't have a chance if I didn't keep moving. Once again I was on a dead run in cowboy boots, stomping hard to catch up to a couple of giraffes, and to my pure surprise, I was gaining on them. It was still country dark, the deep kind right before dawn. I could see the town cop's lights flashing on the other side of the low water bridge. But the rig's lights were still on this side. The Old Man was hesitating. In the rig's headlights, I could see the water running over the bridge, which wasn't much more than a big chunk of reinforced concrete dropped into the stream. The giraffes, heads out, were rocking the rig, surely skittish over the sound of the water—until they got the new whiff of me. Both those necks swung around to watch as I clomped toward them as fast as my boots would go. I was only a few steps away when the Old Man put it in gear. I eyed the water and eyed the back of the rig, desperate. And when you're desperate, you'll try even your most desperate plan.

In full view of my giraffe audience, I took a running leap, jumped on the back of the rig like I was hopping a freight train, and caught a slight hold as the rig rolled into the stream, my boots struggling to stay put on the splashed bumper. Somehow, when the rig bounced onto the other side, I was still attached. With every moment that passed, though, I was losing more of my grip, and it didn't much help that the giraffes' necks were so long they'd both bent them around to watch, Boy so close his tongue was licking my *hair*. I almost fell off trying to bat the snaky thing away.

As the rig entered the little sleeping town and my boots struggled to keep their toehold, I looked for something, anything, to snitch before I fell off. Nothing. As light broke, we passed the city limit sign on the other side of town, the cop car already turning around to head back. I tell you, I despaired. My grip was about to go and my boots were losing their bumper toehold. I either had to go up or was going to go down. In a matter of seconds, I'd be tumbling into the ditch and that'd be that, nothing left to do but lick my wounds as I watched the rig and my dream disappear for good. So, with no help from Boy, who continued to lick my hair, I reached high and pulled my beat-up self on top of the rig. There I lay, spread-eagle, grasping for handholds and dodging bugs as the Old Man lurched us all down the road.

Until, that is, the morning's first rubbernecker appeared.

Stunned at the early-morning sight of giraffes on his country road, the driver swerved way too close to the rig, and the Old Man must've jerked the wheel the other way—because I was suddenly airborne. Bouncing once on my bad rib, then again on my side, I landed spread-eagle in the ditch, and I must've howled pretty loud doing it. Because next thing I knew the Old Man was in my face.

"Holy *hell*, boy, were you on top of the *rig*? You should've broken your fool *neck*! What kind of stunt were you trying to pull? *No*, don't answer that." He yanked me to my feet. "Anything busted?"

My britches were split and my knee was bloody. As the giraffes snorted at me, he ran his rough hands over my limbs. Leaving me wobbling, he retrieved the zoo doc's kit, ripped the tear in my britches wider, and bandaged up my bloody knee, taking a little too much pleasure splashing Mercurochrome—nasty red stinging antiseptic we used to call "monkey blood"—on all my skinned-up parts, which had me yelping so loud the giraffes upped their snorting.

"You'll live." Pulling a dollar bill from his wallet, he flicked it at me. "Here's a dollar. Put out your thumb," he said, grabbing up the kit and heading toward the rig.

"You're *leaving* me here?"

"Somebody'll be along to give you a lift back to town so you can use that dollar to call your people and go home."

"I don't *have* people and I don't have a home," I called after him. "I want to go to *Californy*."

"That's not my problem," he called back over his shoulder.

The giraffes were snuffling loud and jumpy, swiveling their necks back and forth between us. At the sight, I swallowed hard, squared my shoulders, and called out, "No, *your* problem is your bad driving is going to give the giraffes whiplash—and how's Mrs. Benchley going to like *that*?"

He got a hitch in his step at the mention of this Mrs. Benchley I remembered from the telegrams. Pulling his fedora low, though, he kept walking.

And I heard myself yell, "You need a *hand*!"

With that dunderheaded choice of words, the Old Man stopped all right, pivoting full around to catch me staring at his gnarly hand.

"What did you just say?" he growled, shooting me the stink eye of all stink eyes, to which I wisely kept my trap shut. He threw open the driver's door, climbed up, and cranked the motor.

It sputtered and died.

He cranked it again.

"Don't flood it! Go easy on the pedal!" I hollered. When it rumbled to life, I yelled, "What if that hadn't started? You *need* me!"

What I really, really wanted to say was that I needed them.

Grinding those gears rougher and jerking the giraffes' necks harder, the Old Man bounced the rig back on the road. As I watched the giraffes rolling away once more, my heart dropped all the way to the Land of China.

Then the rig stopped.

The Old Man was waving me up.

I ran as fast as my bloodied knee would let me, and when I got to his door, he said, "You really good with engines? Don't lie to me now."

"I'm a true genius," I lied to him.

"You got a license?"

"'Course."

"And you can drive this thing?"

"It's got gears and a clutch, doesn't it?" I said.

"Let's see. I only need you to get us to DC."

"But . . . you're going to Californy."

"We are. You're not."

"But why DC?"

"Southern route starts there. Wasn't stopping, but Earl the *sumbitch* changed that," he answered. "We'll be getting a new driver with their zoo's help. That is, once the Boss Lady asks, and I don't look forward to that chat with her. Worst of it is we'll be hung up there for at least a day, maybe more. Every day we tarry is more dangerous for the darlings. But I got no choice," he added, muttering another *sumbitch* under his breath. "When—if—you get us to DC safe, I'll buy you a train ticket back to New York."

"I don't want to go back. I can get you to Californy. I swear on my ma's *grave*, I can."

The look he shot me could've stopped a rhinoceros. "You'll be OK with DC, boy, or you can stay here on the side of the road waiting for the kindness of strangers. What'll it be?"

So I nodded. He swung the door wide, moved over, and I pulled myself up quick before he changed his mind.

Jangling all our molars, I found my way through the first few gears. As each mile got smoother, though, I started feeling something new—I wasn't quite sure, seeing as I'd never felt it before, but I think I was feeling lucky.

That's when I noticed a car behind us growing bigger in my sideview mirror with each passing second, until it slowed and began to follow from way on back.

It was a Packard. A green one.

Feeling my first fit of pure happiness, I'd have bet the farm that inside it was a flame-haired, camera-toting woman in pants.

. . . "Hon, I got your breakfast!"

Pushing the door open with her hip, it's Big Orderly Red again. Just as I'm putting the period on the end of my sentence.

"Don't want it," I call over my shoulder.

"I warmed it back up for you," she says, setting the tray of powdered eggs and godawful coffee on the bed nearest the window. Girl takes one sniff and shakes her big head.

"You've got to keep your strength up for your writing, don't you?" Rosie tries.

I keep scribbling.

"Why don't you take a break? We can play a game of dominoes—a game and a story—like old times," she says, looking over my shoulder. "It looks like it's getting good, too!"

I keep scribbling.

"So, who did you say you're writing to?" she tries next.

I keep scribbling.

She sighs. "OK, you're onto me. I'll go." As she does, though, she gives my shoulder a squeeze and says, "But, hon, *are* you writing to Augusta Red? Because if you are, where're you going to send it?"

My heart flutters at that. I glance back at Girl in the window, peace-fully chewing her cud. Then I take out my pocketknife, sharpen my pen-cil, and get back to driving the hurricane giraffes.

Newark Star-Eagle

OCTOBER 8, 1938

FANCY MEETING THEM ON THE HIGHWAY

ATHENIA, NJ—Oct. 8 (Evening edition). Did you see a pair of giraffes this morning on the road? Don't call your doctor. Those spots before your eyes were real . . .

Los Angeles Examiner

OCTOBER 8, 1938

HEAD-TURNING GIRAFFES ON SECOND DAY

NEW JERSEY—Oct. 8. The cross-continent motor truck dash of Southern California's first giraffes is into its second day to the consternation of motorists, the joy of newspaper reporters, and the pleasure of village wits along the way, according to national wire services. Small-town folks are turning pop-eyed and foreswearing strong drink, and wisecrackers are calling after the truck with their best quips . . .

Jersey Journal

OCTOBER 8, 1938

GOOD STUNT IF HE DOES IT

ATHENIA, NJ—Oct. 8 (Special). How would you like to go truck, truck, trucking across the nation with a pair of giraffes? Mr. Riley Jones has a neat little job on his hands . . .

Boston Post

OCTOBER 8, 1938

GIRAFFES TO NECK WAY CROSS NATION

NEW JERSEY—Oct. 8. The first giraffes ever to cross the continent by truck are racing against time, according to Mrs. Belle Benchley, San Diego Zoo directrix, the only lady zoo director in the world, traveling fast as they can for the delicate-boned creatures' health . . .

4

Across Maryland

So. There I was—Woody Nickel—driving giraffes with a freckled red-headed beauty hot on my trail. Since every dog has its day, maybe it was just that my stray-dog-boy day had come. God knows I was due a little Light Shining on me from Above, whether I believed in such things or not. Like most people, denying it never got in the way of relying on it. Here and now, older than old, I've lived long enough to believe then not believe, then believe and not believe more times than I can count, life being the bumpy ride it is. But I can say this. Luck it may have been. Yet if ever I've known a destiny feeling, the kind that makes you feel bigger than you are, moving you to something better than you are, it was that moment driving those giraffes with the green Packard in my mirror. I didn't know quite what to do with it, barely able to breathe for fear I'd scare the grand thing away. Every few seconds I checked my mirror, squinting hard back at the Packard until I was sure it *was* Red behind the wheel. Alone.

"Button up." The Old Man was frowning at my shirt.

My snitched shirt was too small to button all the way, but I gave it a good try with my free hand. "Sorry I tried to punch you back at quarantine," I mumbled, cutting my eye his way.

"If you'd done more than tried, you wouldn't be sitting here," he said, eyeing my last button, both of us knowing it wasn't going to budge. "Fine. Drive."

I drove us around a curve. We leaned into it, both glancing in our sideview mirrors at the giraffes. They leaned fine, too. We were up to thirty-five miles per hour.

"That's good. Right there," he ordered. I could feel the Old Man's eyes still on the woebegone sight of me, and they stayed on me long enough to make me antsy.

"What happened to your people?" he finally said.

"All in the ground."

"What happened to your farm?"

"Dust took it." I glanced back at Red, and my flickering hope flared up sky-high again. "I can go the distance. I can. I want to go to Californy."

He fumed. "You and every other Okie."

"I'm not an Okie."

"Sure you are. I hear your twang."

"I'm from Texas. The Panhandle."

"Same thing," he said. Back home, those were fighting words. If you were on the road with your life on your back, though, it didn't matter if you were from Kansas or Arkansas or Texas—you were an Okie. "Don't be having that *Californy* dream. Things aren't like you're thinking." He eyed me again. "When's the last time you ate?"

"I'm not hungry," I lied, thinking he was still looking for an excuse to boot me. "I don't eat much."

Next he was studying the bruises on my arms, the scrapes on my face, and the loose tooth I kept tonguing. "You in the hurricane?"

I nodded, tonguing the tooth.

"You want it to fall out, keep doing that."

I stopped.

"You get that scab on your face from the hurricane, too?"

I nodded.

"Looks older," he said, "and a bit like a bullet graze."

I didn't answer that, realizing he was the kind of man who'd be prying the truth out of you in seconds if given half a chance, and I wasn't ready to tell him the truth.

"What's your name, son?"

My mind still on *bullet graze*, I snapped, "Don't call me *son*." Quickly swallowing down the fury flit that made me say it, I added, "Sir."

The Old Man was now eyeing me like a prized pig at an auction. So I sat up and answered properly. "My name's Woodrow Wilson Nickel. I answer to Woody."

He glanced at me sideways and started chortling. "Your name's Woody Nickel?"

"Don't see what's so funny," I muttered.

But something about that seemed to simmer him down. "Riley Jones is mine," he said. "I answer to Mr. Jones." With that, he propped an arm on his open window and started giving me giraffe-driving orders. "All right. Listen up. We drive no more than three hours at a stretch before we stop to rest them. We find us some trees and open the top for the darlings to stretch their necks and snack, and we don't leave until they're chewing their cud. We stop morning, noon, and night to feed and water, even if we get waylaid going through towns. We watch to see how they're riding as we go. They'll be sticking their heads out at their whim from the side windows unless they're latched. So, watch your sides as well as your overhangs. You give one of the darlings a whomp on their big heads and you'll find yourself on the side of the road again. We only got twelve feet eight inches to work with on underpasses, so move slow toward each one. We don't go over forty, traffic be damned. Watch your speed and watch your animals. Got all that?"

I nodded and he went quiet. I knew I should, too, but glancing in my rearview, I caught a glimpse of the shotgun on the gunrack behind our heads. "Would you have shot those yahoos last night?" I heard myself say.

"If they needed it," he said a bit too quick for comfort. "But I'm not much of a shot."

I paused. "So . . . you'd kill for the giraffes?"

He snorted. "The Boss Lady will kill *me* if I don't get them there safe." Then he saw I was serious. "Would I kill for the darlings? Might as well ask me if I'd die for the darlings. Sane answer's no, I guess. But if you really want to know, it always seemed wrong to think an animal's life isn't worth as much as a human's. Life is life."

Gazing in my sideview at the sight of two mighty African giraffes sniffing American air, I asked what I'd been wondering since I first laid eyes on them. "How did they even get here?"

Something dark passed over the Old Man's face. "They were minding their own business, being the youngest or slowest giraffes in their herd, the ones lions have for lunch every day. Until loud two-legged lions on wheels with rifles and big ropes came roaring up, making the whole herd bolt so they could grab the stragglers. Or worse. Some trappers thinking nothing of shooting mothers to nab the orphans. What dies you leave for the hyenas or sell as bushmeat in the nearest village."

"Bushmeat?"

"Meat from the bush—the wild."

"They eat *giraffes* over there?"

"It's Africa. It's a *gotdam* buffet," he said. "We're all lions except a few like these darlings, God love 'em."

I flinched and the Old Man saw, studying me like he knew what was on my mind with me knowing he couldn't be more wrong. "You don't think so, boy? You never shot a jackrabbit for dinner?"

"'Course I have," I said, chin out. "I can drop a buck a quarter of a mile away and field dress him on the *spot*." Hearing my pa, I added, "They're just animals."

"If that's really what you thought, you wouldn't be sitting here," the Old Man said back. "Well, you'll be happy to know that the Boss Lady doesn't abide trappers. Trades mostly with her zoo pals all over the world. But these two darlings got rescued after a trapper left them to starve. They couldn't be taken out and set free, being herd animals without their herd. So she got a call and here they are, because everybody wants to see a giraffe. Some folks need to. Considering what you went through to be here, seems you're one of those that needs to."

All I need is to get to California, I was thinking.

"Oh, you say all you want is to get to California," he went on before I'd even finished the thought, "but you also needed to see a giraffe. You just don't know why, do you? I'll tell you why—animals know the secret to life."

The only secret to life I was interested in was how to stay alive. Besides, I was *sure* he was snookering me and waited for another chortle. Instead, gazing back at the giraffes in his sideview with the same feisty tenderness I saw in quarantine, he kept talking. "Animals are complete all on their own, living by voices we don't get to hear, having a knowing far beyond our paltry ken. And giraffes, they seem to know something more. Elephants, tigers, monkeys, zebras . . . whatever you feel around the rest, you feel different around giraffes. It's sure true of these two, despite the hell they've been through." Eyes still on the giraffes, he actually smiled. "Don't you worry about these darlings, though. They're headed to the San Diego Zoo, where it's warm as toast and green as a garden and washed in sea breezes all year long. Where they'll never have to worry about their next meal or being safe from lions, and where they'll be loved by a whole city just for allowing us to know them. Well they should, I say. This world of misery is in dire need of some natural wonder to learn secrets to life from." He glanced my way. "Here you got two darlings in your back seat. You should be asking them about those secrets while you got the chance."

A gust of wind blew through the window, and he took off his hat to fan the air between us. "For sweet chrisesakes, boy, you've *got* to clean yourself up. You're a walking pigsty!" We spied our first town a couple of miles ahead. "There. We'll stop for some grub and the mercy of a water pump. Then we'll find a good rest stop for the giraffes down the road."

Excited that Red might see me in giraffe-driving action, I glanced back. The Packard wasn't behind us anymore, though, which seemed odd.

Then the Old Man did something odd himself. When a yellow-and-red panel truck in front of us pulled over near a railroad crossing, he tensed, and as we bumped over the crossing, he stared down the tracks.

By that time, though, I was doing my own staring. A patrol car was parked by the city limit sign up ahead . . . It was the exact model as my Panhandle sheriff's. I stiffened bad, before I saw it was only the town's cop, hopping out of his cruiser to wave us over.

As round as he was tall, the cop guffawed and headed our way to meet the giraffes. Then he led us to a diner, where customers rushed out and waitresses appeared carrying two plates piled high with ham and eggs. They laid them on the truck's hood and I'd wolfed down both before I realized I'd eaten the Old Man's, too. The town newspaper's editor was posing him with the giraffes for pictures. Then Boy gave the round cop a snake-tongue lick as Girl flicked off his cap, and the crowd hooted with delight.

As the Old Man waited for another breakfast, he said, eyebrow cocked, "You get enough to eat?"

I nodded, sheepish. To please him, I went around to the diner's water pump out back and did a little dabbing. I was still a Dust Bowl boy never trusting a full stomach, though, so I came back through the market next door and pocketed a potato. As I settled into the driver's seat, the Old Man crawled in the passenger side, dropped a package of dry goods and a gunnysack full of onions and apples between us, and said again, "You get enough to eat?"

I nodded again.

"Good," he said, "because if you ever steal anything else, I *will* leave you on the side of the road. I cannot abide thieves or liars. Don't make me say it again."

"Yessir," I answered, clutching the potato in my pocket, sure he was about to make me hand it over. Instead he shoved the dry goods package my way. "Open it."

I tore at the brown paper. Inside were work clothes, a whole outfit. Brand-new.

"Put 'em on," he said.

I stared at them, not quite sure what to do, as if I didn't know how to put on clothes. The thing was, I didn't—not new ones. I was seventeen years old and never had a thing new, not even skivvies, nothing but hand-me-downs my whole life. I started peeling off my snitched shirt.

"*Jesus-Joseph-Mary*—farmboy!" the Old Man groused. "Change out back. And this time, *really* use the water pump."

So, after finding a suitable tree to change behind, I shed my raggedy things, did a true cleanup with the help of the water pump, and started putting on my new clothes. They were only work clothes, but they felt like a millionaire's luxe duds. To this day, I don't know if I've ever felt the same sensation those first new clothes gave me. I whipped off my holey undershirt and pulled on the new one, savoring the thought that mine was the first skin it'd touched. Next, I slipped on the new cotton twill shirt, smoothing down the fabric as I fastened each new button. Then I stepped into the denim pants, rolled up the bottoms that were amazingly too long, and cinched the new belt as far as it would go. He'd even gotten me a pair of socks. So, last, I shook off my boots and eased those beauties on, them offering the most sinful-rich feeling of all.

Tugging at everything, I headed back to the rig. The Old Man looked me up and down, giving the air between us a sniff. "Better."

Not having much practice with thanks, I didn't know what to say. "I'll pay you back," I mumbled. It was as close to a thank-you as I knew how to get, and from the shrug the Old Man gave me it was probably as much of one as he'd take.

I started up the rig. A cheer came from the crowd.

"Don't take any wooden nickels!" the round cop called as we pulled away.

The Old Man outright cackled. *"Too late,"* he called back, cutting his eye at me.

But I didn't care. I was driving the giraffes in a big, fancy rig. In new clothes. Me, Woodrow Wilson Nickel. I sat up tall, glancing back at the empty road, wishing Red could see me now.

"Remember, you're only getting us to DC," the Old Man said, my fine feeling being deaf to any such truth. In fact, the Old Man's gift began to poke at some part of me wanting to confess what happened my last Dust Bowl day that was fueling my nightmare. That's what the smallest bit of kindness could do to a seventeen-year-old orphan feeling his first bit of luck. But I knew no good could come from a guilty spiel about a sure crime when it came to my chances to keep driving to California. So I kept my mouth shut.

For a few miles, we rocked along as the Old Man looked for a good giraffe rest stop. When he spied a tall leafy tree nicely off the road, he motioned us over. As I rolled us to a stop, he popped on his fedora and got out, so I followed. "Think you can do some climbing without getting yourself killed?" he asked.

"Yessir," I said.

"Hear me now," he said. "These are wild animals, not farm animals. With wild animals, there's predators and there's prey. Predators use claws, prey use hooves. Giraffes, being prey, can kick with every hoof they got deadly enough to crack a lion's skull or break its spine. You rile them, their front hooves can kill you and the back hooves can maim you. So don't rile them. Just making 'em jittery can get them kicking, and I've got to deal with that splint. Clear?"

"Yessir."

"OK, pop the top to let the darlings munch."

By the time the Old Man had gotten out of the cab, I'd already climbed up and unlatched the top. Girl's snout poked out quick, but I didn't see Boy. I peeked over the side. He was on the floor, his big body curled up, legs under him, and worst of all, his neck looped over his back. Jumping to the ground, I gasped out, "Boy's *down*—"

The Old Man flipped open the wild boy's trapdoor. There was the giraffe's whole body close enough to touch. Spreading the fingers of his bad hand as far as they'd go, the Old Man placed them on the wild boy's looped neck and began to stroke. Boy uncurled it to flick his tongue at the pleasure of the Old Man's touch, and instantly rose to his feet by Girl.

"It's a good sign," the Old Man said my way. "They like your driving. Which means I like your driving."

I was still rattled. "Giraffes lie down?"

He shrugged. "Back on your Okie farm, you never saw a horse lie down?"

Sure I had. But they weren't giraffes. Then I thought about the Old Man's shrug. "Have *you* ever seen a giraffe lie down?"

"Can't say I have," he answered, unlatching Girl's trapdoor. "In fact, the few zoo bigwigs that have had giraffes will tell you they don't. Except to die."

Die? "How do you know it's OK then?"

"I can feel it," he said. "If either do it again, though, they'll never do it at the same time, I suspect. Least as long as the female's leg is in a bad way."

"Why?"

"Lions. Somebody's got to keep watch." Gearing up to check her splint through the trapdoor, he leaned sideways, surely thinking he was going to have to do their dance. She was already stomping a bit, knowing he was there. "Keep back," he ordered.

"I can help," I said.

"You'll do no such thing," he said my way, leaving his shoulder wide open, and Wild Girl kicked.

WHOP.

Groaning, he staggered back.

So, before he could tell me not to, I grabbed the cab's gunnysack, climbed up the side of the rig, and held out a sweet onion to Girl, who lapped it right up and waited for more. Soon, like the first night in quarantine, both giraffes were sniffing me all over for onion delights. The Old Man watched for a minute, then carefully finished his splint inspection as Girl kept getting onions for no more whops and Boy got them just because Girl got them, fair being fair.

As the giraffes went on nudging me with their snouts, I could feel the Old Man eyeing me again. He took his Lucky Strike pack from his shirt pocket, tapped out a smoke, lit it, and hunkered down on his haunches against the tree, motioning me down. I hopped to the ground. He held out his pack. Tobacco might as well have been chewing gum back then—my churchy ma even dipped snuff, nastiest stuff you ever saw. I'd already done more than my share of coughing in my young life, though, and wasn't stupid enough to take up smoking until the War. When I shook my head, he stuffed the pack back in his pocket, took a long suck of his Lucky, and settled back against the tree, resting both arms over his knees. The cigarette was dangling between his mangled fingers. It was the first time I'd had a real good look at them—one finger was half gone, and the others looked like they'd been chewed on by something fierce and spit out to heal all wrong.

"If I let you help me with the darlings," he was saying, "whatever you do, don't let me catch you inside. Big don't know from small. They could love you like their mama but still crush an arm or leg without a clue. And don't be lulled by the fact they're young. After all they've been through, add that to what we're asking of them and they're about as skittish as you'd be in the same situation. You hear?"

I nodded.

Sucking the guts out of the smoke, he flicked the butt in the road, grabbed up a water bucket, and began filling it from the rig's jugs as the giraffes bent his way. As he cooed his giraffe-speak to them, I felt as if I were eavesdropping on something personal.

"You got a feeling for animals, don't you?" I heard myself mumble.

He held out the full bucket until I took it. "That's a safe bet."

"My pa said it's a weakness."

"Did he now," said the Old Man, filling the other bucket. "I look weak to you?"

". . . No, but he said animals were put on earth by God for our use, that it's the natural order, and bucking it's childish for a grown man since we got to either eat or kill them to survive."

"And God knows you got to survive," the Old Man said under his breath.

"You agree with him?" Sarcasm wasn't a thing I heard much down on the farm.

"What?" he said, only half-listening.

"You agree with Pa?"

"Well, now," he said, handing me the second bucket, "I did say we're all lions. Lions got no choice but to always be lions. We do. By the way, you got a feeling for animals yourself whether you and your pa like it or not." He nodded up at the giraffes. "The darlings know it. They knew about Earl, the sumbitch, and they fixed that, didn't they?"

The giraffes were stomping a little for us to get a move on with the water buckets. So I did, as the Old Man sat down on the truck cab's running board, lit up a new Lucky, and began eyeing me again. I felt the hackles rise on the back of my neck as he kept it up, like he was a mountain lion sizing me up on the Panhandle plains. The longer it went on, the sorrier I was I'd kept him talking.

Finally, he said, "You know what an abattoir is? My first job was in one, younger'n I had any business being in such a place, not even twelve years old. They bought old horses on their way to the glue factory to shoot 'em, skin 'em, sell the hides, and feed the meat to the animals. The keepers' job was to keep their string of animals alive and healthy, and old horse flesh was how it was done. They'd bring their big knives and take what they needed for the carnivores—the tigers and lions."

"At the San Diego Zoo?"

"You going to let me talk here? No, not the zoo. My job was being the Judas goat, leading the horses peaceful to the slaughter. All too soon I was the one cutting off meat to feed the carnivores. But I never got used to it, the horse being as noble a beast as they come. So, seeing as I was still a boy and didn't have the luxury of quitting, I got philosophical about it. I got to thinking it was sort of a last noble duty of a damn noble breed, and I'll tell you a secret. Early on, I started thanking each one of them—just like Hawkeye."

I looked at him funny.

He bounced it right back at me. "Hawkeye—*The Deerslayer, Last of the Mohicans* . . . Good God, boy! They're books. By Mr. Fenimore Cooper. Didn't you read 'em in school? Hell, I barely got enough schooling to learn my ABCs and I read 'em all." Eyes shining, he gestured grandly with the hand holding his Lucky and said, "'A man can enjoy plunder peaceably nowhere.'"

I was pretty sure he was quoting from a book, but the only quoting I'd ever heard was from the Good Book, and I never saw anybody do that gesturing with a cigarette.

He leaned my way. "Hawkeye was a frontiersman back in colonial days—a legend with his long rifle. He could drop a stag springing in the air at one hundred paces. Back then," he went on, waving the Lucky overhead, "flocks of passenger pigeons were so big they blanketed the sky, blacking out the sun. Everybody else plundered them for sport and silly hat feathers with their blunderbusses, blasting away—until the birds vanished forever. Not that magnificent ol' bastard, though. Hawkeye never killed a living thing without good cause, and whenever he shot a stag to eat, he always paused to thank it for its life to save his own." The Old Man leaned back. "That spoke to me as a kid in a slaughterhouse. So I started doing like Hawkeye. I still do. Other people say grace. Me, I say thanks to what I'm eating. Its life for mine." He paused, absently rubbing his sorry-looking hand. "Soon enough, I'll be returning the favor even if it's only to the worms. We're just meat when it's all done. That's the natural order. What do I care where my meat goes after I'm not using it anymore?" he said, standing up. "Not that I wouldn't mind being thanked."

With that, he took a last suck of his smoke, crushed the butt with his boot, then climbed into the truck cab. The Old Man had left all the get-going chores for me to do, either lost in his Hawkeye thoughts or trusting me. I figured it was the former, but I was going to prove him right if it was the latter. So I put the water buckets back in their place by the jugs, then closed the trapdoors, and when I climbed into the cab to get us going again, he was sitting there gazing out at the road. As I put the rig into gear, he finished answering the question that I'd all but forgotten I asked.

"Life is life no matter who or what is living it, boy—a thing to respect," he said. "You don't get that, then you're just a waste of skin." Then he flipped a hand toward the road. "Now, daylight's burning."

As I steered the rig back on the road, I was a bit flustered, having gotten more than I bargained for with all his talk. The Old Man was about as different as different could be from Pa and Cuz and any other full-grown man I knew, though you couldn't tell by looking at him. On the outside, he was as rough-looking as any outdoor man, but inside he was one surprise after another. Little did I know there were some mighty big surprises yet to come. In fact, I was so awash in the Old Man's words, a mile would pass before I thought to check behind us for Red.

The road was still empty.

For a while we rode in blessed silence. When we spied a railroad crossing up ahead, though, I felt the Old Man tense again. As we got close, the signal went off and the arms went down. A train was coming. It wasn't a passenger train or even a freight train like the ones I'd hopped. It was a circus train—painted in bright yellows and reds—the same colors as the panel truck that morning. The circus train couldn't have been twelve cars long, but to my eyes it was big-time. The crossing was on flat pastureland with only a few scraggly trees between us, and I could already see the signs on the train cars. We were going to be so close, we'd be locking eyes with both men and beasts.

But the Old Man was having none of it. "Stop—*back here*," he ordered.

So I pulled the rig off the road near the scraggly trees. Within seconds, I was having to wave two cars around us, an Oldsmobile sedan with New Jersey license plates and a rattletrap Chevy. While they took their ogling time passing us, they soon were the ones locking eyes with the circus travelers as the train approached the crossing, hooting and tooting.

BOWLES & WATERS TRAVELING CIRCUS EXTRAVAGANZA, said the sign on the train's fancy Pullman car. Here came a circus organ wagon. There went a lion in a curlicue cage. Next came the elephants and horses, lots of horses. But no giraffes. Back then, nobody much this side of Africa got to see a giraffe. Fancy East Coast zoos were always trying to have them, but the cold was too much, killing them fast. Circuses kept trying to have them, but the traveling was too much, killing them even faster. So, while I knew they were special, I didn't know *how* special—to the point of being all-out coveted—but I was about to find out.

The giraffes were craning their necks toward the loud train and the Old Man was all nerves. Throwing open the truck door and tumbling out, he said, "Help me get the giraffes' heads in! We don't want any trouble."

I didn't much like the sound of that, especially since it was way too late to get their heads in. The train was already passing.

And at that very moment, so was the Packard.

A blur of green shot past us as I climbed up the rig's side. Jolting to a stop behind the other cars at the crossing, Red bailed out in all her curly-headed glory, camera in hand. She snapped the train and cars, then turned to snap us. When she saw me, she was so surprised she lowered the camera to look at me looking at her. And I was surely looking at her.

"Hurry, boy!" the Old Man hollered my way.

From the old Chevy, a man rushed toward us. "I'll be darned if those aren't giraffes—you with that circus?"

I was too busy trying to get Girl to let me close the window to answer. After a couple of tries pushing that huge head where it didn't want to go, I threw up my hands, looking back for the Old Man so he could go ahead and chew me out. But the train had finished passing the crossing and he was squinting hard enough after it to pop a blood vessel.

The family from the Oldsmobile then joined the party. "I know who you are!" the mother crowed, scooting toward us with her little ones. "I read about you in the papers. Look here, children! They're going to California! Those are the hurricane giraffes! They're going to live with Belle Benchley in the San Diego Zoo! *We've seen her in the newsreels, haven't we, children?"* she went on. The Old Man wasn't listening. His attention was glued to the circus train's little red caboose with its banner hanging off the back: **DC TONIGHT!** Because as it disappeared around the bend, a big, potbellied, mustached man strode through the caboose's back door in time to stare at us. Hard.

The Old Man cussed under his breath.

When the railroad crossing arms lifted, nobody in line wanted to leave as long as we were there, so we had to pull around them. With the giraffes bobbing their necks back toward the crowd, we crossed the tracks and disappeared around the same bend. I watched Red in my sideview mirror until she was no longer in sight, wondering if the Old Man noticed her. But his mind seemed stuck on that circus train.

As soon as the road veered away from the tracks, the Old Man announced, "We'll stop for the night now and go into DC tomorrow." Since we still had an hour of sun, that seemed like another mighty strange thing to do. I wasn't going to say so, though, considering he was still planning to ditch me in DC and I needed more time to figure out how to change his mind.

In about a mile, we pulled into a little place called Round's Roadside Auto Rest. It wasn't much, four rickety-looking huts and some cane-back chairs set in a circle around a courtyard campfire. A plump gray-bunned lady and her two grown daughters came out with the Old Man to see the giraffes, all three wiping their hands on their aprons. The place was a family thing, you could tell, their clapboard house by the road serving as an office and a little café, too, if you can call a table with six chairs a café. The ma pointed to the corner hut nearest a nice live oak grove, the one she thought best for our rig parking. Soon we were set. As we finished tending to the giraffes, complete with Old Man kick, onion bribes, and tree munching, the three women brought us meat pies, potatoes, and coconut cake. I was amazed by the Old Man's manners. I sized him for someone raised by wolves, roughshod and proud of it. But you should have heard the sweet talk he gave those ladies. "Why, Mrs. Round, you shouldn't have" and "Thank you kindly, ma'am." A real charmer.

When they left, he caught me looking at him funny and waved me toward the hut. "You can take the bed the first shift."

"Can't yet," I said, not wanting to admit I don't sleep.

"All right, I'll relieve you in a few." Then I stood there with my hands in my new pockets, trying to figure out what to do. He pointed toward the campfire. "Go sit in one of those cane-back chairs. You can see the giraffes from over there."

So I went over and sat myself down.

It was dark by that time. There was only one other car at the Auto Rest that night. I couldn't quite see what it was, the only light being from the little courtyard's campfire. I squinted at the car and sat straight up at what I saw.

It was a Packard. The more I squinted, the greener it got.

I positioned the chair so I could see both the rig and the Packard, and waited. I straightened my new duds, situating my scrawny self like a relaxing rig-driving man, and watched the stars come out one by one. By the time the Big Dipper was above me, I saw the door open from the little hut and out she came.

"Stretch, it *is* you!" Red called as she came close. "May I join you?" she said, and sat down. The light of the fire made her hair look so red I thought it might burst into flames. Up close, I saw she had freckles everywhere, the mighty, all-over redheaded Irish kind that women hid under pancake makeup shoveled on with a trowel. Not her. Plus, I could see she truly wasn't all that much older than me no matter how fancy her clothes or car. She couldn't have been more than nineteen or twenty, the way a girl can look too old for her own good—and, at that moment, mine.

"I can't believe *you're* driving the giraffes!" she said. "The other man's gone?"

I nodded.

"I'm not a very good driver. Just started. City girl, you know. You must be first-rate," she said.

I smiled, sitting up tall. If I didn't speak soon, she'd think me dumb. I cleared my throat and found my voice. "You following us?" I said a tad too loud.

"You don't mind, do you?"

I shook my head.

She glanced back at the rig. We could see the giraffes' heads poking out the top as they nibbled at the trees, and she grinned ear to ear. "*Giraffes!* Can you *believe* it?"

I shrugged again, cocky now, like it was nothing. "They're just animals."

"Just animals!" She looked at me like I had two heads. "They're just animals like the Empire State Building's just a building." Then her eyes wandered to the birthmark the size of a state-fair prize tomato on my neck. When she saw I noticed, she held up her wrist—she had a bird-shaped birthmark of her own. "A birthmark is a sign of good luck, you know."

"Don't know about that." All I'd ever heard back home was it was the mark of the devil, and I sure wasn't bringing that up.

"Well, you seem lucky to me," she said. "Very lucky." As we watched the giraffes, there was a long awkward pause until, without looking my way, she said, "Why did you punch Lionel?"

I sat up taller. "He grabbed your arm."

"I can take care of myself, you know," she said. But her face softened enough for me to think—hope—she might have liked it.

Right then, the giraffes started chewing their cud and their snouts disappeared from view. "Oh . . . oh no." Red's face dropped. "Is there any way I might meet them? Is it too late?"

Now I was on the spot. The Old Man'd been letting people meet them all day, hadn't he? Besides, I'd read her notepad. She wanted to touch a giraffe—and I had the power to make that happen.

I hesitated, but her face opened like a rose and I was done for.

Listening for the Old Man's snores, I led her to the rig through the shadows of the campfire light. I started to climb to the open top. As soon as I put a boot on the running board, though, they poked their great heads out their windows, and I heard Red gasp, the kind of gasp you'd want to hear all the time. I jumped down to help her step up, but she didn't need any help. She popped one of those two-tone shoes on the running board, the other on the wheel rim, and reached for both giraffes. As she made the giraffes' acquaintance, her legs stretching this way and that, I couldn't help staring at those trousers. Like I'd caught her looking at my birthmark, she caught me looking at her britches. "Stretch?"

I felt my cheeks flush. "I never saw a woman wearing trousers before."

She laughed. "Well, I won't be the last—you can take that to the bank," she said. Then, agile as a cat, she climbed to the open top, straddled the plank between the giraffes' traveling rooms, and grinned down at me, as if to say, *What are you waiting for?*

My head all but swiveled off looking back at the Old Man's hut. His rumbling snores were still going strong, so, stiffening my spine, up I went. As I eased down on the plank facing her, the giraffes pulled in their heads from their windows and surrounded us in the open air, their snouts bumping our knees. Girl butted me so hard looking for onions, I had to grab her big head to stay upright. Red, meanwhile, had touched one of Boy's horns and got baptized with giraffe slobber, which would've sent most women screaming for the ground. But not Red.

Laughing again, she wiped at her face and silky shirt with one hand, patting Boy's big jaw with the other, and, as her pats turned to soft strokes, the whole of her seemed to unwind. "I'm touching a *giraffe* . . ." She sighed a sigh so full of reverie I thought she might float away. "They fill me up with wonder just *looking* at them. I see Africa as big as day . . . I see all the wonders of the world, waiting out there to be *seen*," she said, giving me a look of such unbridled, overflowing joy, I thought she was going to kiss me. Even though I'd spent every night at the depot imagining how I'd kiss Augusta Red, it scared the bejeezus out of me. If Girl hadn't picked that exact moment to butt me sideways, I would've found out. Instead Red turned all that feeling toward Wild

Boy, her soft strokes turning into glorious caresses. "They *are* hard to believe, aren't they?"

Trying to keep from going to complete mush watching her caress Boy, I scrambled for something, anything, to say and heard one of the Old Man's warnings come out of my mouth. "Careful. Big don't know from small—"

Boy licked at the air as Red kept on caressing. "Surely they're not that dangerous, are they?" she asked.

Right then, Girl's huge head thumped me again. "They can crack a lion's skull with a kick of their hooves," I said, grunting as I tightened my hold.

Red paused. "You've seen them kick?"

"Seen this one," I said, nodding at Girl, who now had her snout all but in my pocket. "She's whopped the Old Man, but not like she wants to send him to kingdom come—not yet anyway."

"So she's feisty. Good." Red reached over to pat her. She looked back at Boy. "But this one's a gentleman, isn't he?" He answered by sticking his snout in Red's crotch, which had her squirming and me this side of bopping him for his bad manners. As he looked up, all giraffe innocence, she laughed again. "A gentleman *rascal*—even better." And she went right back to her reverie, brushing her fingers over a diamond-shaped spot on the wild boy's jaw as if she didn't quite believe it was there. Then her voice turned soft, dreamy. "Did you know that you're not the first to take a giraffe across a country? About a hundred years ago the ruler of Egypt sent one to the king of France. They sailed it over on a boat and walked it the five hundred miles to Paris. Can you *imagine*?" she went on, softer, dreamier. "The whole country went *crazy* for it—women wearing piled-up giraffe hairstyles, men wearing tall giraffe hats. They say *one hundred thousand* people lined the streets and watched in awe as the royal cavalry escorted the giraffe to the king's palace." She moved her hand down the wild boy's neck, and Boy shuddered with delight. "And hundreds of years before *that*, an Egyptian sultan sent one to Florence. It's actually in frescoes and paintings roaming the town squares and gardens! There's *even* a constellation named after it." She glanced up at the stars. "They say you can see it in the northern Mexican sky. Maybe we'll be able to see it in the desert." Then she sighed again, this time so quiet I almost missed it, and I really, really didn't want to miss it.

Boy began chewing his cud again and Girl gave up her onion hunt to do the same, leaving drool all over my new duds. Wiping at the slobber, I said to Red, "You sure know a lot about giraffes."

When I looked back, Red was gazing at the giraffes the same way the Old Man did. "They're so full of everything I've never done or seen except in books that they might as well have floated down to earth from that hole in the sky—blown to earth by a hurricane to land in front of me. When I saw them, I knew exactly what I had to do." With that, she reached to touch both giraffes one last time, then jumped down to the ground before I had a chance to help her.

When I dropped down in front of her, she seemed out of breath, her hand pressed over her heart, but she was smiling all glory at me. "That was—*wonderful*," she gasped. "Oh, Stretch, I—" Suddenly she was bear-hugging me so hard my broke rib was pinching my suffering spine. Then she stepped back just as quick, like the hug even surprised her. "Sorry . . . but you have *no* idea what that meant to me. Thank you so much," she said, working to get back to herself.

I wasn't in any hurry to get back to myself, though, still feeling the warm ache of her body pressed to mine and being so very glad the Old Man had made me hose off.

Taking a deep breath as we headed toward the campfire, she sighed one last time. Back to business, she pushed the curls out of her face, pulled the notepad from her shirt pocket, and said, "Does Mr. Jones know I'm following you?"

"Don't think so."

"Don't tell him yet. I want a chance to impress him first. Maybe you can introduce me then, OK?"

"Sure, but how'd you know his name?"

"He's in the newspaper stories. The giraffes made all the papers." Red pulled a newspaper clipping from the pad and handed it to me. In the flickering light coming from the campfire, I saw it was the same clipping I'd seen in the notepad back at quarantine: **MIRACLE GIRAFFES RIDE HURRICANE AT SEA**, written by Lionel Abraham Lowe, "Mr. Big Reporter"—and there was the Old Man's name, *Riley Jones*.

"Keep it." She grinned. "It's in the papers, so it's part of history. You'll be part of history, too."

As I slipped it in my new shirt pocket, Red was so pepped up, she was bouncing on her heels enough to make her freckles jiggle. But she was movie-star gorgeous to my seventeen-year-old eyes. Feeling my cheeks about to flush again, I looked away, sure not even the shadows could hide the blasted blush this time. Shifting my weight from one boot to the other, I silently cussed myself cool.

"Stretch, tell me your story," I heard her say.

Pretending to study the campfire, I mumbled, "I've got no story."

"Sure you do. Everybody's got one."

At that, I looked around at her. "What's yours?"

Her face went south. So did her happy bounce as she smiled a tight-lipped smile I didn't understand at all. "Nobody likes a sad story," she said. "*You're* the one that's got a good one, I can tell. That face of yours seems right out of a Dust Bowl photo—are you an Okie? Tell me how you got here and it'll be in *Life* magazine."

Even farmboys had seen copies of *Life* magazine, which was the closest thing to having a TV you could get, being packed as it was with pictures of the world, especially beautiful women, on every slick full-color page. "You work for *Life* magazine!"

"I'm doing a photo-essay," she said, making a frame with her hands. "'As the country teeters between a depression and Europe's looming war, a pair of giraffes, survivors of a hurricane at sea, left a wake of much-needed cheer while driven cross-country to the San Diego Zoo, where lady zoo director Mrs. Belle Benchley awaited.'" Then she clicked the frame like she was snapping a photo. "But it's the pictures that'll make it. You don't have the shots, it can be the Second Coming of Christ and it wouldn't make it in *Life*. I plan to do a photo-essay on Belle Benchley, too, when we get there. I'm going to be the next Margaret Bourke-White."

"Who?"

"The first female photographer for *Life*," she said. "If you've read *Life*, you've seen her pictures. She's got to be the greatest photographer on earth."

I felt my ignorance of the world like a load of horse crap around my neck in the presence of a sea of rosewater. Catching a glimpse of the Packard in the shadows, I proceeded to make it worse. Back then, a woman didn't drive by herself on the highway. Definitely no lady. Ever. And I heard myself blurt, "Aren't you scared on the road all alone?"

She paused, studying my face. "What makes you say that?"

"Well, you're a girl," I went right ahead and said.

Something flamed up behind her eyes as she flashed me a look so exasperated it seemed to take on a life of its own, as if to say, *Ah, Stretch, not you, too.*

I should have been apologizing. Instead, melting at the way those hazel eyes of hers looked all fiery, I felt my cheeks starting to flush yet again. Fighting like hell to hide it, I mumbled, "I'm just saying it's not safe out here alone."

I was a goner and she knew it. I watched the flame behind her eyes cool down, until, with a glance back at the rig, she smiled at me ever so slightly. "Well, I'm not really alone anymore, am I?" Back to smooth city girl, she then raised her chin and said, "How about a business proposition? I'd appreciate your help getting this story, and in return

I'll pay you back any way you say." She put out her hand. "Deal?" She wanted to shake, so I did, and she shook it as hard as any man.

"We keep this strictly business," she said again, still shaking my hand.

"OK."

"Strictly," she repeated.

"OK."

"I don't need to be saved or protected," she went on.

"OK," I repeated.

"So we have a deal," she said one more time, and we stopped shaking. Or I should say she did.

We stood there in the dying light coming from the campfire and I felt her leave-taking coming on strong. "My name's Woody," I said. I didn't tell her my last name for fear she'd laugh like the Old Man.

"Mine's Augusta."

"Augie?" I said, remembering what the reporter called her.

"Only one person calls me that, only to vex me," she answered, smiling that tight-lipped smile again. With that, she headed toward her hut, her curls bouncing like they were as alive as she was, and my heart split in two. "I'll see you down the road, Woody," she said over her shoulder.

I wanted to say something a Driver of Giraffes might say, something Clark Gable might say. Instead I called after her, "My last name's Nickel."

She glanced back. "Drive safely, Woody Nickel." And she didn't laugh.

I watched until the dark swallowed her up. Stoking the campfire, I sat down to keep watch for another couple of hours, my mind full of girly trousers and fancy magazines and Paris and old paintings and giraffes floating down to earth. The time flew by. I even thought I heard the giraffes humming again, like I'd dreamed back in quarantine. When

I walked over close to listen, I heard only the wind whistling through the trees, so I went back to the fire and my big thoughts.

The Old Man appeared from the dark as the fire was nothing but embers and the stars had shifted without my notice. "Time for you to sleep, boy. Close the top before you go," he said, already stirring the fire back to life.

5

Asleep

Inside the Auto Rest hut, still feeling the warmth of Red's body pressed to my aching ribs, I found myself back at the depot in my mind, imagining our kiss to end all kisses safely happening just in my head. Instead of it keeping me awake, though, I went fast to sleep, the first real sleep since the quarantine night inside the rig. I was walking across France with Girl, leading her by a halter like I used to do with my mare, then . . .

> *Hush-a-bye / Don't you cry / Go to sleep, little baby.*
> *When you wake / You shall have / All the pretty little*
> *   horses.*
> *"Li'l one, who you talking to?"*
> *Brown-apple eyes stare.*
> *"Woody Nickel, tell me what happened out there*
> *   and tell me now!"*

I knew I was inside my familiar Panhandle nightmare . . . until I *hear a train in the distance and I'm standing in bright sunlight by a*

cornfield . . . as a giraffe bursts from the dried stalks, careening and crash-
ing, to the sound of lassos whipping the air . . .

Falling out of the hut's bed, I threw myself out the door.

It was still dark.

The Old Man, sitting on the rig's running board, got up at the sight
of me in my skivvies appearing out of nowhere, barefoot and big-eyed.
Trying not to think of Aunt Beulah, I slid against the truck, full awake.
I told the Old Man I was staying. He scowled. "Well, you're not doing
it in your drawers."

So, after I came back fully dressed, the Old Man headed for the hut
to sleep the few hours until sunrise, leaving me with the giraffes and my
cornfield worries to greet the dawn. I sat on that running board and
stared wide-eyed into the country dark, as deep a dark as I'd ever seen.
At first light, I moved toward the field beyond the camp area, expecting a cornfield and a train track. There was nothing but pines. I'd never
been happier to see a bunch of trees.

Not until that moment did I remember Red. I looked back at her
hut. The Packard was gone.

San Diego Free Press

October 8, 1938

GIRAFFES TRUCKING OUR WAY!

Hooray! Southern California's first giraffes are on their way from the East Coast. "I promised the children of San Diego they'd have giraffes and nothing is going to stop them now!" said Mrs. Belle Benchley, our beloved Zoo Lady . . .

6

To Washington, DC

Memories stick to things. Out of nowhere, something finds your nose, ears, or eyes and you're on the other side of the country or world or in a whole other decade, being kissed by a doe-eyed beauty or punched by a drunken pal. You've got no control over it, none at all. One whiff of dust whenever they clean my room and I'm back in the Panhandle staring down a brown blizzard. One glimpse of pink peonies and I'm back in WWII France, standing over a fresh battlefield grave.

And one howl of a rolling old police siren and I am back in the moment I'm driving the rig smack into Washington, DC, seconds from a nervous retch.

Just an hour before, as we tended to the giraffes preparing to leave Round's Roadside Auto Rest, the Old Man kept to himself whatever thoughts he had about my peculiar behavior during the night, and I was glad of it. Because as soon as we got back on the road, we started seeing signs for DC one right after the other. When we saw one that said **WASHINGTON DC 3 MILES**, we spotted the city ahead—and in the middle was something big and pointy. It was the Washington Monument. Of course, I didn't know that and I wasn't about to ask the Old Man. He was already fidgeting that fedora of his, but before I could wonder why, I knew. The highway had widened to an extra lane on both sides and cars completely surrounded us. That's when a police car, with that siren a'rolling, whizzed past on the shoulder so fast that I jerked the wheel and threw the Old Man into the dashboard, his fedora flying to the floor. Cussing, he grabbed it up in time to be thrown against the door as the giraffes rocked the rig. Clenching the steering wheel, I thought I might retch as I grasped the full reality of what I had talked my way into—I was driving two colossal African beasts right into big-city traffic.

Feeling the contents of my stomach roaring up, I swallowed it back down, focusing all I had on keeping the rig steady as cars kept whizzing and the giraffes kept rocking.

Parking his fedora on the seat between us, the Old Man went dead still, and in a voice mighty close to the one he used to calm the giraffes, he said, "Now. Take it slow. Slow and smooth. Don't mind a thing around you."

Up ahead, I could see a river and signs. Lots of signs. One of them was pointing the way to the **NATIONAL ZOO** over the **FRANCIS SCOTT KEY BRIDGE**. The traffic was getting thicker, but I kept driving like a granny, slow-slow-slow. So slow a DC motorcycle cop with his lights flashing was driving up beside us. The Old Man, not looking the least bit surprised, gave the cycle cop a nod, and the cop moved back behind us.

I knew, within seconds, he'd be telling me to make the turn to the DC zoo. When I glanced at him, though, he started talking fast. "Listen up. There's no taking the giraffes out of the rig ever, because once they're out, there's no guarantee we'd ever get 'em back in, and that'd be the death of them one way or the other. You don't tell a giraffe what to do. You ask. They may have taken a shine to you, but that'll mean nothing if they decide later on it doesn't. They're not your pets or your Panhandle horse. You respect them as wild animals. Got it?"

I nodded so hard my teeth rattled. I *was* going to California.

"OK then," he said. "You can drive us to Memphis."

I was sure my ears weren't working right. "Californy," I corrected him.

"Memphis," the Old Man said again. "The road to Memphis is smooth sailing, you're driving decent, and we're making good time. Time is everything now, the darlings' bones so gotdam delicate. We still have lots of daylight to get down the road and we should take it. There's another zoo in Memphis where I'll have time to call way ahead for a new driver to be waiting so we won't be wasting a day or more like we'll be doing here," he said as the bridge exit appeared.

"I can go the distance," I said quick.

"Take it or leave it, boy." The Old Man nodded toward the bridge. "Right now."

I took it.

With that, the Old Man turned his gaze back to the road. "All right. Slow. Smooth. Exactly like you been doing."

A second cycle cop appeared, lights flashing and siren rolling. The Old Man made some sort of forward-ho gesture for him and the traffic slowed even more in our wake as we moved on through the city. At the city's edge, the road narrowed back to two lanes, the cycle cops veered off, and the giraffes popped their heads out to watch them go while I forced myself calm. As we moved into the countryside and everything quieted all the way down, I studied my sideview mirror, wishing to see Red but also wondering what had just happened. "Why didn't the cops take us to the DC zoo?"

"'Cause I never called."

I chewed on that a second. "How'd they know about us?"

"The Boss Lady."

And I chewed on *that* a second. "The Boss Lady is Mrs. Benchley?"

"That's right."

"A woman is the boss of the whole San Diego Zoo?"

"That's right," he said, propping his arm on the windowsill. "Looks like a granny, dresses like a schoolmarm, swears like a sailor, and still charms snooty zoo galoots with their fancy educations."

". . . How'd she get that job?"

"Way I heard it, the gent who started up the zoo from a menagerie after the Great War rang up civil service for a bookkeeper since they barely had money for a keeper much less a staff. She showed up and started doing everything from taking tickets to nursing sick animals until she was running the place.

"Then she started doing those radio shows and movie newsreels, and got famous telling stories about the zoo. But, I can tell you for a fact, she's got stories she won't be putting on those."

"Like what?"

"Well, like the time she walked into a pen with an escaped baboon."

"On purpose?"

"The woman wasn't stupid, boy. Why, I've seen a ninety-pound baboon throw a grown man across a service yard. No, it had gotten into the area behind the monkey quadrangle and was having a gay old time, rattling cages of all the screeching monkeys and loping round and round. By the time I got there, five keepers were shouting and swinging clubs trying to scare it back in its pen. The closer the men got, the scareder and wilder and crazier the baboon got—and you hadn't seen crazed until you've seen a crazed baboon. I was sure it was going to charge us. Then, right that holy minute, the Boss Lady appears from the other end. She'd heard us in her office, thought we were chasing rats, and was coming to tell us we were disturbing the visitors. We yelled at her to run, but before she could do a thing, the baboon headed right for her." The Old Man shook his head. "I tell you, I braced for the worst. The Boss Lady knew full well she was in mortal danger. One gnash of that baboon's jaws could break her neck. But what does she do? The woman doesn't run. She doesn't hide. She forces a *smile*—and just opens her arms. And what does that baboon do? It *jumps* into them, wailing like a *baby*!"

"Then what'd she do?"

"What else could she do? She carried that big baboon back to its pen—with six grown men watching, struck dumb at the sight. We braced for a bawling out, but she was so mad she didn't speak to us for a week." He went on to tell me more Boss Lady stories, like the times she picked up an escaped rattlesnake. And took a streetcar home with a sick baby kangaroo in a basket. And mailed fleas to somebody back East for a flea circus until the post office got wind of it.

After that, he told me story after crazy story about life at the zoo, making it all sound mighty exciting, until we came to the Virginia state line. "There you go, boy," he said, pointing to an official-looking sign announcing the road's name: **LEE HIGHWAY**. We'd made it to the Old Man's cross-country "transcontinental auto route," the southern route he'd been talking about, and the farther we cruised down the fine smooth road, the more my destiny feeling returned and the more I was sure I'd make it to California. If I'd had a map, I'd have seen the fancy highway was two lanes paved all the way to San Diego right through the desert, its smooth concrete looking like the world of tomorrow to anybody who'd ever tried to drive farther than the nearest cotton gin.

But I'd also have seen something else—the Lee Highway wasn't going south. It was *already* south. I'd heard "southern route" and imagined what was south to my Panhandle mind, that being Louisiana and Texas Gulf Coast and a skirting of the Mexico border. In only one more day, though, the road was going to turn and go straight-arrow west—right back through the Texas Panhandle where I came from—and I couldn't hazard that for reasons I never wanted the Old Man to know.

Little did I know that being dumped at Memphis might be the saving of me. As I drove that nice highway with the hurricane giraffes, hanging on to my California dream and feeling God Almighty and the Heavenly Host again on my side, I hadn't a clue what I was risking behind that wheel. It was far more than a couple of mighty precious giraffe necks. It was my own.

Before long, we seemed to be gaining alti—

. . . "Lunchtime, sunshine!"

—Rattling me clean out of the story and back into my room is Greasy.

"You interrupted me in the middle of a sentence!" I holler as he busts through the door again.

"But it's lunchtime, sunshine, the best part of the day, and you didn't touch your breakfast. That's a bad boy."

"Quit talking to me like I'm a child, you little pipsqueak! Go AWAY. Can't you see I'm busy?"

He grabs my wheelchair handles again. "C'mon now."

I throw on the brakes.

He pulls them back up.

I push them back down. Dropping my pencil, my heart . . . freezes.

"Hey—" I hear Greasy's voice from far away. "Hey, hey—goddamn! You dying? I'm going for the nurse!"

He rushes out the door as my heart starts up again. *Mmmphgh.*

"Whew." Rattled, I rub my chest, take a deep breath, and look around. Over in the window, Girl is wiggling her rubbery lips at me. "I could've used your help, you know." Uneasy, I pick up my pencil, forcing myself to focus.

And I hear the shuffling of dominoes.

Real slow, I turn around. There, sitting on the bed shuffling, is Rosie. She's younger, though, her hair brighter, longer . . . with no hint of gray.

I blink.

She's still there.

A game and a story . . . she's saying . . . "Then you take your pills. Why don't you tell me about the Old Man, Riley Jones, again? I do love a man with a dark secret. Or maybe the night you slept in the cab with you-know-who! No, wait. The *mountains*—that was so exciting. Yes, that's always been one of my favorite parts."

Then she isn't there anymore.

"Did you see her, too?" I ask Girl.

Girl nods her big snout.

I take another deep breath. "Oh, good. I was beginning to worry I was seeing things," I say, and turn back to my writing pad, headed to the mountains.

7

Over the Blue Ridge Mountains

Before long, we seemed to be gaining altitude.

I could feel us climbing as I began working the gears more. Despite what the Old Man said about the Memphis stretch being smooth sailing, I knew full well that mountains stood between us and the flat side of Tennessee. I'd never even seen a mountain, much less driven up one—much *less* driven a rig with two-ton giraffes *over* one.

But at least mountains, I told myself, wouldn't have cornfields.

By midmorning, right after we'd had a stop by the side of the road for some tree-munching and neck-stretching and bandage-checking and Girl-kicking, we crossed over a stone bridge that looked like it had been crossed by George Washington himself. And we started going up. There was no maybe about it anymore.

At a burg called Thornton's Gap, the two-lane highway narrowed and we went around our first hill, then another and another. I geared down. Up. Then down again. I began to feel heat doing the same up and down my neck. The giraffes were moving back and forth with the rig, their big weight shifting. Even the Old Man had a healthy grip on his door frame.

Then the signs started coming.

ENTRY TO THE BLUE RIDGE MOUNTAINS AND SHENANDOAH NATIONAL PARK, said the first one.

SCENIC SKYLINE DRIVE—FIRST LEFT, said the second.

Any other time, I might've thought something called Skyline Drive was a hot-dog-and-damn sight worth seeing. But now was not any other time.

Then came the third sign: **LEE HIGHWAY—KEEP STRAIGHT AHEAD.**

My spirits rose.

"Just follow that sign," the Old Man said. "I scouted this. It's an easy up and over, then back down to the highway proper."

My spirits rose even higher. Until we came upon the biggest sign of all.

In the middle of the road, at the intersection of Skyline Drive and the Lee Highway, sat a barricade with a **DETOUR** arrow as big as Dallas, pointing up that Skyline Drive.

"What the—" the Old Man muttered.

About fifty yards down the detour was what looked like a football-field-long tunnel clear through the mountainside. A sign announced the name, as if they were proud of it: **MARY'S ROCK TUNNEL AHEAD—TURN ON LIGHTS.**

I pulled us to a stop. The Old Man jumped out and marched past the sign to the bend in the road ahead. What he saw made him cuss and throw down his fedora. Scooping up the hat, he pulled it low over his brow and began pacing the length of the rig, the giraffes moving their heads along with him, until he stopped to stare back the way we came. He was thinking about turning us around. If we did, that would be the end of my rig driving.

He crawled in the cab. "Side railing's gone as far as you can see," he grumbled. "Something took it out, a rock slide or a car going over." He fidgeted with his fedora, then turned to look straight at me. "You ever driven in mountains, boy? Don't lie to me."

I didn't want to lie big so I lied little. "Not that much."

As he stared down the Skyline Drive detour, the whole of him drooped. He took off his hat and slapped it on the truck's seat the way I already knew meant he was tired of thinking. "Guess we should take them back to DC and wait, even though that means taking them outa the rig. Which means losing more days . . . and maybe worse." He turned, stared me full in the face, and said, "Now's the time to tell me if you got any thoughts on the subject."

The Old Man hadn't decided. He wanted bad to keep going. He just didn't want us going off a cliff. All I had to do was say I could handle it. Instead, looking at the tunnel, what I heard myself say was:

"We have to go through that?"

He paused, and I thought that was it. "It's tall enough," he said. "I can talk you through. It's the afterwards that matters."

"The . . . afterwards?"

"Turnouts, switchbacks, and overlooks to grind every gear you got before we level out and ease down back to the Lee."

"How far?"

"That's not your worry right now," he said.

I didn't like the sound of that.

"There'll be no turning around once we start and there'll be no second chances," he went on. "We can go back to DC—there's no shame in it, and I'll still buy you that ticket back to New York. I had my chance to wait for an experienced driver, but we were making good time and the darlings had taken to you. So I didn't. It'll be on me," he said, adding under his breath, "'Course if we end up at the bottom of the mountain the hard way, it'll be on me, too. But in that event we'll all be past caring."

That's the way he posed it. Either he believed my driving-skill lies or he was not telling me something, which was more likely the case. At the time, though, all I could think was what my rowdy young self had been thinking since leaving the harbor dock—*Californy*.

I straightened my spine, and with the hubris of a selfish boy with nothing behind and everything ahead, I said, "I can do it."

"Hope to God I don't regret this," he muttered, setting his jaw. "OK. Here's what you're going to do. You'll move us real slow into the mouth, not jostling our passengers or whomping their heads one little bit. It's a long tunnel, and your first thought is to hug the side of the mountain. But you can't see the side of the tunnel, so instead what you do is follow the yellow line down the middle, keeping your tire right on it. If you don't think you can do that, then we need to put their heads in right now. If we do, though, there's no good place for us to let their heads back out for a while, and that might be a *big* problem if they get jumpy. Because on the other side it's going to curve and curve and curve some more before we level out, and they'll be doing it blind. So we got to decide right now which way to play it—with a couple of two-ton beasts blindly being bunged around inside their boxes or with their windows open, so they can see what's coming and help us balance the rig."

I stared a little stunned at him after all that, then looked back at the giraffes, who were already shuffling so much we could feel it up front.

"Open or closed?" he pressed.

I reached into my pocket to rub Cuz's lucky rabbit's foot. It wasn't there . . . I'd left it back in the pocket of my old pants along with the Old Man's dollar. I almost told the Old Man, but I clamped my mouth good and shut. I'd have sooner gone off that mountain than let him hear me hanging our future on a rabbit's foot. Instead I said, "Open."

"All right then," he said. "You ready?"

So, without the help of Cuz's lucky rabbit's foot, I turned us onto Skyline Drive. At the tunnel's lip, I took a deep breath, fearing it'd be the last good inhale I'd take for quite a while. I turned on the rig's headlights and we entered the black hole, the pinpoint light at the other end of the tunnel all we could see. Edging slow and steady, we moved into the dark, hugging the center stripe, the giraffes riding fine, the darkness quieting them nicely. A car entered from the other end, popping on its own headlights. I felt the giraffes jolt. The headlights grew bigger and bigger . . . until the car passed with a swish, and I swear I heard us all sigh as one.

Finally, we were out the other side, but we didn't have more than a second to enjoy it. Just like the Old Man warned, the road went straight into a curve. Worse, we were in the outside lane with only stacked-log guardrails between us and the valley below. Pulling hard at that wheel, I wanted to fess up I was a big, fat, whopping liar and he was a fool to have trusted me one whit. But it was too late. We were into it. Deadly quick, I learned what a switchback was—we were swerving back and forth and back again, all around that lumpy mountain. I hugged the middle stripe, trying to ignore the little crosses decorating the shoulder of the road, knowing each one was a body that didn't make it, and I'd have wagered not a one of them had a load of jittery giraffes. With each curve I was feeling us sway. Because what do you do with that much weight going around a bend? You lean. Especially if you happen to be a giraffe. The more they leaned and the more I struggled through gear after gear, the more I pictured us taking flight off the back of one of those switches, with the Old Man's screaming regrets the last thing I ever heard. I slowed down. The speed limit signs quoted fifteen miles per hour as the government's best bet for safe curve-taking speed. We weren't even going ten, with me trying out gear after gear, feeling for the one to right us—then I found it—I *did*. It was *working*—we took the next switchback fine and the next one even finer. I was already imagining the praise the Old Man would be heaping on me the moment we were down, when I heard the sound of a sputtering motor coming up behind.

Before I could do a thing about it, a car appeared in my side mirror . . . a green Packard.

It couldn't have been doing fifteen.

But that was faster than ten.

And . . .

BAMMM.

The Packard popped the back of the rig, throwing us forward and jostling both giraffes to the wrong side of the rig—the valley side. Out the Old Man's side mirror, I could see their heads peering clean over the drop-off. The whole groaning rig was leaning about as far as it could without toppling clean over.

"STOP-STOP!" he screamed.

I threw on the brakes. It made the giraffes right themselves slightly, but not enough. They were panicking. The rig started teetering, hanging over the drop-off, with nothing between them and thin air but a railing built for cars.

Behind us, Red threw open the Packard's door and started to jump out.

"You want to get us all KILLED? Stay in the car!" the Old Man hollered back at her, pushing me out the door. "Climb up the side and call the giraffes toward you while I get us moving!" he ordered, jumping behind the wheel.

"But shouldn't you . . . ?"

"Hurry! You know she's not happy with me! Just lean toward the mountain and talk 'em your way! There's a turnout around the bend—we're almost there, but you got to right them or we won't even make it that far!"

It was the first time I'd seen the Old Man scared, so I moved quick. Climbing up, I leaned as far back as I could on the mountain side of the teetering rig and started calling to the giraffes without a single onion to help. Waving my free arm back my way, I used all the animal calls I knew, which were little more than chicken tsk-tsking and horse clucking, while the Old Man gunned the gas. But the rig kept teetering and the giraffes kept panicking—their big eyes wide with terror, their big bodies telling them to stampede, to run. I tried the Old Man's giraffe-speak, but my voice was brittle. The rig lurched worse. As the Old Man gunned it harder, I lost my grip and had to grab it back, the terror in the giraffes' brown-apple eyes now my terror. Then I was no longer giraffe-speaking, I was begging, wailing, pleading—*please, please, trust me, oh please-please-please-please—COME TO ME—please.*

"COME!"

And they did.

Their tonnage shifted, jerking the rig back straight, away from the free-falling death of us all.

If I could've let go of the rig, I'd have hugged both their titanic heads. But all I could do was hold on as the Old Man lurched us forward again, clearing the switchback and heading around the bend.

At the scenic overlook, barely wide enough for the rig itself, the Old Man jolted us to a stop, tumbling out of the driver's seat to catch his breath. I tumbled to the ground, too, but rushed to the overlook, my bladder having all the excitement it could hold. The second I got the job done and was struggling with my new, stiff denim buttons, the Packard inched by.

I stared at Red staring back at me until she was out of sight.

"Let's go!" The Old Man was already back in the passenger seat. "I got to check that splint, but not here."

Hustling behind the wheel, I eased the rig back on the road. It wasn't over. Not only were we still climbing, it had begun to drizzle.

The Old Man was talking fast. "There's a clearing between the peaks with a comfort station and a big lot. Two maybe three switchbacks and we're there . . ."

Running through the gears as smooth and slow as I could on the slickening road, I took the first switchback, and then the second, catching a glimpse of the clearing.

As we made the next turn, though, lining both sides of the road's narrow shoulders was an army of shovelers. At the sight, the Old Man popped the dashboard with his hand loud enough to make me jump.

He was *smiling*. "God A'mighty—it's the CCC! The *WPA* practically *built* the zoo!"

The shovelers were a Civilian Conservation Corps crew, he said, part of FDR's Hard Times program, like the Works Progress Administration that put out-of-work men to building things all across the country. The road crew, not much older than me, were putting down stones and logs, smoothing the edges of the entrance into the station, where another group was clearing trees and putting down dirt, their shovels flashing in the handful of sunbeams streaming into the clearing through the clouds. Traffic was being stopped the other way to let them work, but the signaler wasn't doing much signaling, as he was too busy gaping at the giraffes. Soon, so was the entire road crew. When they caught sight of our cargo, the shovels stopped in a sort of wave as, one by one, the boys elbowed their neighbors, gasps rippling down the line.

Inching the rig around them, I pulled into the comfort station's lot. The buildings and log picnic benches were so new you could sniff the just-cut smell over the wind. Their big nostrils working overtime, the giraffes had their snouts high to the sky.

I stopped under a big tree near the comfort station as the drizzle got stronger and the clouds darker. The shovel army was headed our way. Quick as we could, we gave everything a once-over. I checked the rig and the Old Man eyed Girl's splint. To me, everything seemed better than it had any right to be after that wild ride, but the Old Man wasn't even close to smiling anymore.

By then, the rig was completely surrounded, the entire crew crowding near. Their faces sunburned and rawboned, some were dressed in khakis, some in denims, some bare-chested, some in hats, all of them toting shovels, picks, or ball-peen hammers. The Old Man motioned me to pop the top so the giraffes could nibble at the shade trees for the CCC audience. I climbed up, but before I could pop the top, the view stopped me flat. From up there, I could see over the side of the mountain where the sun was shining down on the Shenandoah Valley.

It was lusher and greener than anything I'd ever seen in my Panhandle life. It was like looking at a Dust Bowl farmer's idea of heaven. It looked like Californy.

"The top, boy," the Old Man yelled up.

Tearing my eyes away, I threw the top back and stayed put to calm the giraffes. But I didn't have to. Despite our big scare or maybe because of it, the giraffes were already gawking right back at the gawkers, bobbing those necks sweetly up and down.

As the crew cheered them on, I saw the flash of a camera. There stood Red. Fast as she could, she was popping in flashbulbs to brighten the drizzly gloom and switching them out for new ones from the camera bag on her shoulder.

Flash. Flash. Flash.

The young shoveling army, with a red-crested beauty near enough to touch, started crowding in close—too close, to my eyes. Jumping down, I shoved my way through the crews to stand in front of her, arms wide. I expected the crowd of boys to take exception. Instead it was Red.

"What do you think you're doing!" she hissed.

"You said you wanted my help," I said.

Her face was as fiery as her curls. "That wasn't the deal—I don't need saving!"

"Fine!" I said, stepping back, allowing the shoveling army to shove back in, swamping her so quick I couldn't even see her.

I was about to push back in again, no matter what she said, when a siren whooped and a state trooper came rolling up on his saddle-bagged cycle. Dressed in a Mountie-style hat and hip boots, he stopped at the edge of the crowd and dismounted. The crew made way for him as he headed toward the Old Man without even glancing at the giraffes. When he passed Red, she stepped back, too, way back, which seemed strange. The trooper hat alone seemed worth a photo.

The Old Man, already talking to the trooper, was waving me to the rig. I looked back for Red. When I couldn't find her in the crowd, something told me to look out on the road, and I looked in time to see a glimpse of the green Packard driving away.

In a few minutes, we were back on Skyline Drive, the trooper riding behind us with his lights flashing, no doubt at the request of the Old Man. After a few more switchbacks, we left the mountain drizzle behind and I breathed easier, even though I was still feeling jangled down to my core. Descending into the valley, we popped out of the mountains near a town called Luray, where the trooper gave us a nice wave and vanished back up Skyline Drive.

We stopped at the first little roadside store we saw, a small clapboard place with a single gas pump, as a mangy mountain man in a flop hat covered with leaves was tying his pack mule out front. As I steered the big rig around them, the store's screen door slapped open. Out came a man sporting a Santa Claus beard dressed in the newest, bluest, starchiest overalls I ever saw, trailed by a towheaded kid wearing his own stiff overalls.

"I'll be darned! You never know what's going to pass by nowadays!" the man said, slapping his knee. "Real live gi-raffes! At my store!" Rushing back inside, he came back out with one of those little cardboard box cameras and took a quick picture. "That one's going on the wall, front and center." Putting his arm around the Old Man, he escorted him inside while the kid bounded over to gas us up.

I sat down on the truck's running board and worked to calm my nerves. Inside, I could see the Old Man setting things on the counter, then reaching for his money and the owner waving him off. So the Old Man shook the bearded man's hand, jotted something on a postcard, and handed it to him. Then, clutching onion gunnysacks under both arms, he came out with a soft drink in one hand and a beer in the other.

"Here's you a sarsaparilla," he said to me. "You're driving. But I'm not, thank God." Dropping the sacks, he plopped down on the running board beside me, pushed back his fedora, and took his first swig of beer.

I held off on my own swigging, though, worried the Old Man would notice my shakes. So I tried chitchat. "You send a postcard?"

He nodded.

"Who to?"

"The Boss Lady."

"You aren't telling her the bad stuff, are you?"

"Not until I can't help it." Finishing the beer, he grabbed one of the onion sacks, climbed up the rig ladder, and split the whole thing between the giraffes, like peace offerings and thank-yous, cooing giraffe-speak all the while. As the giraffes happily chomped, he came down and took a long look at Girl's splint through the trapdoor, then eased back down by me.

"Her leg OK?" I asked.

He didn't answer. Instead he said, "You did good, boy, but no offense, this was my mistake. I should never have asked it of you. I wasn't expecting that *gotdam* detour . . . yet if we had turned back . . ." He paused, cutting himself off. "For sure now, I'll be seeing about getting an experienced man in Memphis for the rest of the way."

Jitters or not, that almost had me loudly taking exception. It wasn't *me* that almost sent us over the side—it was Red and her Packard. I was doing fine before that bump. Once you get that close to going off a mountain, though, I guess you only remember the scare, even if you're the Old Man.

He could change his mind again, I told myself as I watched the mountain man trudge from the store. *After all,* I thought, taking a deep breath, *what can happen now that'd be worse than almost falling off a mountain?*

As if in answer to a young fool's thought, the mangy man yowled.

"Gimme back my hat!"

He was hollering at Wild Girl. Her long neck, stuck full out her window, was moving in jerky, unnatural ways, and from her throat came a sound so horrid the memory can make my skin crawl even now—she was gagging.

The hat was stuck.

The Old Man got quick to his boots as the store's owner came running out. "*Damn* your eyes, Phineas, it thought that twig hat of yours was a tree!"

I was on my feet by then, but all I could do was stare at that gyrating neck, hardly believing what I was seeing. She was fighting for her breath, flailing wild, unable to pull herself back in her window to get her neck straight.

Grabbing the gas pump's water hose, the Old Man turned it on full force and, climbing quick up by Girl, tried to aim the water hose down her throat. "Steady the hose!" he hollered down. I grabbed the back end, and the Old Man shoved the hose past her tongue—the hose water flowing like a mighty river down her massive craw and flooding right back up like a spouting geyser, hat and all.

Girl gave a mighty sneeze and went back to chewing her cud.

The mountain man grabbed his upchucked hat and went back to his mule.

The Old Man climbed down and the store owner turned off the water.

And me—with a death grip still on that hose, I dropped back to the running board, soaked and gulping.

"Huh," mumbled the store owner, surveying the mess. "You'd think it would've gone down, not come back up. Wouldn't ya?"

Plopping down beside me, the Old Man heaved a great sigh, then got right back to his feet. I got up, too, thinking we were moving on. Instead he shuffled toward the store. "You get the darlings ready," he muttered. "I'm having me another beer."

* * *

A few miles ahead, we connected back up with the Lee Highway again. For the next hour, we glided through scenery that I wished I was more in the mood to enjoy—forest on one side and glory-green valley views on the other. I still hadn't quite beat my jitters, though, so when the Old Man had me pull into a log cabin camp nestled in the forest along the highway, I was glad of it. We had it to ourselves from the lonesome look of the place, and after the usual happy ogling by the camp manager, we began our giraffe-tending. But this time it felt different. The Old Man stared at Girl's splint even longer than he did at the store, and I could see why. The wound was oozing through the bandaged splint. The rough ride had banged it up bad enough to bleed.

Frazzled, the Old Man muttered, "Get the onions." He pulled the zoo doc's black bag out of the cab. I stood on the side ladder and offered onions to Girl through her window. At first, she wouldn't take them. When she did, it was only one. I kept on holding them out to her, though, as the Old Man gently unwrapped the bandaged splint, dabbed powder from the glass bottle on the oozing wound, and wrapped the splint again. When she let him without a peep, I knew what he didn't tell me before we headed into that tunnel. Girl's leg was much worse than he was letting on.

Stuffing the black bag behind the cab's seat, the Old Man pushed his fedora back and gazed blankly at the setting sun. "Handle the rest, will you, boy?" he mumbled, and trudged to the cabin without another word.

So I climbed up the side ladder far enough to throw open the top. The sight of the giraffes standing safe in their traveling suites should have soothed my nerves. But when they moved toward me like they'd done on the mountain, the moment came flooding back . . . *I'm on the switchback . . . Red hits us, jolting the giraffes toward the drop-off . . . I'm hanging off the side, begging-pleading-praying for their towering selves to hear me . . . to trust me . . .*

To come to me . . .

Away from free fall . . .

I was safely clutching the side of a parked rig, yet I was quaking in my boots, the way that almost sailing off a mountain can rattle a person to the bone when the near-death truth of it sinks in. I forced myself to breathe until I could loosen my grip on the rig. But instead of climbing down, I crawled up to the open top. I needed the air, I needed the sky, and I needed the company, even if I couldn't admit it. I sat down, straddling the cross plank like I'd done the night before with Red. This time, though, the giraffes weren't bumping me for onions. They moved as close as they could to me, the way they had to each other their first night in quarantine. Like they were circling the wagons around me. Surrounded by such colossals, I should have felt shaky and small, yet their mammoth presence made me feel big, and calm, and sweetly safe in a way hard to describe and even harder to resist. I knew better. Yet I found myself overcome with feelings for them that I couldn't hold back.

They're just animals, I could hear my pa grousing, *and you ain't a boy in knickers no more.*

But they came *to me on the mountain!* I couldn't stop thinking. *They came—and we didn't die!*

It was a full moon night, one of those harvest moons that light up the night so bright that you can see almost as good as day. As the giraffes reached for the branches surrounding us, I watched and listened as their nibbling slowed and their cud chewing began. I lay back on the plank between the two giraffes' traveling rooms, everything lulling me, the giraffes near and serene, the woods hushed, the moon above big and yellow through the trees. I stared at that moon so long and peaceful that, to my shameful surprise, I must have nodded off.

Next thing I know I was bolting straight up in the dark to the sound of splintering wood—the giraffes were kicking hard enough to fracture the crates. Something was so near they thought they had to defend themselves.

Bracing myself, I leaned over the side. Below us was a bear. It was sniffing around the rig's tires, and *then* it reared up on its hind legs and plopped its beefy paws on the side of the road Pullman.

The giraffes had a fit. Girl kicked so hard, I was sure she cracked a hole in the wood, but the bear didn't budge. I squinted through the shadows for something to wave or bang, gearing up to jump down and scare the bear off. Considering that this was the first time I ever laid eyes on a bear, I couldn't quite make myself do it. As I braced to holler loud enough to scare off the furry devil before the giraffes did some real damage, I saw a *flash*—and everything turned blinding white-bright.

For a second, I couldn't see a thing, but neither could the bear. To the sound of it bumping into the camp's trash cans, running away, I grabbed the rig to save myself from falling off. As I blinked back to sight, out strolled Red in the moonlight, popping the bulb from her camera with a *krink* and bouncing it in her hand until it cooled down. You'd have thought she'd just been to a tea party.

Still blinking, I eased down to check the damage to the rig. Sure enough, it was cracked right through. The Old Man was going to love that. To avoid Red, I climbed back up to the cross plank.

"She kicked at that bear through the *wood*!" Red called up in a loud whisper. "They're OK, aren't they?"

As the giraffes moved near me again, I didn't answer.

"I'm sorry about bumping you in the mountains," Red whispered up.

With that, I aimed all my fearful fury from the whole day straight at her. "You about *sent us over*," I hissed down. "I was doing *fine*!"

"Well, don't *yell* at me!" she whispered up.

"I'm not *yelling*!" I whispered down.

"*Yes*, you are!" she whispered back.

We both looked toward the Old Man's cabin at the same time.

She sighed. "I guess I deserve to be yelled at, you're right," she whispered quieter. "I'm so, so sorry, Woody. Truly I am. You and the giraffes . . . you were *amazing*. May I come up?"

Not waiting for an answer, she set her camera down and crawled up to straddle the cross plank, facing me, exactly like the night before, but this time I inched back, away. The giraffes crowded close, so close that their fur was brushing against our dangling legs. I could feel the warmth of their pelts against my denims, knowing that Red was feeling the same against her trousers, and I felt my fury ebb away. "I fell asleep," I heard myself confess. "I don't fall asleep."

She frowned. "What? You have to sleep."

I sure wasn't going to tell her about my nightmare. So I shrugged.

"I love sleep," she said. "Only thing better is being awake. *Really* awake."

We sat quiet for a moment until Boy stepped back a bit, eyeing a branch he'd missed. I saw Red move, and I thought she was climbing down.

Instead she swung her legs over and dropped right into his crate, hitting its padded floor with a *thump* that might as well have been upside my head, I was so dumbstruck. She'd landed knee deep in Boy's peat moss near his hooves, inches from Girl's splinted leg on the other side of the opening. The Old Man's words were popping like firecrackers inside my head . . . *Big don't know from small . . . They could love you like their mama and still crush an arm or leg . . .*

"Look at all this padding, even on the walls," Red whispered up. "This is comfier than my cabin."

"What are you *doing*?" I hissed down.

"I only wanted to see what it was like in here for the story—and I knew he wouldn't mind."

Boy was shuffling his hooves, moving away from Red, and Girl was swaying her neck like she did right before kicking the Old Man. Red was about to get it. I tried to warn her, but I couldn't get the words out. Reaching through the opening, she placed her left hand on Girl's flank over the same sideways heart-shaped spot I'd touched in quarantine, and reaching back to Boy with her right, she patted them both at the same time. Girl's neck stopped its swaying and Boy's fur shuddered with delight.

"I'm going to Africa someday," Red said, patting, patting. "This'll get me there, you wait and see." She glanced up at me. "How do I get out of here? Oh, wait."

She popped open the trapdoor and eased to the ground, smiling at me like she'd been patting puppies. Climbing down, I whapped the trapdoor shut, wanting bad to tell her to never, ever do that again, but what she'd just done belied any such warnings.

"Woody, did you tell Mr. Jones who I was when I hit the rig?"

I barely heard her. "What? No."

"Good. Let's wait on introducing me . . . you know, considering all. I'll hang on back a bit longer." Then, with a kiss on my cheek that froze me solid, she picked up her camera and disappeared inside her cabin.

It wasn't near time for the Old Man to relieve me, but in no more than a minute he came lumbering up, pulling on his suspenders and squinting in the moonlight. "Half woke up a while ago. Never got full back to sleep. The darlings OK? Thought I heard a ruckus."

"There was a bear," I said, standing so he couldn't see the crack in the rig. "It ran away."

"A bear, eh?" he said, already grabbing his Lucky Strike pack and settling onto the rig's running board. "He won't come back. Go get some sleep. I'll wake you at dawn."

Heading to the cabin, I told myself I'd show him the crack in the road Pullman tomorrow if he didn't find it himself first. Right then, though, I'd had enough of that pisser of a day.

As I closed my eyes, hoping for a bit of sleep without nightmares, I saw a flash of bear on the back of my eyelids and felt the touch of Red's lips on my cheek. And I wondered what might be more dangerous, the bear, the giraffes, or a camera-packing redhead in britches.

POSTCARD

Airmail Par Avion

Oct. 8 38

Not a lick of trouble through
mountains. Giraffes quit
chewing their cud but once
down got back to work.

RJ

TO:

Mrs. Belle Benchley
San Diego Zoo
San Diego, California

. . . "Mr. Nickel?"

Rosie, Greasy, and the nurse are standing in my doorway.

"May we come in?" asks the nurse.

"Well, listen to you asking nicely," I say, lowering my pencil.

"I tell you his heart stopped," Greasy is saying.

"Daryl said you had a seizure of some kind. How do you feel?"

"I'm fine and dandy, fit as a fiddle," I say, glancing at Wild Girl, who's blowing a blubbery Bronx cheer Greasy's way.

Greasy throws up his hands and leaves. The nurse comes over, takes my pulse, listens to my heart, and leaves, too.

Rosie, though, doesn't move. "OK, hon, what happened? I won't tell."

I don't answer, turning back to my writing pad. In a second, she sighs and leaves as well, giving my shoulder another squeeze as she goes.

But then I hear dominoes and I turn to see the younger Rosie on the edge of my bed, shuffling away. *A game and a story,* she is saying again . . . "So what's next? I know! We're about to meet Moses, aren't we?"

My chest tightens.

"Oh, hon . . . why are you pushing yourself so?"

Haven't you ever had a story you should've told someone before it was too late? I think, rubbing my heart.

You've told me, she says.

No, not all—and you're not her. "I need to tell *her*," I say out loud. But I'm talking to an empty room. I glance back quick for the darling Girl. She's still there, peacefully licking the air. So, licking my pencil tip, I get back on the road.

Baltimore American

OCTOBER 9, 1938

LOW BRIDGE!

8

Into Tennessee

At dawn, the first thing I saw as I pulled on my boots and stumbled out of the log cabin was the Old Man inspecting the rig's splintered crack as Wild Girl stomped her displeasure. Throwing up his hands, he said, "Let's go."

Squinting through the far shadows, I could see the Packard was still there. The Old Man hadn't noticed, and as we headed out I spied Red watching from her cabin door.

We stopped at the first roadside store we saw for gas and food. As I checked the giraffes and watched for Red, I eyed the store's Western Union sign, wondering if he was sending that telegram for a new Memphis driver like he said. Getting gloomier by the second, I just got back behind the wheel.

In a minute, the Old Man marched out and dropped the food sacks and a newspaper on the seat between us. As he bit into his breakfast salami, I recall looking down at the newspaper. In letters as big as my fist, it said: **HITLER INVADES CZECHOSLOVAKIA: "Thus Begins Our Great German Reich."** I barely took notice. All I could think about was the telegram. Did he or didn't he send it?

The Old Man held out the salami. "Want a bite?"

I shook my head.

Taking another big bite as I pulled us onto the road, he stored it in his cheek to say, "By the way, I wired for the new driver."

There it was.

"So get us there and I'll buy you that train ticket. Anywhere you want to—"

But I was already spewing out what I'd been practicing since the mountain store. "I had the mountain beat till we got hit! I can go the distance! I can go to *Californy*, swear to *God* I can!"

The Old Man chuckled. "Clean the wax out of your ears, boy. I said I'll buy you a ticket *anywhere* you want to go."

"Anywhere?"

"You earned it," he answered, swallowing down the last of the salami. "Even to California, if you're so set on it."

"You mean it?"

"Yep. You'll be getting there before we will."

That quick, I was going to California. *Soon.* My plan had worked. All I had to do was get to Memphis and I'd be on my way straight to the land of milk and honey.

I felt my flickering hope flame up high as all glory.

The next few miles were a blur. I'm surprised I didn't run us into a ditch I was so over the moon with the Old Man's big announcement. I wasn't even looking back for Red. In fact, I don't recall a thing about that part of the trip until we found ourselves in Tennessee, crossing through a nice little pass that rolled us to the other side of the Smoky Mountains, the biggest ups and downs behind us, at least of the geographical kind.

Soon we rocked into a rhythm like the one on our first traveling day. But for me, it was as different as different could be. I wasn't riding on a thieved cycle trying to keep up. I wasn't working an angle or plotting my next move. I was just driving us along, blissful, the hours slipping by, the roadside stops as pretty as a picture, and the trees sheer chomping delights. We passed a horse farm, and the horses began running with us along the pasture's long white fence, tails swishing, manes flying high. Somewhere during that stretch Wild Boy even lay down. At the next rest stop, I popped the top to find him spread across his traveling crate's floor again, his long neck drooping over his back, defying the laws of necks.

This time, instead of telling the Old Man, I leaned in and whispered, "Hey—"

Unwinding his neck, Boy got to his feet, rising like a giraffe prince as if to say, *What?* Then he pushed by me to reach for the new trees with Girl . . . and a wave of something peculiar and bittersweet passed over me. Down the road, I glanced in my sideview mirror at the giraffes with their snouts to the wind . . . and the same feeling washed over me again. Forcing my eyes straight ahead, I pictured myself riding on that California-bound train until my flickering hope was once again aflame.

The rest of the morning's drive was pure traveling peace, the high point being a batch of those old Burma-Shave ads staggered on little signs as we rolled by:

THE SAFEST RULE
NO IFS OR BUTS
JUST DRIVE LIKE EVERY ONE
ELSE IS NUTS
BURMA-SHAVE

***

HE LIT A MATCH
TO CHECK GAS TANK

THAT'S WHY
THEY CALL HIM
SKINLESS FRANK
BURMA-SHAVE

The last one I remember because it made the Old Man bust out laughing. In fact, by the afternoon's first stop we were all in such a good mood that Girl didn't even kick at the Old Man when he inspected her splint.

As we pulled back on the road, though, we heard the sound of a train in the distance and the Old Man tensed.

The sound grew louder and louder, coming from somewhere beyond the trees. The railroad track was moving toward us again. We strained for a glimpse through the woods, and when we saw flashes of yellow and red, the Old Man cussed under his breath.

"What kind of circus moves so much it keeps up with us?" I said.

"The cheap, fly-by-night kind," he said back.

The trees thinned and I caught a glimpse of elephants in a passing cattle car, their ears sagging low. "They don't look happy."

"Nothing much happy going on over there," muttered the Old Man. He took the next moment to spit out the window, which now in memory seems as much a comment as a sudden urge to rid himself of spittle. Because the next thing he said was, "Forget the skullduggery. You'd want to bring the wrath of God down on them just for how they treat their animals."

For over a mile, the train paced us on the other side of the tree line until it began pulling ahead. Through the trees, we could make out the new sign on the red caboose that said **CHATTANOOGA TONIGHT!** as the train chugged out of sight.

Our good mood was dashed. As the land opened up to pasture, I kept checking the giraffes in the side mirror, their road Pullman looking far too much like a cattle car. I noticed the Old Man looking back more, too, but not at the giraffes. He was glancing at the road, and he kept it up for miles. The circus train had already passed, so I couldn't quite figure why. I checked my own side mirror, worrying he'd spied the green Packard, but the road was empty.

Then he was pointing. "Turn off."

I exited us onto a gravel road that ran through a tall stand of nearby trees.

"Pull into that grove," he said, his voice gone odd. "And put the giraffes' heads in."

So I did, and they let me, which was also mighty odd.

We sat there for five minutes that turned into ten, watching. I started wishing for cars to whiz by to kill the boredom. I saw a glimpse of color . . . yellow . . . and red.

A panel truck whizzed by and out of sight—the same panel truck we'd seen back in Maryland.

I cut my eye at the Old Man, busting with questions, but his jaw was set so solid, I knew to let him be. Our nice traveling mood wasn't only broken now, it was roadkill.

We opened the giraffes' windows again, and for the next couple of hours, the highway wound us through town after little town, the roadside sprinkled with advertising billboards, ones like **I'D WALK A MILE FOR A CAMEL** and **DRINK A BITE TO EAT 10-2-4 DR. PEPPER.** Even town wags calling out "How's the weather up there?" didn't perk us up. By late afternoon, the air had turned a tad chilly, so we rolled up our windows, and even the giraffes pulled their heads in. The stop for the night was about two hours away, the Old Man said, so we'd be done before it got any chillier, the air or the mood.

That's when we came to the overpass.

And when I say overpass, I mean what was left of the overpass.

Somebody hadn't quite made it under. The middle section had been hit by something harder than a giraffe head. All that was left of it was dangling pieces of concrete and wire. Below it was another big **DETOUR** sign, plunked down in the middle of the highway.

The Old Man groaned. "*NOW* what!"

I slowed us to a crawl and the giraffes popped their heads out to see why. The detour arrow pointed to a side road that held the promise of looping back around to the highway soon enough. The side road itself looked iffy, though. It was paved, if cracked and weedy, but it didn't have a name or a number. All it had to mark it was a homemade sign announcing **COTTAGES FOR COLOREDS** with an arrow pointing the way.

"What do I do?" I said.

The Old Man fumed. "Take the road."

We went about a hundred yards fine enough, but as we took a curve, I had to stand on the brakes. In front of us was a railroad underpass, the old narrow kind where the road dips down to go under the track instead of the other way around. It looked low.

And when I say low, I mean real low.

Both of us could tell by eyeing the underpass that the clearance was going to be close, plus it was barely wide enough for us to pass through.

I'd have pulled the rig off the road if there'd been a shoulder, but it was already sloping inward to pass under the railroad trestle. So I had to stop in the middle of the road, and the moment we came to a stop, I felt eyes on me. I thought it was the giraffes until I saw a whitewashed shotgun shack right by the tracks. Sitting in a small window in the roof's eaves was a little Black girl, not more than four or five. We were so close, I could see her eyes grow wide with giraffes.

The Old Man was talking. "Go measure the thing quick before some new fool rear-ends us." Reaching under the seat for a big metal tape measure, he thrust it at me. I got out with it and ran, taking the tape high as soon as I was below the underpass.

"Twelve feet eight!" I called.

The rig was twelve foot eight—maybe higher, since tires inflate on the road.

By the time I returned to the rig, the Old Man was standing near the front fender, staring down at the rig's tire. "I was hoping it wouldn't come to this," he muttered as he took the cap off the tire's air valve stem. The rig had single tires up front and double tires in back under the giraffes to help hold the weight and to keep the rig going if one went flat. Within seconds, he'd let a little air out of all of them, each one making a tiny, soft *phhhhhht* sound, that is, until he got to the last right-side double tire that had picked up a nail. The Old Man had no choice. He had to let air out of it, too—and when he did, the tire went full-out flat. After giving it a good cussing, he took a deep breath. We still had the other double tire to get us to our night stop and some gas station help—if we could only get through the underpass.

I measured again. Still too close. He had to let out a bit more on every tire.

As he was all but finished, his fingers pinching the valve stem of the tire by the flat, a two-seat roadster zoomed around the curve, swerved to miss us, and barreled on through the underpass. Having already been hit once by a swerving rubbernecker, I jumped like a spooked bullfrog, stumbling into the Old Man so hard that his fingers, still squeezing the tire's stem, wrenched the nozzle sideways . . . and the *phhhhhht* sound was replaced by another sound . . . the tiniest unsettling *ssssssshhhhhhh*.

And it wasn't stopping. *Both* of the right-side double tires were about to be flat.

For a second, we looked at each other, then the Old Man yelled, "We got to get through to even get off the road! Put their heads in!"

I wasted a full minute trying, but the usually obliging Boy wasn't having it, much less Girl.

"Forget it!" called the Old Man as he ran to the curve, and seeing the Old Man run was a scary sight in itself. "Coast's clear!" he yelled. "Go!"

I hopped behind the wheel, still hearing that tiny *sssssshhhhhhh*.

"Down the middle—slow but *quick*—they need time to get their heads in," the Old Man hollered, "but that tire's about to go!"

With the giraffes snorting and stomping at the ruckus, I put the rig into gear and inched forward, trusting the giraffes to pull their heads out of harm's way on their own . . . and, God love them, they did. Slow, slow, slow, we moved under the rusted old railroad bridge, the top of the rig making screech-scraw wood-scraping sounds to set your teeth on fire.

The rig was *almost* through—only inches left to clear—when the remaining back right tire went flat with one quick, sad *phhwwmphh*. We dropped to a dead stop, plugging up that underpass good.

I jumped to the ground and wiggled between the rig and the underpass wall to join the Old Man gaping at the woeful sight. Both back right tires were flat, all right. In a flash, we saw what had happened. It was the giraffes. As soon as most of the rig had cleared and it was safe to pop their heads out again, they'd done just that. At the same time. On the same side. The extra weight was too much for the single, half-deflated tire on top of what was causing that *sssssshhhhhhh* sound—which, of course, now had *also* stopped.

At that, the Old Man whopped that poor fedora of his to the ground and stomped it flat, produced a rolling cuss I would have admired any other time, creative as sin and the length of a long spiral spit into the wind. Which is probably how it felt, too, his big plan coming right back in his face, because I knew what he was thinking. I was wanting to kick myself. When the giraffes wouldn't let me close one side's windows, I should have tried tricking them by closing off opposite side ones—Girl one way, Boy the other—to keep the rig balanced for the few seconds we needed it to work. Too little, too late, I latched all the windows giraffe-tight to get us balanced again, at least long enough for the Old Man to stop cussing and start figuring out what to do. In the meantime, we were stuck now in almost as much mortal peril as in the mountains.

So I headed in a sprint back to the curve, since one of us had to keep cars from ramming us into a world of hurt.

The Old Man hollered me to a halt. "Get back here!"

I turned to see why, and what I saw was a fool's folly.

Under the back axle, he'd set up the big fancy jack that came with the big fancy rig. He was going to make me start pumping it. But we had one spare, two flats, and two giraffes. Not to mention the underpass right above the last two to three inches of the rig. It wasn't going to work. I knew it in my bones. There wasn't a jack made that a man could pump on his own strength to raise squat with giraffes sitting on top of it over two flat tires. And there was sure no trick to make them not weigh two tons no matter where they stood.

I knew the Old Man saw what I saw, but he looked desperate, half-crazy with it. He marched over and shoved me toward the jack, ordering me to get pumping. So, I started pumping and I kept it up until I heard the Old Man whisper in a voice so spooked the memory of it can still give me the creeps.

"Uhm . . . boy . . ."

I looked where he was looking. Up on the railroad tracks stood a Black man in blue overalls. He was six and a half feet, if an inch. What got me up quick on my feet, though, wasn't so much the sight of the man. It was the big blade he was holding. He had himself a wheat scythe, a nasty-looking farm tool I'd only seen left to rust on barn walls after cotton and tractors came to the plains. But this one wasn't rusty. This one was shiny and sharp. Like the one Death in his flowing robe carries around in ghost stories.

Down toward the front of the rig ambled the man. When he got near, he popped the handle side of the scythe into the soft ground like the staff of Moses. For a very long moment, he stood there staring hard enough to give both me and the Old Man the willies.

"We been watching you," he finally said.

I glanced around, not seeing any "we," and not much wanting to.

At the sound of the booming new voice, Wild Girl's head bopped her latched window so hard that the latch gave and the window popped open.

Moses frowned. "What kind of animals you got there?"

Before the Old Man could answer, the other latched window whapped open as well, Wild Boy wanting to see what there was to see, too, and with both giraffes on the same side again, the rig leaned, the metal groaned, and *thunk*. So much for the fancy jack.

Moses stared at the jack.

Then at the truck.

Then at the underpass.

Then at the tires.

Then back at us. "Got yourself in a tight spot," he said.

"Yes," answered the Old Man.

"Tried to let out the tires to get it under."

"Yes," answered the Old Man again.

"Now you're stuck," Moses said next.

"*Yes*—" repeated the Old Man, getting crankier by the second over all this stating of the obvious.

Moses nodded at the giraffes. "Don't suppose those big fellers can come out of there."

"*No.*" The Old Man's head all but bobbed off he shook it so hard. For all we knew, Moses had some designs on the giraffes, but the truth was the rig was not a back-loading horse trailer. So, even if we wanted to, there wasn't going to be any taking the giraffes out until it was clear of the underpass. The entire side had to come down to do any such thing.

Giving everything another once-over, Moses then said, "We can do what needs doing. But first, things gotta be put right."

I didn't know about the Old Man, but the sound of that did not make me glad all over.

Moses put two fingers to his lips and made a noise that was something between a crow being murdered and a robin being courted. In less than a minute, six younger, burlier copies of the man appeared. They streamed in one by one, dressed in overalls like Moses, some one-shouldered, some two, some wearing shirts, some not—all clutching farm utensils in their big mitts.

They came up close to the rig, a couple of them even reaching up to touch the giraffes without having to step up on a thing to get to them. You'd think they'd have all been chattering upon seeing giraffes, like every other living soul had so far. But they were silent as the wind, all nods of the head, hands on hips, cocks of the brow, repeating Moses's actions without wasting a bit of breath on speech, looking at the tires, the underpass, the rig, and each other.

Then back at us.

The Old Man, meanwhile, was keeping an eye on the farm utensils in the men's beefy fists. I could tell he was worrying which way this was about to go, his eyes darting to the shotgun on the cab's gunrack. "Stay close," he mumbled at me, like I could do a thing if everything went south.

"Better get the uncs, too," Moses said next, and put his fingers to his lips again. This time the birdcall was more murder than courting, and six more burly men come out of nowhere, older than the first group, but the spitting image of each other except for the amount of hair on their heads. Joining up with the rest, they did the very same wordless sizing up the situation, and they did it so long, both me and the Old Man were about to come right out of our skins.

Then they all turned toward the railroad track as here came *another* man. But this one was different. Using a hoe as a walking stick, he was white-whiskered, his overalls were starched, his blue work shirt was fresh-ironed, and, as he came to a stop by Moses, he only had eyes for the giraffes.

I'd heard of big farming families before, even known a few, but this one pretty much took the prize. Taking in the whole clan, I figured white-whiskers had to be the Big Papa, the uncs his brothers, and the rest had to be their sons, Moses being the eldest.

As Big Papa kept studying the giraffes, Moses nodded at the youngest man—all the muscle but not the height—and the son headed toward the curve to stand watch, a human roadblock if there ever was one.

Then Big Papa spoke. "We know what we can do for these towering creatures of God's pure Eden." As Big Papa and Moses let another moment go by without a peep, the Old Man was about to pop and I wasn't doing much better, wondering why he wasn't raising holy hell to hear their game plan before letting these strangers take control. But I knew why. There was only one thing to be done. Move the truck. And how that could be done without some motorized help, much less taking those giraffes out of the truck, neither of us could quite figure.

Then Moses spoke. "Put it in gear."

I looked at the Old Man, who was already looking at me. Although it was clear as day he didn't want to, he gave me a nod. As I got in and put the rig in gear, one thought rushed through my head: *Wherever the giraffes go, I go.* The idea surprised me so much it half rattled me. I got even more rattled when I glanced in my mirror.

At the curve, a green Packard was stalled sideways off the road, like it had tried to go around the roadblock son, and there stood Red in a man's trench coat, clutching her camera, the human roadblock's big fist clutching her arm.

"You ready?"

Moses's voice snapped me back to the rig.

I nodded.

"Stomp it."

The rig, like I said, had almost cleared the underpass before the tires splatted. It just hadn't cleared enough to pull off the road. That's what the Big Papa clan proceeded to do—push us the few inches clear and to the shoulder. It didn't matter a lick that I was adding to the weight. I might as well have been made of feathers. It didn't matter a lick that two of the tires were flat. Or that the road was inclining up. Or that the giraffes were moving around, popping their heads out both sides of the rig, watching the excitement. With me stomping the gas, the Big Papa clan pushed me, two giraffes, two flat tires, and the rest of the big rig into the short roll needed to get us the few feet needed to clear that underpass. When they'd groaned and grunted and heaved and hoed their last, the rig landed on the road's narrow shoulder right beyond the bridge.

As I turned off the key, Moses whistled that robin-courting call again. The human roadblock son at the curve stepped aside to let four cars inch through the underpass, then let go of Red, who, instead of jumping into the Packard, headed straight toward us on a dead run, camera up. By the time I got out of the rig, the Old Man was standing there as slack-jawed as I'd ever seen him, with Red already there, snapping away.

The Old Man gaped at her. "Who are *you*?"

Red put out her hand. "Hello, Mr. Jones, I'm chronicling your story for *Life* magazine. Woody will vouch for me, won't you, Woody?"

"Oh, for the love of . . ." The Old Man groaned. "You're the one who damn near sent us over the side of the mountain! Get away, girlie!" He turned his back on her, which didn't stop her one bit. She turned and aimed the camera at the sons and uncs. By that time, though, the human roadblock had returned, and he placed his huge hand over her camera.

Red gulped.

"Seventh Son thinks it'd be the mannerly thing to ask, missy," Big Papa translated.

Red took a second to hear Big Papa, staring at Seventh Son's paw on her lens. "Oh. I'm sorry. May I take your picture?" That seemed to satisfy Seventh Son, and he dropped his hand.

Moses, meanwhile, had been inspecting the deflated back tires. "You gotcha a spare," he said. "You don't got two. Which you need."

The Old Man bit his tongue over more stating of the obvious. "Do you have a tire this size we could buy off you?"

Moses shook his head.

"How about a motorized pump you could haul down here for us to use to put the single spare on?" the Old Man tried next. "We've *got* to get down the road before dark."

Again, Moses shook his head.

All out of ideas, the Old Man glanced my way. Things were not looking good.

"Sure the big fellers can't come off?" Moses said.

The Old Man hesitated. "You still able to help if they can't?"

Big Papa and Moses exchanged glances, then Moses nodded real slow and the whole clan turned and marched off.

The rest of us had no choice but to wait, the Old Man fuming, the giraffes snuffling, and Red working her camera, fixing knobs and turning rings like nothing else mattered, not even the fancy automobile she'd left on the side of the road. Then her head popped up. Moses reappeared carrying a single truck tire that looked as bald as he was and, behind him, the sons returned in groups. One group was carrying two long split tree trunks as big around as a man's chest, another lugged long steel bars, and another was rolling a boulder—flat on one side, round on the other with a trunk-sized groove—landing it, flat-side down, a few yards behind the rig.

Moving in a way that spoke of them having done this many times before, the sons made a sandwich with the trunk logs and steel bars, shoved the log sandwich under the rig to straddle the back axle, then laid the other end of the log sandwich in the boulder's groove to create the oddest makeshift seesaw you ever saw.

Then, in choir-like unison, all the sons and uncs climbed up on the end of the log sandwich sticking up in the air. The steel groaned, the logs splintered, the truck creaked, and the entire rig rose the two inches needed for Moses to switch out the two deflated tires for the rig's spare and his own bald tire.

As Moses wiped his hands, the sons and the uncs got off the seesaw one by one, easing the giraffes and the rig to the dirt, the tires touching the ground with a bounce—and staying round. At that, all the parts of the seesaw went back the way they came in the hands that brought them, the men moving silent and solemn.

The Old Man and I were knocked dumb with this new feat of moxie and muscle. Seventh Son tapped the Old Man on the shoulder, held out his squished fedora until the Old Man took it, and then disappeared over the railroad tracks, too.

The Old Man, absently dusting off his hat, found his voice and turned toward Big Papa. "What do we owe you?"

Big Papa twirled his hoe in what I now think was a display of family pride. "Don't want your money."

"Well, then, how can we thank you?" the Old Man asked.

Seventh Son returned over the railroad tracks with the little girl from the shotgun shack's window riding on his shoulder, and Big Papa broke into a smile.

"Honey Bee'd like to meet these creatures," he said, "if you'd be of a mind."

Honey Bee whispered into his ear.

"And Honey Bee would like to know their names," Big Papa added.

Despite himself, I could tell the Old Man was charmed. With a glance my way, he said, "Well, Miss Honey Bee, they hadn't told us their names yet. So why don't you call this one Girl and the other Boy. That suit you?"

So Honey Bee got her own private audience, Seventh Son lifting her high enough for both giraffes to have a nice get-acquainted snort-fest with her.

Big Papa then said to the Old Man, "The old tire won't get you far. We can fix both of your'n tomorrow. Getting dark. We'll put you up. Got a growing motel concern." He pointed to a dirt road about thirty feet ahead, leading off toward the piney woods, another **COTTAGES FOR COLOREDS** sign perched by it. "Besides," Big Papa went on, "Honey Bee'd like you to stay. And Honey Bee gets her way around here. Right, Honey Bee?"

The little girl nodded.

"After all you've done for us, we'd be honored to partake of your hospitality," answered the Old Man, sticking out his hand for Big Papa to shake, which he did. Sprouting a big smile, the Old Man then headed toward the dirt road with Big Papa and Moses, turning into the charming Mr. Jones I saw with the ladies at Round's Auto Rest.

"Best you come, too, missy," Big Papa called over his shoulder, and Seventh Son and Honey Bee stepped Red's way.

Red's eyes darted between the **COTTAGES FOR COLOREDS** sign and Seventh Son. "Oh, uhmmm, no, thank you . . ."

But Big Papa was already gone, walking and talking with the Old Man. So, to the sound of a giggling Honey Bee, I put the rig in gear and turned on the dirt road as Seventh Son picked up the flat tires with his free hand and herded Red the same direction, her big trench coat dragging in the dust.

We were headed toward three little cottages, set apart against a nice stand of leafy maple trees along the edge of the woods—Big Papa's motel concern. As we passed the first cottage where a shiny blue Olds sedan with old shoes tied to the bumper was parked, out stepped a Black couple dressed to the nines to gawk at the passing eyeful that was us.

At the second cottage, Moses deposited Red, leaving her clutching her camera on the tiny porch.

Then, heading toward the third cottage set farther back, we passed a Y in the dirt road leading to a two-story whitewashed house with a barn twice as big as the house. The Old Man motioned me to wait as everybody but me and the giraffes trekked down to them. In a few minutes, Moses and the Old Man returned, and as I rolled the rig to the third cottage, the Old Man hopped on the passenger-side running board, opened the door, got in, and started talking fast: "It occurred to me that some Texas farmboys might take exception to staying overnight at these good people's colored motel. Would that be you?"

I shook my head.

"Would you tell me if you were?"

I shook my head again.

"Good. Wouldn't want to hear it. I still want you staying with the rig. The sons want to take turns watching through the night, and I'm sure not saying no. He sent 'Second Son' over, he said, for the first watch. But you're staying with the giraffes. I told 'em it's your job."

"That's why a son's standing there with his scythe?" I nodded toward Second Son—so I assumed—already standing by a massive maple as I pulled to a stop.

"That's why," the Old Man said as he got out. "You can sleep in the truck cab. If anything goes awry, things'll be hard enough to explain to the Boss Lady without adding any undue amount of explaining. So stay put. Now, Miz Annie Mae and the daughters-in-law are cooking up a feast the likes of which I've never seen," he added, cocking his head toward the big house. "And we're getting the bounty, me up there and you out here."

By the time I'd parked the rig past the third cottage, popped the top, and finished watering the giraffes, here came the Old Man and Miz Annie Mae's vittles carried on a platter by Seventh Son, Honey Bee still riding on his shoulders. He set the platter on the rig's hood and went to fetch Red.

While Red took pictures of Honey Bee feeding the giraffes pancakes, I got to feast on food so good it was almost worth being stranded to get it. It was a bounty, all right. When Red put down her camera, she gobbled even faster than me. As we finished, pretty much licking the plates clean, the giraffes started nibbling at the trees, and Honey Bee held out the last pancake to me, which I'm ashamed to say I gobbled up, too. As the sun set, Honey Bee and Seventh Son turned to go, herding Red to the second cottage as they went. The giraffes were contentedly chewing their cud, and the Old Man, picking his teeth and looking mighty contented himself, moseyed toward the third cottage to turn in, too.

So, as night fell, there we were—me and the giraffes—parked in a colored motel in the middle of Almighty Nowhere. With a last glance back at Second Son standing in the tree shadows, I closed up the top and said good night to Girl and Boy. With my stomach as stuffed and happy as it had ever been in my entire life, I felt myself getting drowsy despite being stuck in a truck in the woods with a man holding a sharp blade nearby. Rolling up the windows against the chill, I stretched out on the cab's bench seat and was allowing myself to drift nicely into well-fed slumber when the passenger door handle rattled.

Bolting straight up, I watched the handle turn and the door swing wide.

There was Red landing on the bench seat beside me, still wearing that big trench coat.

Breathing hard, she locked the door and rested her hand over her heart. "I decided to come see you and the giraffes . . . if that's OK." Glancing around like she was looking for signs of the Old Man, she added, "You *are* staying out here for a while, right?"

"All night," I said.

She perked up. "*All* night?"

I nodded.

Patting her chest, she cut her eyes back at the outline of Second Son standing guard with his scythe in the moonlight. Then she reached over and locked my door. "I . . . haven't been around Negroes much. Have you?"

I glanced at Second Son, not knowing how to answer. Fact was I'd never seen a Black person until I was riding the rails on my way to Cuz. If there were any in my corner of the Panhandle, I didn't know where, which to my mind made them smarter than all the White people I knew. That didn't mean they'd be welcome, especially during the Hard Times with so many folks out of work who needed somebody to be faring worse than them.

The sound of Red patting her chest harder pulled me out of my thoughts . . . She was still trying to catch her breath. "You scared?" I said.

She shook her head, mad at the thought. She still wasn't breathing right. I started to apologize, thinking I'd riled her, but then she ran clean out of breath. Hand clutching her chest, she was gasping—short, desperate, hollow gasps, the kind I hadn't heard since hearing my ma's and baby sister's dust lungs. It scared me so bad I couldn't move, frozen by sounds I thought I'd never hear again.

Her gasps slowed, then stopped. Pushing her hair out of her face, she heaved a huge sigh and collapsed against the seat.

I gaped at her.

"I get a little winded sometimes," she said.

I kept gaping. I wasn't over what I'd witnessed.

So Red sighed again and said, "My heart's broken."

I knew she wasn't talking about being lovelorn, and I felt a sense of dread. "What do you mean?"

"I mean it's really broken."

I leaned away. "That's not funny."

"You're telling me," she mumbled.

I didn't know what to think, much less do, and I must have looked it. Because she grabbed my hand and placed it over her heart. On top of her silky shirt. Over her soft, round breast.

"Rheumatic fever. When I was a baby," she was saying. "It sort of flops instead of beats. Feel it?"

The last thing I was feeling was her heartbeat. "What?" I mumbled. "My heart. Do you feel it?"

I forced myself to focus, waiting for the heartbeat to come. It didn't. And now all my focus was on waiting for it. When the heartbeat came, it was . . . *beat-beat . . . beat . . . beat-beat-beat . . .* pause . . . *beat . . .* pause . . . pause . . . pause . . . pause . . . *beat.*

It scared me so bad I wanted to grab her breast tighter, as if I could force her heart to beat right. "You saying it could just stop?" I choked out. "You could *die?*"

"Maybe." She gave me that tight-lipped smile of hers. "But probably not tonight."

Suddenly angry without a clue why, I pulled my hand away. "Then what are you doing way out *here?*"

Cocking her head, she quietly said, "Woody, haven't you ever wanted something so bad you had to do it or die trying?"

I knew that I had. I'd thought as much not two days ago.

But *this* was different.

She was gazing toward the rig. "Did you know giraffes in the wild only live about twenty-five years at the most? Their hearts give out too quick, I guess, pumping up and down that neck. They're truly blessed not knowing it, but oh, those sky-high eyes of theirs. They've seen the *world.*"

My ears still full of her sputtering heart, I seemed to have lost all good sense. She was talking again. "What?"

"I said, wasn't that something yesterday at the mountain work camp?" She was changing the subject, finished talking about the fact she could die right then, right there, like we'd been chatting about the weather. "*Such* fun. It was a corps of Woodys! I felt like Margaret Bourke-White more than ever. Have you seen her Dust Bowl photos? Oh, Stretch, you could be in them with that face of yours." With that, she leaned over and cupped my jaws with her hands. This time, I was *sure* she was about to kiss me on the lips. Instead she trained her whole being on my prairie face like she was taking a photo with her eyes. I was as stunned as if I'd been buckshot. I'd never been looked at this way, and sure not in moonlight. At the time I had no idea what kind of look it was. Now I know it was fueled by the "love of mankind." But like any seventeen-year-old boy, especially one already roiling with too much feeling, I mistook it as personal as the tingling that was rushing from my cupped face to south of my belt buckle. Feeling myself blush at the whole confusing thing, I thanked God Almighty it was too dark for her to see.

"How did you get here, Woody?" she was murmuring. "How'd you survive the Dust Bowl *plus* a hurricane and come to be driving the giraffes?" When I didn't answer, she smiled and dropped her hands. "Well, I'm lucky you did. I didn't know who I could trust on the road, but I trust you, Woody Nickel." She glanced the giraffes' way. "I guess we can't go visit them tonight. I miss them." Resting her head back against her window, she sighed and closed her eyes.

From where I sat behind the wheel, I could see nothing out her window except Second Son's shadow in the tree-filtered moonlight. I could see Red, though, the shadows nicely giving me that. I watched her for what seemed a long time, and when I opened my mouth to speak to her, I realized I'd never used her real name. *Red?* I almost said.

"Augusta?" I whispered instead, the word feeling peculiar on my tongue.

All I heard was her slow, steady breathing. She was asleep. Right at that moment, I wanted to kiss her myself. I wanted to pull her to me, place my hand on those flaming curls, and kiss her like a full-grown man, as if somehow my kiss to end all kisses I'd been practicing since the depot could fix everything. But then Red curled up like a dead bug across the bench seat, her red ringlets flopping onto my leg. I went still as death, straining to hear her breathe. When I couldn't, I put my finger under her nose to feel her breath. When I still couldn't, I panicked, reaching through her curls to touch her neck, waiting for the throb of her heartbeat. Still nothing. It wasn't beating . . . then it was. Then it wasn't again. Each time it skipped a beat, I didn't breathe myself until I felt the next beat. I did it again and again and again. For the longest time, I didn't twitch a muscle. I must have worn myself down and finally conked out. Because next thing I know instead of worrying over hearing the sound of Red's last breath, I hear my ma calling to me—

"Li'l one, who you talking to?"

. . . Then I'm sprinting across my pa's dirt farm in broad daylight, the dirt turning into a cornfield under my boots.

. . . I see giraffe heads above the stalks.

. . . I hear the roar of rushing water.

. . . And I hear the blast of a rifle's report—my rifle—echoing on and on until it turns into a little girl's giggle.

I jerked awake to find Seventh Son and Honey Bee staring at me through my window. It was dawn and Red was gone.

My heart thumping wild, I tumbled out of the truck. Seventh Son, rolling an eye toward Red's cottage, smiled at me, an unsettling sight on its own. Pushing by them, I opened the trapdoors and got busy tending to the giraffes, who were stamping a little, like they were wondering where I'd been. I filled their water pails, shoved them in the trapdoors, then crawled up and popped the top for them to reach for the trees.

Balancing there, I could barely move under the weight of my thoughts. Bad enough my cornfield nightmare was back, but I was still stirred up over Red. And I don't mean the kind of stir any boy feels when a red-crested beauty places his hand on top of her heaving breast. I mean the kind of stir from feeling Red's off-kilter heart. From hearing her gasp so much like Ma had through dust lungs to final death rattle. From seeing the spark of life fade from Ma's eyes, the only eyes that ever looked at me with pure affection.

Until Augusta Red's.

I didn't snap out of it until I heard someone talking below.

"C'mon down, boy."

The Old Man was standing below holding a gunnysack.

"Let the darlings nibble," he called up. "They fixed the tires, day-light's burning, and if you're up there looking for the girlie, she's already gone."

At that, feeling myself about to damn blush, I forced my mind off Red and eased to the ground.

"Come get some of Miz Annie Mae's sausage, grits, and gravy," he said as one of the sons shoved a full plate of vittles on top of the truck's hood. "I already thanked them for the fine night's rest. You should do it, too, if you get a chance. Show your good manners." He opened the truck's door and plunked the sack inside. "Mr. Jackson's giving us some traveling onions from his garden for our 'towering creatures of God's pure Eden.'"

"Mr. Jackson?" I said.

"That's our host's name, boy. You don't look too good. Eat. That'll fix you up."

So I ate, and the comfort of Miz Annie Mae's food calmed me all the way down.

As the giraffes kept nibbling at the trees, the entire Big Papa clan showed up, led by Moses toting two perfect-looking tires. Setting up the seesaw again, they had those tires on the wheels so fast it didn't even take the giraffes' minds off their breakfast.

As Honey Bee's uncs finished up, I felt her eyes on me again. When I looked down, there she was, standing inches from my ankles. She gave me a giggle and grabbed my skinny legs.

Chortling, the Old Man slapped me on the back. "She must think you're a giraffe, what with that neck spot of your own," he said, nod-ding at my birthmark. "That right, Honey Bee?" Honey Bee nodded as Seventh Son raised her up for one last chat with the real giraffes.

Then the Old Man and I crawled into our seats, the giraffes popped their heads out their windows, and we started rolling toward the detour road with Big Papa's whole clan parading behind.

As we drove away, what filled my side mirror was what lingers most in memory all these years since—the giraffes are stretching their necks to look at Honey Bee waving goodbye atop Seventh Son's shoulder, with Big Papa and all the sons standing sentry, sending us safely on our way.

. . . My eyes are getting tired.

And my pencil's getting short.

Yet I can't stop.

I glance back at my window to see if Wild Girl's still there.

She is, God love her. The darling giraffe reaches over and gives me a push with her big snout. "OK, OK," I say. Sharpening my pencil, I take a deep breath and get back to this writing . . . yet I can't help but wonder.

Are your eyes reading these words?

Has this story found the precious likes of you?

My old heart tightens again at the thought, and it's keeping me from thinking straight. I know I'm asking questions that make no sense, but I strain to write down this next day, here almost ninety years later, and that's a curiosity. Lord knows I've done plenty things more shameful after living a century. If I wrote *them* down, they wouldn't even give me pause now that I'm so old. Put next to a man's war days alone, it's nothing but a trifle. Yet this day to come with the giraffes still cuts me deeper than makes a bit of sense. If Red's heart was already broken, mine had barely been used, lacking in any proper language or direction, and that went double for my ruddy little soul. I can only suppose that when you're riding with two "towering creatures of God's pure Eden," and you grasp the first rotten proof of your true self, you never quite forget it, no matter what you do later to make it right.

I glance back at the sweet giraffe in my window and sigh.

I'm sorry, Girl.

I still, truly, am.

9

Across Tennessee

A few peaceful hours down the road, this side of Chattanooga, we pulled into a Texaco gas station and general store surrounded by a nice grove of munching trees. The tires checked out fine, exactly like the Old Man figured. So, as soon as the man in his fancy Texaco star uniform met the giraffes and filled the tank, I pulled the rig over to let the giraffes eat and crawled back in the cab. In a minute, the Old Man returned from the store with a salami, soda pops, and a new newspaper he plopped down between us.

HITLER STILL VOWS WAR, the newspaper's front page hollered in big black letters, and my eyes landed on the day's date—October 10.

Tomorrow was my birthday.

I'd be eighteen.

Right then, a county deputy's car came roaring up with its siren rolling, making the giraffes wobble and me, as usual, tense up.

"Well, whaddya know," the paunchy old deputy said, getting out and hitching up his pants. "I sure thought the bulletin was a joke. It said to be on the lookout for a gal driving a green Packard following a truck carrying African tip-top critters. And here they are."

I flinched.

"A bulletin, you say?" the Old Man said.

"Thassright." Coming over to my window, the deputy propped a boot on the rig's running board. "From all the way up in New York City. I read a lot of bulletins, but that one took the cake. Something about a runaway wife in a stolen vehicle chasing giraffes."

"A runaway wife, you say?" the Old Man said.

I flinched again. Bad.

"Thassright. In her husband's Packard."

At that, I had to clench the steering wheel to keep from clenching my fists.

"And she don't even have a license," the deputy went on. "Could be only a spat gone halfway across the country, but don't matter. A woman on the road alone is suspect all by herself, being as no real lady would be doing such a thing. More likely she's having herself a nice little tryst with another gent," he said with a righteous little sniff. "If so, we still put stock in the Mann Act around here. It being, young fella," the old deputy said, "about the crossing of state lines by any person of the male persuasion for immoral purposes with any person of the female persuasion." He was so close I could smell the snuff stuffed under his lip. "Yeah, my money's on her having a sugar daddy. They always do. Especially the peaches, and from the description, she's a real peach, a fiery redhead floozy."

"*That* doesn't make her a *floozy!*" my fool mouth fired off on its own.

The deputy spit snuff juice over his shoulder and wiped his mouth with his sleeve. "So," he said with a dirty little leer my way, "I guess you seen her."

I dropped my eyes, which I knew was as stupid as my blurt.

"You could say we ran into her," said the Old Man. "Right, boy?"

I shrugged, biting my tongue.

"She alone?" asked the deputy.

"Seemed so," said the Old Man. "She was snapping pictures, saying she was with *Life* magazine." He paused. "Right, boy?"

I shrugged again. Feeling the deputy's eyes still on me, I feared what was coming next.

"What's your name, son?" asked the deputy.

The Old Man cut in. "His name's Woodrow Wilson Nickel, deputy."

"That name's got a familiar ring to it. Have we met, Mr. Woodrow Wilson Nickel?"

I shook my head, certain now that a Panhandle bulletin had been in all his bulletin reading.

"He's named after a president. Maybe that's it," the Old Man cut in again. "Deputy, he's been driving us for days and he's doing a fine job."

"Still. Maybe I should take a look at *his* license while I'm here. Let's see it, son."

At that very moment, though, what did I see coming up the road but a green Packard—and behind the wheel was a flash of red curls. I tried hard not to look. God knows I tried. But look I did. And when I did, so did the deputy.

"What the . . . Was that the *floozy*?" The paunchy old deputy whirled around so fast he all but fell on his fanny as the Packard sped up and vanished around the bend. "Stay here! Don't y'all move!" he croaked back at us, scrambling to his cruiser and peeling out after Red.

"Like piss we are," the Old Man said. "Let's go." As I hustled us onto the road, the Old Man kept giving me his hollow-eyed stare. "Is there something you need to tell me about this girlie?"

I shook my head a bit too quick and a bit too hard.

While I didn't know a thing about Red when it came right down to it, I was acting like I was guilty of knowing something, but the something I knew was more about me. I wouldn't have cared if she'd robbed a bank, since I wasn't but two steps from doing something like that myself. I wouldn't have cared if she was a runaway, because I might have been one myself if Ma and Pa hadn't died first. But a *wife*? That I cared about. Even more, God help me, than the dying heart part. Yet I heard myself say, "You going to turn her in if she shows up again?"

"I've had many a pretty woman turn my head, so I know what you're feeling," he answered. "We've got enough troubles, boy, so yeah. I will. If the girlie's not lying about herself, she'll be fine. And if she is, we'll be finer without—" But the Old Man never finished the thought, erupting with one of his long-string cusses loud enough to make me jump right out of my skin. He was gaping past me. The highway was passing the railyards, and in the field between the highway and the tracks was the circus, packing up after its Chattanooga show. There'd be no hiding the giraffes this time. Not thirty yards from us, two men were hanging the new sign on the red caboose: **MUSCLE SHOALS TONIGHT!**

While the Old Man saw only the circus, I couldn't take my eyes off the railyard. It was where I'd first jumped a freight after my ma's Mason jar money played out on my way to Cuz. Wandering around that station scrounging food and trying to figure out what to do, I'd bumped into railriders about my age. Back then, thousands and thousands of them were hopping freights right along with the hoboes and tramps. I can still hear one of them talking it up: *It's freedom, pally! Plows and cows are for suckers!* So I'd joined up with them, and that's exactly what it felt like to my farmboy self. *Freedom.* We were now so close to the circus, though, try as I might I couldn't ignore the vile racket—animals roaring, creatures caterwauling, men bellowing, whips snapping.

"Speed *up*!" the Old Man yelled.

As I did, though, the paunchy deputy appeared heading back our way, motioning us to pull over.

As I rolled us onto the shoulder, I thought the Old Man was going to bust. We were straight across from the gut-wrenching din, the elephant cattle cars not a stone's throw away.

Steering the cruiser up close, the deputy hollered, "Did you see her? Did the floozy double back?"

We shook our heads.

"Stay put this time! Don't move a lick!" Spinning the cruiser around, off he went again.

So this time we stayed, getting more and more miserable as the bellowing, wailing, and whip-snapping got louder and harder and rougher—until the Old Man came unglued. "*Look* how those sumbitches are treating their elephants!" he yelled.

I didn't want to look. God knows I didn't want to. But I did, and then I couldn't look away. The elephants, trumpeting loud and wretched, were being prodded onto the cattle car by workers with pointed poles.

"You know what circus people call those magnificent creatures? They call them rubber cows!" the Old Man sputtered. "See those poles they keep poking their 'rubber cows' with? They're called bullhooks with three-inch barbed spikes! There are places on an elephant you can stick that spike to make them feel bad-*bad* pain, and in cheap outfits like this one, there are always measly little men who get sick pleasure out of finding those places." Then his voice dropped low, deadly. "To the point you wish elephants were like lions, ripping and reaping . . . to the point it can tear at your heart when they don't . . . to the point that anybody with a heart can only watch a measly little man using a hook with pleasure until it's a matter of time before anybody with a heart is going to give him a taste of that bullhook in his *own* measly, miserable hide." Before I had a chance to think about what I'd just heard, he said, "*Nossir*, that right *there* is the kind of shady outfit that might decide to acquire a couple of giraffes the easy way. To *hell* with that deputy—get us *outa* here!"

And it dawned on my thickheaded self how the Old Man knew all this. He'd worked for a circus, maybe even run off to join one as a kid. As I sped us out of the railyard, I was so sure of it I almost asked. He was still glaring at the elephants, thinking thoughts I didn't want to hear, full of circus things I didn't want to know, and I was already feeling more than I could stand over nightmares and dying hearts and runaway wives. So much so that when I spied a handful of tramps and railriders running to hop a slow-rolling freight train, I was wishing I was hopping it, too, being anywhere but here.

Freedom, pally!

As I watched, though, a tramp with a cooking pot on his back stumbled on the track and as he scrambled not to be hit, I saw his face. It was the face of all tramps . . . weathered, blotched, woebegone . . . *like the tramp's face I saw thrown off to die for his shoes.*

Almost running the rig right off the road with that bottled-up memory, I whiplashed the giraffes and threw the Old Man into the dashboard worse than back in DC. You'd think that would have had him chewing me up and spitting me out, but he barely did more than yowl, still bad-bewitched by his circus thoughts.

Five miles passed before I was driving proper, and it'd be another five before I could rid myself of the tramp's face. By then we were well past Chattanooga, farmland surrounding us again, the road lined with store billboards touting jams and jellies, sorghum and cider, RC Cola and Jax Beer.

On my side, the highway was running along the rail's right-of-way with only a thin line of pine trees as a divide. Mile after mile, the Old Man kept eyeing that tree line and I wished I didn't know full well why. We could hear a train coming, and within seconds, a fast-moving freight train was roaring past the opposite way. The clickety-clack was so loud, both giraffes thrust their heads out the train's side so forceful the rig lifted off the road. I leaned the other way, like that could stop the top-heavy rig from lurching into the trees. When the Old Man did it, too, though, I saw he was trying to yell over the clamor, motioning me to pull over. So I braked hard, jerking us to a stop on the shoulder. As the freight roared on, the Old Man grabbed Big Papa's gunnysack, crawled up the side away from the train, and began pitching those onions in the giraffes' windows, one after the other. He was trying to get the giraffes to pull their heads in—which they did—and, even though we now knew latches meant nothing to giraffes, he latched the windows anyway. After the long train passed, the Old Man and I, ears still ringing, sat inside the truck cab without the will to move until the echoes died away.

"How long's the track going to be right next to the road?" I mustered up the courage to ask.

"All day," was the Old Man's answer.

For the next hour, we rode along eyeing the tracks and our side mirrors, the giraffes riding quiet inside, the skies turning gray to match our mood. I kept looking back for Red. There were lots of cars on that nice highway but no green Packard. If she was back there, and I knew she was, she was hiding pretty good from both the law and us.

Finally, we heard another train, this one approaching from behind. Seeing flashes of yellow and red in our mirrors, we knew it was the circus. Railcars of elephants, horses, and lions draped with posters of clowns and a top-hatted ringmaster inched closer and closer until they were traveling right beside us.

This time there wasn't enough shoulder to pull off. I had to keep going. Frantic, the Old Man searched the road ahead for a turnoff with no luck.

The train was now so close the lions might as well have been in the truck cab with us. The only thing we had going for us was that the giraffes were still riding quiet inside the rig, unseen.

"C'mon, darlings . . . stay put," the Old Man kept saying under his breath, glancing every few seconds back at the latched windows. "Stay put now."

But then one of the circus cats roared, and out popped the giraffes' heads searching for the lions. With that, the giraffes were seen, all right. A bearded lady by a Pullman window noticed first. Then a potbellied man with a handlebar mustache raised his window to lean halfway out the window to look. It was the same guy on the caboose back in Maryland.

I thought the Old Man was going to explode into little pieces where he sat, hollering and pointing at a country road up ahead. Turning so quick, we all but did it on two wheels and we didn't stop until we saw the red caboose pass with its new sign flapping: **MUSCLE SHOALS TONIGHT!**

By the time we found our long way back to the highway on the narrow winding roads, the train track had veered away and the circus had surely made it all the way to Muscle Shoals.

The next twenty miles down the Lee Highway were blessed quiet. We'd traveled a lot of silent miles by that time, but that silence was a loud one. As the sky grew darker and grayer, we drove into a low area with a small storm brewing complete with sudden, dense fog. The cars behind us might as well have vanished.

For ten long minutes, we weren't moving faster than a crawl, hoping everybody else was doing the same.

From the fog, a sign zipped past.

YELLER'S MODERN TOURIST CAMP
100 YARDS AHEAD

"Pull in there," ordered the Old Man. "We'll figure out how to get by that train tomorrow and on to Memphis while they're busy loading. If we time it right, we'll get to their turnaround stop ahead of them and that'll be that."

"They'll be turning around?"

"It's a southern circuit outfit," he said. "Unless things have changed. And things don't change."

A hundred yards ahead, the sign popped into view again.

YELLER'S MODERN TOURIST CAMP
YOU MADE IT

We could make out the tall pine trees framing the entrance, their trunks painted bright yellow. I turned in and rolled the rig toward the red neon **OFFICE** sign glowing like a fog light in the middle of the grove.

The place was an auto-trailer camp, not an auto court. Except for the owner's trailer and what looked like some rental trailers, it seemed we had the place to ourselves, although we couldn't be sure because of the fog. After a few meet-the-giraffes moments for Yeller himself, complete with food right off his own trailer's table, which we devoured on the spot, he lit his lantern.

"Sure glad you saw our sign with this fog, considering those fellers," Yeller said, nodding at the giraffes. "We're the only place for miles this side of Muscle Shoals."

We followed him through the fog as he lit lanterns along the way. Thirty yards past the sleeping trailer we'd rented, he motioned me to park the rig at the camp's edge under a row of leafy trees, their yellow-washed trunks surrounding us in the deepening fog as if framing the whole world. Hanging his lantern on one of the trees, Yeller waved and headed back toward the neon office light.

Dusk falls queerly in a fog. As we cared for the giraffes, the light around us turned from white-gray to gray to gray-black until the only light left was the glow from the lanterns spread around the deserted camp. The Old Man announced he'd take the first sleeping shift as usual and headed back to our trailer.

But I didn't do the usual. I didn't crawl up and stretch out on the plank between the two giraffes to gaze at the stars. I wouldn't be seeing any stars that night, but it wasn't the fault of the fog. In fact, as soon as the giraffes were chewing their cud, I closed their windows and top for the night before they had time to move toward me, closing my heart for the night as well. As I sat down on the running board, tetchy and worn out, my mind still full of murdered tramps and rubber cows and runaway wives, I wasn't sure what to fret over first. I had to remind myself we'd be hitting Memphis tomorrow. *Only one more day and none of it will matter anymore. I'll be on my California way,* I kept repeating, and soon I was lost in puffed-up thoughts of riding in a fancy train Pullman headed to the land of milk and honey, where I'd live like a king plucking fruit from the trees and grapes from the vine and sipping from the cool, clear rivers.

All I had to do was get to tomorrow.

Bracing for a longer night than usual, I looked around for Red to show up before I remembered I didn't much want her to. But that didn't keep me from expecting her. In fact, I expected it so much that when I saw something move, I got up to face Mrs. Augusta Red.

Instead, from the shadows came a tall figure, strolling like he was taking a walk in the woods. He was almost to me before I saw his face, and what seemed to come out of the fog first was his handlebar mustache. It was the potbellied man from the train—wearing a yellow cutaway suit with a red bowtie and knee boots—like he'd jumped off the train's poster, the ringmaster come to life. He even had on the top hat. Then I noticed he had something in his hand. It was an ivory-handled cane, and I was wishing for the Old Man's shotgun, having heard of firearms hidden in such sticks.

"Percival T. Bowles at your service," he said, tipping his top hat. "And who might you be?"

"Not sure that's any of your business," I said, eyes on the cane.

He placed both hands atop the cane. "You look like a fine young man. Maybe you saw our circus train, Bowles & Waters Traveling Circus Extravaganza," he went on, showing his coyote teeth in what I took to be a smile.

"I saw."

He drummed the top of his cane with his fat fingers. "Don't talk much, do you? Mark of a wise man. You like the circus, son?"

"Don't call me *son.*"

"Ah. A particular man as well as a wise man. I respect that," he said, then went right on. "We're right down the road. Two performances tonight. On my way back there now, as you can see," he added, nodding at his clothes. He pulled some tickets from his breast pocket. "Here's some free passes, if you'd care to join us. Ringmaster's deluxe."

"Don't want 'em."

He flashed that coyote smile again. "Don't blame you a bit. You got a circus right here, don't you?"

As he put the tickets back in his breast pocket, his cutaway coat opened enough for me to spy a holstered gun on his hip.

He saw that I saw.

"Ah." He fingered it. "Did I forget to mention I'm also the lion tamer? A lion tamer never knows when he'll have to take down an animal, you know." Resting his hand back on top of the other, he gazed past me at the rig. "This is some fine job you got here."

"Not a job," I said. "Just driving them."

"Well, now, I'd give you a job. I'm about to be doing some hiring. Expecting to have giraffes very soon myself."

The hackles on the back of my neck were standing straight up. It was the feeling I used to get while hunting in the Panhandle brush, like a wild pair of eyes was watching me. I squinted into the fog all around us as the ringmaster parked his cane over an arm and pulled something new out of his breast pocket. He palmed it, then opened his fist and held it toward me. It was a twenty-dollar double-eagle gold piece, the first I'd seen in my life, and the tree lantern's glow made it look all the more golden.

"Heads up!" he said, then *tossed* it to me.

I caught it and it was all I could do not to close my fist around the piece of gold. "Feels nice, doesn't it?" he said, reaching over and scooping it out of my palm. "You a betting man? I'm sure you'd agree fifty-fifty odds are pretty good, correct? How'd you like this double eagle? All you got to do is call heads or tails and it could be yours." He flipped the coin and slapped it onto the back of his hand. "Call it."

When I didn't do so, he cocked his head. "Come now, young man. Which is it? *Heads*? Or tails? If you win, you don't have to take it. It's all in good fun."

I paused. "Heads."

He raised the hand covering the coin. Tails. Then, grinning so big and oily I could've slipped on it, he turned the coin over . . . It was tails on the other side, too.

I jerked back. "What are you trying to pull!"

"Good trick, don't you agree? Works every time. You ever heard anybody say 'tails up'?" He held out the coin. "It's yours. Smart young lad like yourself can make good use of it."

"Don't want it," I muttered. "Don't like tricks."

"Ah, an honest man, too." He flicked his wrist and there were two gold pieces in his palm. He flicked again and there was only one. "Young man, I promise no tricks. Only a proper offering of services. Here's a real double-eagle twenty-dollar gold piece. Go ahead. Check it."

I turned it over in his palm. It had the appropriate amount of sides—one heads, one tails.

"All you have to do is give me a peek at the hurricane giraffes," he said, nodding toward the rig.

"How do you know that?"

"Why, you're famous, young man. You've been in all the papers as you travel. I was figuring you'd come along the Lee Highway, and I was right. So what do you say? A peek and the coin is yours." When I didn't snatch it right up, he pinched it between his thick thumb and forefinger and held it out, the thing all but glittering in the lantern's glow.

With real gold hovering so near, I forgot all about the trick coin, the Old Man's circus outbursts at the railway, and pretty much everything else. In a time when you could buy a hot dog and a soda pop for a nickel, a twenty-dollar gold piece was John D. Rockefeller. I didn't just want it, I needed it. There was no bigger devil-deal to offer a hard-knock boy in a Hard Times world. I'd lived on tumbleweed soup and been tempted with raccoon parts cooked over crazy-hungry bums' fire barrels. Not until years into my army days did I trust that tomorrow would hold food without fear. *I'm back on my own at Memphis, aren't I?* I told myself, staring at that gold. *Even with a ticket to Californy, I could be broke and hungry again soon, couldn't I?* Right then, my fool young self started angling how to get the gold piece with no harm done to the giraffes or the Old Man. I was cocksure I could do it, having yet to learn that nobody gets devil-dealing both ways, there being either heaven or hell to pay for everything in this world and nothing in between.

I reached for the double eagle.

He palmed it. "First, a look."

So I stepped up on the fender to open the giraffes' windows. At the sound of me so near, both Boy and Girl pushed their heads out on their own.

"*Ohhhhhhh,*" the ringmaster moaned with smarmy pleasure, eyes glistening. "They're *sublime*! And so young! Perfect, *perfect.*"

The giraffes, however, took one look at him and pulled their heads back in.

He groaned. "No, no, *no*, make them come out!"

Since I already knew you couldn't *make* a giraffe do anything, which he didn't seem to know, I thought it was over. "You saw them. A deal's a deal," I said, eyes on his clenched palm.

"But I *must* see *more*." He opened his golden palm. "More and it's yours. You have my *word.*"

I glanced back and forth between the coin and the rig, pondering the least I could do to get the gold piece. Considering he'd seen their heads, I opened the trapdoors to reveal both giraffes' lower halves, hoping that'd be enough.

It was not.

"*Come* now, you can do better."

All I could think to do next was open the top for a look down on them. Climbing up the side ladder, I headed up, expecting the roly-poly ringmaster to follow.

"Young man," he called up, rubbing his belly, "there's got to be another way." When I didn't hop right to it, he waved the gold piece at me once again. I couldn't think what else to do. He was now bouncing it in his open palm, just so it would gleam in the lamplight. There was the double eagle, all golden and glittering. Waiting. For me. "It's *yours*, son! Don't you want it?"

Tearing my eyes off the coin, I glanced around me, my eyes landing on a big clamp near my hand, one of the four heavy "ramp" clamps holding the entire side upright. *Maybe I can lower the side—only a bit,* I thought. Never mind I'd hadn't touched the clamps before and never mind I had no idea how heavy the side was. *Halfway down—that's as far as I'll go,* I told myself, temptation as bad in inches as in miles.

I opened the top first, then started working on the side clamps. The Old Man had battened the things down to last for the entire ride, and I had to work them loose. You'd think that would've given me time to think about what I was doing. But that gold piece had me still believing I could outsmart a tricky fat cat making me deaf, dumb, and blind to all but it. When the last clamp opened, I grabbed hold of the middle and stepped a boot down on the fender—as far as I was going to go—and lowered the traveling crate's side for the first time since the giraffes had been put in. I might as well have drawn a diagram on how to do it, Mr. Percival T. Bowles watching my every move. It was worse than a knucklehead stunt, it was a selfish and deadly one that I was to regret the moment I'd done it. Because no sooner had I stepped down, I lost my footing on the fog-damp fender and I fell, landing on my back in the dirt with the rig's entire side flopped down on top of me, chest-high.

That sudden, the giraffes had nothing between them and us but air. They went full tilt into a tizzy, rearing up, rocking the rig, readying to kick anyone near. And I was the one near. I locked eyes with them.

Those trusting brown globes were so full of fear and confusion I felt my insides ripping apart. It was as if I were glimpsing their big giraffe souls, and they, God help me, were glimpsing the sorry state of mine, because they started clawing their fragile legs up the sides, *away* from me. The giraffes had seen me for the lion I was. Any second, they'd do what they do to lions. They'd kick me dead as I deserved, tumbling down the panel to do it.

If I didn't do something and do it quick, we were all done.

Scrambling up and throwing all my weight under the downed panel, I somehow shoved it upright, jumped back on the fender, and thrust the heavy thing over my head, clamping as fast as I could until the top and sides were fixed back tight.

Tumbling to the ground, I stared at their windows, praying for the giraffes to appear. Instead I heard the beginning moan of the sound I'd hoped never to hear again—the giraffe-terror caterwaul from the night of the yahoos. Climbing halfway up the side ladder, I began cooing the Old Man's giraffe-speak the best I could through the slats, fearing—*knowing*—they'd never trust me again. To my shock, though, as I kept on cooing, their moans began to soften. I upped my cooing. Within seconds, the giraffes had quieted all the way down, and then, forgiving me all my treachery, they moved toward me.

It was too much. For an instant, I was seeing my mare's trusting brown-apple eyes in theirs, reliving the sure crime that sent me running toward Cuz, and I wanted to yell at the giraffes, *Don't you forgive me—don't you dare!* Instead I dropped to the ground and bent over to keep from passing out, knowing I'd dodged a bullet of my own firing.

"Get ahold of yourself, lad," I heard Bowles say. "They're just animals." Upon hearing my pa's words spewing from his mouth, the only thing that kept me from punching his porky face was the pair of eyes I still felt watching us from the fog. "You've got to remind them who's boss, that's all," he kept on. "Now, let's try once more."

I straightened my sorry ass and forced my eyes off his golden-coined fist. "I'm not who you need to ask for any more looking."

He considered me for a moment, the lantern glow now making him look like Lucifer himself. "Ah, and who might that be?"

"Mr. Jones," I mumbled.

"And where is this Mr. Jones?"

"Don't want to wake him."

"Well, then." He flashed his toothy coyote grin. "The twenty-dollar gold piece is still yours, and there's lots more of those where that came from. We are living in a time of opportunity, young man. It pays to take what you want, remember that. The job offer stands. Percival Bowles is a good friend to have." He looked back at the rig. "Such a pity, isn't it? These animals are so hard to get yet die so quick, and they never breed before they die. But, oh my, there's money to be made while they last. Here you go."

I'd quit listening after "the gold piece is still yours," not realizing until much later what he'd said and what it all surely meant. Because, right then, he opened his fist. There was my double eagle. I snatched it up, looked quick at both sides, and shoved it in my pocket before he could change his mind.

"I'll return to speak to your Mr. Jones in the morning." He tipped his silly hat and then disappeared into the fog, which was spooky enough on its own without a yellow-suited, top-hatted, black-booted man being swallowed up into it.

Easing down on the running board, I pulled out the piece of gold to gaze at it in the lantern light. I must've stared mighty hard and *mighty* long, because I was still gazing at it when the Old Man appeared from the fog to relieve me, and I stuffed it back deep in my pocket.

"Everything all right?" the Old Man said.

Nodding, I hustled past him to the rented trailer, flopped down on the trailer's cot, and stared into the dark. Until daylight, I spent the hours waiting for the night to end, fingering my new gold piece and thinking only of my Memphis ticket to ride.

By dawn, though, I must have dozed off, because I thought I heard the giraffe-terror wail again, far away, like in a dream.

I sat up to listen, but what I heard sounded like . . . Red.

"WOODY! WOODYYYYYYY!"

In nothing more than my skivvies and boots, I threw open the trailer door to gaze through the remains of the fog hanging in the trees, and what I saw chilled me to my marrow.

A cornfield.

"WOODY!"

Thirty yards away, Red was standing by the rig. The entire side looked open to the ground facing the field, and she was gaping up. Into the traveling crates.

Sprinting across the gravel and pine cones, I looked where she was looking, and what I saw all but dropped me to my knees. Boy was still in the road Pullman, barely, leaning so far into the open that gravity would soon be making the next move.

But Girl was gone.

From behind me, I heard the giraffe-terror caterwaul again—this time loud and long. Jerking full around, I could see a ruckus on the far side of the field, cornstalks flattening every which way. There was Girl, her long neck stretching above the dried cornstalks. Two men were moving toward her, one pulling at a lasso around her neck, one twirling another . . . and she was kicking . . . kicking at the lions.

If that sight wasn't horrifying enough, halfway between me and them was the Old Man, wobbly as a drunk, shotgun aimed their way. If he took a shot like that, with a gun like that, he'd be more likely to hit Girl than the demons after her. I had to stop him.

Hearing Boy stomping behind me, though, I spun back around. He was pawing at the downed panel. He had to get to Girl. Once again, I threw my full weight under the panel, rushing to get it up in front of him, Red pushing, too, then snatched the rifle from the truck cab and sprinted toward the Old Man.

I was halfway to him when I heard the shotgun's blast.

Stunned, I stumbled, dropping the rifle in the cornstalks, and braced for what I'd see.

But the Old Man had missed and fallen to his knees.

Across the cornfield, the men, knowing the Old Man couldn't stop them now, were back at it. One was wrestling with the rope around Wild Girl's neck, Girl throwing him around like a puppet until she reared up and the second man's rope found its mark—her front leg. Pulling the rope taut, he now had Girl splay-legged and they were closing in.

For a moment I stared at the sight, deaf to all but my own thundering heartbeat. Then scooping up the rifle, I stood, aimed, and fired.

As the leg-rope lackey dropped into the flattened stalks and the other took cover, I was hearing nothing but my nightmare's rifle report . . . because this was not the first time I'd shot a man.

The lackeys disappeared into the cornfield, and within seconds, I spied streaks of yellow and red careening through the stalks.

To the sound of their truck barreling away, I stared at the gut-wrenching sight before me. Girl was wandering slow among the cornstalks, a rope dangling from her neck.

Struggling up on his boots, the Old Man lurched her way. Heart in my throat, I remembered word for word what he'd said in DC.

There's no taking the giraffes out of the rig, because once they're out, there's no guarantee we'd ever get 'em back in, and that'd be the death of them one way or the other.

The Old Man fell again. I ran to him. Blood was running down his face. He tried to get to his feet and couldn't. Grabbing him by an arm, I was struggling to get him up, when there was Red, camera swinging from her neck, grabbing his other.

"Get the rig," he gasped as we got him to his feet.

I ran to the truck. Wires were dangling behind the starter. I shoved them back up and got the engine going, then rolled the rig and Boy into the cornfield, splaying stalks as we went.

We jolted to a halt behind the Old Man, who was now down on his haunches, cooing his giraffe-speak to Girl twenty yards away. Girl's matchstick legs were swaying, the rope moving with them, like she was readying for more lions.

"Let her see Boy," the Old Man called over his shoulder.

I swung the wild boy's trap window open. Boy's head popped out, and as soon as he saw her, he started bumping against the rig's side to get to her.

"*Easy . . . easy, Girl,*" the Old Man kept cooing, all the while whispering back my way. "Lower the side—we've got to get her back in."

"But couldn't Boy be out, too?"

"Not unless he falls out. He'll want to, but he won't step down on his own. Unless Girl starts loping away. Then I don't know what the hell he'll do. But it won't be good."

Boy, head still out, was bumping the rig so hard the frame was shuddering.

Seeing him, though, Girl slowed her swaying and took a halting step toward us. The Old Man cussed under his breath and I saw why— the splint on her wounded leg was half unwound. And it was bloody. Balancing on three legs, she was now doing her best not to use the wounded one.

The Old Man moved toward her, and the Girl kicked—a heart-crushing weak one—and it loosened the bandage even more. Another kick could have her falling to the ground and, once down, maybe never getting back up.

"*Onion—*" the Old Man hissed back. I grabbed an onion, pushed it into the Old Man's waiting fist, and stood back.

Girl's snout caught the scent. So the Old Man tried moving toward her again, holding out the onion. She still wasn't having it, readying a weak—and maybe last—kick.

The Old Man stepped back quick, lowering the onion.

A second went by. I moved nearer to get a better view. The Girl's neck moved with me, and the Old Man saw.

"Step closer," the Old Man whispered my way.

I stepped closer.

She moved her neck back, forth, eyeing me up, down.

"Closer!" the Old Man hissed.

I forced myself to do it again. I was close enough to be kicked. Again, the Old Man was holding out the onion, this time toward me. I should have taken it, but I couldn't make myself do it. Instead I was fighting the urge to disappear into the cornstalks, too, so I wouldn't be the Old Man's last-ditch chance at saving the terrified giraffe above us.

"Take it!" the Old Man ordered. When I still couldn't make myself move, he scrambled to me, stuffed it in my pocket, and shoved me forward.

Nostrils quivering, Girl stepped wobbly toward me, close enough that the useless rope was dangling near enough to touch. Then, exactly as she'd done the first night in quarantine, she lowered her neck to sniff out my onion. I pulled the onion from my pocket and held it up. Her tongue snatched, her neck rose, and the onion slid down.

Sidling near, the Old Man dropped Big Papa's gunnysack at my feet. *"Give 'em to her!"* he whispered. As I was giving her the first onion from the sack, I heard a *whap* behind me. The Old Man had let down the rig's side, exposing Boy to the open air, and was pulling out a long, wide plank from below the rig that I didn't even know was there, placing it like a bridge into the crate for her tall spindly legs.

He motioned me his way.

I began taking tiny steps backward, sack in hand, stuffing an onion in my pocket every few steps, and waiting for Girl to come get it. She

stepped slow. But she stepped. Each time she came near, I'd give her the
onion, her tongue pulling it past her lips and down that throat, while I
stuffed a new one in my pocket.

We did it over and over, until we were at the rig.

I stepped up on the plank, the panel, and into the traveling crate.
There Girl stopped.

Boy began snuffling and stomping his hooves in the peat moss. Yet
Girl kept swaying her neck at me like she was weighing the value of the
next onion's taste upside where she'd have to go to get it.

The onion sack was almost empty. I stepped toward her from her
boxcar suite, waving the onion sack her way, then stepped back into
the crate.

And she decided.

One leg, two, then three. Her bandaged leg struggled to find the
last bit of plank. I could hardly watch. Then she was up on the panel,
the whole of her standing on it at an angle . . . the next second would
have her either going forward or back faster to the ground than anybody
could stop.

I threw the rest of the onions into the peat moss and scrambled up
to sit on the cross plank by Boy, one last onion in my hand.

She bent her neck forward, thrusting her long tongue into the pile,
and came up with one dropped onion after another. Then her long neck
rose up, up, following the scent of the last onion in my hand, until she
had stepped all four legs into the peat moss.

Wild Girl was in.

Faster than seemed Old-Man possible, he had that side panel
upright and clamped all by himself, dropping to the running board to
catch his breath. I wanted bad to join him, but I couldn't move. Girl
had her massive head stretched across my legs. The moment the side
panel was up and latched, she'd reached past me to sniff at Boy. Then,
leaning her quivering body against the crate, she dropped her heavy
snout into my lap and shut her eyes, and from her nostrils came the

thundering whoosh of a sigh as big as Wild Girl herself. I put my hand on her shuddering head and from somewhere deep below my clamped-down insides burst a mighty fount of forgotten emotion. It was my boy-in-knickers feeling I'd allowed myself to feel—for a moment—the night after the mountains. Now, though, with Girl's sweet head in my lap, it was rushing through every last inch of me, my heart swelling full and warm and pure and kind in a way I'd clean forgotten it could. I was lost in it, its surging tenderheartedness taking my breath clean away.

Girl opened her eyes, looking far too much like my mare's brown-apple eyes. As the tender feeling turned into my nightmare secret's purest pain, I lifted the lasso from around her neck and flung it deep into the cornstalks.

It took us a while to get on the road after that. Still parked in the middle of the cornfield, the rig looked no worse for wear, which was more than I could say for the rest of us. I gazed back toward the trailer camp for Red. Once again, though, she'd vanished. So I stood there still dressed only in my skivvies and boots, watching the Old Man work through the trapdoor applying all the sulfa we had left to Girl's wound, which was now not only bloody but also covered with pus. Infection had set in. She was so worn out, she leaned against the crate and let him. He rewrapped the splint the best he could. As we held our breath, she wobbled a second and stood straight again on all four legs.

Closing the trapdoor, the Old Man sank onto the truck's running board, only then raising a hand to check his own wound. The gash on his head had stopped bleeding but still looked as angry as the Old Man felt about it being there. Watching, I felt the full weight of Mr. Percival T. Bowles on my chest, the gold piece in my pocket burning like sin, because I hadn't warned him. If I didn't tell him now, I'd keep feeling like a Panhandle Judas. *But what good will telling him do? He'll leave me on the side of the road right here before Memphis,* I reminded myself.

I had to say *something*, so I said, "Can I help clean that up?"

He didn't answer. He looked at his gnarly hand's fingers that didn't quite bend and cussed them good, then fingering his gashed temple, he cussed it good, too. Whatever had happened, he wasn't in the mood to share.

Shifting from one boot to the other, I tried again. "Girl's going to be OK, isn't she?"

That got him on his feet. "We're lucky we don't have a dead giraffe to be burying out in this *gotdam* cornfield. And we better hope our luck holds until we can get more sulfa, or we still might be doing it."

I braced for what was surely coming next, a calling of the law and all the questions that'd go with that. Instead the Old Man reloaded both guns, put them back on the rack, and said, "If anybody asks, boy, I shot that rifle. You could have killed a man, and I wouldn't wish that on you."

I frowned, puzzled at what seemed like a questioning of my shoot-ing skills. "I winged him," I said. "If I'd aimed to kill him, he'd be dead."

The Old Man's bushy eyebrows popped high, like he didn't know quite what to make of what I'd said. For a moment he gave me his hollow-eyed stare again, but with a flicker behind it I couldn't quite name. "Go put your shirt and pants on," he finally said. "Fast as you can. We got to go."

"You're . . . not calling the law?"

"Haven't you been listening? We need to get to Memphis," was his answer. "Right *now*."

I'd like to say that was the last we saw of Percival Bowles, but it was not. Back on the highway, we watched the railroad track in the distance edge slowly closer. By the time we got to Muscle Shoals, the highway once again took us right by the train station with no place for us to hide—and there was the circus pulling up stakes.

About ten miles on the other side of town, the tracks hugging the road again, we saw a roadside store with old-timers rocking on the porch. We hadn't had a thing to eat since Yeller's leftovers the night before, and we were getting dangerously low on gas. We could go without food, but we couldn't go without fuel. We had to stop.

I pulled the rig up to the pumps. As the old-timers on the front porch stools geehawed and made their way over to get a better look-see at the giraffes, the Old Man put on his fedora and pulled it low over his gash. "I know you got questions," he said my way, "but first we need to get you and the darlings to Memphis." With a tense glance back down the road, he got out and marched into the store, the giraffes watching him go.

As the attendant, staring at the giraffes, pumped the gas about as slow as I ever saw, a panel truck pulled up on the other side of the pumps—a yellow-and-red panel truck. And out from the passenger side crawled Bowles. No longer in hat, boots, and ringmaster outfit, his mustache bushy and unwaxed, he was as pure ugly as a devil should be.

He's going to spill the beans on me, I thought, looking back for the Old Man. Giving the giraffes a soulful look, I eyed the railroad tracks for a place to hop a freight if it came to it, and then, squeezing the gold piece in my pocket, I stepped toward Bowles and his driver. I was going to say something, anything, to stop what I thought was going to happen next, even arguing with myself over handing back the gold piece if that would end it.

But Mr. Percival Bowles had no interest in a measly double-eagle coin. As he and his driver moved my way, he pulled a wad of money from his breast pocket. It was a roll of hundred-dollar bills held together with a single rubber band, and it was big as his fat fist.

If the gold coin looked like John D. Rockefeller to my orphan eyes, then that roll of bills looked like Fort Knox. This wasn't a double eagle to bribe a fool of a boy . . . this was a full-grown man's bribe, the kind of fortune a fella could put in his pocket and go. Never mind the giraffes were worth thousands more than whatever he had, and never mind that his lackeys had tried to abscond with the giraffes that very morning, Bowles thought he could buy the Old Man off, mistaking Mr. Riley Jones for another Hard Times chump like me.

Here and now—with the decades fading from living memory the outright chicanery of that "time of opportunity," as Bowles called it— you might be thinking it folly for anybody to believe they could bribe for, much less steal, two giraffes and get clean away with it. A giraffe is a mighty hard thing to hide, as we already well knew. There was good reason the Old Man called outfits like his "fly-by-night," though. It was still a time of medicine shows, Bible salesmen con artists, and all manner of flimflammers leaving town under the cover of darkness, and that included one-night-stand traveling circuses. To live before the War was to believe you could be or do whatever you wanted by just moving on down the road, especially with the Hard Times turning even good people bad. Fat cats like Bowles relied on it, as much as the greed or hunger of every soul he met, and he was relying on both right then.

"Hello again, young man," he said, flashing the cash roll my way as the beefy driver came around the front of the truck to stand beside him. "I have a proposition for your Mr. Johnson. But I want you to listen very closely, because if he's not wise enough to take it himself, it can be yours. Possession is nine-tenths of the law, as a smart lad like you knows, and you are, after all, in the driver's seat." Then he held out that roll of bills close enough for me to touch. "Do you understand what I'm saying?"

In the glow of that small fortune, I lost any good sense I'd redeemed that morning. My eyes stuck on Fort Knox, I heard myself mumble, "Jones."

"Hmm?"

"Not Johnson—Jones," I mumbled. "Riley Jones."

He jerked a step back, taking the cash roll with him. "What did you say his name was?"

"Riley Jones," I said again.

His face dropped like he'd seen a spook. What he said next made me forget all about bills and beans and bribes.

"Young man," he muttered, "you're traveling with a murderer."

There were few words that could have gotten my eyes off that cash wad, and that was surely one of them.

His gaze darted past me. "You best watch yourself driving such delicate creatures in this ridiculous rig. You'd be better off with me. At least I know the value of a man's life over an animal's."

From behind me, I heard the slap of the store's screen door. Next thing I knew Bowles had shoved the cash roll into my chest and let go, making me grab it to keep it from dropping in the dirt. Just that quick, I was touching more money than I'd ever again hold in my hands. Men have died for less. At that moment, I knew why.

I'd like to write that I never wavered, full of moral fiber to burn. That, chin high, remembering the giraffe larceny and my shot-firing part in stopping it, I flung the cash roll back at him. And don't think I wasn't tempted to tell the story that way, being forced to make full use of the eraser end of this pencil. But you know that's not what happened. I surely understood that Mr. Percival Bowles expected a certain obligation from any poor soul taking his money, be it thrust on them or not. Dealing with any attached fat-cat strings, though, had to wait. Because once my hands touched that roll of cash, it wasn't about the fat cat. It wasn't about the Old Man or the giraffes. It wasn't even about right or wrong. It was only about a Dust Bowl orphan and a big roll of cash. I did what you'd expect such a boy to do. I pushed that pocket fortune deep into my right front pocket on top of the gold coin, my fingers clutching both good and tight.

"BOY!"

The Old Man was by the screen door, still in his bloodied shirt. Then he was marching at us double time, onion sack in one hand and a bag of supplies in the other. He dropped the supply bag into the cab's open window and threw the passenger door wide, ignoring both the fat cat and the driver. "Get in the truck, boy."

"Now hold on," Bowles said, moving toward the Old Man. "All I want to do is talk."

The Old Man turned his back on them both, still clutching the gunnysack. But then the driver went and clamped a paw on the Old Man's shoulder—and with a one-two punch I'd never see the likes of again, the Old Man swung the onion sack, smacking the driver full in the face while he socked Bowles square in his double chin, knocking him on his butt.

"MOVE!" the Old Man yelled.

We jumped in the truck and screeched away as fast as a big rig could go, my sideview mirror full of scattered onions, old-timers, and the circus driver trying to pull the roly-poly ringmaster out of the dirt.

There was, of course, a big flaw in our getaway. A panel truck without two-ton giraffes can travel faster than a top-heavy rig with them. I was driving us faster than the Old Man had ordered me ever to go, bouncing the giraffes around, inside and out, their heads banging against their windows. Yet all too soon, the panel truck caught up. For a mile they dogged us, as the railroad tracks veered even closer to the highway, sometimes not ten yards away. The circus truck kept pulling into the wrong side of the road, until, on an empty stretch, it came up beside us like it was going to pass. But it didn't. It rode right along with us, weaving back and forth inches from my door.

"What the hell's he pulling?" yelled the Old Man.

Bowles was trying to get my attention. Clenching a new wad of money in his fist, his arm resting on his windowsill, he was signaling me with every look his way: *Pull over, young man. That's all you have to do . . . You have the money. And here's more . . . if you pull over.*

You might think it'd be easy to keep my eyes to myself, that one wad of cash was surely enough. For a stray-dog boy, though, enough is never enough. If one pocket fortune could save me from feeling the

desperate gnaw of an empty stomach forever, another could make forever last longer still. Never did it cross my mind to wonder what they'd
do to the Old Man, much less the giraffes, if I chose to add a new wad
to the old one. There are far more salvations than the kind you find in
church, and I was in need of one right then to save me from myself.
Because here was where I would begin to grasp not only the first stink
of my waffling young soul but also that destiny is a mobile thing—that
every choice you make, along with every choice made around you,
can cause it to spin this way and that, offering destinies galore. I had a
choice to make. Yet as I kept glancing at the new cash roll, the future
in which I had all this fat cat's money came full and irresistible to me.
It was a blinding, sparkly, full-table thing in the way only an orphan
could see it. In my gut, here and now, I know *that* destiny would have
been my choice and my, our, undoing.

And I was saved from it only by a bump in the road.

We hit a pothole so molar-rattling hard it bounced my glance off
the new wad and onto Bowles's other hand, which was gripping something on the seat beside him. It was the gun from his holster, an old
pistol like the kind my pa brought home from World War I, and he was
clutching it in a way that said he'd use it. Bowles had a backup plan. If
I didn't stop the rig, he was going to do some brandishing of it. Maybe
aiming for our tires. Or back at the giraffes. Or at me, never mind his
high words about valuing a man's life.

That shook my mind free of the devil-deal just long enough to grasp
all the other destinies spinning out from what I'd do next, what we'd
all do next. Because, with one eye still on Percival Bowles's pistol, I saw
the Old Man ease the shotgun from its rack. As the seconds ticked off,
with our vehicles filling both lanes of the empty highway, the future was
waiting for me to choose a destiny. Choices are as bad as plans, though,
and as you already know, I was very, very bad at plans. If I stopped, all
hell would break loose. If I didn't, all hell could still break loose.

I couldn't decide.

As I kept not deciding, I kept on squirming. The more I squirmed, the more the cash roll in my pants pocket slipped higher, until the top bills were fluttering in the breeze—and the Old Man saw.

Reaching over, he grabbed the cash roll and pulled it out.

I jerked my head around to see him gazing at me with wounded eyes that said he knew exactly what it was and where it came from. I waited for him to aim the shotgun righteously my way. Instead, his gaze never leaving my face, he tossed the cash out the window, bills scattering to the wind. I didn't have a second to yelp or to mourn. Because the next moment was to be a reckoning.

On my left was the devil packing a pistol and cash roll, on my right was the Old Man packing a shotgun and the judgment of the Almighty. The future was waiting for me to make that choice.

For the first and last time in my life, though, not being able to make a choice was the right choice.

Because the fat cat's plan had its own flaw, and it was coming right at us. A logging truck appeared over the rise. The driver eased on the panel truck's brakes to pull back behind the rig. What he couldn't see was that there was now another car behind us. A sedan had pulled out from a farmhouse's driveway, weaving in and out of my sideview mirror. It was a Packard and a woman was behind the wheel. I blinked at the sight, thinking it to be Red so much I wondered if I'd conjured her, but this Packard was brown and the driver was a granny in white crocheted gloves and hat. She'd pulled so close gaping at the giraffes, Girl's head out one way, Boy's the other, she didn't seem to know what was happening, and *worse*, neither did the giraffes. Boy's head was sticking much too far over the road.

The logging truck driver laid on his horn.

The circus truck driver stomped on his brakes.

Bowles's pistol jolted to the floor.

Wild Boy, God bless him, pulled his head in.

And the Packard granny slammed on her brakes. But it was too late for the circus truck to swerve behind her. The logging truck was already on us. Bowles's driver did the only thing he could do. He swerved left, bouncing across weeds and dodging trees to land full on the railroad right-of-way. He hit the track so hard we could hear all four tires blow—*pop pop pop pop*—followed by the sound of the logging truck horn's *AAAAAAagngngggggggngg* as the big truck roared past and gone.

Quaking down to the tip of my boots, I slowed the rig so much that the brown Packard passed us, the granny's face white with fright, and I had no doubt mine looked the same. As the train track began mercifully veering away, I pulled myself together and geared the rig back up. The Old Man, though, was still gripping the shotgun and eyeing the road. I could barely look at him for fear of what I'd see in his face. I wanted to explain. There was a stray-dog truth behind it all, though, and how did I explain that? I barely was aware of it myself. All I could do was blurt out, "I *didn't* . . . I *wouldn't* . . ."

"Was that all of it?" he said, not looking my way.

"Yes," I lied, unable, even then, to part with the gold piece still in my pocket.

We rode in silence for miles. Then we began seeing signs for Memphis. The Old Man, shotgun still in his lap, had yet to look my way, so I braced myself for what he'd do. I was sure I'd kissed the California ticket goodbye, but for all I knew he was planning to hand me over to a Memphis sheriff as well, and *that* I couldn't let happen, still strapped with secrets of my own.

Up ahead, the **MEMPHIS CITY LIMIT** sign appeared.

I geared down.

"Keep driving," the Old Man said. "Let's get ahead of the sumbitches' turnaround and stop this once and for all. If the darlings let us keep this pace, Little Rock's only another four hours."

I wasn't quite getting it. "We're not stopping?"

"Keep driving," was his only reply.

That quick, I wasn't leaving one way or the other at Memphis. Yet I still had the Old Man's precious cargo in my lying blackguard hands. *Why isn't he yanking me from behind the wheel while he has the chance?* I wondered. Was he planning some kind of Old Man justice up the road? My discombobulated young self was getting more so by the second, with four more hours ahead to ponder every awful way the day might have gone and how it would shape the days to come—including Bowles's murderous claim at the mention of the Old Man's name.

And if *that* wasn't enough, as we passed a roadside fruit stand, out pulled a green Packard.

I glanced down at something flapping with the breeze in the Old Man's floorboard. It was yesterday's newspaper he'd bought in Chattanooga.

Tomorrow had turned into today.

It was my birthday.

I was eighteen.

San Diego Daily Transcript

GIRAFFES TREKKING WITHOUT A HITCH

SAN DIEGO—Oct. 11 (Special edition). Animal lovers across Southern California wait with bated breath to meet their first giraffes. Our Zoo Lady, Mrs. Belle J. Benchley, announced at the San Diego Zoo's birthday party Sunday that the two elongated ruminants' cross-country motor-truck dash is "continuing on schedule." According to progress updates from zoo man Mr. Riley Jones, most recently a telegram from Tennessee, she was happy to report that the trip has been "nothing but smooth sailing" . . .

. . . "Pops?"

Someone's knocking on my room's door *again*. This time, it jars me from these scribbles enough to make me all but jump out of my skin.

"Leave me *be* for the love of *GOD!*" I yell, patting my heart as the orderly marches right in like the rest.

Catching my breath, I pull myself off the Memphis road to take a good look at him. "You're Black."

"Nothing wrong with your eyes, Pops. I was told to come check on you, since you hadn't eaten all day."

"Who are you?" I say.

"Ah, Pops, you say that every night."

I'm not anybody's Pops and sure not his. But he reminds me of Seventh Son, so I don't growl at him. "I stayed at a colored motel once," I tell him. "It was nice."

"*O*-kay," he says.

"The giraffes liked it, too. Didn't you, Girl?" I say toward the window.

He frowns. "You seeing an old girlfriend right now, Pops?"

"No, my friend Girl."

"You mean your girlfriend."

"No. Girl." I point back over my shoulder at her.

"O-*kay*," he says again, looking right through Girl like she isn't there.

"She's a giraffe," I say. "You're staring right at her. She's in the window."

"Pops—" He screws up his face like he doesn't have good sense. "We're on the fifth floor."

"Yeah?" I pause. "Yeah." I turn toward the window.

Girl is gone.

"Listen," he is saying, "maybe you should take a break from whatever that is you're doing. You've got to pace yourself at your age."

My age? I look down at what I'd just wrote.

It's my birthday.

Wait. No, it's not.

It was.

My heart stutters again as I remember.

I'm over one hundred . . .

"If you promise not to attack the new TV, we'll let you come down to the rec room if you want. Nothing's worth making yourself croak, right? Pops?"

With a glance back at the empty window, I start writing again.

Faster.

10

Into Arkansas

I once knew a man who didn't know his own birthday. He was a lucky man. He lived his life each day like any other, never quite knowing his age, therefore never knowing a birth date's yearly tyranny. I can do without them, thank you, having had many, many more than my share. The thing about birthdays is you're rocking along drawing breath, living sunrise to sunrise, becoming who you'll become without a thought put to it—until the day you popped into this world arrives. Then whatever happens, good or bad, you'll forever mark it in memory along with the passage of ticking time, a date on a calendar forcing you to look behind with no way to change things and look ahead with no way to know what's coming. When I reach back for this birthday on my ride with the giraffes, that's what I recall my new eighteen-year-old-self feeling as I stood on the banks of the Mississippi River, a river so wide that, if you try crossing it, you can't see where you're going. With no idea what was ahead for me and no time to ponder what was behind, I was traveling blind.

We'd just passed through Memphis proper after the fat-cat chase. The giraffes were riding heavy, the green Packard was either hiding or waiting down the road again, and I was still discombobulated. With every sign we'd seen pointing back to the Memphis Zoo as we drove through the city, I had mourned my lost California ticket, eyeing the Old Man for any change of heart and still worrying about some Old Man–style retribution. But he kept on looking back, shotgun in hand, until we saw the bridge up ahead and he motioned me to stop near the riverbank before we crossed over.

As the Old Man parked the shotgun under an arm and started checking the rig, out popped the giraffes' snouts, their nostrils sniffing the watery smell. But I couldn't make myself move. All I could do was stand and stare at the skinny bridge disappearing over the river like it was falling off the edge of the world—and I felt my stomach do the same. **HARAHAN BRIDGE**, the sign had said, **4,973 FEET LONG**. Almost a *mile*. I had come over it heading toward Cuz, but at night on a train down the middle. From what I could see, cars and trucks were crossing on single lanes slapped on either side that were scarcely more than boarded-over tracks.

"I'm driving the rig over *that*?" I mumbled.

"No choice," the Old Man said. "Plus, it's rough. So help me get their heads in and let's hope they keep 'em there."

No choice. My gut, though, was telling me if I went over that bridge, I *was* making a choice, one that I wasn't quite understanding. And I still wasn't ready. Not yet. Maybe not ever.

Right then, one of the giraffes kicked the rig and the Old Man sprung up the side to latch their windows himself. "Let's *go*," he called down to the sound of stomping and snorting.

I'm jumpy about the water, that's all . . . like the giraffes, I kept telling myself as I crawled behind the wheel and pulled us into the traffic entering the bridge. Taking one last look over his shoulder, the Old Man placed the shotgun back on the rack.

With a thump and a bounce, we were on.

Every tire taking a beating, every tooth in my jaw rattling, we crept along. On my side was the track going down the middle, and I tried not to think what would happen if a train came along. On the Old Man's side was water, water, and more water, the jutting trestles the only thing between us and a free fall of giraffe, truck, and body parts to a muddy Mississippi splashdown.

"K-keep it s-steady . . . ," the Old Man said as we jolted along, cars stacked up behind us and getting more so with every minute.

WELCOME TO ARKANSAS, said the sign halfway across the bridge.

"S-s-steady—" the Old Man kept on saying. "Steady-y-y."

With one last bone-jangling bounce, we were on the other side, rolling once again onto solid ground, both giraffes popping their latches to sniff the good earth.

The delta land spread out flat on either side as far as all four of us could see, and the Old Man started showing signs of relaxing. The racked shotgun stayed put and his glances over his shoulder stopped altogether. Heaving a hefty sigh, he leaned back, took that fedora off his head, and set it on the seat between us. Soon, as the railroad track once again veered out of sight, we were back to good traveling speed and the soothing rhythm of the road. That was nothing, though, compared to the soothing sight of that fedora lying quiet between us.

For a couple of miles, we rode in silence, watching the black delta land stretch into cotton fields from here to yonder. I could see acres and acres of pickers' backs bent low, pulling their "whole-9-yards" cotton bags behind them, only a few near the highway unbending in time to see the giraffes go by. Still looking plain pitiful with dried blood on his shirt and a crusted-up gash on his temple, the Old Man then spied a grocery and dry goods store on the dirt road skirting the highway and ordered me to stop. Steering around a farmer driving a mule-driven rickety wagon, I parked us this side of the store.

The Old Man got out and flipped open Girl's trapdoor, and she was still so exhausted she didn't even kick when he dared to touch the rewrapped splint.

"Water 'em," he ordered as he flipped the door shut, his face grim, and headed into the store. When he returned, he was wearing a new shirt, his head gash was cleaned up, and he was carrying a gunnysack of onions to replace the one used to smack the driver.

"I called Little Rock," he said as we climbed back into the truck cab. "We'll be overnighting at their pint-sized zoo." Then he said, "I haven't forgot what I promised you about Memphis, boy. But things have changed. We'll talk about it tonight."

I started to reach in my pocket for the comfort of the double-eagle gold piece. Glancing at the Old Man, though, I thought better of it and put the rig into gear.

For the next few hours, the Old Man was lost in his thoughts, with me worrying what those thoughts were. It was October but the air was so thick with heat and moisture, you'd have thought it was hot-damn August. The giraffes, though, seemed to like it fine, having not pulled their heads in once since the Memphis bridge.

By the time the sun began to set, we were getting close to Little Rock, piney woods framing the winding highway. All seemed normal enough as we approached a tiny town that looked like every other tiny town we'd been through . . . until we saw the big homemade sign:

NIGGER, DON'T LET THE SUN GO DOWN ON YOU HERE

Riding the rails, I'd heard of "sundown towns" with signs warning "colored" travelers not to be caught there after dark. Now I was seeing one. I was staring so hard at the thing, I almost ran the rig up on a wreck not twenty yards past it.

There, spun around sideways to the highway, was a rusted-out Model A truck with **PECANS FOR SALE** painted slapdash on the side.

The entire head of a very dead big-antlered buck was stuck in the front grill, and the radiator was gushing pink water. I veered in time to miss the truck but not the buck's back end. Blood, deer parts, and pecans sprayed across the highway—and as we passed, parts squishing and pecans crunching, a Black man in a straw hat scrambled for the tree line.

Both the Old Man and I looked back. I was staring at the deer parts we'd flattened. The Old Man, though, was staring at that tree line.

"Pull over," he ordered.

I thought he wanted to check the rig's front bumper. Instead he climbed out, walked to the tree line, and called out something I couldn't quite hear. He must have gotten no response, because he started up again, this time pointing toward Little Rock, then back at the sign, then up at the setting sun. With that, the pecan man eased out from the trees, straw hat in hand. They talked a second, then the pecan man followed the Old Man to the rig, eyes darting between the road and the two giraffe heads swiveling to get a good look at him. When the Old Man opened the cab door and pointed to the bench seat's space between him and me, the pecan man shook his head.

"Nossuh," he said.

The Old Man tried reasoning with him, but the pecan man kept glancing down the road and shaking his head.

"Nossuh. *No*-SUH."

Not until we heard a car coming did the situation change—the pecan man sprinted back to the trees.

As the car passed, the Old Man fumed, picked up one of the water cans between the rig and cab, and shoved it into his floorboard. Then he called toward the pecan man, pointing to the now-empty water-can space behind the cab.

The pecan man peeked out. Shoving his straw hat back on his head, he rushed to his wrecked truck and grabbed up as many lumpy gunnysacks from the wrecked truck as he could handle. Hustling back to the rig, he squeezed himself into the water can's empty space behind the cab, pecan sacks cradled in his arms.

After the Old Man did his own squeezing into his seat, legs straddling the big metal water can, I put the rig in gear and steered us onto the road, eyeing what I could see of the pecan man in my rearview. Stretching out her front window, Girl's long tongue was nibbling at his straw hat, making the pecan man weave and bob until another car whizzed by and the pecan man pulled his straw hat as low as it would go.

As we entered the one-horse town, I recall feeling the sweat pop out on my forehead. I'd already felt scared lots of times in my young life, but this was a different kind of scared. It wasn't like we were going to roll through unseen with a couple of giraffes, and if somebody, *anybody* in this damn town, noticed the pecan man, there might be forewarned hell to pay. The sun wasn't down yet, but it wasn't far from it. I didn't feel a bit better when the Old Man moved the shotgun from the rack back to his lap.

The burg's downtown was only four blocks long, barely more than a wide place in the highway. As we rolled slow through it, a handful of people, all unsurprisingly White, came out of the storefronts to stare. I glanced back for the pecan man.

He wasn't there.

"STOP!" the Old Man yelled, and I stomped on the brakes.

A red-faced yokel in a shabby tan uniform with an old sidearm on his hip had stepped right in front of the moving rig and put up a hand. Eyeing our bloody front bumper, he walked over to look in at us from the Old Man's window. On his uniform was written in what looked like leaky blue fountain pen ink: "Sundown Peace Officer." It didn't take much imagination to see him in another kind of uniform, the kind with a hood . . . and I found myself wishing for Big Papa's clan complete with those sharp, nasty-looking scythes.

"You're creating a hazard, mister," the yokel grumbled. "What the heck are you toting there?"

"Giraffes."

"Uh-huh. You with a carnival? We don't much cotton to carnivals around here. Too much riffraff among other undesirables. We like a peaceful town after sundown," he said, tapping his uniform's inky title. "And it's almost sundown."

"We're only passing through, if you'll let us on by," the Old Man said. "Trying to make the Little Rock Zoo before dark."

"Uh-huh." He eyed the Old Man's head gash and nodded toward the rig's front. "There's blood on your bumper."

"We hit a buck about a mile back," the Old Man said.

The "sundown peace officer" stepped back to the bumper and flicked off a piece of bloody deer pelt. Meanwhile, in my rearview I could see Girl craning her neck to sniff at the space where the pecan man had been. The yokel looked up at Girl. "That animal agitated about something?"

"Deer riled him," the Old Man said. "That's all."

The scruffy officer scratched himself. Then, resting a hand on his sidearm's grip in the way he must have seen lawmen in Westerns do it, he started moving toward the space where Girl was still sniffing.

At that, the Old Man raised the muzzle of the shotgun to rest on the windowsill, just high enough for the sundown peace officer to see. "You know, *officer*," said the Old Man, "I'd keep my distance if I were you. Those are dangerous animals. *Real* dangerous."

The yokel paused, staring between the gun barrel and the look on the Old Man's face, and slowly lowered his hand from his sidearm.

"Like I said," the Old Man went on, "we're passing through to get to Little Rock before sundown. We should go."

"Well, OK then . . . I don't mean to keep you nice White folks," he mumbled, then stepped back, stuck out his chest, and waved us by. "You can move along."

As we picked up speed hitting the open highway, I heard the wind whipping what sounded like the rig's stashed tarp meant for cold nights or heavy storms, neither of which we'd had so far. When I looked back in the rearview, I saw the tarp rise into view, and with it the pecan man's face. He had pulled out the tarp enough to skinny under it to cover him and his pecans, his broken straw hat the only casualty. Not until we'd left the town far behind, though, did he ease the tarp all the way back and sit up, Girl greeting him with a lick and a nudge.

The Old Man and I didn't say a word. There wasn't much to say, at least not much either of us wanted to say. So we stayed silent, both of us glancing back at the pecan man every few seconds. Soon, he was sitting tall enough to reach up and touch Girl's snout like he wasn't quite sure he was touching something real.

On the outskirts of Little Rock, the pecan man tapped on the back window. I pulled over near a dirt street and he hopped down, straightened his broken straw hat, grabbed up the pecan sacks, and, chin up, held one of the sacks up to the Old Man's window. I could tell the Old Man really wanted to let the pecan man keep his pecans. But when there's a debt to pay, a man has the right to pay it. So he took the sack. With a nod our way and a last glance back at the giraffes, the pecan man disappeared into the shadows.

We sat there a minute, watching the shadows grow deeper where he vanished, even the giraffes straining for a last look. Then the Old Man set the shotgun back on its rack and said, "Let's go."

Putting the rig in gear, I heard a vehicle roaring up behind us.

I looked back and froze.

It was a panel truck . . . a *yellow* panel truck . . .

ARKANSAS EVENING GAZETTE DELIVERED TO YOUR DOOR, said the truck's sign as it whizzed by.

Swallowing my heart back down my throat, I let off the clutch and moved us on.

Soon as we passed the city limits, we saw a sign pointing to the **FAIR PARK ZOO**. It led us onto an old cobblestone bridge across a railroad crossing and into the city park, straight to the zoo's entrance. The zoo's single building looked like the stone structures I saw in the mountains, no doubt built by the WPA, too. The entrance was set up on a little rise, and the park surrounding the zoo was full of people. Not like you might think, though. Everywhere we looked were down-on-their-luck folks lying about, on benches, in makeshift lean-tos, and in rain tunnels, like the people in Central Park I passed in New York City chasing the giraffes.

"Stay here," the Old Man ordered, getting out. Moving around a beat cop rousting a tramp away from the entrance, he made his way into the zoo.

"We're getting giraffes!" screamed a kid who broke away from his mother to run up to us. "Giraffes! Giraffes!" he kept saying, jumping up and down.

A crowd formed, already oohing and aahing as the giraffes stretched down to be touched. I could tell it was like a sweet chorus to the giraffes after the day we'd had, and despite myself, it made me feel good.

The Old Man returned, motioning me to bring the rig around to a gate in the zoo's high stone fence. By the time we caught up to him at the open gate, he was already talking to a short man in wire-rim glasses dressed fancier than you'd think any zoo man should be—all gussied up in suit, tie, and bowler hat. Soon as we were in, he closed the gate and headed us toward a spreading sycamore along the back wall, perfect for giraffe-feasting.

The zoo was as tiny as the Old Man said. Even in the growing dusk, I could see it all from where I parked the rig. To the left, the front entrance part was a long building housing monkey cages that opened into a breezeway leading to outside paddocks to our right—a buffalo roaming in a big pen, tortoises and prairie dogs inside a dry moat, peacocks, some camels, a lion, a zebra, a brown bear. That was it.

The Old Man and the bowler-hat zoo man stood in front of the rig chatting as I popped the top for the giraffes. When I jumped down, the Old Man waved me over.

"My apologies about the trouble out in front," the bowler-hat zoo man was saying, his voice as high as a woman's. "We've got the same Hooverville problem blighting our nice park like most cities these days, no matter what we do, and it's always worse at closing time. Who do we have here?"

"This here is Woodrow Wilson Nickel, my young driver," the Old Man said. "We had a bit of miserableness this morning in Tennessee that made us wish for a secure night's sleep this side of the river. So we thank you in advance for the short-notice hospitality."

"Any friend of Mrs. Benchley is welcome here," the bowler-hat man said, his eyes darting past me to the giraffes already nibbling the tree. "Where's your home, Mr. Nickel?"

Home? I didn't have a home, least not one I wanted to chat about.

The Old Man piped up. "We met young Mr. Nickel back East, and he's been helping us out in a pinch."

The bowler-hat man wasn't really listening, though, his social nicety already forgotten under the spell of the giraffes. He sighed, staring up at them. "What we wouldn't do for giraffes. Sure you don't want to let them stay awhile?"

The Old Man didn't even dignify that with an answer. I didn't know what to think until both of them broke out laughing.

"Mrs. Benchley would have us both tarred and feathered!" hooted the bowler-hat man. "For what it's worth, I called our vet to come look at the female's leg. It'll make his day. Don't think he's ever seen a giraffe. Ah, here he is."

The zoo's vet was as far from the white-coated Bronx Zoo vet as he could get, dressed in stained khakis, smelling of manure, with a pop-eyed look on his face to rival my own at my first sight of the giraffes. He forced himself to focus on Girl's leg. "You say she's been in the rig the whole time? That must've been *some* miserableness you had. Looks more like she's been running and kicking to beat the band."

When the Old Man didn't answer, I made the mistake of looking at her leg myself, and I thought I might retch. It was way worse than back in the cornfield, blood and pus oozing from everywhere. *Because of me,* I thought. I had lowered the side. I had taken the twenty-dollar gold piece. I hadn't warned the Old Man—and I'd hurt Girl. I couldn't breathe, feeling a weight pushing against my lungs so bad that Mr. Percival T. Bowles might as well have been sitting his fat ass right on my chest.

"Get the onions," the Old Man said.

Grabbing the sack, I crawled up the side and started feeding onions to the Girl as fast as she'd take them. While the vet doctored away, medicating and rewrapping, I kept feeding the Girl until the vet called it "done as done could be" for traveling. "Don't suppose you can leave her here until that leg decides if it's going to heal," he said.

The Old Man shook his head.

"Well, then, it goes without saying that it'd be good if you can get her on solid ground as soon as you can," the vet said. "I'll come in early to check her in the morning before y'all leave and give you more sulfa and supplies for the road. It'd be an honor."

At that, the bowler-hat man slapped the Old Man on the back, like we were all having a gay ol' time, and said, "Let's go send Mrs. Benchley a telegram."

"I'll catch up with you," the Old Man told him. As the two zoo men left, he motioned me down. Pushing back his fedora, he settled his hands on his hips and waited until I was standing in front of him, then leveled his gaze at me and said, "I know what I promised you at Memphis, but I had to make a choice for the darlings' sake. And now it looks like I need you to keep going. Otherwise, we're stuck here for longer than her leg might stand. If we can dodge any more bad luck, we're only about three days out and we'll be to California, like you wanted." He paused. "You OK with that, Woody?"

It was the first time the Old Man had called me Woody. He wasn't turning me in to the cops . . . and I was still headed to California. I couldn't find my tongue. All I could do was nod.

"All right then." He gave me a couple of awkward hard pats on the shoulder, something he'd never done before, either, and said, "It's safe in here. We should both get a good night's sleep. What's ahead is as different from what we've already gone through as the moon is from the sun. But you already know that," he added, "since we'll be passing through your old stomping grounds."

That zapped me like a thunderbolt out of blue sky. "What?"

"The highway," he said. "It crosses Okie-land and the Texas Panhandle to get West."

"But we're going the southern route," I mumbled. "That's what you said, the *southern* route . . ."

"This *is* the southern route." He cocked his head. "We're in Arkansas, boy. Did you think we were going by way of New Or-leens?"

Yes! I did! I wanted to shout. *That's a southern route!* Cussing myself for being so lamebrained, I didn't know what to do. *I can't go back through the Panhandle! I can't even go near—I'd be chancing too much after what I did!* I kept thinking, my mind screaming with it. Yet I couldn't tell the Old Man. He'd want me to tell him why, which I wasn't about to do. It even occurred to me that he might somehow know. *Is that why he kept me on after finding the cash roll in my pocket—to take me back to the Panhandle county sheriff for a reckoning there?*

But he can't *know . . .*

The first time a poor soul gets a bit of grace in his wretched life, especially from a man who, by his own pronouncements, abides no chicanery, it's a hard thing to recognize let alone accept, and even harder to trust. I knew what to do with judgment, having a young lifetime of experience with that. This level of kindness, though, if kindness it be, only made me prickly and even a bit fearful, since I hadn't forgotten what Percival Bowles had warned at the mention of the Old Man's name.

The Old Man was talking. "You've never been to a zoo, have you? Don't tell fancy four-eyes, but while the animals seem healthy enough, this zoo's a sideshow compared to the San Diego Zoo." He waved toward the front. "Stroll around if you want, but don't let the darlings out of your sight. I'm going to get a real meal with this sawed-off pal of the Boss Lady's, and I'll bring you some back in an hour. Best I relieve you early as well, to make sure you sleep good. Here on out, who knows what kind of sleep we'll be getting."

Then he was gone.

I stood there feeling buckshot, gazing up at the giraffes in a way I hadn't allowed myself since Yeller's because of guilt. Girl's and Boy's mighty snouts were peeking out the top, their tongues reaching for the sycamore branches, and the sight gave me a stab of such pure feeling that my knees buckled. I had to put a hand on the rig's fender to steady myself, overwhelmed by the full weight of the last two days as I drank in the sight of the two gentle, forever-forgiving giraffes . . .

. . . *who deserve better than me.*

Something had gone and changed without me looking. I was barely recognizing myself. Keeping Percival Bowles's double eagle and pocket fortune? That didn't surprise me a lick. I did both without a thought. The shot I fired to protect Girl from the lackeys? I did that without thought, too, like I was protecting my own. But they weren't my own. I had as little claim on them as I did on Red. And now I was about to hazard going back through the *Panhandle* for a couple of animals that weren't even mine? I rocked back on my bootheels, skittish as a calf, knowing this time I *had* to cut and run . . . yet each glance at the giraffes was like a knife to the heart. I didn't want to go back to the life of a stray-dog boy, but wasn't it better than what might be waiting for me if I drove back into my Panhandle past?

At that moment, like a sign, I heard a freight train. It was coming this way.

Forcing my eyes from the giraffes, I moved toward the front of the little zoo. The chattering people still inside were all heading for the exit. Muscling up my runaway courage, I stared at the exit, my fist clutching the gold coin in my pocket. *I can find my own way to Californy,* I told myself. *I still got the twenty-dollar gold piece . . . I'll be fine. The giraffes don't need me. They'll be fine, too . . . They won't even notice I'm gone. And the Old Man? He'll stomp on that crummy fedora, then the bowler-hat guy will find him a real driver to get the giraffes to Mrs. Benchley just fine . . . more than fine . . .*

People were trickling by me, vanishing through the exit. I took several big breaths and joined them. As I stepped into the crowd, though, someone grabbed my arm. I whirled around, ready as always for a scrap.

It was Red, holding her camera with one hand and putting her arm through mine with the other.

"Stretch, there you are!" she was saying. "Are the giraffes OK? Who were those awful men yesterday? I almost lost you in the fog, and found the rig like *that* and—"

"Where did you go?" I said, cutting her off.

Her eyes took on the look of a doe in headlights. "Nowhere. I was a bit delayed."

"I keep thinking I'm saying goodbye to you."

She squeezed my arm. "Everything holds a goodbye someday, Woody. But not us, not yet. Now *tell* me what happened! Those men were trying to steal the giraffes, weren't they? And you *shot* one—I *saw* you! You could've *killed* him!"

"I winged him," I grumbled, wondering why everybody was questioning my shooting skills. "If I'd wanted to *kill* him, he'd be dead."

Red gave me the same funny look the Old Man did. "What did the police say?"

"They didn't say anything. He didn't call 'em."

"Mr. Jones didn't call the police? Why not! Tell me *everything!*"

But I didn't feel much like doing that, thinking more about police bulletins and runaway wives than fat cats and circus lackeys. Instead I said, "Why didn't you stay to see for yourself?"

She paused. "I was certain Mr. Jones would call the authorities, and I thought it best if I didn't get involved."

"Why not?" I pushed.

Letting go of my arm, she changed the subject. "Isn't that the saddest thing outside?" She nodded toward the park's Hooverville beyond the exit. "Look what the man by the entrance handed me after I took his picture." She pulled a card from her shirt pocket.

Intern'l Itinerant Migratory Workers Union

HOBOES OF AMERICA

NATIONAL MEMBERSHIP CARD No. 103299

Thank you for considering a token contribution
to my continued existence.
I am deeply in your debt.
May God bless your bounteous heart.

(over)

She flipped it over. "Look at all this on the back, too."

Hoboes' Oath

I <u>John Jacob Astor, Esq.</u> solemnly swear to do all in my power to assist all those willing to assist themselves. I solemnly swear never to take advantage of my fellow men, or be unjust to Others, to call out those that do, and to do all in my power for the betterment of myself and America—so help me God.

"It's only a hobo card," I muttered.

"Bums have *cards?*" she said.

"A hobo's not a bum. A hobo's proud of being a hobo."

"Really! Well, it worked. I gave him a penny. It'll be a great shot," she said, replacing the card in the breast pocket of her white silky shirt, and despite myself, I couldn't help but stare. It was like something movie stars wore, that shirt, just like her trousers.

As I watched Red pop a new flashbulb in her camera, happy as a hog in rain, I felt my fury flare high and hot and straight her way. I wanted her to feel as bad as I did for her own piece of traveling treachery—and worse, I *needed* her to. I couldn't take it a second more. "Why was that Chattanooga deputy after you?"

She stiffened. "What?"

"You sped up. I saw you. He said you stole the Packard."

At that, her face fell. "I didn't *steal* it. I borrowed it."

"I borrow things all the time," I kept on. "And what I'm doing is stealing them. Did you *borrow* the Packard guy's money, too, for all this traveling?"

"Don't be fresh, Stretch," she snapped, and then paused again. "Did Mr. Jones hear this, too?"

"Sure he did."

Her face fell lower, but it wasn't low enough for me.

"Are you running away to have a tryst with some gent?" I went right on.

That made her jaw drop. "What kind of question is that?"

"The deputy said you might be violating some 'man act' about husbands' wives running away with other men. Are you?"

"You know good and well I'm by myself!"

Then are you somebody's wife? I longed to say next.

But she was already waving a hand like it could dismiss the whole thing. "Lionel will get his Packard back when I'm done. He's the one who refused to come."

My gut did a backflip. *Mr. Big Reporter? But he's old, pushing thirty if a day.*

"I have to do this story whether he likes it or not," she was saying. "I'm trying to make us all famous! Don't you want that?"

"You're already doing the story."

She rolled her eyes. "Yes, yes I am . . . but I have to have the photographs . . . It's *Life* magazine! Stretch, *please* let's stop. You won't understand," she said, moving toward the monkeys.

I *didn't* understand and I needed to. Maybe the guy was as much a lout as he looked. Maybe he needed another punch in the face. I had to know, so I followed her to the monkeys. As she raised her camera, I reached over and pushed it down. "Tell me what was so bad back home that you didn't want to stay."

What she said next she said so quiet I almost missed it. "Home's not the place you're from, Woody. Home's the place you want to be."

I waited for her to go on. Instead, staring at the whooping, screeching caged monkeys, she said, "Do you ever think about the fact they'll never be free again?"

"The monkeys?"

"All of them," she said. "Even the giraffes."

Still feeling full contrary, I said the most contrary thing I could think of. "Well, maybe they like it fine. They don't ever miss a meal. Or have lions nipping at their heels. Or dust blizzards killing off everything they ever knew. Some of those folks right outside would probably trade places with them on the promise of such alone."

She screwed up her face. "That's not what I mean . . . I mean what if you had to live the rest of your life not spreading your wings?"

I was pretty sure we weren't talking about monkeys or giraffes anymore, but didn't care. "Giraffes don't have wings."

Knowing she wasn't going to charm me this time, she sighed. "We still have a deal, don't we?" She held out her free hand. She wanted to shake again.

I didn't.

"Woody, please."

I slowly put out my hand, and she moved right past to hug me, head against my chest, her camera digging into my still-hurting-like-hell rib. Then she looked up and gave me that sad, tight-lipped smile of hers. Suddenly I wanted to kiss her like I'd been imagining ever since the depot, despite all my pent-up fury—and it made my bewildered heart hurt so bad I wished I'd never laid eyes on her. So when she aimed that camera my way and clicked, its flash blinding me all over again, I welcomed it. I was blinded by her the first time I saw her, I'd been blind the whole time I'd known her, and I was blinded by her the very last time I was ever going to see her. It was almost a relief.

"You know, I better keep on seeing you down the road. We're more than halfway, and, oh, the *pictures*, Woody. They're *incredible*."

I felt a kiss on my cheek and she was gone.

Blinking myself back to sight, I just stood there until I heard the sound of the freight train again, and I set my mind to catch it. Marching to the exit, I pushed my way through as the park's streetlights came on, and bumped square into a beat cop giving the bum's rush to a hobo.

"Sorry, sir," said the cop—to *me*—and went right back to yanking the collar of the smiling hobo, who kept trying to give him a card.

Set back on my bootheels, I paused to get my balance. As the last of the exiting visitors streamed past, I was bombarded by the sights and sounds of the Hooverville straight ahead—the clamoring noise, the trash-can fires, the shelters of cardboard and huddles of tar paper. It was all I could hear and all I could see.

Above the racket, though, I thought I heard the echo of a giraffe wail. I knew that couldn't be. The Hooverville din was far too loud to have heard any such thing.

I shook it off.

Then I heard it again.

Stepping back through the zoo entrance, past the monkeys, I inched toward the rig, sure I'd only imagined it.

As I turned back toward the exit, though, I felt a soft crunch under my boots. I seemed to be standing on what looked like oats . . . There was a trail of it coming from the direction of the buffalo pen, like something had snitched feed from a trough and scurried past. The giraffes were stomping. Looking up, I saw something crouching in the truck's shadows. Wishing for the shotgun, I crept closer, readying for anything with claws.

Instead, there stood someone holding the onion and pecan gunnysacks and staring up at the giraffes. He was so caught up, I almost got to him before I stepped on a twig.

He whirled around, clutching the sacks to his chest.

As Boy and Girl upped their stomping, neither of us moved. I could see him in the faint light coming from one of the park's streetlamps. Raggedy and barefoot, he was about my age but much, much scrawnier, nothing but scary skin and bones. Where I was sporting a birthmark on my neck, he had a half-healed burn across both neck and jaw, the kind of burn you get from a fall on a hot rail or a scuffle over a bum's fire barrel. Too wretched a sight to be a hobo, too young to be a bum, he'd been a luckless railrider—I was sure of it. But he wasn't now. Now he was stealing food meant for animals, hunched over like a junkyard dog.

We locked eyes, and what I saw gave me the willies. There was nothing left there but fear and hunger and what he'd do to keep both at bay.

Right then, one of the giraffes kicked the rig hard enough to shake the frame. When I glanced up he ran right at me, knocking me flat on my ass—exactly like I'd done to the Old Man in quarantine—and I hit the ground hard, the stink of him on my new clothes. The last I saw of him were the gunnysacks slipping over a stone wall too smooth for scaling. Yet there he went. Just like a cat.

Lying there in the dirt and spilt oats, I stared after that raggedy boy, stuck in the moment. In the years since, I have sometimes seen his face in the mirror for no reason I can say. Back then, though, the only thing that snapped me out of it was the sound of the rig rocking, swaying, the axle groaning to breaking. The giraffes were about to flip the rig where it sat. Scrambling up on my boots, I kicked a loose onion and scooped it up. Then I was straddling the cross plank between the Old Man's darlings like I'd thought I'd never do again. Girl and Boy moved close and the rig went still. I stroked both their mammoth jaws, cooing the Old Man's giraffe-speak and feeding them the onion, peeling off its layers one by one. As their big heads lingered, surrounding my young self like living shelter, my heart swelled with the boy-in-knickers feeling from the cornfield again, making me feel lighter and shinier and safer in a way I still can't explain. We stayed that way for a good long time, until the two reached once more for the sycamore's leaves, their quivering nostrils the only reminder of the latest lion at their heels.

I lay back on the cross plank to watch, seeing their outlines against the stars and hearing their soft nibbling against the sound of the freight train dying away.

Next thing I heard was a gruff voice.

"You up there again, boy?" called the Old Man. "You're going to break your fool neck doing that."

Certain I was in a moving boxcar, I grabbed at the plank under me. I'd dozed off. Above me, the stars had moved. The giraffes were still surrounding me, and I sat up feeling as untroubled as I'd ever hoped to be again.

"Come on down," the Old Man ordered. "The grub's cold but good. So eat up and go stretch out on the nice cot that fancy four-eyes set up in his office. I'll wake you when I need to."

Back on the ground, the raggedy boy's oats crunching under my boots, I gobbled up the grub, and instead of leaving, I turned to look at the Old Man. He'd plunked down on the running board and was pulling his smokes and his Zippo from his shirt pocket.

"Something on your mind?" he asked, lighting his Lucky.

"I pocketed that cash roll," I said. "Why didn't you dump me?"

Clinking the lighter shut, he took a puff, looked my way, and said, "You think I've never been hungry?" He left his eyes on me longer than he had to, giving me the same look, full of mercy, that the giraffes gave me after I'd opened their rig for my piece of gold—and it hit me like a punch in the gut.

He was forgiving me, too.

"Now get on to sleep," he said, and waved me away, the giraffes peacefully chewing their cud above.

As I took in the whole of them, the whole of me welled up . . . and I let a new, clearheaded thought sprout inside my walled-off heart. If home, like Red said, was not where you came from but where you wanted to be, then the rig, the Old Man, and the giraffes were more home—and more family—than any home I'd ever had. For a stray orphaned boy, *this* home seemed fiercely worth holding on to, with both fists, as long as I could. No matter what might be waiting for me up the road.

With a glance back at the raggedy boy's stone wall, and another toward the Panhandle, I sucked in all my fearfulness and headed for the bowler-hat zoo man's office, knowing I was staying put—come what may.

In the tiny zoo office, even with the peace of having made a decision, it took a while to settle down. I lay wide-eyed on the cot in the dark, listening to the monkey sounds and missing the serene silence of the giraffes, until I must have dozed off. Because I found myself *standing under a glaring red-dirt sun . . .*

. . . I hear Ma: "Li'l one, who you talking to?"

. . . I see animals in cages, a bear, a raccoon, a mountain lion, and rattlesnakes.

. . . I see giraffes floating by in rushing water.

. . . I see a sawed-off double-barreled shotgun aim and fire.

. . . And as the boom-boom ricochets off the office walls, I bolted upright in the dark, hitting the floor in a crumpled lump, cot and all.

I rubbed my head where it hit the concrete, my mind reeling with floating giraffes and caged animals. I couldn't place any of it. The only thing I recognized was the sight of the gun—until I remembered it rightly. My nightmare's gun was a rifle. This was a sawed-off double-barreled shotgun. I could not recall ever seeing such a gun in my life.

I pushed the cot off me and sprinted from the office, not stopping until I'd climbed up the rig and laid eyes on the giraffes safe inside. Only then did I look down at the Old Man, who was staring at me exactly like the first time I'd run to the rig in my skivvies, back at Round's Auto Rest.

Heart thundering, I asked, "Do you have bears in cages in San Diego?"

"We got bears, but in a nice big pit."

"Mountain lions?"

"No. Not a one."

"A raccoon?"

"Now who'd want a raccoon?"

"Rattlesnakes?"

"Those we got. We've dug thousands out of the zoo's hills to trade to other zoos. Australians even got some."

"How about rushing water? You got rushing water?"

"Well, we got the ocean," he said. "What's wrong? This little zoo got you going?"

I shrugged. It was all I had the energy to do.

He ordered me down. "Sit."

I dropped down beside him.

"Let me regale you a bit more about the place we're headed," he said. "You think that prairie dog dry moat over yonder is good? In San Diego, you got African lions with nothing between you and them but a moat. In fact, if the Boss Lady had her way, the weather's so nice they'd fence in all of Balboa Park and let the animals roam. The fencing may be rusty and the money's always tight, but it's about as aces a place to be an animal among us humans as there is. I ever tell you about the penguins?"

Leaning back on the cab door, I listened to the Old Man talk, wanting to tell him about this new nightmare and even about Aunt Beulah, yet knowing it wouldn't help a thing.

Instead I gazed again toward the road.

West.

WESTERN UNION

11 OCT 38 = 702P

TO: MRS. BELLE BENCHLEY
SAN DIEGO ZOO
SAN DIEGO, CALIFORNIA

OVERNIGHTING AT LITTLE ROCK. CANCEL
MEMPHIS DRIVER. GIRAFFES ACES. WILL
CONTACT IN OKLA.

RJ

WESTERN UNION

12 OCT 38 = 710A

TO: RILEY JONES
WESTERN UNION OFFICE

[HOLD]

NATIONAL COVERAGE 500+ ARTICLES. LIFE
MAGAZINE COVERING ARRIVAL.
SENDING PHOTOGRAPHER VIA AEROPLANE.
WIRE E.T.A. A.S.A.P.

BB

. . . "HON!"

I'm on the floor. I don't know how I got here. "Where's . . . where's my pencil?"

"Let me help you up, then we'll find your pencil."

I feel Big Orderly Red grab under my armpits and set me back in my wheelchair. "Oh, hon, you hit your head. That's going to leave a mark. What happened?"

I think my heart stopped. But I'm not telling her that. I look around for Girl. The window's open, but she's not there.

And I remember why.

Rosie reaches toward the window. "You're cold as ice. We better close this."

"Girl might come back!" I roll to stop her, hit the bedstead, and start tumbling out again.

Rosie grabs me. "I better call the nurse."

"*NO, NO, don't!* A nurse'll drug me and I can't stop, I have to finish! I'm past my time, *way past*—you know I am! The rest is all I have left to tell her, and for her it's the most important part! It won't make sense to her unless I finish—you *have* to let me *finish!*"

Sighing, Rosie glances down at the last thing I scribbled.

Across Oklahoma.

"I don't recall Oklahoma, hon," she says. "Now that I think of it, I don't recall anything past Arkansas. Did you tell me the rest?"

"Yes," I lie.

"Well . . ." She pauses, pushing the same graying strand of hair behind her ear. "If you lie down awhile, I won't call the nurse for now. Deal?"

I nod.

"There," she says as she helps me from my wheelchair onto the bed. "You haven't eaten all day bent over that desk. That's probably what happened."

I know it's not, my heart missing a beat. "Where's . . . where's my pencil?"

She picks it up from the linoleum and lays it on the desk. "You can go back to your trip once you've had a nice nap. Rest first, promise?"

I nod again.

She leaves.

I lurch back in my wheelchair, grabbing up the pencil. Taking a deep breath, I place my hand on my heart a moment. Then keep on going.

Here's where I begin to wish . . .

11

Across Oklahoma

Here's where I begin to wish.

I wish I could jump ahead.

I wish I could skip to the finish without having to ride through Oklahoma and the Texas Panhandle again in those Hard Times.

The land you grow up in is a forever thing, remembered when all else is forgotten, whether it did you right or did you wrong. Even when it flat near kills you. Even when it invades your dreams and stokes your nightmares. Even when you run from it never to return, then find yourself headed straight back for it, and the best you can wish for is to drive through it with your head down and your wits about you, dodging the worst of it so you can get on with your young life somewhere else.

Like they say, if wishes were horses, beggars would ride. But that never kept a beggar from wishing.

There were two main roads to California from the Dust Bowl. Route 66 took most of the load and the fame, swooping down the plains from Chicago through Oklahoma toward Los Angeles. The other, the "southern route" heading to San Diego, cut across the bottom part of the Texas Panhandle, my part. Nobody I knew called it the Lee

Highway. It was just the road west, and it was the road we were traveling whether I much liked it or not.

The green of the land began to fade not far over the Arkansas state line into Oklahoma. Even the blue of the sky changed as we drove deeper into the state, the color lighter, hazier, thinner. My ma used to tell me tales of the clear big beauty of the Texas Panhandle sky when she and Pa first started homesteading their piece of land, but it might as well be a fairy tale to me, my childhood sky always an iffy thing and soon a deadly one. You may have heard of the worst day, the duster of all dusters, called Black Sunday. In April of '35, a black cloud came roaring onto the horizon enough to scare a multitude of saints. It was the Great Plains blowing at us, the storm from hell that blew three hundred million tons of topsoil off Texas, Arkansas, Oklahoma, and Kansas. When it hit, it blackened the skies so bad that your hand in front of your face went unseen, the static in the air so bad that the slightest touch of anyone or anything turned sparks into black magic flames. And it kept blowing. In fact, the dirt blizzard blew east so thick and hard and swift that it actually darkened the skies of Washington, DC, even the congressmen, they say, having to close their windows to stave off the dust. That day is a point of historical fact for most. It was point of no return for me and mine. That was when, cough by cough, my baby sister and my ma began to die of the dust pneumonia, along with an earthly host of other folks young and old. For months on end, it was all anybody could think about. The dust never quite left the air, descending and rising like a biblical plague with yellow clouds of swarming grasshoppers and brown skies raining down mud. Even after the air cleared, the worry never did. Each year brought more dusters, each holding the dirt in the air longer and spreading the dust pneumonia deeper, real rain only the stuff of unanswered prayers. Nesters and tenant farmers alike left in droves. Those who stayed would talk about little else right up to the very day we came riding through. Because that day there was wind. With wind came a hint of dust. And with dust came the old dread—even with a pair of giraffes from the other side of the world passing right in front of their eyes.

Less than an hour over the Oklahoma state line, the wind began gusting enough to sway the rig. We pulled under a sturdy tree grove to check Girl's splint and let the giraffes nibble and rest, since it was the last such grove I knew we'd see for a good long time, the trees sparser with each mile. Before we hit the road again, we tried to get the giraffes' heads in and latch the windows, but they were having none of it and we were too late to try any tricks.

"You got any idea how long this'll last?" the Old Man said, holding on to his fedora.

I didn't and, more than ever in my miserable farmboy life, I wish I did.

For a couple of hours, as the wind got worse and the land turned flatter and flatter, we drove slower than usual. A few miles this side of Comanche, we made a stop at Loco, a crossroads with only two buildings on opposite sides of the main highway. One was a two-pump gas station, all red and black and shiny as the new Texaco sign above it. The other was a ramshackle general store and post office that looked like it might topple if you gave it a good push. The store had more metal signs on it than wood, outsized signs for Coca-Cola and Brylcreem and Carter's Little Liver Pills tacked everywhere you looked. While it seemed odd to the Old Man, it looked normal to me. Metal signs stopped the dust and wind that could even beat tar to seep through a shack's cracks.

I pulled the rig into the tiny Texaco station and a gap-toothed, bow-tied gas attendant greeted us, the giraffes leaning down to greet him on their own.

"Don't that beat all!" he kept saying.

On the far side of the pumps a carload was pulling onto the farm road north, whooping back in Spanish at the sight of the giraffes.

"Migrant workers," said the gas pumper, holding his cap on against the wind. "That time of year. Been a stream of 'em all week passing through on their way up to Michigan for cherry-picking season. If this dust gets bad again, I swear, I'm heading that way myself."

The Old Man watered the giraffes himself so he could give the Girl's splint another quick check, sending me to the store across the highway for food and a new sack of onions.

Behind the store counter, a rawboned man sporting a neck goiter the size of a corn ear shoved the last of a biscuit into his mouth. "Whatcha got over there?" he said, wiping his lips with his sleeve and squinting through the screen door.

"Giraffes."

"Don't say! The things I see going by. Passing through quick, I imagine."

I nodded, grabbing up the supplies and plunking them down on the counter.

The man harrumphed. "Better you do, what with the wind getting up. Critters with throats like that won't like it if the sky turns brown. Woke up to the dang dust. Hadn't seen it in months. Whole state's still recovering from '35, ya know."

"I know," I said.

"Which made the dusters of '34 and '37 look like church picnics, ya know."

"I know," I said.

"But rain's coming," he added. "You can feel it."

Hearing that turned me cold—it was a phrase as familiar to my ears as the wind itself, like an anthem of all Dust Bowl hangers-on, the ones too stubborn to leave. My own pa used to say it, right before things usually got worse, and that made me turn around to get one more thing—a jar of Vaseline. Then leaving it all up front for the Old Man to pay for, I went to use the indoor privy at the back of the store.

Passing by a big barrel of apples, my old pilfering reflex almost had me easing one into my pocket. As I came out of the privy door, though, who do I see standing by the apples but Mrs. Augusta Red. The sight of her twisted me up like a pretzel, especially since I thought back in Little Rock that I'd never see her again. Despite all her sweet talk at the zoo, I wasn't through with my pique at her, and I was in no mood to hear more. I inched back behind the door to wait her out, and I almost missed what she did next. Glancing toward the clerk still staring out at the giraffes, she stifled a cough. Then, slick as you please, slicker than *I'd* ever done it, she picked up one of the apples herself, slipped it in her trouser pocket, and strolled out the back entrance to where the Packard was parked.

For a second I stood there flummoxed, not sure that I saw what I saw and not sure what it meant if I did.

As I hustled across the road to the rig, craning my neck back for Red, I almost ran right into a pole by the gas pumps, looking around only at the last second.

"Whoa!" exclaimed the bow-tied gas attendant. "That was close."

"Better watch where you're going, boy. Fast as you were moving, that pole would've knocked you on your can," the Old Man said, closing the trapdoors. "Looks like that store's got a Western Union shingle, so I might as well check for a telegram from the Boss Lady. Did you get the supplies ready for me to pay for?"

I nodded, still watching for Red. There she came, leaning into the wind, camera up, scooting across the highway toward us.

The Old Man fumed at the sight of her. "She keeps turning up. Like a bad penny," he muttered, then headed around the far end of the rig to avoid her.

I was sure the Old Man was going to call the law on her, like he said he would, and I had a sudden urge to warn her. But I didn't. I could only stand there watching her snap pictures of the bow-tied gas pumper and the giraffes. Then she looked up and grinned my way, and I thought

I heard singing. I started to pop myself upside the head until I saw a tent out beyond the station surrounded by trucks, tin lizzies, and farm wagons. The sound of singing voices was wafting on the wind from it. I figured it must be a church "revival" like the ones I got dragged to every year of my life, complete with a pulpit-pounding evangelist and soul-saving altar calls, so I wasn't about to bring it up.

But Red sure did. "What's going on over there?"

"Oh, they're having themselves an all-day community sing," the bow-tied attendant said. "Mostly the Jesus-jumpers. You know, the Holiness crowd. I wish it was the Baptists. Now, they can sing, and they don't use them jangle-banging tambourines."

Red's face lit up.

Just then, it began to drizzle.

A lady near the tent's opening warbled, "Rain!" and half the crowd came out to see.

"Praise Jesus!"

"What a blessing!"

One soprano thought it worth a few high shout-outs.

That's when the lady near the opening saw us. "Brothers and sisters—*look*!"

As the rest of the crowd streamed out to gape at the giraffes, the singing died off. For a moment, the only sounds were the wind and the last little tinkles of a tambourine. Then the rain started coming down in a heavy pitter-patter.

"It's a *sign*!" somebody hollered.

Two different groups broke into two different songs. Somebody started singing a favorite gospel song . . . "I'll fly away, oh glory, I'll fly away . . ." while a second bunch burst into another standby . . . "Oh, come to the church in the wildwood . . ." The racket sounded like dueling tambourines on top of a mess of screeching cats. While the song leader broke a sweat trying to get the singers on the same song, the giraffes craned their necks toward the rumpus, their ears swiveling back and forth almost in rhythm with the tambourines.

As the crowd started holy dancing over to serenade the giraffes, mouths wide to catch either the rain or the ear of the Lord, the Old Man came out of the store across the highway. Arms full of supplies, he had a look on his face that said he was wondering what fresh hell was this.

"Want me to try putting the giraffes' heads in?" I asked over the din as he hustled toward us.

"You think they're going to let you with all that caterwaulin'?"

Jumping into the cab, we rolled up the windows as the singers crowded near. Red was snapping pictures in the middle of it all, and at the sight of her, the Old Man's face went as dark as Black Sunday.

"Did you call the law on her?" I said.

He gave me a look like he'd forgotten all about it, like something else was on his mind.

That gave me pause. "You get a telegram?"

He motioned toward the road. "We'll talk about it later. Let's *go*."

I started the rig and, over the engine rumbling, the song leader waved his arms and hollered, "Page 351, brothers and sisters! Let's send them off proper!"

At that, the singers and the tambourines went silent, the mood turning sweet and light and angel-chorus bright. In four-part harmony, they began to sing the most perfect hymn for that singular moment that could ever be. I'd heard it all my life. Yet only then did I hear the words' meaning:

> All creatures of our God and King
> Lift up your voice and with us sing
> Allelluia
> Allelluia

Even I had to admit it sounded beautiful.

For a mile, the Old Man and I rode in blessed silence, the giraffes looking back like they'd acquired a taste for gospel singing, with the windshield wipers slapping time. In another mile, the green Packard was back in my sideview mirror, and I didn't relax until she slowed and disappeared from view again as we passed through Comanche.

Five miles past, the spattering rain stopped and we rolled down the windows.

In another five, you couldn't tell it had rained at all. The dust was kicking up again, the grit in the air bad enough to leave a mark on my skin, making me pull in my elbow from the window, so it was surely getting into the giraffes' eyes and nose. We *had* to try putting their heads in, so we stopped at a wide crossroads. An old-timer with more wrinkles than skin was sitting at the stop sign in a tin lizzie pickup with more rust than paint.

"You got giraffes in that thang!" he guffawed. "You putting those big heads of theirs in because of the dust?"

I nodded, then got to it, and the giraffes, having had enough, let me.

The old-timer was still talking. "First sign of dust in quite a while. Might get worse fore it gets better," he called to us as we pulled away. "But rain's coming. You can feel it."

We drove like that for a few miles slow and steady, the wind dying down a bit, which made the dust still lingering in the air all the more worrisome.

The giraffes began to cough.

Even now, the thought of it can still make my skin crawl. It was a sandpaper on stone kind of sound, half moan, half rattle, and all bad. By then, even the Old Man and I were coughing with the windows up.

Feeling the rising panic of a Dust Bowl boy who knew a cough was like an invitation to a funeral, I pulled over.

"What are you doing?" the Old Man said, coughing into his fist.

I grabbed up the jar of Vaseline I'd added to our supplies at the sound of my pa's rain curse—it was my ma's answer to the dust storm's worst. Whether the giraffes would even let me try it, I hadn't a clue, but I had to try. With the Old Man following, I climbed up, opened the top, and slopped every bit of the Vaseline in that jar all over those cantaloupe-sized nostrils, wishing I had more. As the Old Man and I stroked their necks and cooed giraffe speak, their throats moved in ripples like small convulsions . . . until the sandpaper-scratch sound slowed. Less dust was getting in those big snout holes of theirs. Still, I feared it was too little, too late.

"Let's wrap the tarp, too," the Old Man ordered, and I wished to God we'd done it sooner. Once the dust gets in, it keeps going round and round if you're moving, and we had no choice but to keep moving.

We rode for a good thirty minutes that way. Their sandpaper wheezing was gone and the wind was now barely more than a breeze. The giraffes, though, were still snuffling and sneezing loud enough for us to hear with the windows up, so we pulled over again and undid the tarp enough to peek in the trapdoors. Heads and necks hanging low, both giraffes were drooling spit, snot, and saliva. Their big bodies were trying to flush out the remaining dust on their own.

The Old Man ordered me to throw back the top while he filled up the buckets from the rig's metal jugs. Soon as I was back on the ground, he crawled up the side with one of the buckets, eased it onto the cross plank, and with a grunt, sat down on the cross plank himself. Pocketing a couple of emergency onions, I grabbed the other bucket and followed.

"Stay right there," he ordered as I hit the top rung of my side ladder. "Get their heads up," he said next, "then *hold* them."

Like I could do such a thing if they didn't want me to. Setting the second bucket down, I waved an onion Boy's way. Up his slobbery snout came. As I fed him the onion, I put my arms around Boy's jaw as tender as I could without spooking him, ready to grab when the Old Man was ready. Cooing his giraffe-speak from the other side, the Old Man raised the bucket of water and nodded. I clamped. With a mighty heave, he sloshed the entire bucketful of water at Boy, hitting him full in the face and up those big nostrils. Boy whipped me like a bucking bronco, and then let go a sneeze that covered the Old Man with more spit and snot than I'd seen in my entire life. As the Old Man cussed and wiped and cussed and wiped, I all but bit through my tongue keeping a straight face. Then we moved to do the same to Girl, who'd seen all she needed to see and had her payback ready. The Old Man picked up the bucket and nodded. I grabbed. He sloshed. And Girl, shaking off my paltry arm hold, reared back and let go with the sneeze of all sneezes, sharing the wealth with me as well.

We slopped to the ground and plunked down on the rig's running board. As we wiped at ourselves, we listened for more worrisome noises. But we heard nothing more than some righteous stomping and slavering. So we offered the giraffes new buckets of water, which they eyed a moment before gulping down, then stashed the tarp and pulled back onto the road.

We had to keep moving.

Soon we were into the worst-hit part of the Okie Dust Bowl. The farther we went, the more barren the view turned. At first, as the clouds began drizzling again, we didn't much care. After an hour passed with us being the only vehicle on the deserted highway, though, the road itself started looking abandoned.

All of a sudden, we weren't traveling alone. Wave after wave of small brown birds were flying along with us in the drizzling rain, sweeping into bubbles and ribbons, flowing close, then away. The miles ticked off and there they still were, a rippling flock with no beginning or end, going on and on across the flat, empty land.

Even the Old Man was impressed. "Now *that* is a natural wonder right there."

The giraffes noticed, too, their necks swaying along with the endless bird wave.

"Where are they all going at the same time—and why?" I said, watching as the ribbon fluttered across the barren land only to sweep back again.

"Maybe it's about something that just happened," the Old Man said, his voice quieting as the wave whipped close. "More likely it's about something that's about to happen."

"But how could they know that?" I said.

"Animal instinct. Built in since the dawn of little brown birds," he said. "It's not like we don't have vestiges of it ourselves. Like when you feel somebody watching you, or why, at the last moment, you didn't walk into that pole back at the gas station. Some people feel it so much they believe they got a sixth sense, a second sight, and you can't tell 'em any different."

Well, that made me twitchy as quick as you might think, wondering if the Old Man somehow knew about Aunt Beulah and my new mixed-up nightmares. His eyes, though, never left the birds.

"'Course, such people are called quacks or nuts," he went on. "But seems to me, such things could be echoes of what birds and animals never lost—tiny leftovers, say, of some built-in survival instinct that thousands of years of human civilizing hadn't quite quashed." He shook his head as the birds looped over us in ringlets only to sweep yet again over the plains. "Yeah, I tell you I've seen strange things working with animals all these years, strange and wondrous things . . ."

We both fell silent, mesmerized by the rippling birds, so much so that I forgot about everything else. For two full hours, my sideview mirror was brimming with both birds and giraffes, framing it all like a picture, the giraffes' long necks swaying along with the billowing birds, and each glance surprised me with what I can only describe as a jolt of joy. On and on it went. The sky kept drizzling, the giraffes kept bobbing, and the birds kept flying, giving the Old Man and me plenty of time to muse. I've been told since that there's a name for something like it—a *murmuration*—a rare bird gathering that looks like a dancing cloud. Nobody ever explained the forever-flowing ribbon quite to fit my memory, though. Against the unforgiving land of my hardscrabble childhood, where the term *natural wonder* had no meaning, the sight filled me with a sense of exactly that—wonder.

By late afternoon, the birds had been with us so long they seemed like passengers hitching a ride on our journey.

Until, without a bit of warning, a bend in the road took them away. They were gone.

The land emptied back to ugly and barren so fast, I all but got the bends. Forced to once again stare at nothing but dead Okie-land, my mood flipped into a flat-out brood that even glimpses of the giraffes couldn't fix. Glancing at the Old Man, who was himself looking way too brooding, all I could think about were those passenger pigeons from the Old Man's Hawkeye story with flocks so huge they'd black out the sky—until they were blasted clean off the face of the earth. *Extinction* was a word nobody much used back then. As a boy who barely escaped that dead prairie landscape alive, though, I pondered it while we rode on, thinking about all the frontier folks with their blunderbusses who wondered where the pigeons went—like the Okie pas and mas with their plows who wondered where the soil went.

In the years to come, as the War took over the world and the prospect of going extinct ourselves, by our own hands, became a thing we were forced to ponder, I'd find myself thinking back to that moment of the vanishing murmur, feeling a soul-weary loss beyond explaining. That day, though, it was only an odd traveling melancholy without a name, a feeling as drizzly as the rain still spitting at us from above.

In that way, we drove until we were almost out of Oklahoma. The Old Man broke the silence by announcing we'd stop for the night at the next auto court that had the tiniest bit of trees.

About an hour from the Texas state line we spied the Wigwam Trading Post Auto Court & Campsite with stucco teepee-shaped rooms set apart like an Indian village. The nice line of tall planted trees along the back fence sold it to the Old Man, though, who was surely the last person on earth who'd ever spend the night in a plaster room shaped like a teepee. But for the giraffes, that's exactly what we were about to do.

At the sight of us, the owner and his wife came scooting out of the office and trading post, the owner whooping with delight and the wife waving souvenir paper Indian headdresses—two for us, two for the giraffes—which the Old Man declined for us all. Soon, the rig was settled back by the trees. Staying there that night with us were only a couple of well-scrubbed traveling families in nice automobiles whose kids thought they'd hit the jackpot with teepees *and* giraffes. Plus, in the campsite area beyond where we parked, there was one big Okie family who'd pitched a tent, their belongings strapped down over their old Model T.

As dusk fell, the Old Man and I tended to the giraffes. We checked Boy and Girl for any lingering giraffe ear, nose, and throat problems and got covered with new giraffe spit for the trouble. Girl was so tired out that she barely snuffled when the Old Man checked her bandage. So, to lift the giraffes' spirits, we let the new crop of giraffe admirers from around the teepee village come close, allowing Girl and Boy to have fun leaning to lick on the kids' faces and lop off the men's hats. Even the Okie family couldn't resist. First came the ma with a baby in her arms, and next the granny who had her menfolk unload her rocking chair and haul it over for her to sit and watch. The Old Man, almost smiling, even let the children feed the giraffes some onions.

As all the parents corralled their children and their granny either inside their plaster teepees or back to their campsite, a green Packard pulled up a few wigwams down, sending the Old Man's good mood south. I thought I was finally going to hear the tirade percolating since Chattanooga. Instead he turned to me and said, "We need to talk about

the Boss Lady's last telegram. Right now, though, I got to wire a reply."
Then he headed back toward the office.

The sky had cleared a bit, the dust gone, the clouds high and
patchy, racing past the stars. With a trading post handy, the Old Man
cooked us a hot meal of beans and cornbread over a firepit not far from
the giraffes. Despite myself, considering the ups and downs of that
Oklahoma day, I felt untroubled, the way clean air and a full stomach
can make you forget about all your problems for a while. The Old Man
must have felt the same, since whatever he wanted to talk about didn't
come up. That was fine by me. Dousing the firepit, he headed to our
wigwam with his usual promise to relieve me. So I climbed up top to
straddle the cross plank between Girl and Boy for the pleasure of their
company as they settled into their cud chewing. The only light was the
reflection from the Okie family's campfire across the way, and it made
everything all but glow.

That is, until I heard Red below.

"Woody?" she said, stifling a cough. "May I come up?"

Untroubled no more, I wanted to say no. Instead I nodded, if
prickly. Hitching up those trousers, she climbed up to my perch and
straddled the cross plank, facing me. I eased back, away from her, like
I'd done the night after the mountains. She noticed. Girl greeted her
and then returned to her cud chewing, but Boy snuffled up close.

Red reached out to stroke his jaw, then had to stifle another cough.
"I cannot get the dust out of my nose," she mumbled. In the scant light
from the Okie campfire, she looked at me and my "prairie face" the
same way she did at Big Papa's. "Tell me your story, Woody," she tried.
"Please. I truly want to hear it."

I didn't say a word and she knew full well why.

"OK," she said, taking a deep breath. "Ask me anything. I promise
I'll answer."

So I set my jaw and said, "Are you married?"

"Yes," she said, holding my gaze.

I flinched. "To that reporter?"

"Yes."

I flinched again. "Then why are you here and not with him!"

"Because I want to be here more."

"But you got a husband."

She leveled her gaze and again said, "Yes."

I'd never been around any married women except my ma or women like my ma. The idea of her being hitched but not hitched to his side wasn't sinking in. "But he wants you back with him."

"Maybe," she said. "Or maybe he only wants the Packard back."

I then heard words come out of my mouth that I'd have thought chump talk only two weeks ago. "You don't love him?"

That got her squirming. "What I feel is between us." She sighed. "He's a good man, whatever he thinks of me."

"A *good* man? He put out a police bulletin on you!"

"Yes."

"But why'd you marry *him*?"

She sighed again. "You won't understand." She was fighting with herself, turning as red as her hair.

I didn't care. "You *said* you'd answer any—"

She cut me off. "You think you're the only one with a story you don't want to tell?" Hand to her chest, she started talking fast. "I was in a bad situation and I needed out." She dropped her hand. "So, I did it the usual way women do. I got married."

"But why him? Why *Mr. Big Reporter*?"

"Because he *was* Mr. Big Reporter," she answered. "With his big job and big car. I was seventeen. He was *safe*. That was all I thought I needed, and it was for a time. It truly was." She paused. "But then, every week, he'd bring home another *Life* magazine. I started seeing the world through those photos. And I started to want . . . to need . . ." She stopped to cough, then the cough turned to a gasp, another and another, like back at Big Papa's—short, desperate, hollow gasps—and they shocked me all over again, sounding so much like my ma's death rattles. She pressed her lips tight against each new gasp like she was mad at having to do it and throwing all her will at them to stop.

Until, at long last, they obeyed.

For a moment she sat clutching her shirt and breathing small, quieted breaths. Then, hoarsely, she mumbled, "I know I promised, Woody, I thought I could . . . but I *can't* . . . *please.*" With that, she struggled to swallow, like the truth was stuck in her craw. "You don't have to tell me anything, *honest* you don't."

As I watched her push her cascade of curls back from her face, I lost all my contrary. I couldn't tell if what she'd said was the truth or not, since it wasn't the whole truth. Right then, though, I didn't care a fig what the whole truth was. I had my own truth stuck in my own craw, didn't I? Even if she told me all that only to hear my miserable Dust Bowl tale, I didn't care. I wanted to tell her. But it didn't make it any easier to put words to the misery.

I wasn't even sure where to start . . .

You ever wake up covered in dust, the air so thick with it you have to suck it in or die? You ever wake up with the fear that another of your animals, sucking in the same dust, didn't make it through the night? You ever spent years of such days, living in fear and dirt, from the day you bury your baby sister to the day you bury your ma? And what you don't know, what you can't know, is that same day—that day of days—will end with you the only living thing left on a patch of worthless Panhandle land, your face and boots splattered with blood?

But *my* whole truth—the truth I still don't have the grit to commit to this writing pad just yet—*that* truth I wasn't telling.

Instead I told her the story of every Dust Bowl orphan . . . that women like your ma died from dust pneumonia from too much honoring and obeying, staying through all the signs of a biblical curse, because men like your pa said to. That if you were unlucky enough to be born to such mas and pas, you were halfway to dead yourself. That the animals that kept you alive were on their way to dead, too, starving from the inside, how farmers like yourself cut open dead cows to find only dirt. How you had to endure each morning knowing you could wake to find another one laid out on the ground, needing to be put out of its misery. And how, after a while, you were half-crazy with it, realizing that all of us needed to be put out of our misery. The land was having its revenge, ashes to ashes, dust to dust, and it was past time to quit even if you didn't know what to quit to. Some folks couldn't do it, couldn't let go, men like your pa who didn't know how to quit without ending up dead himself . . . which is what your pa goes and does . . . with a smoking rifle still in your grip . . . raised and aimed *right* at him.

That is what I tell her. All but the rifle part. I say such a story is just one of a thousand ways you get to be an orphan in this land, a thousand ways that are all the same way. "The only thing left is to find somewhere else, somebody else, to be," I ended, jaw set to keep it that way.

"But, Woody . . . you've come right back *here*," she murmured. "*Why* would you do that?"

I gave her the answer I'd been giving since the hurricane. "I want to go to Californy." With that, I glanced toward Girl and Boy chewing their cud. When I turned back to Red, her eyes were wet. She placed her hand on mine as comfort. I pulled it back, still too raw with memory. So she leaned over to hug me like she'd done in Little Rock, and I let her. Then, like hugs sometimes do, it was followed by a small peck of a kiss more comfort than caress, even if on the lips. Yet I knew nothing of such things, and even if I had, it wouldn't have mattered. Because it was Augusta Red I was finally kissing and I wanted it to last—to be the first kiss to end all kisses I'd been imagining since the long nights at the depot. So, when she started to lean away, I put my hand through her curls at the back of her head to hold her there, to make the kiss mean worlds more than she ever meant it to mean, to make it mean what *I* wanted it to mean.

She pulled back with the strangest look I'd ever seen.

Then she threw up.

WESTERN UNION

12 OCT 38 = 1012A

MRS. BELLE BENCHLEY
c/o SAN DIEGO ZOO
SAN DIEGO, CALIFORNIA

   E.T.A. SUNDAY. IF NO HITCHES.

                                    RJ

12

Across the Texas Panhandle

Hush-a-bye / Don't you cry.
"It's time I made a man outa you!"
"Woody Nickel, tell me what happened out there
*   and tell me now!"*
"Li'l one, who you talking to?"
Brown-apple eyes stare.
Rushing waters roar.
. . . As the air fills with bellowing, moaning, gi-
*   raffe-terror caterwauls, growing louder and*
*   LOUDER and . . .*

A thunderclap jerked me straight up in my wigwam's bed, hands over my ears, a gully-washing downpour splashing in the window. Heart pounding, I slammed the window shut, cussing Aunt Beulah, hurricane-whops, guilty Dust Bowl nightmares—and whatever the hell else might be causing my mixed-up dreaming.

The door flung wide and in stomped the Old Man. Sopping all over the floor, he kept the thunder going inside the stucco teepee until he'd gotten himself into dry skivvies and pants. As quick as the rain had started, it stopped, and the Old Man stepped back outside to eye the sky.

"Looks like it's over," he grumped. "The sky's clearing west."

Dawn was breaking, so I pulled on my boots and pants and followed. I wasn't looking at the sky, though. I was gazing three wigwams down.

The night before, after Red threw up, she'd dropped to the ground before I could think to say a thing, mumbling "I'm sorry" and rushing away. I'd called after her with the only words of comfort I could think of. "It's OK! The giraffes'll eat it." Upon hearing that fool thing fly out of my mouth, I went full speechless, then she was gone, swallowed up by the dark.

But now I was hearing the same upchuck sound. There was the green Packard, parked three wigwams down.

The Old Man looked where I was looking. "Is that her spewing?"

I nodded.

He marched straight over and banged on the wigwam door nearest the Packard, already talking. "Girlie, don't come near us if you've got the heaves. We don't have time to be sick."

The door swung wide and there stood a bald man with two sleepy towheaded boys peering out from behind him.

The Old Man scowled at them. "Who are you? Where's the girlie?"

A mousy woman appeared behind the boys.

"What did you call my wife!" the bald man snapped.

Red's head popped up from the other side of the Packard. Pushing her curls out of her face, she wiped at her lips . . . and, staring at those lips, I was back on top of the rig in the middle of our giraffe-surrounded kiss.

Then Red's head disappeared again.

To the sound of another heave, the wigwam door slammed shut, and the Old Man and I headed toward the other side of the Packard where Red was once again wiping her mouth, looking miserable. She had the same man's trench coat from Big Papa's draped around her, like she'd been sleeping in it, and the Packard's back door was open. One peek inside made it clear where she'd slept. Plus, being a poor farmboy who rarely changed flour-sack drawers much less my clothes, I hadn't noticed until that very moment she'd been wearing the same clothes this whole trip—the same trousers, the same white shirt, the same everything, down to her scuffed two-tone shoes—all of it now looking rumpled and dingy in the daylight. I was beginning to understand a few things I'd been too thick to grasp before.

"I must have eaten something spoiled back down the road," she muttered, cleaning puke from her curls. The Old Man cocked his head, staring at her left hand. She was wearing a thin gold band, which I hadn't noticed, either.

"You better hope so," the Old Man was saying. "Otherwise, it sounds like you're in the family way."

Red looked at him all but cross-eyed. "That's not possible, I *assure* you."

"Why not?" the Old Man said, nodding at her ring. "You're married, aren't ya?"

Grabbing a towel from inside the car to wipe her face, she snapped, "I don't see how that's any of your business, Mr. Jo—"

He cut her off. "Or maybe you're the Virgin Mary?"

She lowered the towel to gape at him. "What did you say?"

"Or you could be a floozy," he went on.

She was halfway to slapping him, and, heat rising up my neck, I suddenly wanted to punch him myself.

"You know what I mean," he said next, "maybe you got a fella along the way?"

He was trying to get a rise out of her, but I didn't know that, my brain still stuck on our kiss. I rocked back and forth on my bootheels, clenching and unclenching my fists. "Now, *wait* a—"

But the Old Man cut me off, too. "Shut up, boy."

"What kind of girl do you take me for!" Red said.

"You tell me," the Old Man said back. "Everybody knows a lady doesn't travel alone. So I guess you're no lady."

She gasped. "You've got a lot of nerve!"

Burning with righteous fury, I was barely resisting the urge to punch him. "Now—*wait just a*—"

"I said shut up, boy!" He leaned into Red's face. "Yeah, only a *floozy* would be on the road by herself."

With that, forgetting all about the Old Man's forbearance and my own lying treacheries, I threw that punch.

Of course, the Old Man knew it was coming. Red wasn't the only one he was egging on. Grabbing my fist in full swing, he bellowed at Red, "*Look* at this—you got this boy's head turned full *around*. You should be ashamed of yourself for that if nothing else!"

He let go and I stumbled back, landing on my shocked young ass at her feet.

Red's face turned so white I thought for sure she'd puke down on me. "I *told* you," she said, swallowing hard. "I'm on the road by myself because I'm taking photos for *Life* magazine. I *assure* you, Mr. Jones, it's normal vomit," she added, pulling the trench coat tight around her like it was her lost dignity.

"Have it your way," the Old Man said, "but you're done here."

She paused. "Are you saying I can't follow you?"

"I'm saying I'm onto you. I don't know what your game is, girlie, trailing us all this way and lying the whole time. But I want you to keep the hell away from the rig and the giraffes, as of now."

Red went stiff. "What do you mean?"

"I mean you're no *Life* magazine photographer."

I gawked at him, then back at Red.

"Of course I am!" she said.

I started to get up.

"Don't you move," the Old Man ordered, turning back to Red. "I truly cannot abide a liar. I'm going to ask you straight out. Are you with *Life* magazine or not? You'd better be able to prove it."

I recall the way Red gulped. Like she was gulping down something more wretched than puke. I was about to find out what.

She started talking fast. "OK, I'm not yet . . . but I will be, I *promise* you! I couldn't risk you not letting me follow, because I had to get the pictures first—and I *have* them! They are amazing! You have no idea!"

Then she remembered me.

Sitting there in the dirt, gazing up at Red gazing down at me, I took in her face and then pushed it far, far away.

"Get up," the Old Man was saying. "Let's go."

I pulled myself up, looking anywhere but at Red.

The Old Man and I needed to take care of the giraffes and get on the road. That's what we did without another word.

When we left the Wigwam Auto Court, Red was nowhere in sight and I was glad of it. Considering I'd gotten this far by lying my own deceiving self, though, I couldn't quite let her go. Instead, as I began moving through the gears, I looked over at the Old Man and said, "Maybe she *can* do all she's saying."

At that, the Old Man pulled out a folded piece of paper from his front pocket and handed it to me. "Read it, then I don't want to hear a thing more about her, you hear?" It was yesterday's telegram from his Boss Lady, Mrs. Benchley, with these words on it:

```
...LIFE MAGAZINE COVERING ARRIVAL.
SENDING PHOTOGRAPHER VIA AERO-
PLANE...
```

I read it. Then I read it again. As its full meaning sunk in, I was sore at everybody but the giraffes—sore at Red for everything all over again, sore at the Old Man for only now showing me the telegram, and sore at myself for being such a farmboy sap.

Fifty dead-silent miles passed before I could look at the Old Man. The only reason I did, even then, was the sign up ahead:

TEXAS STATE LINE—1 MILE

By the time we crossed the state line, I was so light-headed I must've been holding my breath the full mile. The sign greeting us as we passed into my home state was as big as all get-out, like you'd expect.

WELCOME TO THE LONE STAR STATE

Taking deep breaths, I began aiming to be into New Mexico before nightfall. I kept thinking that if we could make it across the Panhandle with nothing bad happening that I'd be fine—that *everything* would be fine—all the way to California, and all that thinking made me so fidgety that the Old Man noticed.

"Your twitching is giving me the motion sickness," he said. "Is it the girlie or being back in Texas?"

Corralling myself, I cut an eye his way. "Sorry I tried to sock you again."

"You telegraph your punch," was all he said, looking back at the road. "You should work on that."

As we got deeper into the Texas Panhandle, though, I started fidgeting again. Not until we passed the abandoned road that was causing it could I stop, yet soon as we did, I let out a sigh of relief so loud it got the Old Man's attention right back on me.

Eyeing me, he said, "Your home anywhere near here?"

I stiffened. There it was. He was going to make me lie to him, and we all knew what he thought of liars. Besides, I was still stinging bad from Red's lying load of crap myself. The last thing I wanted to do was serve the Old Man a new lying load of crap of my own—especially after I'd just tried to slug him again. *All I want is to get through Texas still driving the giraffes and on the Old Man's good side,* I kept thinking. *That's all I want.*

Like so many times before, though, the road forced us to forget everything but it. Traffic was downright heavy for the Texas Panhandle, something that *never* happened. Odder still, it came to a full stop right by a sign that said **SIDEWINDER WASH**. Two patrol cars were parked sideways across the concrete, and I was sure it was somehow my county sheriff come for me. But they were highway patrolmen. They were standing in the middle of the road and they were stopping all traffic, here in the middle of nowhere.

The Old Man leaned forward, studying the sign. "I saw this on the trip coming out. The highway got finished all the way West only last year, except for some bridges over bone-dry shallow washes like this one. It shouldn't be stalling us. The concrete goes in and out and on its way."

As we pulled close, one of the troopers adjusted his Stetson and headed to my window as the giraffes popped their heads out to investigate.

"What in the Sam Hill . . . where are you taking a pair of giraffes? There's nothing ahead but desert," he said.

"San Diego," the Old Man called over me. "We don't have the time to get stuck. Can you let us through?"

The highway patrolman, flipping back to john-the-law mode, rested his hands on his gun belt. "Sorry, sir, no can do. You need to get off the highway. It's closed until we see what's going to happen with the water in the wash."

We both stared at the dry gully. "What water?" the Old Man said.

"There's a thunderhead stalled about a hundred miles up north, raining like a son of a gun. Been gully-washing the place up there for over twenty-four hours now. They're already calling it a century storm," the patrolman answered.

"Did you say *a hundred miles north*?" the Old Man repeated.

"That's what I said, sir. With the topsoil gone after years of dusters, we don't know how all that gully-washing's going to break. So since we've got three washes like this in the next ten miles, we're shutting the highway for now."

"But if it's a hundred miles north it's not going to happen in the next minute, is it?" tried the Old Man.

"We won't know until we know, sir."

The Old Man looked around at all the dry dirt and the clear sky and tried again. "We *need* to keep the giraffes going. We're traveling fast as we can to keep 'em *alive*."

The trooper rested a hand on my windowsill. "Sir, I don't think you're comprehending the gravity of the situation. Either of you ever see a flash flood? They come out of nowhere in seconds and take trees and livestock and houses clean away. You can drown in two feet of water, swept away with it all."

The Old Man sized up the trooper. "That so."

The trooper sized up the Old Man right back. "That so."

"You ever see such a thing?" the Old Man said next.

The trooper leveled his gaze. "Never saw a duster before I found myself in one. This land has a clock all its own. Out here, where you got plants that bloom once a century and varmints that stop their hearts beating when they need a break from the sun, you don't believe in such things at the risk of your own neck," he said, glancing up at the giraffes. "Those are some valuable necks to risk." He turned to me. "Son, I'm sure you got the sense not to buck me, what with that prized cargo in your care. Just take these special animals on back up the highway a bit for the night. Back all the way to Muleshoe if you need to. Stay safe, until we know what's what."

Then he took a few steps back, placed both hands on his gun belt, and waited for us to obey.

My insides were pitching a fit. We were only minutes from getting out of Texas. So I wanted to buck him, all right, as if the rig could do any such thing. Because what nobody knew but me was that on back "a bit" was the abandoned road to my pa's farm.

The trooper wasn't budging, so, taking a lung-busting breath, I swerved the rig around cactus and tumbleweeds on the road's edge, half hoping the tires would sink in the dirt, then headed back by the place I thought I'd finally put behind me forever.

The Old Man was talking.

"What?" I said.

"You ever seen such a thing?"

I shook my head.

"I think that trooper's been in the sun too long," the Old Man grumbled. "We could've already been *past* it all by now. Besides, they're giraffes. No water coming down a shallow wash is going to drown a giraffe. Not in this rig and not on pavement. We could ford a stream with the rig on pavement." He paused to fume. "Well, we're not going all the way back to Muleshoe. I seem to recall some dump a mile back."

Perking up, I agreed.

So we pulled in to the next overnighter we saw, a run-down tourist court and campground so ratty we'd passed it the first time with barely a notice. It was already filled up with other stalled travelers. The Old Man stepped down from the rig anyway, pulling out his wallet as he went. Getting out to stretch my legs, I could see him inside the office, handing a scruffy man bill after bill from his billfold, until he was marching back to the rig.

"OK," he said, "we're here for the night, hiding as best we can behind that line of pitiful-looking mesquite trees out back. They're not even nibbling prospects for the darlings. It'll be hay for them tonight. But I'd rather not be here for the next couple of hours until it gets dark. Considering that stinky fella inside didn't blink taking my money, even more folks are sure to be piling in. I'm not going to let the darlings be the sideshow. Besides, we should keep a breeze going for them as long as we can. So let's go find that gas and grub store I remember a ways back. We can waste some time filling up and getting provisions for the night cheaper than from this scalper."

Well, that had me fidgeting once again so bad, there was no hiding it. Because I knew exactly where he wanted to go. It was the only gas station and supply store for miles around my pa's farm, and I was about to stop at it with a couple of giraffes.

"What's wrong?" the Old Man said, watching me squirm. "Did a scorpion crawl up your pant leg?"

We wasted a couple of minutes scorpion-searching. I even jumped out and dropped my pants. When we didn't find anything, the Old Man said, "All right, let's go."

Breaking out in a cold sweat, I pulled up my pants and got back behind the wheel.

The thing about destiny and fate and God-sized coincidences is that they fly in the face of being the master of your own life. When things are falling your way, it's an easy idea to give up. But when they're not . . . well, I'd already grappled with those feelings back in Tennessee and didn't much care to again. Besides, no eighteen-year-old is going to believe he's got no choice in what he does. So I told myself that whatever the thundering crap was going on, I still had choices—not yet knowing that having a choice can be worse than having none at all.

So we went. In a few miles, we passed the abandoned asphalt road I knew all too well, and I made sure not to even give it a glance. When I spied the gas station up ahead, though, I thought I might come right out of my skin. "Why don't we go down a little farther," I tried again. "I don't like the looks of this place."

"Looks fine to me," he said. "Pull in."

I stopped the rig by the station's gas pumps.

"I'll stay out here," I said a little too quick.

Eyeing me, he headed inside as the gas pumper came out, the same toothless goober in overalls who had been there since the world began.

I ducked my head.

"Mister, you got giraffes in there!" he crowed as he started pumping. "You truck for a circus? I love a good circus, but last I heard of one in the Panhandle was up in Amarillo back in the '20s. Now that's been a while!" He finished filling the tank and was wiping the windshield when he leaned around, ready to jaw on about giraffes and circuses. Then he squinted. At me.

"Hey . . ."

I ducked lower.

"Heyheyhey—ain't you Ned Nickel's boy? From out at Arcadia?"

The passenger door creaked open and the Old Man got in, clutching a bag of supplies. He barely had his butt in his seat when I pulled us out of there. As we passed the same deserted asphalt road I'd done such a good job of ignoring before, I couldn't help myself. This time, I cut an eye at the old sign:

ARCADIA →

"How far is it?" the Old Man asked.

"What?" I mumbled.

"Your pa wasn't a sharecropper—he was a homesteader, a nester, wasn't he? You had a place down that road." When I didn't answer, he cocked his head. "Pull over a second."

As I veered the rig onto the shoulder and stopped, I could tell the Old Man was waiting for me to explain, gazing at me as confused as I'd ever seen him. All he knew up to that point was that my ma and pa died and the dust took our farm. Now he'd just found out that we'd passed close by it twice without a word from me. My options, though, were paltry. I could swear he heard wrong and try to stick to it. God knows I could lie with the best of 'em. Considering how the day was already going, though, I knew that wouldn't last long. He'd soon be having me swear on my ma's grave or the like. And who could blame him? I'd shot a man for him and the giraffes, but I'd also been caught pocketing the fat cat's cash, and that very morning I'd tried to punch him again. If mercy there'd already been from the Old Man for whatever reasons, I kept poking it good. He'd forgiven me twice already. But like my ma used to say, only God can keep on forgiving. Maybe making good time for the giraffes' sake would be a good enough reason to keep me on, I told myself, no matter what he found out about me. Or maybe, like most such things, how he'd respond would be a mixture so personal that you'd have to know his whole Old Man story to even venture a guess. So I kept sitting there like a bump on a log. Or worse, a deer in the headlights.

"Look at me," he ordered, having enough of my stalling. "That true?"

I didn't know what else to do. Giving up, I nodded.

"How far?"

"Two miles," I mumbled, gazing down the old farm road. "Off the pavement." The land was so flat you could see the cotton gin at the end of the asphalt from where we sat.

More turned-around cars were passing by, honking and whistling and making an unholy racket at the sight of us. Riled by all the noise, the giraffes had stopped chewing their cud.

"Aw, dammit," the Old Man muttered, leaning out his window to look back at them. "We need to get off the highway, but hell if we're going back to that packed rattrap yet. Is there a decent tree anywhere up this road for the darlings?"

"Not hardly," was my half-ass reply.

The Old Man frowned. "Not hardly, meaning there is one?"

I nodded slow. "If it's still even there." I glanced at the blue sky. "The trooper also said it might start up raining . . ."

The Old Man paused long enough to make me look around at him. "If it's too much for your gut, say so." That's the way he put it—like any eighteen-year-old would admit he didn't have the stomach to visit his own homeplace. I stalled again, this time too long.

"Is there something you're not telling me?" he said, those bushy eyebrows as low as I'd ever seen them.

Now I'd done it. He thought I was hiding something. Because I was.

A car pulled to a stop behind us. It was the green Packard. Nothing would have surprised me right then, swear to God. Yet I recall wishing that, just once, Augusta Red would take a wrong damn turn. The Old Man saw her in his sideview and hit the roof, which at least got his mind off me.

"That bad penny keeps showing up!" he grumbled. "I'm getting pure tired of worrying about her. If she wants to follow all the way to San Diego, I should let her. She's in for a rude awakening."

I glanced at her in my mirror, sitting there in the idling Packard, no doubt trying to figure it all out—why we were stopped and how she was going to talk her way back into our good graces—without a clue what was waiting for her in San Diego.

Two more cars whizzed by, one of them honking loud and long. With a glance back at the giraffes, whose necks had begun to sway, the Old Man gestured toward the farm road. "Listen, boy, we need to get the darlings off the highway for a bit. This is going to have to do."

I didn't move. Instead I turned toward the Old Man and said the only thing I had left to say. "It's too much for my gut."

A truck passed so loud it made the giraffes bolt, rocking the whole rig. The Old Man jerked his head around to check on them, and when he turned back, something in his face had changed. He looked like a whole other person, who was now looking at *me* like I was a whole other person. I'd found the limit of his forbearance—the giraffes.

"Let's go," he ordered.

"But you said . . ."

"We go up the road or I let you out right here and I'll find that tree myself. You can catch a ride with your bad-penny girlfriend. Me and the giraffes have had enough of sitting here."

My gut now doing backflips, I backed us up and turned down the old road I thought I'd never travel again. I glanced in the mirror. The Packard turned in, too, and I recall thinking how Red was tailing me right back into my nightmare.

As we kept dodging tumbleweeds, I noticed the abandoned road's asphalt was turning crumbly and pointed it out to the Old Man, hoping I could still change his mind.

The Old Man studied the road, then studied me. "That's the tree straight ahead, right? We'll be fine that far." Then the Old Man spotted the dry gulch that had begun to wind alongside the road. "Hold on, is that a wash?"

I glanced at it. In the Panhandle, with the land being flatter than a pancake, people called any bump a hill and the slightest dip a ditch. That's what he was staring at—a dip I'd been looking at my whole life stretching away from the asphalt and back again. "That's only a ditch," I mumbled.

"You ever see water in it?"

I shook my head.

But he wanted a real answer. "Never?"

"Never."

"Pull over," he ordered.

We lurched to a stop. The Old Man got out, squinted, kicked at the dirt, and got back in the truck. "Oh, for sweet chrisesakes, what am I worrying about? It's not even much of a ditch. This dirt's so packed it's hardpan. I'll be damned if a flood's coming into that today."

So we moved on, the giraffes sniffing the air as if they could smell the rain up north. Soon we came to the asphalt's dead end. On the right was the abandoned cotton gin. On the left, this side of the ditch, was a tumbledown church surrounded by wooden homemade crosses, the graveyard full before its time. In front of it all, shading a place that needed no shade, was the leafy tree, a rangy but hardy bur oak, the only thing alive in miles of tumbleweeds and dead dirt, nourished by the pine-box-buried dead below its roots.

The Old Man was almost smiling at the green tree in the middle of so much brown. But I was looking straight ahead. At the top of the asphalt road's dead end was the weathered **ARCADIA** signpost. A dozen dirt paths splayed out in all directions from it toward deserted barns and shacks dotting the land as far as you could see. Still tacked to every inch of the post were name-carved chunks of dangling board pointing every which way, even down to the ground, telling the sorry tale of the whole place in one glance. And, there, on the bottom was our sign—**NICKEL**—still directing the way down the dirt path beyond the graveyard, like nothing had changed, as if you could find my ma waving you in to join us for supper.

The giraffes lurched the rig. Looking back, I caught the Old Man staring where I'd been staring—my pa's sign. He started to say something, but the rig lurched again. We poked our heads out to see what was going on. From where we were parked on the edge of the asphalt, the giraffes were already stretching to reach the tree. Just like in the mountains, it was making us lean.

"Inch over closer," the Old Man said, getting out. "The hardpan will take the rig."

I rolled the rig half-off the asphalt, its left side parked on the hard-packed dirt directly under the tree. As I crawled up to pop the top, the giraffes began making happy snorting sounds at the sight of the day's first leafy lunch. Feeling woozy, I had to look away, my eyes landing on my family's unmarked graves, which made me woozier still. I closed my eyes a second, then opened them to see Red snapping photos from the Packard's window where she'd stopped a ways back, and I had to look away from her, too.

Because I knew what was about to happen.

I edged my way to the ground and waited for it.

The Old Man was gazing down the dirt path to the left—where the carved **NICKEL** sign was pointing. Not a hundred yards along the ditch was my pa's dead dirt farm. You could see it all from the church. There was the leaning, ramshackle barn. There was Pa's broken-down Model T truck. But the Old Man wasn't looking at either of them. He was squinting at the charred stone fireplace standing like a tombstone over little more than a piece of scorched earth.

He looked back at me, again waiting for me to explain. I knew there was nothing I could tell him to keep the rest of the questions from coming, so I couldn't make myself say a thing.

With a last look back my way, the Old Man marched through the graveyard and crossed the ditch, heading straight for it all. There was nothing left for me to do but follow, head down, knowing the way by heart. By the time we passed the barn, I was so woozy I could barely walk. As the buzz of flies grew loud, I watched the Old Man stare down at the rifle and pistol rusting in the dirt, then move to the fireplace and the ash heap and the singed metal bedframe and the charred stove until there was nothing left to see.

Except the shallow grave beyond. The shallow, dug-up grave full of picked-clean broken bones.

I felt the ground start to spin. *The buzzards and coyotes found her anyway.*

The Old Man whirled around. "*Tell* me those are animal bones."

I was out of time.

"*BOY,*" he had to yell, "what happened here?"

I could refuse to tell him. But he would ditch me for sure, wondering who he and the giraffes had been spending their days with. I wouldn't be able to blame him a bit, since I didn't know my own self.

So I was down to my only choice, and then all the choices would be his. He'd either believe the story I told or he wouldn't. He'd either let me keep on to California or he'd leave me in the place I'd run from like my life depended on it, because I was sure it did. As I opened my mouth to answer, I looked behind me to drink in Boy and Girl.

That's when I saw the water.

I couldn't quite take it in. I'd spent my entire life *not* seeing water in that ditch. It was like a mirage, like I'd conjured it by saying it couldn't be. Yet there it was . . . a trickle. And then, faster than possible, more. Much more. The ditch *was* a wash, filling up with water from nowhere. The land with a clock of its own didn't care a whit about the entire life experience of a Dust Bowl boy. Stranded, invisible thunderstorms were gully-washing Panhandle dirt that couldn't hold squat. The trooper had been right.

A flash flood was on its way.

By then, the Old Man was standing slack-jawed beside me. We looked at each other and at the trickle that had already turned into a stream, snaking back along the ditch toward the church's graveyard oak and the giraffes peacefully nibbling at its leaves.

No flash flood can get as high as a giraffe, I told myself, trying to keep calm.

"What's happening!" Red was standing in the dirt path hollering our way. "Where's the water coming from? Where are the storm drains?"

"Where do you think you are, girlie, New York City?" the Old Man hollered back. "This is the *gotdam* High Plains edge of the *gotdam* screwy desert! There's not even supposed to be water much less a *gotdam* storm drain!" I watched him gesturing, throwing his hands this way and that, as if he could scare the whole absurd danger away with his own thundering.

Then I was suddenly in motion.

The thing about finding yourself in the impossible-turning-possible right under your feet, you aren't quite in control of all your faculties. I recall heading back toward the rig and the graveyard. I recall splashing through the ditch water, already ankle-deep, hearing the Old Man behind me. I recall upping my pace, gazing at the giraffes still nibbling at the leaves above graveyard crosses, as tall as tall could be. I recall yelling at Red to back the Packard down the paved road to where it veered away from the ditch—aiming to do the same for the rig and the giraffes as fast as I could.

But I have no memory of the rest of the way there. I found myself already behind the wheel, grinding the starter, stomping the clutch, and gunning it, doing the worst thing I could do. I was flooding the engine, panicking like only a Panhandle flatlander would in a flood. Because there was so much at stake in this wretched place I'd brought these towering creatures of God's pure Eden. Not the Old Man. *Me.* I was the reason we were here—I had driven the hurricane giraffes from a killer ocean straight into a desert flood, and not even floating giraffe nightmares had woke me up enough to stop me.

I ground the starter this side of ruin before I could make myself stop. The water was rising in the ditch, lapping at the graveyard's edge. Smelling the danger, the giraffes had started to stomp and shuffle. The rig was wobbling. *Drown in two feet of water,* that's what the trooper had said. My common sense told me that couldn't happen. Maybe it could to stupid eighteen-year-olds, but not to twelve-foot-tall giraffes. As I tumbled out of the cab to stare up at the giraffes, a hand clamped on to my arm and whirled me around.

"Are you *hearing* me!" It was the Old Man, his face flushed with new fear. "That's not *pavement,*" he said, pointing down to the hardpan under the left-side tires. "The rig's top-heavy! The water's not the danger—it's the *surge.* If rushing water jumps the wash and that hardpan goes soft and the giraffes panic—the rig *could* . . ." He couldn't make himself say the next word—*topple.*

"What do you want me to do!"

"Get the rig started and move it full back on the asphalt! It's not even two feet over!"

"The engine's flooded," I moaned. "What else can we do!"

He threw up his arms. "I don't know! I never drove giraffes into a sun-drenched flood before!"

"Close the top and windows?" I tried.

"What good would that do? You think this is an ark?"

"Get 'em out?"

"They won't come out—not in time!"

"Open the top and sides to the ground?"

"They'd be thrown out and injured trying to get to their feet, and that'd be the *end* of *her*."

"What else . . . what else?" I babbled. "There's got to be something!"

"The pavement's right *there*!" Throwing his entire weight against the rig like frustration alone could move it, the Old Man slammed his fist down on the hood. "Just get it *started*!"

Knowing it was too much too quick, I got in and tried anyway while the Old Man grabbed some onions and climbed up to coo his giraffe-speak, hoping to keep the giraffes from tipping the rig over themselves.

"C'mon-c'mon-c'mon," I begged, grinding the ignition, stopping again this side of draining the battery dead. Throwing my door wide, I dropped to the ground, fingers digging at the left tires' dirt. The hard-pan was still rock-hard and bone-dry. I told myself it would be enough to keep the giraffes upright, because it had to . . . because I had nothing else to tell myself . . . because the water in the wash was spilling over.

The flash flood had arrived.

I blinked and it jumped the ditch's edge, rushing across the graveyard.

I blinked again and it was sweeping away the crosses, spreading across the dirt like it was searching for us until it was pouring over my boots.

That quick, all the ways in the world to describe moving water were happening where I stood. And because water finds what it wants, it was also filling the crumbly asphalt behind us, flowing toward the paved road's bend away from the ditch where Red was supposed to be—but where, of course, she was not. She had stopped only halfway back and was snapping pictures. Now the water had found her, too.

The giraffes began kicking the rig, the water's roar drowning out the Old Man's coos. I got back behind the wheel, grinding the starter again until I heard the battery dying—and it was all I could do not to grind it dead for fear there'd be no reason not to if it didn't start now.

Instead I crawled up with the Old Man and the giraffes, telling myself over and over, *The water will stop . . . the water has to stop . . .*

But it wasn't stopping.

In fact, we could now see what the giraffes had already seen. The worst—the surge—was still coming. Debris-filled water, crap from one hundred miles away, was on us. Limbs and rocks and mud pinged the rig as the water rushed past. Then, like it fell from the sky, an entire uprooted tree appeared, bouncing off one side of the wash and back to the other, until the surge raised it up and slammed its trunk into the church, collapsing the whole rickety thing. Before we could do a thing but holler, the trunk and half the church swirled around the graveyard oak and slammed into the left side of the rig, making the Old Man lose his fedora and almost take a header into the water before I grabbed him back.

With the water forced to flow around the tree trunk jammed now against the rig, no longer was the worry how deep or how fast, but how heavy. Just like the Old Man feared, we felt the hardpan under the rig's left tires begin to go soft.

The rig began to lean.

Scrambling to the other side, we started calling Boy and Girl to come our way. But the giraffes, caught again at the mercy of roiling water, were panicking. As the rig leaned nearer and nearer to the point of no return, from the bottom of their long throats came the bellowing, blood-boiling, giraffe-terror caterwaul.

Down the wet asphalt road, Red stood on the Packard's hood watching. I gazed at her, longing for the next moment never to come, wishing I could stop time.

But time doesn't stop.

The next moment came . . . and, with it, came the sound of a revving engine.

Driving straight for us was the Packard.

Speeding faster and faster, the Packard began to hydroplane along the wet pavement, water spewing up on both sides until it was right on us, seconds from crashing into the rig. Then Red jerked the wheel left, plunging the Packard between the surge and the rig, and as the water grabbed it, she jerked the wheel right, slamming that big Packard broadside against the leaning rig, wedging us tight against the surge.

By the time I'd grasped what had happened, Red had wiggled out her window and climbed up to us, as the worst of the flash flood hit. For the eternal seconds that followed, we couldn't do a thing but watch and wonder if the rig would stay tall, if the Packard's heft would hold, if the giraffes would stay on their feet—trying not to think about how dirt is dirt and mud is mud and rivers create mountains by rushing and roaring.

Then, quick as it came, the water was gone.

As the debris settled and the flood sounds disappeared, we sat there. The silence was crushing. Yet still we sat. We stared at the bright sunny day. We stared at the giraffes as Girl sniffed and Boy sneezed. We stared at the bent graveyard oak and the crosses strewn helter-skelter as far as we could see. The feeling was like the hurricane shock in my memory, coming down off the moment, waiting for my mind to catch up with my body. When mine did, I saw I had grabbed hold of Red, and the Old Man had grabbed us both. We untangled, easing a few inches apart, all staring down at the wedged Packard, watching water leaking from every door.

Only then must Red have remembered what she'd left behind.

With a strangled cry, she tumbled down, wrenched open the Packard's door, and pulled out her soaked camera bag—its cameras, film rolls, and plates all tumbling into the mud—and then sank in the mud beside them and covered her face with her hands.

I eased to the ground. I didn't know that the Packard had more chance of coming back from the dead than waterlogged film or fancy cameras. But when I sloshed over, picked up some of her film and heard the water squishing inside them, I knew it was bad. And I knew enough to leave her alone.

The Old Man, now on the ground, too, was staring back up at the giraffes, their heads hanging over the snarl of wood and metal and mud below. The rig was still leaning but the giraffes were calm, as if they knew the worst of the lions were gone.

I went down on my haunches and dug into the mud near one of the rig's tires. The hardpan was dry not three inches down. If we could get the rig started and the giraffes upright, I was pretty sure we could pull out.

Meanwhile, the Old Man had unjammed Girl's trapdoor to check her bloodied bandage. When he saw that the wound had only been scraped, he gently placed his hand over the bandage and left it there a moment, heaving a great sigh.

Next, I opened the truck hood to check the motor. When we saw it was dry, I placed a hand on the engine and heaved a sigh of my own.

Red, though, was still sitting by the Packard, staring at her soaked cameras and film. As the Old Man went looking for his fedora, I moved near, hoping she'd look up. When she didn't, I stepped around her. Eyeing the blown tires and what looked like a bent axle, I lifted the Packard's crushed hood as far as I could. The motor was drenched. I tried starting it anyway, but it wouldn't even click over. The truck, being flooded with gas, not water, would start if I waited long enough, but the Packard was done.

So, taking the keys, I looked in the car for a suitcase. All I found, though, was the man's trench coat she'd been wearing, the pockets stuffed with hairbrush, toothbrush, a wrapped bar of soap—and her notepad. I opened it. She'd written most of it with a fountain pen, and the water had turned it all into smeared lines of blue. The only thing left readable was what she'd written in pencil long ago—her list on the last page:

THINGS I'M DOING BEFORE I DIE
-Meet:
    - Margaret Bourke-White
    - Amelia Earhart
    - Eleanor Roosevelt
    - Belle Benchley
- ~~Touch a giraffe~~
- See the world, starting with Africa
- Speak French
- ~~Learn to drive~~
- Have a daughter
- See my photos in Life magazine
- Pay Woody back

I stared hard at what had been added—*me*—and what was crossed out, feeling the beating of her broken heart at Big Papa's and knowing the list now for what it truly was. If I'd had a pencil I'd have crossed out the last one without hesitating. Slipping it back into the trench coat's pocket, I folded the coat and turned toward Red, who was still sitting in the mud. I started to say something to her. Yet what was there to say? I placed the trench coat in the cab and gazed around for the Old Man. About two hundred feet down the wash, he'd found his hat stuck to a wooden cross and was whopping it against his pant leg to dry.

After that, for a good long while, we went around gathering broken boards to put under the tires for traction, gathering far more than we'd need to give both the rig and Red more time. As the afternoon sun began to set, I got up the courage to try the truck's ignition. On the first try, I pumped the pedal too hard. It gurgled and died. I let off. When I tried again, it gurgled once, twice, and then roared to life. Back in my right mind, I popped it quick into neutral and revved it a few minutes to make sure it wouldn't die on us again. The Old Man actually smiled.

Before we could go anywhere, though, we had to right the rig, moving it away from both the Packard and the wedged tree trunk, which meant getting the giraffes to help. The Old Man, onions in hand, crawled up the right side and asked the giraffes to come get them. When the giraffes did, I called down for Red to move. But I might as well have been talking to the mud. So, with one eye on Red, and the other on the Old Man and the giraffes, I put the big rig into gear, screeching metal against metal away from the Packard, and metal against wood away from the uprooted tree trunk, until the rig was free and all four tires were back on the asphalt.

With that, the Old Man patted and stroked the giraffes, now shuffling upright and looking mighty happy about it. Then he climbed down to inspect the damage. The rig was bunged up and battered, with a crack full down the tree-trunk-smashed side. But it would get down the road.

"We've got to go," he said, cutting an eye at Red.

With the engine idling, I climbed out and went over to Red, who still had yet to move. I shoved all the ruined cameras and film back in the soggy bag, stuffed it with the folded-up trench coat in the truck cab, and went back to Red, grabbing her hand and closing the Packard keys inside it. "We have to go. We've got the giraffes," I said as tender as I could muster. "We'll get you somebody to haul the Packard somewhere, if you want. Right now, though, you've got to come with us."

She let me help her to her feet. Keys clenched in her fist, she paused for a moment to take a last look at the drowned, smashed Packard, then she tossed the keys in the open window and climbed into the truck.

As we drove back down the asphalt, the Old Man and I eyed the flood's havoc. By the time we got back to the highway, though, there was nothing to see. The flash flood had followed the wash away from the road, no doubt toward the washes of the closed highways west.

Red, though, still silent, had looked nowhere but straight ahead until we eased onto the highway, headed back to the run-down tourist court. Then she said, "Mr. Jones, would you be kind enough to drop me at the next city's train station?"

With a look as close to gentle as I'd ever expect to see on Mr. Riley Jones, the Old Man said yes.

As the sun set, we pulled into the auto court, surely looking like a pack of drowned rats with a couple of hitchhiking giraffes. None of us were in the mood to make new friends, so the Old Man decided it best to close the road Pullman's windows before making our way to the scraggly line of mesquite trees, hoping the giraffes were tired enough to oblige—and they were.

Every type of vehicle you could think of was parked around the little circular drive of the auto court—motorcycles, trailers, fancy sedans, long-haul trucks. Most everyone had already turned in early, considering we'd all been forced into this overnight stay. The only people we ended up seeing were the ones camping near the edge of the property where we'd be parking—some Okie families, their old Model T Fords packed high with belongings and family members, huddled together around their makeshift campfires.

The Old Man had hopped out at the office to throw some more money at the owner for dry towels and blankets. By the time he returned, arms full, I had parked us as good as I could behind the scraggly trees and was opening the top for the giraffes. Hopping down to grab the blankets, I turned to hand one to Red.

She was gone.

For the rest of the evening, under the cover of dark, we tended to the giraffes. The trapdoors, warped because of the flood, took some elbow grease to open and even more to get closed again. But the tending in between was pure pleasure, especially hearing Girl kick at the Old Man as he tried replacing the bloodied bandage with a clean one. "Get me some more *onions*, will ya!" he grumbled. "We got to end this day, swear to God."

After the giraffes were chewing their cud like it was any other day, we decided we'd leave the top open through the night for the giraffes, and the Old Man went to talk to the manager about the Packard before we took turns sleeping in the truck cab for the night. As I watched him pass the first of the makeshift campfires, I recognized the Okies from last night's Wigwam Auto Court, and I noticed what the Old Man didn't. Sitting with them, wrapped in a homemade quilt, was Red. The granny had wrapped Red in one of their blankets, strung a clothesline, and hung up her clothes to dry and was sitting by her at the fire. I grabbed up her soggy camera bag and folded-up trench coat, and headed that way.

The granny waved me over. "You OK, dearie?"

I nodded. "Yes, ma'am."

With a smile, the granny left us alone as I eased down beside Red, placing the camera bag and coat at her feet. She didn't touch either. She sat there staring at the campfire, her face chalk white like she'd upchucked again. After all we'd been through, I was surprised I wasn't puking myself.

"The Old Man is talking to the manager about the Packard," I told her. "We'll be leaving before dawn. We'll take you where you want."

When she didn't respond, I fumbled around for more words. I wanted to say what neither the Old Man nor I knew how to say. I wanted to thank her for plowing her Packard into the flood to save the giraffes and our own hides. I wanted to say I was sorry it meant the loss of all her film and the dreams wrapped around them.

Instead I heard myself asking what my clueless young self most wanted to know. After everything she'd risked to get this far—the lies she'd told, the customs she'd flouted, the husband she disobeyed, the laws she'd stretched—I blurted, "Why did you do it?"

She shot me a glare that could've turned fire into ice. "How could you *ask* that?"

This time I knew to keep my mouth shut.

She sighed, her eyes wandering back to the giraffes. "May I go see them?"

The Old Man was already asleep and snoring in the cab, but I wouldn't have cared if he wasn't. I stood up and so did she, the quilt wrapped tight around her. When we got to the rig, ready to climb up, she dropped the quilt, even though she had nothing on but her unmentionables, and just like her trousers, this was my first time to see such a sight in real life. I never saw my own ma in her bra holding up her massive bosoms, much less wearing only her drawers. But now, seeing Red not caring a whit about herself, it was all I could do to not pull her to me—not for what I was seeing, but for reasons I had no words for, ones that had more to do with how *she* must be feeling. That was another first for me.

I helped her climb up to the top again, grabbing a towel for her to sit on. Girl came over close, happy to see her, sniffing at her unmentionables, then Boy came up to do the same, but easier, sweeter, snuffling at her hair.

The next moment I have studied in my mind through the years, and the feeling from it has always remained the same. Red leaned over them both, her wild curls falling over her face, letting the giraffes nibble at them as if she was cherishing each little snuffle and nip from the two. It seemed like a thank-you she was offering the giraffes . . . and a goodbye.

I felt it so strong that I even said so at the time. "We'll see you tomorrow. This is not goodbye or anything."

She didn't answer. Instead she reached out to touch Boy and Girl one more time and then climbed down, wrapped the quilt tight around her, and went back to the Okies' fire.

The granny sat down beside her, offering her something in a tin cup to sip. As Red began to talk to the old woman, I was too far away to hear, but I knew what she was saying. I watched as she told the women about the whole day, nodding toward the rig. I watched as the ma with the baby in her arms joined them. I watched as Red coughed, then opened her quilt and took the granny's hand, placing it over her heart exactly as she had done with mine. I watched as the granny moved her hand from Red's heart to her stomach. Then I saw Red glance quickly toward the baby.

And I knew what the Old Man had guessed about Red was true.

From the looks of it, now so did she.

13

Into New Mexico

Our plan was to leave in the dark right before dawn to avoid the other stalled travelers, deciding we'd tend the giraffes down the road. But when we were ready, there was no sign of Red.

"I can't find her . . . ," I whispered to the Old Man as I ran back to the rig, trying not to wake anyone else at the place. "The Okie granny told me she disappeared as soon as her clothes got dry by the fire. Her camera bag's still over there, though. There's no place else to look."

"Maybe she's changed her mind or decided to wait for the Packard," the Old Man whispered back, climbing into the passenger seat. "Or maybe she's gotten new help that isn't us. Wouldn't blame her, would you? My guess is she doesn't want to be found. Probably best to leave her be." He pointed back at the rig. "Close up the top."

"We can't just *leave*."

He propped an elbow on the open window and sighed down at me. "All I know is she's not here and we've got to go, boy. We've got the darlings."

So quietly I closed the top, the giraffes barely noticing in the dark. Climbing down to the ground, I took one last full-circle look around the auto court. Then I got behind the wheel and took us off slow, glancing back every few seconds until we were long out of sight, not wanting to believe this *was* goodbye. Things didn't feel right, I recall thinking, as if yesterday wasn't finished with us even with a new dawn on its way. There was only one thing I knew for certain. However much I looked, there'd be no green Packard in my sideview mirror ever again.

As dawn broke, we drove over the three low wash places in the highway pavement, exactly like the trooper described. We took all three in first gear, the flood debris far worse than at Pa's farm. A crew had already cleared the highway lanes, but there was still some water in all of them. So, pavement or not, it didn't do much for my nerves as we splashed through them. Crossing each wash, the rig wobbled and I had to force it straight. The last one was the worst. The giraffes, their heads still inside their windows, were bouncing around more than usual, banging against the sides, the whole battered rig shaking bad.

"Should we stop?" I asked the Old Man.

He shook his head. "Let's get past all this."

We crossed the state line, once and for all out of Texas. Within another mile, we were already into the scrubby hills of New Mexico that wanted to be full-out desert but weren't quite ready to do it yet. The sun was almost up. We needed to be looking for a place to pull over and take care of the giraffes. But I was only half seeing anything at all, still thinking about Red. And the flood. And the farm. I guess the Old Man was doing the same, because he looked at me and said, "I think I need to hear what happened out at your pa's farm."

My eyes landed on a passing Joshua tree, sprouting arms toward heaven. I was out of time again, and this time there'd be no flash flood to save me.

Ever since running toward Cuz's, I'd been rehearsing a good lie, fearing that what happened would find me no matter where I went. Yet, after the flash flood, I wanted more than ever to stay with the giraffes, to see them safe to California even more than getting my own hide there.

I didn't know which would keep me driving—the lie or the truth. You can carry around a heavy load only for so long, though, before you've got to set it down, and that goes double if you're only eighteen.

So I took a deep breath, squeezed the wheel tight, and told the Old Man the truth.

"We were about to put my ma in the ground," I began. "Only a burial, me and Pa, at the church graveyard by my dead baby sister . . ."

We didn't have money for a real funeral, I tell him, and there was nobody to come anyway, the rest of Arcadia either dead from dust lung themselves or lit out along with the ginner, who was the closest thing to a preacher the tiny church had. As Ma got sicker, I kept thinking we'd pack up and go, too, but we never did. We had nothing left. Less than nothing. So all we could do for Ma was swaddle her as best we could, Pa pulling wood off the barn to make her a pine box. With our truck broke down again, we were planning to hitch our old mare to the wagon and pull Ma to the graveyard. We'd set Ma and her pine box in the wagon, put on our best Sunday go-to-meeting clothes, and then Pa had gone to get the mare.

When he doesn't come back, I go looking for him and I find him on the far side of the barn, standing over the mare. She was the last animal we still had, the pigs and chickens all eaten when the last crop failed and the cow dying in the last dust storm. I figure she's dead, too.

As I come closer, though, I see the mare's brown-apple eyes move to stare up at me. I feel sick, because I know she *is* dead, but she just doesn't know it yet.

Then, and only then, do I see the rifle in Pa's fist. He is holding it out to me, ordering me to put the mare out of its misery, because I should learn to accept death as part of living, because I should start acting like a man. He is saying it in a way he knows I will obey or wish I had.

But I don't take it. I gaze back at the horse's wide, scared, suffering eyes and I know I should. And I know I can't. I don't have it in me.

Because that old mare is the only animal I've known for my entire miserable life—since I first pulled breath. Since I was big enough to jabber at her and tend her and plow behind her. God help me, I know, at that moment, she is the only living thing I have ever loved besides my ma. I cannot be the one to take away her life, not when her life takes in my whole life. Not even if it is an "act of mercy," because *mercy* holds no meaning for me. It is all I can do not to yell this at Pa, even though I know he does not abide such disrespect, and I have felt the whip of his belt at even the hint of it. This time, though, I don't care about his belt. I don't care about his hollering. I just stand there. So, he shoves the rifle into my ribs until I take it.

"Time you carried the load around here!" he says. I notice a thing in his eyes that isn't ire or panic or grief but something cold beyond them all, like his small, pitiful heart has shriveled and died with Ma, and I was about to find out what was left.

"Do it!" he yells.

I still can't.

Marching back to the house, he returns with his Great War pistol, loading it as he comes. "*Do* it!" He slaps the barrel shut and, brandishing the revolver, marches straight at me. "Do it *now!*"

But it's not the pistol that scares me most. It is the wild, gone-wrong look in those eyes that is sending a shiver into my bones. So I point the rifle in my hands at him, sure that he will lower his pistol at the sight. Yet he does not, as if I'm pointing a toy at him, as if I'd never shoot. He is still marching toward me, pistol still up, aiming those crazy eyes at me so devil-fierce I forget to breathe.

"It's just an animal!" he is hollering as he gets close enough to slap my rifle barrel away. "And you ain't no boy in knickers no more. It's time I made a man outa you!" Pistol to my neck, he is shoving me with his free hand, pushing my rifle barrel toward the mare's head, her scared eyes looking straight at me. "*Do* it! Or as God is my witness, I'll do it to *you* . . . you lily-livered, yellow-bellied worthless excuse for a son!"

And I do it. The mare jumps with the power of the shell hitting her head and goes limp, her blood splattering my face and my boots, her dead eyes still staring my way. I begin to blubber like a baby, feeling the puke rising, hating my pa for making me shoot my horse, and hating God Almighty if mercy be a thing so hateful.

Pa is talking, his pistol bowed only slightly. I think he will surely say what will save us both. That it's time to give up. Time to go to Californy like everybody else. Time to live instead of die.

Instead, his voice oddly quivering, he says what I cannot abide. "All right then, let's get it hauled into the barn. We'll skin it, sell the hide, and dry what meat there is to eat. That should keep us going till we get a new crop in the ground. Rain's coming, you can feel it."

With that, I swivel the rifle back his way, because I know he is never going to leave. He's going to stay and breathe dirt until his lungs fill up like Ma's and my baby sister's, and he thinks he can make me do the same.

I move in front of the mare, and I am now the one hollering. "I'm not skinning her and I'm not eating her—and *you're* not either—I'd sooner shoot *you* dead!"

Gaping at me, his spineless son talking back for the first time, Pa lowers his gun. I know if I lower mine, if I pull myself back from the fury that's possessed me, this will stop. I will feel the sting of the back of his hand and it will be over. We will go on with our misery, since there's no one to put us out of it. Because that is what we do. Because quitting the misery takes the kind of heart and soul neither of us has ever had.

But I do not lower my rifle.

Instead I keep spitting out words I know he can't abide. "If that made me a man, I should put you out of *your* misery!" I holler, now the one brandishing a firearm. "If that made me a man, then *you're* not a man or you'd have put Ma out of *her* misery!" I holler on, now the one spewing, seething. "If that made me a man, then *you're* not a man or you'd put *yourself* out of *my* misery—"

The crazed thing in Pa's eyes disappears. I watch it go, my fury tamping down as it flickers. In its place, though, something dead passes through his eyes that I shudder to see even now. He raises his pistol again, training it on me. I see his finger moving. He is squeezing the trigger. I scramble backward, rifle up, gaping at that trigger finger, not believing what I am seeing. My life slows to nothing but staring down my rifle barrel at my pa's trigger finger. For all of my flamed-up fury talk, I am sure I could not shoot my pa—nor could I believe he'd shoot me. Yet there we are, two dead-inside beings holding guns on each other.

Until I realize something new . . . I'm seventeen. I don't have to stay even if he does.

I can leave. I *will* leave.

Time to live instead of die—without him.

I take a step back and then another, lowering the rifle to turn and just walk away, when I hear the click of his pistol's hammer.

Whirling around in time to see the pistol blast, I feel my cheek burn, grazed by his pistol's slug. Then hearing my own rifle fire, I see his shoulder pop back, hit by my rifle's bullet—

—and there we stand, two dead-inside beings who have shot each other.

I find my feet if not my balance, and I throw down the rifle.

Pa, standing like he doesn't even feel my bullet in his shoulder, lowers his pistol, too.

Then he shoves it under his chin.

And shoots.

I reel back, spattered now in both bloods, both bodies at my feet, my lungs forgetting how to breathe. As new puke mingles with the blood on my boots, my mind is stuttering with only one thought—

I made my pa kill himself.

Until another thought comes home to roost—

I could have been the one doing the killing. If he hadn't done it, my young fury would have. I'd have shot my pa for making me shoot that mare. I'd have shot him for letting the dust take my ma and my baby sister. I'd have shot him dead if he'd tried to make me stay. I knew it to be true beyond true.

". . . I could have been the one," I finished telling the Old Man, squeezing the wheel even tighter.

For a long moment, I couldn't go on, until I heard the Old Man speaking in the same timbre he used for the giraffes.

"Son," he murmured, and I tensed at that word, "you need to tell me it all."

Sinking back into my own skin, I braced to tell the rest. "The dust was so bad that static electricity was always in the air like black magic," I told him. "Any spark could set it off, sometimes flaming right in front of us, silver-blue flames we'd have to stomp out before they set ablaze. So the shooting must have started the fire."

I paused, parsing my words, because it wasn't *our* gunplay that started the fire, it was mine. I had staggered back from the puke and the blood, and I started firing at the house. I emptied the rifle, and I picked up Pa's pistol and did the same, clicking long past empty, screaming myself hoarse as the silver-blue sparks began flying like the hell I felt I was in . . . until one took to the wood and burst into true flames, taking my homeplace back to the devil. I did not tell him that. I lied by omission, as church people call such sins, desperate for the Old Man to not know my own dust-fever crazy.

Instead I said, "The place was matchsticks. There was no saving it and nothing worth saving." So I'd sunk to the ground, I told him, watching my house burn until the flames had taken it full. When it was over, when I found my feet again, I pulled more wood off the side of the barn and built another pine box. I put Pa in by Ma, hitched myself to that wagon, and pulled it to the churchyard to bury them both by my baby sister. After I finished, I sat there letting evening turn into morning, then stumbled back to my ma's dead garden to dig up her Mason jar of coins from its hiding place, before I lit out.

But not before digging another grave, as best I could, for the mare where she lay. "Because nobody was going to eat her—*nobody*," I mumbled, "not even the buzzards and the coyotes."

And they found her anyway.

Then I was done, but it was not done with me. The reliving of it had fired up my leftover fury so bad, I thought *I* might burst into flames right there behind the wheel. I knew I had to tamp it down, but I wasn't quite doing it. Feeling a tug from the rig, I slowed, focusing hard on the gears, on my driving, on anything but the burning inside, until I found the courage to glance at the Old Man.

He'd pushed his fedora back on his head and was sitting silently, eyes on the road, arm propped on his open window. When he spoke, it was barely above a mumble itself.

"People look at you peculiar if you talk about the feeling you got for animals, saying animals have no souls, no sense of good or bad, no value up next to humans," he said. "I don't know about that. Sometimes I think animals are the ones who should be saying such things about us." He shook his head. "Animals can tear your heart out. They can maim you. They can kill you dead on instinct alone and saunter into the next minute like it was nothing. But at least you know the ground rules with animals. You can count the cost of breaking the rules. You never know with people. Even the good can hurt you bad, and the bad, well, they're going to hurt you but good." He dropped his arm from the window to rub his gnarled hand. "It's why I keep choosing animals. Even if it kills me. One day, it probably will."

He stopped talking. Yet I kept listening. I thought for sure he was going to tell me about that hand. Or why Percival Bowles had called him what he called him. Or both. I yearned for it, for anything to help free me from myself. But he propped his arm back on the window and went the kind of silent I knew I was supposed to leave alone. Instead I squeezed the wheel near to bending and asked what I feared most. "You going to call the sheriff?"

He cut his eyes back at me. "Now why would I do that! We got giraffes to get to San Diego."

"But I made my pa shoot himself."

"You did no such thing. He did it to himself."

"But I shot him. I could've killed him."

"You winged him."

"What?"

"That's what you said back in Tennessee," the Old Man answered. "'I winged him,' you said. 'If I'd wanted to kill him, he'd be dead.'" As if that was enough for the Old Man, he looked back at the road and said, "That's your first story, but it doesn't have to be your only story. That's up to you."

What he was going to say next I'll never know, because right then the rig wobbled so bad it felt like the tires lifted off the road. Then it did it again, this time knocking us both off our seats. We both jerked around to look back at the road Pullman at the same time.

"There!" the Old Man pointed. "Pull in."

Up ahead was a dusty, weathered sign.

COOTER'S
GAS. WATER. FOOD.
DESERT ANIMALS COME SEE

The place was set back from the road and we had too much on our minds to give it a once-over. As we got close, though, it started looking bad. Except for the water cistern on stilts, the building was ramshackle, its roof already half caved in. I rolled the rig toward the gas pumps. They were both broken and had been for a long time, so I pulled on past them and stopped.

"I don't like the looks of this," the Old Man said. "Let's check the giraffes and get going."

The giraffes were pushing their heads out their windows and pulling them right back in, making noises I'd never heard before. It sounded like one of them was going to kick a hole in the trapdoor, it was rattling so hard.

Hustling back to open the warped trapdoors, I glanced toward the far side of the tumbledown building and froze at what I saw.

A bear. A mountain lion. A raccoon. Rattlesnakes.

All in cages.

In the glaring red-dirt sun . . .

"Howdy, strangers!" came a high-pitched voice from beyond the cages. Out stepped the shortest, hairiest, most googly-eyed, leathery geezer I'd ever seen—one eye milky and one not exactly looking our way. "Welcome to Cooter's," he said, picking up a stick and poking the animals.

"Stop that!" the Old Man yelled.

"Just trying to get 'em to put on a show for you," the milky-eyed coot said, still poking. "You're the first customers I've had in a coon's age."

"You're *killing* them like this," he said, waving at the cages set out in the sun.

"Oh yeah? What do you know?"

"I work at a real zoo!" the Old Man spit out. Then, with a glance back at the rig, he sucked in his fury and pulled out his wallet. "We only need to check on our giraffes. We'll pay you for the trouble and be on our way."

"Hot diggity-*dang*, I was right!" the man crowed, rushing over to grab the money from the Old Man. "When I saw you drive in, I said to myself, 'Cooter, that truck's got a load of giraffes.' But I wanted to make sure you saw them too before I said anything. Didn't want you to think I was crazy. Hold on."

He disappeared inside the building.

Remembering the rest of my Little Rock nightmare, I scrambled for the truck's gunrack as out came the man with a sawed-off double-barreled shotgun.

"No, no, leave those be," said the man, aiming both barrels at me. Skittering over, he grabbed both the Old Man's rifle and shotgun off the rack and flung them deep into the scrub, the shotgun skidding all but to the road.

"What the—what is *wrong* with you?" the Old Man roared. "I just gave you money! You want more? What the hell do you want?"

"Whaddya think I want, mister real zoo," he snapped. "I want them giraffes. Still, I'm a reasonable man. You got two. I'll take one. That way we'll both be happy."

The Old Man gave the desert coot a look that should have sent him straight to hell. "I'm not giving you a giraffe! You're not going to shoot us. You'd be hanged and you know it."

Then Cooter smiled a smile that still can make me cringe now almost ninety years later. Because the next thing he said was this: "True enough. But nobody's going to hang me for shooting critters, and a giraffe's a critter. So if you don't choose, mister, I'll shoot one and feed it to the critters I already got." At that, the crazy geezer banged on the rig until both giraffes popped their heads out again, so he could point the sawed-off shotgun at them. *"Boom!"* he shouted. "Boom, *boom!"*

The Old Man was ready to tear the man's head off, and the old coot knew it, swiveling the gun his way. "Perhaps this moment calls for a demonstration," he said. He backed up to the row of cages and shot the caged raccoon dead, the shotgun pellets splattering guts all over the cage.

"Got-*dam!"* howled the Old Man.

The coot narrowed his gaze. "You know, I've been mighty profane myself in this life, but I don't think I'm tolerating any blasphemy in my establishment since God's being good to ol' Cooter today. So you watch your language. That goes double for your young'un toting that devil mark on his neck," he said, waving the gun at my birthmark. "I'll be taking one of your critters now. I'll give you a moment to decide."

"Now *wait*—" pleaded the Old Man.

"Mister, I can do this all day. Nothing to me." The coot opened a cage holding nothing but jackrabbits, grabbed one by the scruff, and dropped it in the top of the mountain lion's cage. At that, my leftover fury burst into full flame. Because I knew what we were about to hear. A jackrabbit's scream sounds exactly like a human baby if the kill isn't quick. I'd become a crack shot by the time I was ten to avoid ever hearing it again. As the mountain lion ate the rabbit alive, its entrails hanging from the cougar's teeth, the jackrabbit's screams filled the air. The shrieks went on and on and *on*, and the part of me still holding together after telling my story came undone. I lunged for the sawed-off coot and found myself instead facedown in the dirt. The Old Man had tripped me before the coot blew me full of buckshot. Under the Old Man's glare, I pulled myself up, the air filled now only with Cooter's cackling.

Until we heard the sound of a muffled wretch.

"Don't *shoot* . . . ," came a whimper from inside the rig.

"That a *woman*?" The coot whirled around. "You got a woman in there, too? Let's see!"

I yanked open Boy's warped trapdoor. There was Red, huddled under the giraffe's legs.

The Old Man groaned.

Cooter cackled louder. "You made the woman ride in the back! I always wanted to do that!"

As Red crawled out, batting straw off her face, a leering Cooter sidled up close. "Now that you've got her trained, maybe we can make a bargain for her *and* the giraffe," he said, circling his gun muzzle around her breast.

Red pushed the barrel away and tried moving toward us, but he poked her to a halt and went right back to pawing her with that gun.

Watching that and not being able to do a damn thing to stop it, my leftover fury flamed even higher, as high as the morning I shot Pa. A moment before, with the jackrabbit screaming me clean out of my mind, the coot could have gone right ahead and shot me and I wouldn't have cared a lick since I'd already have pounded his sawed-off ass to a mighty-fulfilling pulp. Now, standing there watching him grope Red with that gun, I was back to thinking the same daft thing. It must have been written all over my face, because suddenly the Old Man was standing close and talking loud.

"We've got to tell him, boy—it's the right thing to do," he boomed, giving me the eye. Turning to the coot, he pointed at Girl. "This one's hurt."

Cooter squinted, pointing the gun at the Old Man. "I don't want no hurt giraffe. Let me see."

As Red rushed out of reach, the Old Man yanked open Girl's trapdoor, then stepped back.

"You get back, too, the other way," the coot said to me, and waited until I did.

The trapdoor was shoulder-high for the Old Man and me. The coot's head, though, was right at the opening, Girl's shuffling front legs only inches away.

"See it?" the Old Man coaxed Cooter. "On the back leg. You got to look close."

Gun still cocked at the Old Man, Cooter stuck his nose into the opening exactly like Earl had done the night of the yahoos. His face was almost in the Girl's range when he pulled his head back out. "Hold on." He turned his good eye to the Old Man. "Does it kick? You'd like that, wouldn't ya?"

Smooth as buttermilk, the Old Man said, "Animals don't kick with their front legs. Everybody knows that."

"Oh yeah," said Cooter, leaning back in.

The Old Man and I held our breaths, waiting for him to get close enough for the Girl to kick and save us.

The coot did.

Girl, though, did not. Watching us wild-eyed from above, she stomped and shuffled and snorted and swayed.

But she didn't kick.

Cooter pulled his head out. "*Waaiit* a second. Why'd you tell me that? You doing the ol' switcheroo? If you're telling me this one's hurt, maybe it's the other that's hurt. Or you could be telling me this one's hurt, so I'll think it's the other'n, when it's really this one's that hurt and the other one that's not. Ha! Nice try." He waggled the shotgun my way. "Let me see the other'n."

The Old Man could barely look at me. We both knew the easy way out was gone. Boy had never kicked anybody.

It was then that I knew this was going to end bad. I could not let that happen. Not after hurricanes and mountains and bears and fat cats and flash floods—let alone reliving the worst day of my life. Cooter leaned into Boy's open trapdoor, this time aiming the gun up at Boy, and even seeing that did not stop me. Because when you're eighteen, burning with furies from within, there is a moment when you cannot count the cost a second more.

I lunged for the gun.

Hovering over the shrimp, one hand on the barrel and the other clenched around the old coot's grip, my young self was cocksure I could yank it free.

Yet I wasn't quite doing it.

The shriveled peewee didn't weigh a hundred pounds, and he was fighting like Lucifer himself had pitched in. I was still shoulder-high to the trapdoor. Cooter's head was still leaning in the opening, and the gun muzzle was still aimed up at Boy. I glanced back for help, but the Old Man had run for one of his flung firearms, and I could barely see Red out of the corner of my eye. The rig began rocking fierce, and it was all

I could do to hold the coot's gun steady. The giraffes were panicking, banging the crates, kicking the cracked wood, rearing up the sides . . . until up from Boy's throat came the beginnings of the horrible giraffe-terror caterwaul.

Hearing that, Red did the one thing she should never have done. She lunged for the gun, too.

Grabbing the only place left to grab, she clamped onto the ends of the short barrels and pulled, trying to help get them off Boy. The three of us were smashed against the rocking rig, pulling, yanking, twisting, until, from one second to the next, the gun wasn't pointing at Boy—it was pointing at Red. The coot had somehow swiveled and used our own strength against us to jam the sawed-off muzzle into Red's ribs.

All the blood in my body rushed to my head, because I knew that with one jerk of his trigger finger, Red was gone. No one comes back from a gut wound like that. Not back then. Not in the middle of nowhere. Even if she tried to let go and run, the gun would go off before she could get out of its way. Red's slow, brutal death would be the cost I thought I could no longer count.

Her gaze jerked to meet mine. She knew.

Right then, though—as if the giraffes knew, too—both Boy and Girl reared up at the very same time, banging the traveling crates so hard that Red lost her footing, a shriek knocked out of her as she fell.

And at the sound of Red's own caterwaul, Boy did the one thing we never thought he'd do.

The blessed beast kicked.

His hoof thwacked Cooter's skull with a sick, hollow pop.

The gun went off, spraying the air.

The geezer crumpled to the dirt, blood oozing from an ear, and I stood stunned over him, both hands still clenching the gun.

The Old Man careened into view, rifle up. "That was a fool stunt— *both* of ya!" he wheezed. "The giraffe saved *both* your worthless hides!"

Watching Red get to her feet, I shuddered at what I'd almost done. Then I looked down at Cooter, who was very, very still.

"Is he dead?" I mumbled.

The Old Man pried the coot's gun from my grip. "Don't know. Don't care," he said.

That's when we heard the water. The sawed-off shotgun's blast had hit the cistern up on stilts, and water was spewing from the puncture holes. The Old Man scowled up at the emptying water tank without a bit of surprise.

"Are you calling the sheriff?" I asked for the second time that day.

The Old Man turned full around to gape at me, like I was the one with the sun-fried brain. "You want to hang around to make friends with the local law enforcement?" he bellowed. "What about the darlings? You even thinking about them in this civic duty? What do you think they'll do with the Boy? It won't matter a good *gotdam* he saved us from a nutcase. He's still an animal and that sumbitch's still something they'd call human. We'd be stalled here for weeks. Even if they don't order him put down, that could kill the both of them all by itself. No! *Nossir!* They're going to San Diego. Right. Damn. *Now.*" He set both firearms on the truck's hood, reached in the window for his fedora, and stalked off.

"Where're you going?" I called after him.

"One more thing needs doing!"

Shoving the fedora on his head, he headed out to retrieve his shotgun from the roadside scrub, then marched past us to the animals and opened every cage, one by one. The jackrabbits and the bear ran for the hills without looking back. Even the rattlesnakes went slithering off. The mountain lion, sated with fresh rabbit, still licking the blood on his whiskers, was a different story. It watched the Old Man with cold eyes, studying him as it leaped to the ground from his cage. The Old Man fired his shotgun in the air, and the mountain lion slipped into the scrub.

"Let's go," he ordered, coming our way.

I kept staring at the coot's sprawled body. "What if the mountain lion comes back?"

"I say let him," the Old Man snapped, then must have thought better of it, because he grabbed Cooter by a leg and began to pull. I grabbed the other. The Old Man, though, wasn't heading to the building. We dragged him to the bear cage, stuffed him in by the bear's half-full water bucket, and slammed it shut.

"Now *move*, before I throw the raccoon's carcass in there with him," the Old Man said, marching toward the rig. "If he's alive, he can get his sorry self out. If he's dead, he'll rot in one piece. He doesn't deserve to be an animal's supper."

The giraffes were still stomping and snorting. The Old Man put the guns back on the truck cab's rack, then flung the coot's sawed-off shotgun deep into the scrub, and we all got in. With Red sitting between us, we headed toward the highway as the spray from the water tank's holes turned the dirt into its own muddy lake. Straight ahead was the **DESERT ANIMALS COME SEE** sign. I aimed the rig right at it, flattened it into kindling, then turned us onto the road west.

For two miles, the only sound in the cab was me repeating a soft "Sorry" as I kept brushing up against Red's trouser legs to change gears. I felt like I was moving through molasses, my body having yet to catch up with my brain. I wasn't alone. Red's hands started to shake, and she began to sniffle, then the dam busted wide.

"Stop," she begged. "Stop, please—"

Up ahead was a dusty rest area of stone picnic tables overlooking a small outcropping. Pulling in quick, I hustled out of her way. Red stumbled over to a table, and she didn't just cry, she sobbed. The Old Man averted his gaze, but I couldn't take my eyes away until, running her hands through her hair, she stopped, and I felt a reckoning of my own coming on strong.

We tried giving the giraffes water. They wouldn't drink. Climbing up, the Old Man opened the top and began cooing his giraffe-speak, stroking the giraffes as best he could, so I climbed up and started stroking, too. Leaning over the giraffes, though, I had to work to keep my own balance, feeling wobbly inside and out. I was waiting for the sky to fall, for the sirens to sound, for something to happen as big as the feelings still rolling through me after dodging the crazy coot's worst.

"Is it over?" I mumbled, looking back down the road. "Is that the end of it?"

"You think you always get to know the end of a story?" the Old Man said. His voice faltered, giving away his own Old Man shakes. "Most times you're lucky if you get *your* ending. If this is our ending, it's a *gotdam* happy one."

As we kept on stroking and cooing, the giraffes began believing all was safe again. Girl stopped her stomping, and Boy, snorting a massive sigh, slowly laid himself down to rest.

So the Old Man and I eased to the ground, sat down by Red, and did the same.

Associated Press Wire Service

... ST. LOUIS POST-DISPATCH
SAN FRANCISCO BULLETIN
SAN JOSE MERCURY HERALD
SYRACUSE POST STANDARD
ST. CHARLES BANNER WEEKLY
ST. JOSEPH NEWS-PRESS
BUFFALO COURIER EXPRESS
LAFAYETTE MESSENGER
WATERBURY REPUBLICAN
PROVIDENCE JOURNAL
LOS ANGELES AUTONEWS
FT. DODGE MESSENGER
KANSAS CITY STAR
BALTIMORE AMERICAN
GRAND RAPIDS PRESS
SACRAMENTO UNION
HARTFORD COURANT
EL CENTRO POST
WASHINGTON STAR
DETROIT NEWS
AMARILLO GLOBE ...

CROSS-COUNTRY GIRAFFES OFFER JOY, RELIEF

AP Special—Oct. 14

Two British East African giraffes have been offering coveted relief from the daily ominous reports of looming war in Europe, as they continue their travels by special truck to the San Diego Zoo, delighting townspeople and travelers. Blazing a trail of nationwide publicity for the young zoo out west, their odyssey has caught the weary public's fancy like no other story in years . . .

14

To Arizona

There are times in life when everything shifts so fiercely you can only hold on, the Dust Bowls and graveyards and hurricanes all forging the You, and the fury, left behind. There are other times, though, when you feel a shift down deep in your bones. Quiet, clean, pure. As we moved on that morning, shaken but alive, I felt that kind of bone-quiet shift. The fury that had ahold of me ever since shooting my pa was gone. In its grip, I thought I could rescue us. Instead I'd almost killed us. It had taken the gentlest of giraffes to save us from the fiercest of lions, and somehow Boy had melted away my fury in the doing. In the days ahead, I'd have reason to ponder whether it was gone for good. But by the time we left the outcropping's rest stop, I'd felt free of the fury long enough to know I wanted to stay that way.

A few miles down the highway, we felt the morning's heat begin to rise. Then the land went off the caprock like a shot and we found ourselves in low red desert land. There was nothing as far as I could see—a different kind of nothing than the Panhandle, a bigger, wider, redder nothing.

At the first sign of a real gas station and store, I turned in. As the gas pumper came out, already geehawing at the giraffes, the Old Man said to Red, "The road turns south for a few hours before heading back west to Phoenix, bypassing El Paso, but we can detour over to that train station for you, Mrs. . . ." He paused, not having a name to go with his politeness, then glanced at the bell-shaped public telephone sign hanging over the store's front door. "Looks like they got a phone if you need it," he added, climbing out and going inside.

Red, though, didn't move, having yet to look up, much less talk.

As I opened the door to get out, I looked at her sitting there so silent in the middle of the bench seat. A piece of hay was still stuck in one of her curls. I almost reached to pluck it. Instead I said, "I'm going to check the rig." I fumbled for my next words. I wanted to say I was glad Cooter didn't shoot her. I wanted to say how sorry I was for almost getting us both shot dead. I wanted to say more—so, so much more, something that would matter. Like always, I said something else. Staring at the hay in her hair, I heard myself say, "What were you doing inside the rig?"

At that, she looked up, all right. "You think I did it on *purpose*?" She sighed. "Last night the nice Oklahoma family offered to let me sleep in their Model T, but I knew I wasn't going to do any sleeping. So, I sat by the fire until my clothes dried and kept sitting there for I don't know how long. I watched you and the rig through the shadows, and when I saw you take your turn sleeping in the truck cab, I watched Mr. Jones. The longer I watched, the more I wanted to be near the giraffes one last time . . . by *myself*, you know? So, when Mr. Jones went off to relieve himself in the bushes, I climbed up to the open top and dropped into Boy's side like I'd done in the mountains and I stroked his pelt for the sweetest time."

Pausing, she sighed again. "I was only going to stay a minute, but then Boy *lay down*—I couldn't believe it. So, I eased into the corner in all that padding to watch him drape his wonderful neck over his back and close his big eyes. When I felt my own eyes close, I let them. I knew I'd wake up when you tended them before we left. But you took off!" she said, throwing up her hands. "I didn't even hear you close the top! Next thing I know, Boy is up on his feet and we're bumping down the highway. And I couldn't open the trapdoor from the inside like I had before, because of the flood." She took a breath. "I even started yelling and banging, until I saw I was upsetting Boy. It was all I could do to stay out of his way." She took another breath. "Then you turned into that *maniac's* place . . . !"

Stifling a gasp, she had to stop. "I . . . only wanted to say a proper goodbye to them," she added softly, then shut down again, hand to her heart. I almost reached over and took her other hand, I *so* wanted to touch her. But I got out and slowly closed the door.

The Old Man appeared with his arms full with sacks of apples, onions, bread, and a salami big enough to feed a work crew. He handed me the bread and salami and climbed up to feed the rest to the giraffes.

"They OK?" I asked.

"They always are, God love 'em. Despite everything we've done to them," he said, offering up the delights.

As I set the bread and salami in the cab's open window and climbed up to help, Red went into the store. Within seconds, though, she was back in the truck.

Jumping down, I went over to her window. I still had an apple in my hand, so I shined it up on my shirt and offered it to her. She barely noticed.

"What happened?" I finally said.

"I tried calling collect, but he didn't accept my call."

I shoved the apple in my pocket. "I thought you said he was a good man."

"He is," she mumbled. "He just needs time to remember it."

As I pulled us onto the road, a highway patrol car whizzed by—back the way we came. I cut an eye at the Old Man, who was gazing, untroubled, in his mirror at the giraffes sniffing the wind.

For the rest of that day traveling down the length of New Mexico, we barely saw another soul. One Okie family came up behind us, their old Model T stuffed to the gills. The tin lizzie even had a basket strapped to its running board with a goat in it. As they passed, they didn't seem a bit surprised at seeing giraffes. Why would they? They were already riding on dreams. They waved, all wearing big Californy-bound smiles. Even the goat. It made me melancholy, but nowhere near as bad as the furniture peppering the roadside like a relic trail of the Hard Times. We started seeing such things—a chifforobe, a broken rocker, a lamp, and the like—Dust Bowlers' worldly goods either fallen off or dumped when they got too much to carry. It would be that way for the rest of the trip.

At each stop with a phone booth, Red went in to call again. I figured she was trying to remind the guy he was a good enough man to wire her ticket money to El Paso. Each time, though, she returned looking more and more unhappy, and I didn't have the gumption to pry. Yet we were getting closer and closer to El Paso. Soon we were on the outskirts of Las Cruces where the Old Man said there would be a Y in the road, one way leading south to El Paso, the other way headed west to Phoenix and California.

When we spotted the Y, the Old Man motioned me to pull over before we detoured, and as I got out to check the giraffes, Red grabbed my sleeve.

"Woody," she whispered, "I need to tell you something."

I didn't like the sound of that.

"I never made those calls," she confessed, wringing her hands. "I tried to. But I *couldn't* talk to him yet . . . and I *still* can't." Dropping her

hands into her lap, she stared straight at me. "So now I've got to convince Mr. Jones to drop me at the Phoenix station tomorrow instead.
Do you think he'll agree? I'll call Lionel on the way. Cross my heart.
I only need a little more time . . ." Her face said she wasn't lying this
time, but who was I to say?

The Old Man slipped back into the truck cab and turned to Red.
"The detour to the El Paso train station is that way. We'll be there in
less than an hour."

She breathed in, raised her chin, and said, "Mr. Jones, I'd be much
obliged to you if—"

"She needs to take the train from Phoenix, and there's no detour
for that, right?" I cut in, giving him the eye.

The Old Man had been busting a gut to be nice, so I was praying
he wasn't going to launch into his whole "not abiding a liar" spiel, if he
suspected such.

Instead he said, "I'll pay for your ticket from here. Least I can do."

Neither of us was expecting that.

"That's very kind, Mr. Jones," she said quick. "I'm certain, though,
the money will be waiting at Phoenix. Truly."

I was giving the Old Man the eye so hard I wouldn't have been
surprised if my eyeball had popped right out. But he nodded, giving
me the eye right back.

So we took the Y toward Phoenix, heading into the deep desert.
We still weren't talking much, except for my apologies every time I
sideswiped Red's leg shifting gears. Red, though, didn't seem to notice,
a far-off look taking over her eyes that I'd seen before. It was the same
look she had at the quarantine station, sitting alone in the Packard and
staring toward its front gate. Before everything.

At dusk, we pulled into a place the Old Man had chosen on the
way out. It was not an auto court. It was a "motel," a newfangled place
that wasn't much more than a strip of rooms with a space to park your
car between each room, but they were fronted by a little oasis with real

palm trees, and we had the place to ourselves. Parking the rig on the desert dirt a few yards past the end, we took the room right by it, and the Old Man sprang for the room next to us for Red. Thanking him for his kindness again, she went in, glancing back at me with those hazel eyes as she closed the door.

The Old Man went to tend the giraffes, but I kept standing there until I heard him calling me to help. By the time I'd blinked away Red's glance and caught up to him, he was already checking the Girl's bandaged splint. He looked so relieved I figured she had to be doing OK, but I wasn't sure until he stepped up the rig's ladder to the open top to pat the Girl, who was already contentedly chewing her cud. Then, without another word, he came down and headed to the motel room, leaving me the first shift, as usual, with the giraffes. Instead of climbing up the rig, though, I found myself at Red's door, heart pounding, feeling a pining I couldn't quite name, much less handle. Every tingling, yearning muscle of my eighteen-year-old body wished for something I didn't have the courage to ask for.

Not until I heard the sound of coyote howls in the hills was I able to move—and it was back to the giraffes.

Heart in my throat, I climbed up the rig. Breathing deep to calm down, I eased onto the cross plank between the darlings while they went about their cud chewing, taking passing whiffs at the sudden cool change in the air with nightfall as well as every inch of me. I must have smelled like part of the desert. Maybe that night, I was. The moon wasn't out yet and the sky was something to see. The dark of the desert you'd think would be total on a moonless night. It isn't. Everything is shades. Maybe because there is so much of nothing between you and the horizon, the stars shine brighter and bounce off what is there more. The stars were so clear I decided to look around for Red's giraffe constellation since we were close to the Mexican sky where it was supposed to be easiest to spy, and I felt less heavy just in the looking.

In a few minutes, the coyotes seemed to up their howls across the desert, and their echoes made it sound like they were lurking right on the other side of the dark. So when I noticed movement below, I readied for a wild thing.

"Woody?"

Red.

The howls got louder and she climbed up double time.

With a quick pat for Girl, Red sat down on the cross plank by me, her legs dangling over Boy's side, and Boy brought his mammoth head around to snuffle her. She rested her head on his muzzle, her arms reaching full around his neck, like she was giving him the thanks he deserved after saving her, saving us all, from the desert coot. She stayed that way for as long as Boy let her, which was a mighty long time.

When she let go, I started babbling. "Nice out here, huh? The desert smells real different, seems to me. The giraffes sure love it. Where they come from must be more like this than anything else so far, I was thinking. Or maybe they know they're about to get out of this rig. They're sure due, all right . . ."

Red touched my arm to stop my chattering, and then turned to straddle the cross plank facing me. The giraffes moved their big selves even closer, their pelts warm against our legs, so Red stretched her arms out to touch both of them at the same time. As her touch turned to strokes, she said, as gentle as a whisper, "Do you know what I like best about photographs?"

"What?" I said.

"They stop time." Then she smiled that sad, tight-lipped smile I hoped never to see again.

She was starting her goodbyes.

The thing about knowing you're doing something for the last time is that it takes the joy right out of it. I've done lots of things for the last time in my long life, but I didn't know it. This time I'd know it. The goodbyes were near . . . tomorrow from Red, the next day from the giraffes. I could barely abide the thought. I watched her there, in the glow of the motel sign, her arms wide, her curls wild, her trousers and shirt rumpled to ruin. She looked exactly like she should for someone who'd gotten stuck in a moving rig with a pair of giraffes and who'd lost everything but the clothes on her back. Yet she looked like a picture to me.

We sat like that a long time and no time at all, the way that such things can be both, the only sounds the snuffling of giraffes to a chorus of coyote howls. The air was getting chillier. I knew she was about to say it was time to go back to her room. That's the way it always had been. Instead she said in a voice so soft, so weary, I barely recognized it, "Woody, could I stay? I'd rather not be alone tonight . . . and you and Boy and Girl are . . ."

When she couldn't finish the thought, I finished it for her by asking the giraffes to allow me to close the top. They agreed. So, easing onto the ladder, I motioned Red to climb down and I closed it. Then, as if it were the most natural thing in the world, I dropped down, took Red's hand, and led her right back up. As Boy and Girl popped out their windows to surround us, I was still holding her hand as we lay back on the flat top. Side by side. Eyes to the sky. Full up once more with yearning, I admit I wanted to touch much more than her hand, although I had no experience in doing any such thing. The Old Man had been calling me a boy all this time, and rightly so, because even at eighteen I was still one in all the ways that mattered, like this one. Yet even if I could do as my whole body was telling me to do—to lean over and try the kiss again, offering up my longing in the slightest hope she felt the same—I knew it was no good. It was not what she was asking for. How I knew, I didn't know, still surprised by any notion that was the least bit selfless. Even though every last inch of me was on sweet fire, I wasn't going to hazard a thing that would not keep her there beside me that night. So, when she shivered and I slowly put my arm around her, she let me. I pulled her close. After all we'd been through that day, that was enough.

That was glory. There we lay safely, together, under a sky bursting with shimmering stars, surrounded by the giraffes, the night quieting us so full that we both fell into a deep and abiding sleep.

When I opened my eyes, a half moon was far above, the giraffes had pulled in their own heads, and Red was no longer beside me. I gazed a moment where she'd gone and back to where she'd been, committing the night to full memory—the chill of the desert air that pulled us near, the feel of her thick curls against my arm, the snuffling giraffes surrounding us, and the position of the stars above us—savoring every little thing, exactly as I'd done at the depot after first laying eyes on both her and the giraffes. This far down the road, though, the giraffes seemed to be the only part of the whole world left unchanged.

I got up and opened the top again. The giraffes raised their heads to meet me, Girl laying hers for a fine moment in my lap, just like back in the cornfield. Then I stretched out again on the plank between them, their breath warming me in the cool air, and went back to searching for a constellation in the shape of a giraffe, filling an empty space in the sky.

The next day through the desert was what the Old Man would surely have dreamed every day on that trip would've been, the passage through such wide-open space a surprise in its pleasure. In the deep desert back then, if something went wrong—a rod blowing in your engine, a radiator overheating, even a flat tire—there was a whole lot of nothing you could die in. Even if we were lucky enough to have somebody come along to help, they wouldn't have room in their vehicle for a couple of giraffes. So we should have been all weep and worry about making it through such a dangerous space without a hitch.

But it lulled, that day. No people to speak of, no trouble to bear.

It was a day of no lions.

We had left an hour before dawn again. By the time we were watching the moon set on one side of us and the sun rise on the other, we'd all fallen into a moving bit of peace. I'd felt a sliver of that peaceful feeling after we'd made it through the mountains. This time, though, it was long and lingering and soul-soothing deep. It seems now like the closest thing to praying I'd ever done. When I'd lived a little longer and heard people talking about such things, calling it by spiritual names, I'd want to scoff but couldn't. In the years ahead, through the War and beyond, it was this quiet day moving through the unmoving land with Boy and Girl and the Old Man and Red that I returned to when I needed it most. Like the jolting joy of giraffes amid the traveling bird wave, its peace passed any understanding, any attempt at words. You only get a few of those in your whole life if you're lucky, and some only get one. If that be true, this was my one. When I remember it, I'm not eighteen in the memory. I am whatever age its comfort came to me, be it 33 or 103, and I am driving us all, through the timeless red desert, headed nowhere in particular, just someplace good. Together.

We stopped twice that morning, once this side of Silver City and once more near Globe, long enough to water the giraffes and stretch our legs. We did it without more than two words between us, the lull was so deep. Not even the train track in the distance trailing us all day wrecked my lull. It should have shook up all sorts of fretful thoughts of murdered bums and raggedy boys and fat-cat pocket fortunes, not to mention the twenty-dollar gold piece still tarnishing the inside of my pants pocket. But it didn't. Despite those things happening to the Dust Bowl boy I was only days before, I didn't feel much like that boy anymore.

Red had finally called Mr. Big Reporter at Silver City. "Lionel . . . ," I heard her say as she closed the phone booth door. I didn't eavesdrop. Didn't have to. I could make out what was happening by watching her from a ways off. It was the same high-volume talk I'd heard them have back in New Jersey, if now one-sided, until she got to the news that'd shut any man right up. Then she leaned on the back of the wooden phone booth, and it seemed neither of them said a thing for a long time.

She came back to the rig saying he promised to wire the money to Phoenix for her train ticket before the end of the day. There was no reason not to trust the louse since she hadn't called him until that moment. But of course, I still didn't. As we pulled up to Phoenix's big fancy train station, peaceful was the last thing I was feeling. This was only a drop-off, the Old Man had made plain. We still had several hours of daylight left and the Old Man wanted to keep going, San Diego less than a day away, so I stopped the rig right in front of the station and hopped out to make way for her. The Old Man showed his manners by getting out, too.

Red stepped down and collected herself.

"Thank you, Mr. Jones," she said, straightening her clothes, hair, spine.

"Goodbye, Mrs. . . . ," he said back, stumbling again over what to call her. He also seemed to be struggling to say something else. In my memory, I like to think it a thank-you of some sort or even an apology, but it was probably neither. Whatever it was, it didn't come. All he could muster was a tip of that fedora. With a glance my way, he then turned to deal with the crowd already ogling the giraffes, who were already happily ogling them back.

I walked her to the big arrivals and departures board outside the station doors. That day's streamliner, the only East Coast–connecting train, had already left, and there wouldn't be another until the same time tomorrow. The telegraph office where any wired money would be waiting was inside the station, though, and the Old Man was already waving me back.

I started to walk inside with her anyway.

She stopped me. "No, Woody, you're not going in with me."

"But you've got to stay all night and you've got no cash," I said. "What if the money's not there before the wire place closes? What if you need to take Mr. Jones up on his offer?"

"It will be," she said, "and I won't. Don't worry."

Then she touched her stomach, and that made me ask what I had no business asking. "What're you going to do?"

"I'll wait," she said.

"No, I mean . . ." I didn't know how to say what I meant. "Your heart."

Flashes of something sad and tough passed over her face. "Ah, Stretch, I made that up. Never trust a woman who wants to meet your giraffe." She was lying. I saw it plain. Just when she was leaving, I could tell. "I'm still going to be the next Margaret Bourke-White. You wait and see," she went on, offering up that tiny tight-lipped smile.

Reaching into my pocket, I pulled out the twenty-dollar gold piece and held it out.

"*No.*" She shook her head so hard her curls bounced.

Grabbing her hand, I pushed the twenty-dollar piece into it, and I took my time being sure it was square in her palm and a longer time to let go as her fingers closed around it.

There was that tight-lipped smile again. "I don't know when I can pay you back."

"Don't want it back," I said. "Not mine. Not Mr. Jones's, either."

"Oh," she said, as if she figured I'd snitched it. Which I deserved.

Squeezing the coin tight, she started to turn toward the depot but stopped and gazed past me at the giraffes in a way that was more drinking-in than last-sight . . . and then did the same at me.

"We had us an adventure, didn't we, Woody Nickel?" she said.

Before I could answer, she hugged me hard and kissed me square on the lips long enough for me to place my hand on the back of her head, lace my fingers through her soft curls, and kiss her like a full-grown man, exactly as I'd always imagined. Then, stepping back, that far-off look taking ahold of her face once more, she said, "I'd do it again, you know."

Whether she was talking about stealing the Packard to follow us, lying to keep it up, dashing her magazine dreams to save the giraffes, or kissing me with a kiss to end all dreamed-upon kisses—it didn't matter. The goodbye had come.

By the other side of Phoenix, the Old Man was talking. *A lot.* I needed desert silence again, bad. He was having none of it. The man was a blasted magpie. The closer we got to San Diego the happier he got and the moonier I got. It was only hours away now. I half thought he was going to make us keep driving, but there was a mountain pass to get through and we'd be hitting it at night. Considering our less-than-dandy mountain experience, I was mighty glad to hear we'd be waiting until morning. Of course, that meant more Old Man chatter. Maybe because we were driving through desert sand, he couldn't talk enough about how lush the zoo was, how anything'd grow there. How the founder, a man he called Dr. Harry, walked all over the grounds poking the soil with the tip of his cane and dropping seeds he'd brought back from around the world, and how, abracadabra, the place was now brimming with greenery from all over. To hear him tell it, the Okies got it right when it came to San Diego. Any other time, listening to all he was saying, I'd be salivating for it, too. Now all I was hearing was another goodbye. So, I spent his magpie-chattering miles staring at either the road or the giraffes, ignoring his paradise talk altogether, holding on hard to the paradise I still had.

Somewhere along that stretch, we heard a train whistle. The train track was trailing the highway off in the distance. The tooting grew louder and louder until a freight train was passing with railriders hanging out the empty boxcars all down the way. It wasn't until the long train was clean out of sight that I realized the Old Man had stopped talking. He was studying me with that right-through-me stare I thought we'd left back in Texas. He opened his mouth to comment, like he always did after one of those looks, and I tensed. Instead he hung his elbow out the open window, cocked that cruddy fedora back, and said, "Did I ever tell you my life story?"

Well. That perked me up. Maybe I was finally going to find out about that hand of his and even about what Percival T. Bowles had called him. If so, I could already tell he was going to take his sweet time getting to it.

But what did we have but time?

He was born, he said, back East "to a wastrel" who had thirteen sons by his first two wives, and six more with his third one, the Old Man's ma. By the time he was in knickers, his pa had up and died and his ma was supporting the whole kit and caboodle with a boarding-house. That, he said, was when things got "interesting."

"It was around the corner from the Barnum & Bailey winter grounds," the Old Man went on. "Soon as I could, I started sneaking in to see the elephants and the lions and tigers and monkeys."

"That when you started at the abattoir?" I cut in.

"You gonna let me talk here?" he said, and went right on. "After a while, the kinkers and the roustabouts got tired of running me out, so I got chummy with the funambulists, you know—the tightrope walkers. They got me rope walking with them."

"You're kidding," I said.

He chortled, popping the side of the cab's door. "I got so good, they said they'd take me with them when the circuit began. I would've done it, too, if one of my older brothers hadn't hauled me back home before they hit the road. By the time I was about your age, though, I caught the consumption. The only cure for a lunger back then was to head out West. So I did. It was the making of me, I tell you what. I highly rec-ommend it. For four years, I rode as a cowboy, punching cattle on the Colorado plains, riding night herd, living on sowbelly and sourdough biscuit, and I got my cure. I never got the elephants and the lions and tigers out of my system, though. Next circus I saw, I signed on."

"As a ropewalker?"

"Naah. They didn't have any of that. They weren't Barnum & Bailey. Not even close. No, I only signed on to be around the animals. Before long, though, I was in a fistfight every day with some razorback who was mistreating an animal. So, before I ended up dead or in jail, I headed to San Diego and their new zoo, where I'd heard that the animals get treated better than the people. I hope to die there, I do." He smiled so nice I hardly recognized him. "Not before we get these darlings into its gates, though. Right, boy?"

It was a kindness the Old Man was performing, getting my mind back where it belonged, for the giraffes as well as my own moony self. It was working, maybe a little too well. We were pulling into Gila Bend, which was nothing much more than a little oasis with a well and a fountain in sight of the mountains, when I realized he hadn't told me what I wanted to know.

"Wait, what about your . . ." I pointed to his gnarled hand. "Was it lion taming?"

"Well, now, that's a whole other story."

That's when we saw the elephant and the dog.

A short, wiry man wearing a straw hat was just walking his dog and his elephant along the road.

I was sure it was a mirage, but the Old Man saw it, too.

The wiry man gave the dog a boost on top of the elephant, and the elephant wound his trunk back to touch the dog. Everybody was smiling, including the dog. *Especially* the dog. If ever I was speechless on this trip, and there were many such times, that was one of them.

The Old Man guffawed. "I know that galoot! That's Maroney. He's got himself a little traveling show, going around giving rides to the children on that Asian elephant of his. I heard he came out to the desert towns for the winter."

"But . . . ," I mumbled, "where'd he get an elephant?"

"Same place anybody gets an elephant," was how the Old Man answered. Like that explained it all. "Don't worry. Those animals are having a good time and being treated dandy."

"How can you tell?" I said.

As we watched the elephant put its trunk in the fountain to spray the wiry man and the dog, the Old Man smiled at me as if that was better than any answer he could give. Shaking his head, he glanced back at the giraffes and said, "There's no explaining the world, boy. How you come into it. Where you find yourself. Or who your friends turn out to be—be you man or be you beast." With that, he got out of the truck and headed toward Maroney, arms waving, already talking, and I realized he still had yet to tell me a thing about his gnarled hand.

On we went for another hour. Until, near sunset, at the foot of the mountain pass, we pulled into the second desert motel the Old Man had pegged for us. This one was fancy. I mean fancy-fancy. It was called the Mohawk, with twelve pink stucco "cabanas" circled by palm trees that looked like they'd been hauled in complete with water and soil, all green and perky. The place was full up, big-ticket cars parked in front of every room, more fancy vehicles than my farmboy eyes had ever seen, and it was the quietest place I ever saw to be so full. I wasn't quite sure what to think. As we pulled to a stop past the office, a ritzy couple who looked like they stepped out of a Hollywood movie was getting out of a baby-blue convertible only to disappear inside their pink cabana, ignoring us completely. Even the manager didn't seem impressed with us, like he saw trucks full of giraffes every day. Which was fine by me since I wasn't in a mood to share the two of them anyway.

We headed to the motel's far corner and started our nightly routine of feeding, watering, and tending to the giraffes . . . for the last time. I could no longer put off thinking it so.

Soon as we finished, the Old Man was already closing his motel door behind him, antsy to get the night over so tomorrow would finally come, so I climbed on up to the open top's cross plank, like always. Girl's breath hit me hot and fusty, and Boy greeted me with a slobbering snuffle. Wiping giraffe spit off my face with pure pleasure, I settled in to share the sky with Boy and Girl one last time.

It was a warm night. So, about midnight, as they started their sleep-standing, I hopped to the ground and opened their trapdoors for more air. As I stared at Boy's hooves, I was back at Cooter's, seeing Red crawl out from between them. I was still seeing her when I climbed back up top. Yet it wasn't at Cooter's. It was on the night of the bear, the night she ignored my Old Man warnings and dropped into the road Pullman to be closer to them. Trusting them to trust her.

With Red before my eyes, I slipped down slow and easy into Boy's crate, right by the cut-through opening between their traveling crates, until I was standing directly between them both. For a moment, I drank in their mighty selves exactly as I had back in quarantine, their tall flanks no longer smelling of ocean but of earth. Then, like Red, I stretched out my arms, until I was touching them both . . . and, at my touch, the two blessed giraffes begin to *hum*! They *had* been humming to each other back in quarantine, and now they were humming with *me*. The deep, rolling thrums were so mellow that, standing there touching their hides, I could feel my chest vibrating with them, their rumbling African croon echoing deep into the night and deep into my marrow. Even now, its memory is so clear and rich that I can place my hand over my old chest and feel it still. When they stopped, I might have wondered once again if it had happened at all, except for the humming deep in my bones, and I recall my young self wishing I could stand there forever between them, just another scrawny young giraffe they'd adopted on their long, strange trip to California.

By the time the Old Man appeared out of the moonlight to relieve me, I'd forced myself back up top to keep watch over the sleeping giraffes from above. I braced for his usual questioning of my eighteen-year-old common sense.

Instead he said, "I thought I heard a rumbling, thrumming sound a while ago."

I pointed at the giraffes.

"Well, I'll be damned," he muttered.

As he sat down on the running board to light up his usual smoke, I dropped to the ground in front of him and stood there.

"You want to stay?" he said.

I nodded.

"All right then, boy, all right."

I climbed back up to the cross plank. The giraffes stirred from their sleep-standing to watch me settle back into my sentry spot. Then they lay down . . . *both* of them together . . . with me and only me standing guard for lions above.

And I thought my heart would bust.

San Diego Union

OCTOBER 16, 1938

GIRAFFES 'TRUCKIN'' INTO ZOO TODAY!!!

SAN DIEGO—Oct. 16 (Special edition). The San Diego Zoo's young giraffes are scheduled to come "trucking" into San Diego today around noon. A telegram yesterday from Riley Jones, head keeper and cross-country giraffe escort, announced the good news and estimated arrival, reported an ecstatic Belle Benchley.

Off will come the top of their crates.

Out will pop their gargantuan giraffe heads at the ends of their streamlined necks.

And up will go the cheers from all across our fair city.

In the meantime, harbor employees will have moved the harbor's big crane into the zoological gardens where it will be used to lift the giraffes, crates and all, off the three-ton truck that two weeks ago pulled out of New York City bound for San Diego . . .

15

Into California

We left by moonlight again, right before dawn.

By the time the sun was peeking out, we'd hit the mountains going through what they called Telegraph Pass. We did it so slow and smooth in first light that the giraffes, thank God, barely knew we'd done it.

Popping out the other side, we rolled right into Yuma. That was where the Old Man said we were going to cross into California on what was called the Ocean-to-Ocean Bridge over the Colorado River. When it was built, it was the only place for 1,200 miles that a vehicle could cross and go—like the name said—ocean to ocean.

From the looks of it, the river had recently done some flooding, debris littering the ground all around us, and the sight sent a small shiver down my spine. But there were more spine-shivering things to look at than that. This side of the bridge was another Hooverville of tents and tin lizzies and campfires and huddled people. I had to slow the rig to a crawl as a clump of grimy children began to run alongside us.

"Welcome to Okie Town," muttered the Old Man as we joined the line to cross the bridge. He was staring ahead, toward the bridge's middle, where several California state policemen were stopping traffic.

A Model T pickup was being forced to turn around. The truck was piled high with stuff barely tied down, including a mattress with half a dozen kids riding on it. When it passed, I caught a glimpse inside of a stone-faced pa and a weeping ma.

"What just happened?" I said.

The Old Man didn't answer, his eyes on the drama still ahead. Between us and the troopers were only two cars—the tin lizzie with the ride-along goat that passed us in New Mexico and the shiny baby-blue convertible carrying the ritzy couple from the Mohawk.

One of the troopers motioned up the family with the goat and started grilling them.

"Know what he's asking?" the Old Man muttered. "'You got money in your pocket? You got a job?' If the answer's no, they don't let you cross. They're calling it the Bum Blockade."

I glanced back at the old Model T pickup as it rolled to a stop back on the Arizona side. "What if they got nowhere else to go?"

"They stay right here." He nodded back at the shantytown. "This close to the Okie Promised Land and not an inch more."

Eyeing the goat riding in the basket on the tin lizzie's running board, the California trooper must have thought it looked like money, and he waved them by.

Then he waved the fancy convertible through without a glance.

We were next, and I thought we'd surely be stopping if for nothing else than the usual meet and greet with the giraffes. I even put on the brakes. But the trooper took one look at the giraffes and I guess saw money as well. Without cracking as much as a smile, he motioned us through, too.

As the giraffes rode high over the rest of the bridge, both the goat Okies and the Hollywood couple waved back at them, all of us entering the land of milk and honey together.

After that, things started coming at us fast.

We saw canals and green fields and orange groves and trucks hauling workers.

We saw more Hoovervilles set up helter-skelter.

We saw crowds of beat-down men with farmers' faces.

We saw signs that said **JOBLESS MEN KEEP GOING. WE CAN'T TAKE CARE OF OUR OWN** right alongside other signs that said **WORKERS UNITE!**

We kept on moving.

We passed through a tiny town called El Centro, and then, like a bit of abracadabra, the people and the signs and the towns disappeared, and we were driving through dunes high enough to be the Sahara, the sand blowing and shifting like sugar across the road. As we wound through the dunes, the Old Man pointed at an abandoned "plank road" made of wood railroad ties, warped and rotting alongside the paved highway. "Be happy you're not driving on that," he said. "That was once the only way across these dunes."

We kept on moving.

For a while, Mexico was within spitting distance on our left. Or so the Old Man said. But I didn't notice one bit of difference between over there and over here except the highway itself—until the road curved north and headed again for some more blasted mountains. I jerked my head toward the Old Man, who hadn't mentioned any such thing.

"No problem," he promised. "It's only a short pass with a couple of switchbacks and turnouts."

A sign zipped by:

DANGER AHEAD: STEEP NARROW CLIMB

"If a little steep," the Old Man added. "And narrow."

As the road divided into one-way single lanes, he leaned back, cucumber cool. "You know how to do this and so do the darlings. On the other side is home, boy."

So we went into the climb, the rig giving it all it had, the giraffes and me eyeing the "Engine Overheat" areas at every turn, moving up, up, up . . . then racing like a son of a gun down, down, down, with me standing on the brakes fighting to shift into a gear low enough to slow us back near legal limits. We barreled straight past the rest stop at the bottom as the split road joined again, my stomach sliding back down my throat and the giraffes' snouts bending back with the wind.

That quick, we seemed to be in San Diego proper and you can bet we were met by a police escort. A dozen motorcycle cops and city patrol cars were scattered all along the city limits. When they spotted us, they circled the rig and turned on their rolling sirens, waving us to follow.

Before my eyes could take it all in, we were seeing our first glimpse of water—the road had led us straight to the city's bay.

We'd made it. Ocean to ocean.

Everywhere I looked there were coast guard cutters and tankers and navy ships, all coming and going like a picture postcard against a big, beautiful hill at the mouth of the bay. I'd never seen such a sparkly place. Instead of harbor rats and hurricanes, there were pelicans and sun and docks so gleaming they would have made Cuz itch. Both giraffes popped their snouts out to sniff at the new ocean.

And still we kept on moving.

The front motorcycle cop did a little circle wave in the air, then led us into a sharp turn by the bustling train station, a towering building covered in Spanish curlicues with fancy vehicles of every kind parked in front, including a shining cream-and-blue Harley that caught my eye.

From the road, I could read the station's big arrival and departure schedule board outside, announcing the next departure: **THE SAN DIEGO & ARIZONA RAILWAY, EXPECTED ON TIME—DESTINATION EL CENTRO, YUMA, PHOENIX CONNECTING WITH ALL POINTS EAST.**

I slowed the rig to stare. Then, with a last, long glance, I pulled my eyes away from the board as we moved on.

The Old Man noticed. "She'll be fine, boy. For a girlie, she knows how to handle herself and any husband she's got, I suspect."

Up ahead, the cycle cops passed a sign pointing to Balboa Park. Within seconds, we were following them across a tall, slender bridge straight through an archway that led us into what looked to me like a fairy-tale cobblestone plaza—where another sign waited to point the way to the San Diego Zoo.

The Old Man could barely sit still. Pulling on his fedora, he positioned it for business with more pleasure than I'd ever seen. "Now you're going to see the show of your life!" he crowed. "I rang up the Boss Lady when we started out this morning. She's alerted the papers as well as the police, rousting them soon as we hung up, I bet. It's going to be a sight, a true sight." He pointed. "When we make that turn up ahead, all the reporters and picture-takers are going to be waiting. If the word's spread, probably half the town. The Boss Lady already got a crane from the docks, so we'll be hauling the darlings' traveling suites off the rig into their big new home and opening 'em up. Then, tomorrow the rest of the town that's not up there already will turn out. Even got a ceremony lined up. All for the darlings. We're *home*, boy! Yessir, you are in for a treat!"

That was exactly what I saw waiting around the bend—a hullabaloo the likes of which my young self had never seen. Lining the road on either side of us were people of all shapes and sizes, crowding against fancy red ropes. As the crowd roared, the front gates opened. I saw a plump woman in sensible granny shoes, schoolmarm bun, and church-lady dress coming to greet us, arms wide. I saw the camera guys begin snapping and the flashbulbs begin popping. Inside, I saw a harbor crane hovering high with men in dungarees waiting below. Rolling us to a final stop, I realized, with a last look in my mirror at the giraffes, that I was once again just a boy, on another coast, watching a sea of dungarees studying how to get two giraffes where they needed to go—a lucky boy who somehow got to tag along for the ride in between.

The Old Man was already grabbing for the door handle. As I sat in that cab with him for the very last moment we'd ever be doing it together, I heard the arriving San Diego & Arizona Railway train blow its horn pulling into the station, and I knew there was one more thing I had to do. "Mr. Jones . . . I've got to go."

The Old Man jerked his head around as the arriving train blew its horn again, and he saw me glance its way. At that, he fumed. "All right, boy. It's not your brain that's doing this thinking, but I guess it'd save me a lot of explaining to the Boss Lady that I'd rather do later than sooner." He took out some cash from his wallet and stuffed it in my shirt pocket. "That's enough for any round-trip ticket you need, got it?" Then he stuck out his hand. "The giraffes can hold on to their thanks until you get back. But as for me—you did a man's job and you deserve a man's thanks, right damn now. Shake my hand, son."

And I did.

Then he gave me a shove out the cab door, which was the only kind of farewell he was willing to give and the only one I was willing to take. I'd be back in a day, after all. It wasn't goodbye. I glanced up at the giraffes, their heads swiveling my way, and felt my heart drop into my boots. *I'll see them tomorrow, when I'm back,* I told myself, then headed on a dead run toward the train station. I wasn't much clear what I was going to do when I got to Phoenix besides find her before she left. Maybe I was going to come up with something that a full-grown man might say or do. Maybe all I wanted was to make sure she wasn't stranded, that Lionel Abraham Lowe, Good Man, had wired the money. Or maybe it was just that after seeing the giraffes safe to the end of their trip's story, I couldn't rest until I knew the end of Red's. I didn't much know. Like always, when I didn't know, running was what I seemed to do.

As I got closer to the depot, though, I could hear the conductor yelling his "All aboard!" I could see the last passenger get on and the train begin to move. I'd hesitated too long. It was pulling out and I was still a block away. Dodging cars and statues and benches and fences, I sprinted down the tracks after it, high-stepping to keep from stumbling over the rails, my heart pumping so hard I was gulping air as the train picked up speed. Still feeling Red's kiss on my lips, I kept telling myself that I'd hopped freights before. *I can do it, I can catch it, I can—*

I couldn't.

On such small things, entire lives turn.

Stumbling on the track's cinders, I staggered to a halt, so light-headed I had to throw my head over my knees. When I looked up, all that was left to see of the train as it slipped away was the caboose . . . the brand-new, redder-than-Red caboose . . . and the old do-or-die fury I thought was gone came roaring back. Moving on stray-dog-boy reflex alone, I found myself beside the shining cream-and-blue Harley still parked where I'd spotted it. Next thing I knew I was on it and gone.

For miles, as my head began to clear, I kept telling myself I should pull over, should go back, should rethink this stupid old move, and when I didn't, I told myself that after I caught the train I'd never, ever do such a thing again.

I kept up with the train as the highway followed the rails, until the tracks headed straight through the mountains. As the train disappeared, I kept zooming along the winding highway, hoping to catch up at El Centro.

But I missed it again by seconds.

So, I kept on going. To Yuma.

I made it to the other side of the Ocean-to-Ocean Bridge, ripping through Yuma looking for the station, before I got nabbed, the sound of the coming train cruelly filling the air.

To the Arizona sheriff I was only another lying, thieving Okie orphan who had no business on a shiny new electric horse, stealing people's motorcycles on my way to stealing a little of everything from everybody for years to come. Who's to say that wouldn't have been true only a few weeks before? The reason I gave for stealing the cycle was even a poor one to my own ears. He didn't believe a word of my tale of trains and giraffes and highways, despite my pleas to go ask the California trooper back on the bridge. "Do you think I'm a fool?" the sheriff growled. He'd had his fill of boys like me, which he proceeded to make mightily clear, his hooked nose stuck all but up my own.

Right then, the boy I was back on Cuz's boat dock would've pitched a hollering fit to call the Old Man or even Belle Benchley herself. The giraffes' boy, though, the one I'd become between the Atlantic and the Pacific, couldn't bring himself to do it. Maybe because I couldn't abide the Old Man knowing the throwback piece of thieving I'd done after everything we'd been through. But maybe more because I knew it wouldn't change a thing, this sheriff not letting me off even if the Old Man showed up riding the giraffes themselves. The sheriff didn't know the Old Man. Or Belle Benchley. This wasn't California. This was Yuma, home of Okie Town, with hundreds of boys exactly like me. I stole a motorcycle. Simple as that.

Since this was 1938, and Hitler was already starting to stomp across Europe, the choice I got was the choice all such thieving orphan boys got to avoid going to jail—joining the army.

"It'll make a man outa you," he said, making my choice for me.

It would be seven years and a world war before I found out whether Red got on that train, and even longer before I got back to San Diego.

San Diego Sun

OCTOBER 17, 1938

NEW GIRAFFE RESIDENTS ARRIVE

SAN DIEGO ZOOLOGICAL GARDENS—Oct. 17 (Special edition). One of the most astonishing zoological spectacles ever attempted, the zoo's great giraffe trek, ended safely and successfully yesterday when Riley Jones, head keeper of the San Diego Zoo, drove the first giraffes ever to be seen in Southern California up to their new home after a 3,200-mile trip from New York.

Still in their traveling crates, the long-necked beasts were lifted from the truck by a big harbor department crane. A 2-hour task of coaxing them into the strange surroundings of the outsized new enclosure with its tall house, fitted with an 18-foot-high door for the benefit of its long-geared residents, followed. After a branch of acacia leaves, alfalfa, and other vegetarian dainties had failed in the coaxing process, onions turned the trick.

"Onions," Jones said, "have got power."

Today, in a ceremony Mrs. Benchley christened them "Lofty" and "Patches," the winning names selected by the children of San Diego, and head keeper Jones brushed their high foreheads with a branch of black acacia from Balboa Park trees, which they proceeded to eat. Crowds from across Southern California came to be the first to see the exotic creatures and were instantly enthralled by their serene grace and ethereal beauty . . .

16

Home

About the time I'd put in my army stint and was ready to get out, the Japanese bombed Pearl Harbor and I got put right back in, along with every able-bodied American man for the duration of the War.

I was twenty-five before my return to the USA.

I'd like to say I saw action on the battlefield and returned a hero, war making a man of me like the sheriff said. But war's a cruel place to grow all the way up. I was part of the Quartermaster Corps in Europe. I worked with the dead. We were the ones that came in after the battles, collected the bodies and dug the graves. The army said I had an "aptitude" for it, and I still don't know what that means. What I do know is my sudden aptitude appeared after I told the wrong officer that I'd had my fill of death, and he said, "Fill of death, huh." Suddenly I had the aptitude and would soon have more than my fill of death. There was no glory in it, just duty. And it made me wish my eyes were filled with Panhandle dust again, until I learned how not to see and not to feel so as not to think as I performed my duties, day after horrible day of death.

Such things beat memories of your life before the War right out of you unless you hold on to something and hold on tight. Most soldiers held on with sweethearts and family, writing letters to people writing letters back. What does an orphan hold on to, though? So, as the days with the dead turned into years, I let myself slip away.

When it was over, I came home by transport back across the ocean, heading to New York Harbor, still carrying the War with me. But as we traveled through a storm at sea, I began to feel something again. What I felt was the giraffes. As the ship bucked and swayed, I realized I was riding the same ocean Boy and Girl had. I closed my eyes, and instead of being strapped in the hold of an army ship in 1945, I was strapped in a crate on the deck of the giraffes' transport in the Great Hurricane of 1938, heading toward America. The other soldiers couldn't sleep for thinking of home and family. Me, I couldn't sleep for thinking of the hurricane giraffes. I *had* held on to something. As we rode the swells of the storm, I was once again driving two "towering creatures of God's pure Eden" cross-country. I was seeing the Packard in my rearview and hearing Girl kick the Old Man. I was leaning off a mountain, meeting Moses's clan, spying the fat cat, and shooting the thieving lackey. I was bucking a flash flood, wrestling a desert coot, watching Boy save us, and feeling Red's lips against mine. I was again hearing what the Old Man said about the wiry man with the elephant and dog—that there's no explaining the world, where you find yourself in it and who your friends turn out to be. And I began to remember who my friends were.

As I rocked and rolled in that transport, riding those waves, I planned what I'd do the moment we docked.

I'd find them.

I'd find her.

And I'd find you.

I tracked down Mr. Big Reporter, Lionel Abraham Lowe, to a little New Jersey house with a green grass yard. When he opened the door, the way he eyed my uniform I'd have bet all my army pay he was 4-F, probably for flat feet or flat head.

So, I quickly said what I came to say. "I want to speak to Red."

He stiffened. "Who?"

"Augusta, your . . . wife."

Easing the door shut behind him, he looked me in the eye. "Augusta died years ago. Who's asking?"

I staggered back like I'd taken a punch. I must have looked seventeen again, all the years and all the graves falling from my face, because he recognized me. His eyes grew wide and fierce, his face flushed, and his fist came flying.

And I let it.

I staggered back another step with the blow and just stood there, blood gushing from my nose. He stared at me bleeding all over his stoop until I crumpled down on his front step, then, fetching me a towel, he eased down beside me.

A moment passed, the two of us hunched there, waiting for the towel to staunch the blood.

"How'd she die?" I mumbled.

"Her heart, of course," he answered. "In her sleep. About a year after our daughter was born . . . That's how we met."

"What?"

"Her heart," he said, looking off. "I found her on a curb holding her heart, unable to catch her breath. I offered to take her to the hospital. She had no money, but when I offered to pay, she said no. So, I took her to the indigent clinic and waited with her, those gasps not stopping until they gave her a shot of some kind." He paused. "She came from money, you know. Her father was one of the ones who jumped from their Wall Street windows in the crash of '29, when she was twelve. For years she and her mother were shuffled between relatives, most scratching to get by themselves, until her mother lost her mind and went wandering. Augusta was out looking for her. I spent days helping her look, figuring I'd get a story out of it, considering the Wall Street jumper angle, whether we found her mother or not. That happened all the time during the Depression, people vanishing, never to be heard from again. But we found her, all right. Too late. By that time, though, I'd forgotten all about the story and Augie didn't have anywhere . . ."

The front door creaked open.

There you stood. With his face. And her red curls.

"Go on back inside, sweetheart," he ordered, "go on." He looked at me more anxious than fierce. "Leave my daughter out of this. She's only six," he whispered. "She doesn't know a thing about her mother's wild streak . . . running after *giraffes* of all things . . . by *herself.* You and that zookeeper *letting* her! She was a woman, for God's sake! With a heart condition! She could have *died* out there alone. She asked too much . . . she *always* asked too much!"

With that, he fumed and stood up. But there was more I wanted to know. Did Red get in her magazine? Did she ever see Africa? Did she get to stretch her wings?

Before I could ask, though, the door opened again.

"Lionel? Who is that?" There stood a pretty brunette wearing a print dress and smelling of lavender with a baby on her hip.

I got to my feet.

"Just a soldier looking for somebody who no longer lives here, dear," he told her.

"You're bleeding," she said.

"Yes, dear," he answered for me. "He had a sudden nosebleed, but we fixed it, didn't we, soldier? I've already offered him a towel. No need to worry. Now he has to be on his way."

"Well, God bless you, sir. Augie Ann, this man won the war for us!"

Augie.

You came close, and I got to see you smile.

Herding his family back inside, he said loudly my way, "Sorry not to have been able to help you, soldier." Then Lionel Abraham Lowe closed the door on me, his eyes telling a tale of their own. He'd loved Red. I wasn't sure of it until that moment, and it made me feel better for you.

I found a library and went scouring through back issues of *Life* magazine. I'd hoped she'd made it in somehow, even without us. Of course, she wasn't there. This Margaret Bourke-White photographer she loved was everywhere, taking pictures of the War all over the world. But no Augusta Red.

Yet as I sat there in that library, safe if not yet sound, I heard Red's last words to me as if she were still standing in front of me. *We had us an adventure, didn't we, Woody Nickel?*

"Yes," I answered, right out loud. "*Yes*, we did."

I wanted to run back and tell you. Your ma *did* have an adventure—a proper one that made her heart sing for a time even if it couldn't make her heart strong. Along the way, she *did* see Africa—in the back of a truck, in the eyes of the giraffes, down the road going west—and she was as daring and brave as could be. I ached for you to know. The War had made me an honorable man, though, if it did nothing else. I was asked to leave you alone, so I did. You being their daughter, I had no rights in the matter, despite my deep feelings for Red. Truth is, I'm not sure what your ma was to me, even now. Nothing I come up with rings true. I didn't know her long enough to say she was the love of my life, although it can deeply feel that way here and now as I write. But if a man leads a handful of lives inside a long life like mine, I can say she was the love of my first life. That I can surely say.

So, from that library, nursing more than a broken nose, I headed cross-country to San Diego to find the giraffes. I walked through the zoo entrance, which was unchanged from the day I'd seen it from afar. I wandered a moment, turned a corner, and there they were. A sign announced them to be "Lofty" and "Patches." But, make no mistake, they were Boy and Girl, full grown, healthy, and tall as tall can be—Boy now taller than Girl and regal as a prince. I sat my blissful self down on a bench to let my eyes drink them in, and out from behind them scampered a giraffe calf. The sign on the fence said his name was "D-Day," being born on that day of days, June 6, 1944, while the Allied armed forces were invading Europe—what do you think of that? And he was already taller than me.

I spent a week off and on there on that bench. I didn't expect them to remember me, but I wanted to give them a chance. For two days, they didn't notice me among the crowd. On the third day, when the keepers weren't around, I snuck in a couple of onions to offer through the fence—to see what they'd do. Girl ambled over first. Her back leg was scarred but working dandy. She bent her neck down to snuffle me head to toe, exactly like the first night in quarantine, then curled her tongue around the onion in my hand and lobbed it down her throat. When Boy joined us, baptizing me with a blow of giraffe spit, nobody could convince me they didn't see the boy they used to know.

I planned to find Riley Jones, too, of course. I wanted to see him with the giraffes and hear a bit of his giraffe-speak. I'd walk over close and say, "Hey there, Old Man." Each day, though, another keeper, younger than the Old Man but just as leathery, came out to tend the giraffes. Each day, he'd nod and I'd nod back. Until one day, he caught me feeding the giraffes onions.

"Hey, you, soldier!"

Some long-gone reflex made me want to run. Instead I came to attention. "Yessir."

He looked me up and down, eyes lingering on the birthmark on my neck. "What's your name?"

I paused. "Who's asking?"

"Is it Woody Nickel?"

"How . . . ?"

He grinned ear to ear. "Riley said you'd show sooner or later. Come with me." His name was Cyrus, he said, Cyrus Badger. As we walked, he put a hand on my shoulder and told me the bad news. The Old Man was dead, too, that very year. I'd missed him by a month.

"Mabel, this here's Riley's boy," he announced as we stepped into some sort of paymaster's office. "This is the famous Woodrow Wilson Nickel."

Before I knew it, I was being handed a check for driving services, back pay.

"Oh, wait," she said, rummaging in her desk. "Riley left you something." Laughing, the woman handed me a sack of wooden nickels. "I was supposed to give you the wooden nickels first and call that your pay, but I didn't have the heart." She held out the sack until I begrudgingly took it. "Look closely at them, Mr. Nickel. It's a gift from him," she said, handing me one. Each nickel was a token good for a visit to the zoo. There were hundreds of them.

Cyrus walked me out, enjoying the look on my face as much as the Old Man would have.

When I found my tongue, I said, "What got him? Did the consumption come back?"

"Consumption?" Cyrus screwed up his face. "He wasn't a lunger. It was the smokes that did him in, got the cancer of the throat. Where'd you get it being consumption?"

"He said he had it when he was my age after he almost ran off with the circus as a kid. He came out West to work as a cowboy and got his cure cow-punching and eating sowbelly."

At that, the Old Man's pal slapped his knee and guffawed. He laughed so hard and long I began to take offense. Wiping tears from his eyes from all the hooting, he said, "Woody, that ain't Riley's story, that's Dr. Harry's, the founder of this zoo. Dr. Harry tried to run away with the circus as a kid. Then he caught TB, and got his cure by heading West and cowboying—all before he ended up a doctor, moved here, and started up the zoo on a lark. Riley Jones never punched a cow in his life!"

The Old Man lied? I couldn't believe my ears. "But he couldn't abide a liar!"

Cyrus smiled. "Well, now, I wouldn't go so far as calling him a liar. Nobody abides a liar. But everybody sure likes a good storyteller, don't they? Sometimes the best medicine is a good story. I bet you found that out."

I threw up my hands. "Well, what was his *real* story?"

He shrugged. "My money's on him being a foundling. He never mentioned an orphanage, but he once told me he was on his own by ten. Used to happen in his day more than you'd care to know. Being with the circus, now that was true."

I was so rattled I couldn't find my voice, and when I did, I couldn't do much more than stutter. "Well . . . how about his hand? A lion mangled it in the circus, right?"

Cyrus roared again. I was cracking the guy up. "God love him, I bet ol' Riley had a thousand stories about that hand," he said, shaking his head. "Don't feel bad, son. He did it to us all. I once caught him telling two different stories about it on the same day. He was born with it, dollars to doughnuts. Or it might well have been caught inside a big cat's mouth. If not, whatever happened to it was so bad he never told it true. Which was his right. Some things are so much yours, you just have to keep 'em to yourself. But I guarantee if he could've had his ending be a lion's lunch instead of the cancer, he dang sure would have," he said, and walked off, with me standing there gaping like a blessed monkey. A few steps away, he stopped and looked back. "Well, come on. You need to meet the Boss Lady."

In a minute, I was standing in the presence of Mrs. Belle Benchley, the famous Zoo Lady. She still looked so much like the schoolmarm at the zoo entrance back that October day in '38 with her arms stretched wide for the giraffes, I felt a rush of feeling that almost bowled me over. She was coming out of her little office behind the boiler room when we walked right up.

"Guess who this is!" Cyrus beamed. "This here is Riley's boy he talked so much about. Mr. Woody Nickel."

"Well!" She stuck out her hand to shake. "How do you do? How *do* you *do*!" We had the nicest chat you'd ever want to have, until the phone jangled behind her and she disappeared back inside.

Cyrus walked me back through the zoo to send me on my way. Before I left, though, I wanted to ask one more thing about the Old Man if I could make myself do it.

"Don't take this wrong . . . ," I started up, fumbling for the words. "But back in his circus days, did Mr. Jones ever get in a scrap over some animal cruelty with a man . . . dying?" It was as close I could come to the fat cat's murderous name-calling.

At that, Cyrus's face went sober. This is what he said a touch too quick in my memory: "Nope, never heard that. Wouldn't put it past him when it came to animals, but you could probably say the same about most of us here if push came to shove." He cocked his head my way. "Besides, everybody deserves a second chance. He sure gave one to a certain Dust Bowl young'un, didn't he?" He patted me on the shoulder. "Did he ever tell you why he did?"

I shook my head.

"He said 'the darlings' told him to." With a sly grin that seemed more for the Old Man than me, Cyrus turned to go. "Don't be a stranger, ya hear?" he called back. "He loved telling stories about your ride, and Lofty and Patches will always be glad to see you."

Lofty and Patches. I went to correct him but stopped short, knowing it didn't matter, that nothing mattered except they were alive and so was I. Red was gone and so was the Old Man, but I still had the giraffes—and because I did, I also had Red and the Old Man. It's a strange thing how you can spend years with some folks and never know them, yet, with others, you only need a handful of days to know them far beyond years. As I headed back to the giraffes, I knew I was never letting the Old Man's darlings far out of my sight again. I was in California and I was with the giraffes. That was as much of a Promised Land—or home—I figured I'd ever need.

So I got a job at the city cemetery. After all, I had an aptitude. On the way out West, I kept thinking I'd hit up the Old Man to be a keeper, maybe even for Boy and Girl. Mrs. Benchley, though, had saved the jobs of all the zoo's keepers who joined the Armed Services during the war, to give back to them on their return. Plus, within a month, a disk in my back gave way. One too many graves dug, I suppose. So, the job I ended up with was a graveyard night watchman, a position you might find surprising, considering the dead don't usually need much watching. But it suited me fine, sleep still not being something I was ever good at, the War making it worse. To pass the long nights, I took to reading those books the Old Man loved, the ones by "Mr. Fenimore Cooper," and while their old-fashioned words could come close to putting even me to sleep, the best Hawkeye parts were dog-eared glory. And soon I had a routine, spending my nights at work and my days at the zoo. Every morning I'd get off as the zoo was opening. I'd grab a salami, some bread, and a pocketful of onions. Then, using one of the Old Man's wooden nickels, I'd have breakfast with my friends the giraffes, thinking about the Old Man and wishing the magnificent ol' bastard could join us. Sometimes, Mrs. Benchley herself would stroll by and sit down beside me to watch the giraffes. Before too long, the keepers even started calling me Giraffe Man. Which was fine by me. Fine, indeed.

As the years went by, life slowly became the ordinary thing it was always meant to be. I tried to be a good man, which surely would have surprised the piss out of the boy I was back at Cuz's. I never passed up the chance to feed a stray dog or cat or stray anything that passed my way, and I never trusted a soul who didn't like animals. I loved some respectable women and some not so much. I married three, all redheads, you might not be surprised to hear, and I outlived them all. The closest I had to a child of my own was a grown stepdaughter, gone now, too, who once gave me a plaque that said "Time spent with animals is added to your life," joking how I'd live to be a hundred, if that isn't a kicker.

But the truth is I kept up my relationships with Girl and Boy better than I did any human, *family* having become a word without boundaries for me. I made sure they never wanted for onions, leaning in for Boy's slobbery hello and to pat Girl's spot in the shape of a sideways heart. I watched them thrive in all the love coming their way, feeling it as full as if it were my own. I saw how their lives lived among us did exactly what the Old Man said they would, making all who met them more alive to this world's natural wonders most people would never know or care about any other way. Before they were gone, I even got to see them running free in a farm-like park the zoo built out in the desert with a herd of their own making, along with some from other zoos—a "tower" of giraffes, they call it, if you can beat that.

As for what the Old Man said about animals knowing the secret of life? While there were moments I thought they just might speak, his darlings never shared a secret with me in so many words. It didn't take me long to grasp, though, that in all the time I was spending in their presence—reveling in their company like the Old Man did, seeing the world through their serene sky-high eyes like Red did, and sensing creation through two "towering creatures of God's pure Eden" like Big Papa did—I had found me *a* secret to life, and it was the secret to a good life. Maybe that's what the Old Man meant for me all along.

The years, though, kept passing, and the keepers kept changing. So did everybody else at the zoo, including even the Zoo Lady, Belle Benchley. I bet I told my story a thousand times before all who knew the Old Man were gone. After that, I must have started a thousand times to tell the new folks, too. Yet I never did, sure that my story now mattered only to me, just the twice-told tales of the old man I had become. I wasn't much of a chatty man anymore anyway, the silence of the graveyard slowly quieting all within me and without. After a while, though, I think it was more than that, more like what Cyrus Badger said about the Old Man's gnarled hand. Some things are so much yours that you've got to keep them to yourself. For thirty years, that's what I did. I shared my life with the giraffes and they did the same with me, us three keeping our story our own, until the day Girl and Boy were both gone.

Then the years turned into decades.

And I kept on living.

Time heals all wounds, they say. I'm here to tell you that time can wound you all on its own. In a long life, there is a singular moment when you know you've made more memories than any new ones you'll ever make. That's the moment your truest stories—the ones that made you the you that you became—are ever more in the front of your mind, as you begin to reach back for the you that you deemed best.

So it was that after every living thing I'd ever loved was gone—taking with them big chunks of my very soul—I stumbled upon an old *Life* magazine. As I thumbed through its pages, I found myself thinking about Red, the Old Man, and the giraffes more than I had in decades, my mind traveling back, back, back to the boy driving the hurricane giraffes. I quaked at the raggedy man I'd have surely become without a hurricane blowing me to the giraffes, and I marveled at the power of a soul's truest story to staunch life's cruelest ones. I could've lived my entire life in the shadow of Dust Bowl miseries and Hitler horrors. Instead such times held less pain because of two animals I once knew.

But time just kept on passing and I just kept on living.

Until, deep into my nineties, time got away from me.

I had quit going to the zoo, spirit willing but body worn out. What I hadn't noticed was that my mind was wearing out, too. Time plays its cruelest trick without you knowing it. Even the memories a body holds most dear become like scratchy old phonograph records played too long, fading in and out, with little sound and even less fury. Until you're only another old man sitting in a wheelchair in a crowded VA room with other old men staring at a parade of TV pictures and stories not your own.

That's how my own story could have ended, the long goodbye of older-than-old World War II vets like me whose bodies outlasted their stuttering minds.

Yet that's not what happened.

Yesterday, long after I was told I'd lived over a century, which was as strange a thing to hear as you might suspect, I saw a giraffe filling the screen of the crowded room's TV. I stirred from my foggy mind to hear a deep-voiced TV man talking. Giraffes had all but vanished from the earth, he said, like the elephants and tigers and gorillas and rhinos. Warring, poaching, and encroaching, he said, were emptying the jungles and silencing the forests and turning zoos into arks enough to make Noah weep. Thousands of animals and birds and even trees were at the point of no return, he said, going the way of the Old Man's sky-blanketing passenger pigeons.

Gone as gone could be.

The TV kept talking, and pictures of doomed birds and animals and plants kept rolling—as if it would list all the world's wild things if someone didn't stop it—so I rushed over in my wheelchair and punched the TV to stop it myself.

As the orderlies came running, though, I sank back into my wheelchair, realizing that punching all the TVs in the world wouldn't save the giraffes. There wasn't a thing an old man could do. *How could this happen?* A world with no jolting giraffe joy or traveling bird waves or soaring forest glory seemed an ugly, barren, and soulless place fit only for the dust storms and the cockroaches and the likes of us. *If they can go extinct, dear God Almighty, let me go extinct too!* I was desperate to be gone—graveyard gone—fearing, like always, I'd just keep on living.

Then, for the first time in eighty years, I dreamed.

My nightmares had pretty much stopped after my ride with the giraffes. Whatever had stoked them seemed gone with the stray-dog boy I left behind. I went back to no dreams at all. But after the War's end, I went to find Red and met you. That night, after dozing off on the train to San Diego, I saw Augusta Red as an old woman. She was standing in a little red house, opening a package, and inside was a giraffe. I tell you it rattled me good. I feared Mr. Big Reporter's punch had started up my nightmares again, and cruelly so. Never mind the mailed giraffe. Red was never, ever going to be an old woman. Yet I dreamed no more. For decade upon decade upon decade, I went back to a life without dreams of any kind, which suited me fine.

Last night, though, after getting rolled back here and put to bed by a pack of orderlies, I closed my eyes and heard a sound I hadn't heard since I was eighteen . . . the soft, rich, purring *thrummmm* of humming giraffes . . . and I knew I was inside a dream. Because there, in my room, was Girl poking her long neck into my room's fifth-floor window, snorting at me to get out of bed and through the window. So, in my dream I do. I am back on top of the rig somewhere in Virginia, wrestling with Girl's head as Red is telling stories of giraffes in the sky, in paintings, in Paris, and I find myself awash with those stories she told from long ago as if they were alive, as if we could all live forever inside their telling.

Then the rig vanishes. I'm back in bed, once again dreaming the dream of Red as an old lady in a little red house, opening a package and finding a giraffe.

And I see it's not Red.

It's *you*.

At that, I bolted straight up in bed, full awake, and in my mind's eye, the dream finished itself like a vision—I am once again on the road with the giraffes, the Old Man, and your ma. But this time *you* are there, too. You are there in the Packard as Red snaps her pictures. You are there in the flood as she sacrifices her dreams to rescue the giraffes. You are there as Boy saves her and the you that will be you from the coot's gutshot. You are there on the rig's top as Red is telling giraffe stories of masterpieces and legend. And she is telling another story—*our* story.

To you.

That's when I knew I'd been a foolish and selfish man.

It is a foolish man who thinks stories do not matter—when in the end, they may be all that matter and all the forever we'll ever know. So, *shouldn't* you hear our story? Shouldn't you know how two darling giraffes saved me, you, and your mother, a woman I loved? And it is a selfish man who takes stories to the grave that aren't his and his alone. *Shouldn't* you know your mother's brave heart and daring dreams? And shouldn't you know your friends, even though we're gone?

I knew, then, there *was* something an old man could do. I found a pencil and I began to write.

Few true friends have I known and two were giraffes, one that didn't kick me dead and one that saved my worthless orphan life and your worthy, precious one.

They're gone now. So surely am I. If the TV was right, there are no giraffes in the world to boot, gone with the elephants and tigers and the Old Man's sky-blanketing pigeons.

Yet, somehow, I know there is still you. There is still this story that is yours as good as mine. If it goes extinct with those creatures of God's pure Eden, that'd be a crying shame—*my* shame. Because if ever I could claim to have seen the face of God, it was in the colossal faces of the giraffes. If ever I had a story I should be leaving behind, it'd be this one, for them, all of them, and for you.

So, here and now, before it's too late, I have written it down. If there is any magic left in a world without gentle giraffes, if that bit of God I saw in those sky-high wonders is still alive somewhere holy and true, a good soul will read these pencil scratches of mine and do this last thing I cannot do.

And one bright and blessed morning, the giraffes, the Old Man, me—and your ma—will find our winding way forever to you.

. . . As I lower my pencil, I hear a noise at the window.

It's *Girl*.

Her glorious giraffe neck stretches near again, and I feel the same clutch around my heart on first spying her and Boy down the dock so long ago.

"We *did* it, Girl," I say, pointing at these words. "You happy? I'm happy."

Snuffling, she blows a satisfied spitball my way.

I start to ask the darling why she's back. But, as my heart misses a beat . . . then another . . . and . . . another . . . I know. I drink in my final look of my true friend as she fades away.

Goodbye.

Shaky hand to old, old heart, I smile down at these last scribbles.

Time to stop.

Time to go . . .

. . . and I reach over and close the window.

EPILOGUE

The VA liaison put down the last writing pad from Woodrow Wilson Nickel's antique footlocker and gazed around. It was already late afternoon, and she was now far behind schedule. But she didn't look at her watch. Instead she gently bundled up the pads scattered around her, placed them neatly back in the footlocker along with the tiny antique porcelain souvenir giraffe, and walked in to see the hospital administrator.

"Do you have a moment?" she said. "There's something I should show you."

———— ✦ ————

A few days later, inside an office past a mural of legendary "Zoo Lady" Belle Benchley, the current director of the San Diego Zoo leaned back in his chair. On his desk lay stacks of scribbled writing pads that had been sent over from the VA Center, the last of which he had just finished reading. He gazed out the window at the forest-like grounds in the direction of the zoo's new Institute for Extinction Prevention, where, nearly a century before, an enclosure had housed the zoo's first giraffes.

Then he touched the screen on his desk monitor, and the zoo security director appeared.

"Yes, sir?"

"If we wanted to find someone," the director asked, "where might we start?"

———————•◆•———————

In that way, one bright and blessed morning, a slim, freckled eighty-six-year-old New Jersey woman with a shock of once-red curls sat reading a special-delivery message—as she had done a dozen times since it had arrived—when the doorbell of her little redbrick house chimed. She whisked the door wide to find two delivery men holding a World War II–era antique trunk, and she motioned them to set it down gently on her hardwood floor.

As the door closed behind them, she opened the military footlocker and found a giraffe. For a moment, she admired the tiny porcelain San Diego Zoo souvenir. Then, closing her fingers around it, she picked up the first batch of writing pads, eased herself into the nearest chair, and began to read.

AUTIIOR'S NOTE

In 1999, while doing deep dives in the San Diego Zoo's archives for a project, I uncovered a batch of yellowed news clippings chronicling the kind of story that captures the imagination and never quite lets go. A place as colorful as the San Diego Zoo has stories galore, but the scope and audacity of this one was remarkable:

In September 1938, on the orders of the zoo's famous female director, Belle Benchley, two young giraffes survived a hurricane at sea, then were driven cross-country for twelve days in little more than a tricked-out pickup truck to become the first giraffes in Southern California. While the giraffes saw the USA from their sky-high windows, over five hundred newspapers carried the story day after day to their readers' delight.

As I read those old clippings, I kept seeing a bored little farmgirl staring out her window when suddenly two giraffes whiz by. Finding a telegram from Lloyd's of London insuring them, as I recall, for "blow-outs, acts of God, tornadoes, dust storms, and floods," I was hooked all the more. I searched for a trip diary by the keeper who managed the feat, a man named Charley Smith. Like most rough-and-tumble zoo men of the time, though, he wasn't the kind of guy who wrote in diaries.

So that was that.

Then, a few years ago, I began thinking about those giraffes again—but for a disturbing reason. Here in the early twenty-first century, giraffes along with far too many other species are now threatened in what is being called "the sixth extinction," which is about as scary-sounding a name as it should be. As I brooded over the future of the world's most iconic wild animals, I found myself back in 1938, traveling the winding roads of America with two young giraffes, seeing things in my mind's eye no one will ever see again and imagining how those two animals must have made people they met all the more human. Maybe that's what really had me. Realizing we could lose them, I wanted to spend time thinking about why creatures who share our world can move us so. Belle Benchley's memoir *My Life in a Man-Made Jungle* being an international bestseller during one of the worst eras of the twentieth century proves that connection. There's more going on than the "circle of life"—Hitler was threatening, the Great Depression was persisting, yet two traveling giraffes lightened the load of an entire country.

The challenge of creating historical fiction inspired by a true event like this one is to research well enough to capture what life was like when such a crazy idea seemed feasible. At the same time, a story is always a reflection of the present, since that is where it's being read. We have big, big things to worry about in this new century, extinctions of beloved animals among the most heartbreaking. But there's good news: all over the world, conservation organizations, research centers, aquariums, sanctuaries, foundations, and zoological institutions like today's San Diego Zoo Global are fighting the good fight for endangered species—and for ourselves, since we now know there will be a human toll for losing even creatures as small as bees and butterflies.

In the decades ahead, when or if someone finds this novel on a bookshelf or in the stacks of a library, God forbid the world's a place without elephants, pandas, tigers, butterflies—and giraffes. In a famous 2014 TED talk, nature writer Jon Mooallem suggested how we feel about an animal dramatically influences its future survival. In his words: "Storytelling matters now. Emotion matters. Our imagination has become an ecological force."

May it be so.

For now, we may not have the chance to ride cross-country with a pair of giraffes, falling in love with them and each other while learning secrets to life, but we can still be charmed and inspired by them. They are still with us. Here's hoping that will never, ever change.

HISTORICAL NOTES

Belle Benchley

An early glass-ceiling breaker, Benchley came to the fledgling San Diego Zoo in 1925 as a civil servant bookkeeper and quickly began doing everything from taking tickets to sweeping cages in the burgeoning but always-cash-strapped zoo, until she soon took over directorial chores after a series of male directors didn't last. While she was known in newsprint and popular culture by the time of our tale as the only female zoo director in the world, the official title given her by the zoo's 1927 male board of directors was "executive secretary," until voted "managing director" just before her 1953 retirement. Through her long tenure, she became affectionately known as the "Zoo Lady" and in 1949 was the first woman elected president of the American Association of Zoological Parks and Aquariums. Her first book, *My Life in a Man-Made Jungle*, was published in 1940, becoming an international bestseller, and was sent to soldiers overseas as a morale booster. She followed it with three more. One of her most forward-thinking ideas was a school bus program that brought second graders to the zoo, fueled by her belief that the only way people will care about nature's wild animals is to meet them, which now infuses all conservation-minded zoological institutions' missions.

Burma-Shave Ads

A brand of brushless shaving cream, famous for its advertising gimmick of posting humorous rhyming poems, phrase by phrase and spaced evenly for full punch-line effect on a series of small signs along the roadside.

Dapper Dan

A famous hair pomade used in the early twentieth century to give a greasy and waxy hold on hair.

Great Hurricane of 1938

Also called the Long Island Express and the Yankee Clipper, the Great New England Hurricane of 1938 was the first to hit the upper East Coast in over a century and was the most destructive storm to strike New England in recorded history until 2012's Hurricane Sandy. The hurricane was so devastating that several shore communities simply disappeared, along with the people who lived in them, with houses and people swept out to sea. Katharine Hepburn famously was caught in it at her family's beach house. As for New York City, the Empire State Building reportedly swayed in the high-powered winds as the East River overflowed.

Giraffe Hum

Giraffes have been caught on tape by biologist researchers humming at night on a very low, rich frequency. Speculation abounds, such as the hum being a giraffe snore, a sound made when they dream, a sound made when they are content, or even a way to communicate with each other like dolphins or elephants.

Hobo Cards

Despite public perception, hoboes weren't just tramps who happily rode the rails. They began as nomadic workers who roamed the United States, taking jobs wherever they could, and never spending too long in any one place—enjoying the freedom of the traveling life. To avoid police harassment, a group decided to form a union, which created hobo cards to flash, touting a hobo pledge. Dues were a nickel a year.

Hoovervilles

Shantytowns pieced together by the homeless in the United States during the Great Depression, nicknamed after Herbert Hoover, president during the onset of the Depression.

James Fenimore Cooper

Considered the first true major American novelist, he most famously wrote adventures of the frontier American life. They were called collectively the Leatherstocking Tales, about a wilderness scout named Natty Bumppo, known as "Hawkeye." While they tend toward old-fashioned verbosity, they still endure in our culture, his most famous novel being *The Last of the Mohicans*, a tale that included the last two members (both male) of the Mohican tribe and now is a common phrase used to connote the last of a type, which resonates for our tale.

Lloyd's of London

The legendary insurance group, established in 1688 by a seaside coffeehouse owner named Edward Lloyd to insure ships, is famous for insuring the uninsurable (such as giraffes being driven across the entire USA). Interestingly, it's able to do that because it is not an insurance company but a "market" of financial backers, underwriters, corporations, and single members who pool and spread risk.

Lee and Lincoln Highways

The Lincoln Highway was the earliest transcontinental highway route for automobiles across the United States, running through northern states and finished in 1913. The Lee Highway followed, finished in 1923, running through southern states starting at Washington, DC, and ending at the Pacific Highway in San Diego.

Mann Act

Signed into law by President Taft in 1910, the act, named after its author, Congressman James Robert Mann, made it a crime to transport women across state lines "for the purpose of prostitution or debauchery, or for any other immoral purpose"—the last phrase allowing liberal, often racial interpretation. Celebrities such as Charlie Chaplin, Frank Lloyd Wright, Chuck Berry, and Jack Johnson were caught in it. Johnson, the first African American heavyweight boxing champion, was among the first to be charged under the act after a road trip from Pittsburgh to Chicago with his White girlfriend.

Rube Goldberg

An early twentieth-century American cartoonist, inventor, and Pulitzer Prize winner, best known for his popular and often hilarious cartoons depicting complicated gadgets performing simple tasks in convoluted ways. The cartoons led to the expression "Rube Goldberg machines" to any invention that looked overly complicated, and continue to inspire national competitions for fun to this day.

SS Robin Goodfellow

The merchant marine ship carrying the giraffes was famous for surviving the Great Hurricane of 1938. It didn't survive World War II, though, when it was torpedoed and sunk by a U-boat in the South Atlantic on July 25, 1944, with all crew lost.

Sundown Towns

After Reconstruction and before the civil rights era, signs like the one in our story popped up on the outskirts of thousands of small towns across the country, warning "colored people" to keep moving. This created a huge problem for the Black traveler and inspired an annual publication guidebook from 1936 to 1966 for African American motorists, called *The Negro Motorist Green Book*, or just the *Green Book*, after its editor, Victor Hugo Green. It also inspired the title of the Academy Awards' 2019 winner for Best Picture.

Tin Lizzie

A nickname for the Model T Ford that dominated the early automobile industry, being cheap and dependable, especially by the time of the Great Depression, after many of the earliest ones became dilapidated yet were still roadworthy.

WPA/CCC

The Works Progress Administration (WPA) and the Civilian Conservation Corps (CCC) were two New Deal programs created by President Roosevelt in 1935 to combat the Great Depression. The WPA employed mostly unskilled men to carry out public-works projects, creating new school buildings, hospitals, bridges, airfields, zoos, and roads, as well as planting an estimated three billion trees. The CCC was a public work-relief program for unskilled, unemployed young men, ages eighteen to twenty-five and later twenty-eight, that offered shelter, clothing, food, and a small wage. The young men lived in work camps most prominently in the country's national parks. They planted more than three billion trees and constructed trails and shelters in more than eight hundred parks between 1933 and 1942.

ACKNOWLEDGMENTS

Every book is a bit of miracle, and I'm deeply, humbly grateful for this one.

I will miss hanging out with the giraffes, Woody, Red, and the Old Man. It's been a wild ride—a wild yet uplifting one that I got to share with you because of all who helped make this literary trip happen and who deserve my profound thanks.

Most exceptionally:

Jane Dystel, who may love giraffes more than I do and whose skill as well as attention continues to be a thing to behold. And Miriam Goderich, who so quickly saw the potential of this unusual story.

The people of San Diego Zoo Global, especially CEO Douglas Myers, for all you do every day for the world's endangered animals. Words fail.

Danielle Marshall, whose book sense is extraordinary.

The remarkable sources that made the research for past-world building possible—San Diego Zoo Global's archives; the San Diego History Center; newspaper databases and oral-history accounts of the 1938 hurricane, WPA/CCC, Great Depression, and the Dust Bowl; and book, film, and photo publications, including *The San Diego Zoo: The First Century 1916–2016*, John Steinbeck's 1939 *The Grapes of Wrath*, Victor Hugo Green's 1936 *The Negro Motorist Green Book*, Timothy Egan's 2006 *The Worst Hard Time*, Ken Burns's 2012 documentary film *The Dust*

Bowl, plus the timeless documentary photography of Dorothea Lange and Margaret Bourke-White.

And, of course, my nearest and dearest, both human and animal, who continue to put up with the writer in the house.

ABOUT THE AUTHOR

Photo © 2019 Korey Howell

Lynda Rutledge, a lifelong animal lover, has had the joy of petting baby rhinos, snorkeling with endangered turtles, and strolling with a tower of giraffes in her eclectic freelance career writing nonfiction for well-known publications and organizations while winning awards and residencies for her fiction. Her debut novel, *Faith Bass Darling's Last Garage Sale*, was the winner of the 2013 Writers' League of Texas Book Award. It was adapted into the 2018 French film *La dernière folie de Claire Darling* starring Catherine Deneuve. Lynda, her husband, and their resident dog live outside Austin, Texas. For more information visit www.lyndarutledge.com.